KILL PROMISE

A JACK WIDOW THRILLER

SCOTT BLADE

Black Lion Media

CHAPTER 1

The woman woke naked, and bound to a large tree, like a human sacrifice to some prehistoric creature living in the North Dakota wilderness. At least, she assumed she was still in North Dakota. That's where she'd been at the last moment she remembered. The last memory she had was getting into her car. *Her destination?* She couldn't remember. It eluded her.

Fear overwhelmed her, at first. *Don't panic!* she told herself. Dangerous situations came with her job. She had never experienced anything like this before. Her instincts were good. And they told her to stay calm. She trusted them. She had to trust them.

A heavy draft blew in from out of the darkness and wafted across her body, like an icy caress. The cold stung. She shivered, realizing for the first time that she was naked. Her vision was hazy, but she could see. She searched the base of the tree for her clothes, but there was nothing. Her clothes were nowhere to be seen.

Again, she tried to calm herself, to let her training kick in. She was an investigator. She remembered that. *But what kind?* She wasn't sure. Her skills were good. She knew that too. Staying calm and levelheaded under pressure was one of the best skills she'd developed. At first, it worked to a certain degree. But then she remembered something else, a new piece of the puzzle.

It wasn't her car. The car she remembered getting into. It wasn't hers. It was a rental. She'd flown in from someplace else. She wasn't from here. She'd come here on assignment, to investigate something, a long-forgotten crime. That's how she'd pieced it together so far. It was hard to be sure about anything, including her memory recall. Her brain was foggy. She knew her name and her occupation, sort of, and her boss and her contact. She remembered the case she was working on. And she remembered the town she'd been in for the past week. It was called Sawyer Lake, in North Dakota, where she believed she was. It was hard for her to know for sure since she didn't know how she got on this tree, or who strung her up, or why.

She was scared. *Who wouldn't be?* She wouldn't get any answers from being terrified. It wasn't going to get her out of this. It wasn't going to get her down from the tree. She also started thinking that whoever did this to her, if they wanted to kill her, they would've just killed her. *Why all this?* She remembered a time when she'd been blindfolded in the Middle East by men with guns. It was another investigation she was a part of. So, she'd been in sticky situations before and gotten out alive, even if she couldn't remember the details.

The bark of the tree brushed against her skin. Her arms and wrists and hands were looped above her head, tied to the tree. She couldn't move them much. She couldn't move much of anything. The first thing she did when she woke up was try to move any and every part of herself to see what could move and what couldn't. Her fingers and toes wiggled. That was good. *What use would that be to her?* She could turn her head from side to side. And her chest expanded and deflated as she breathed. This was the extent of her mobility. Every other part of her was tied too tight to move, making any effort of wiggling her way out of the ropes nearly impossible. She could do it with enough time and effort and energy. But she'd die of old age long before she was successful.

The woman was completely naked—no shoes, no socks, and no underwear. Her toes were grimy, like she'd been dragged through the dirt and snow. The blood flow to her extremities wasn't completely cut off, but it wasn't looking good. The good news was she didn't feel the pain. The bad news was that instead of pain, she felt cold numbness across her body, like undergoing surgery. That wasn't good.

People fear the unknown, like going under the knife, under anesthesia. They pray that they'll wake up, only they never really know until they do. The naked woman's fear was worse. She wasn't under anesthesia. She was wide awake, feeling the fear. It flooded over her like a fire blanket trying to snuff out someone who was on fire. The fear engulfed and burned her as if she were actually on fire.

Big, thready knots of rope coiled around both of her wrists, her abdomen, and her legs like fat serpents. The rope was thick and bulky, but tight. It looked navy blue in the darkness. But it was hard to tell the rope's exact color because the moon was the only source of light she had to go by. In moonlight, everything looked blue, like it was the night's default color.

The time of year was autumn, not winter—not yet. Still, there was light snow on the ground. The night temperatures dropped after sundown. They dropped dramatically. It was cold, very cold. It was too cold for a person to stay out there, naked, and survive the night. Even though the naked woman was healthy and in her mid-thirties. She'd kept up with basic cardio, three days a week. Cycling had been her go-to weekly workout.

Good cardio was more than a lifestyle choice for her. Her job required it. She interviewed witnesses and walked a lot. She always had to be on her toes. It was an occupational hazard. Still, all the exercise in the world wouldn't stop hypothermia from killing her. Like every other mammal, she could only take so much cold weather.

The naked woman wondered how long she'd been out there already. Her contact would be worried about her by now, surely. Her boss would also be worried about her. Unless it hadn't been long enough since her last check-in. Maybe it hadn't. Time was hard to grasp at that moment. Plus, her profession gave her a certain amount of freedom, a certain amount of slack. She checked in with her boss, but not day-to-day. He may not be aware that she's in trouble. In fact, she may not even be considered missing yet. Not technically. The time since she was last conscious and free could've been hours ago, or it could've been days ago. The headache pounding in her skull could've signified either.

It all depended on how she got there. If she could remember that important detail, then she could figure out the time-lapse since she'd been taken.

How much time had passed? she asked herself, but she had no idea. Without the exact last conscious memory—the moment she was taken, and the time in between—she would only be guessing. Guesswork wasn't going to help her. She could've been abducted and put into a coma for a year. A big enough team of expert abductors could pull that off, theoretically.

The tree she was strapped to looked wicked and monstrous, like it was a creature concocted from her nightmares. It was as if it were tailor-made to scare the living daylights out of her. If she survived the night, this moment in time would haunt her for the rest of her life. *If she survived the night.*

Her mouth wasn't gagged. She could breathe and speak and scream. Which she did. She shouted into the night over and over.

"HELP!"

No answer.

"HELP!" she repeated.

No response.

The naked woman continued to shout for help until she lost track of how long it'd been since the first attempt. The only response she'd heard was the constant, yet subtle, sound of the wind and the creaking of the trees.

No one was out there in the dense darkness. She was alone.

Her brain forced her into survival mode, which was not a good place to be. The brain gets desperate. Mistakes are made. The wrong thoughts surface. People make mistakes when they're desperate, grave ones. She knew that. She'd seen it thousands of times in her work. The realization helped her to stop and breathe. She stopped shouting, to conserve her energy. She only concentrated on breathing, taking in several deep breaths and releasing them, until her mind slowed and her breathing became normal.

You can work this out, she told herself.

The naked woman took another deep, deep breath, as deep as she could, against the ropes. They were tied tight around her. There was enough slack to allow her to take deep breaths, but not enough for her to wiggle her way free. She squirmed and writhed for several minutes, fighting against her restraints and making certain that she wasn't getting free. She did this until she ran out of energy. It made no difference. The ropes didn't give. They weren't going to.

She focused on her surroundings, peering around slowly, like a night owl scanning the darkness for moving prey. She started with the trees nearest her.

The trees' branches twisted and distorted outwards from thick trunks, like petrified tentacles of nightmarish beasts. That's how the trees looked in the dark, like phantom monstrosities from another hellish world. They reminded her of something out of an HP Lovecraft story. Those were books she wished she'd never read. They were required reading in college. Right then, they filled her mind with images of horrific, out-of-this-world creatures.

As she glanced around, all the trees looked terrifying. There were so many of them. Thousands of trees surrounded her in all directions. Some were close, and some were far across the open field. The trees twisted in the gloom, like an army of giant, contorting creatures. The sight was even more horrifying than old HP Lovecraft could've dreamt up. It scared her more than her darkest dreams. It terrified her more than the monster she imagined lurking under her childhood bed at night, so many years ago.

In reality, the only monster more terrifying was the one she was here to catch. The human brain will fill in the blanks when confronted with terror.

The monstrous trees were everywhere. They surrounded her. It was like they were slowly closing in on her. She shut her eyes and counted to ten. She hoped they'd vanish. But they didn't. Closing her eyes only made it worse because the sounds multiplied in her head. The forest of trees rustled and creaked in the wind. It sounded like they were slowly uprooting their trunks, revealing a horrifying secret. As if the trees had legs and feet underground. As if tonight they'd reveal this secret to her.

She had to be imagining it, hallucinating it. That couldn't be real. *Could it?*

Maybe it was all a dream. Maybe the whole scene, the whole experience, was a dream and nothing more. *Could it all be just a terrifying nightmare?* She wished she'd wake up. She wanted to wake up—desperately. She wished her eyes would just open, and she'd be back in her hotel room bed. She wished that she'd jolt awake, like when that falling feeling would jar her awake at night from a deep, dead sleep.

The naked woman kept her eyes shut and squeezed them tighter. Again, she breathed in and breathed out, waiting for the falling feeling, for the wakening jolt. It never came. She prayed the nightmare would end. That it was all triggered by a hard night of drinking. Only she couldn't remember drinking. Still, she couldn't remember much of anything about the time before she ended up on the tree.

She tried to remember, but not much was there. It was all a blur. She was dazed and confused. It was possible she was hallucinating. At least, she hoped she was. Her head throbbed and ached. She felt like she was experiencing the worst hangover of her life.

The same questions continued to torment her. *How did I get here? Where am I?*

She opened her eyes. It was all still there. The trees. The wind. The darkness. The nightmare. Nothing had changed.

The wind blew and howled around her, passing unforgivingly through the leaves and branches. The old, monstrous trees groaned in the stillness. The sounds echoed through the woods, carried by the wind, like something out of a fever dream—a fever nightmare.

Clouds floated across the sky, but sparsely. Billions of stars twinkled above her. The sky looked big and infinite. The stars blanketed across it all. The horizon stretched on for miles and miles. It was so vast that it was possible to see Canada from there. If she were out camping, this would be a beautiful spot and a beautiful night. But she wasn't camping. She'd never been here before. She was certain of it. Another question popped into her mind. *How far was she from Sawyer Lake?* That was the name of the town she'd been staying in for the last several days.

She was in Sawyer Lake to investigate an old crime. The crime had long since been forgotten by the public, by most people. Only the affected family still remembered it. They remembered it because it tore them apart. They had once been a happy Native American family. But the old murder case shredded and fragmented them into a family unrecognizable to the people who used to know them.

Hundreds of Bur Oak trees stood tall and thick around her. The one she was tied to sat at the edge of a dense forest and a wide open prairie. Tallgrass and slender wheatgrass and little bluestems rolled across the field in front of her. Wind gusts tossed and bent the grass like hammering waves out on the open water.

She recognized none of her surroundings. Not the area. Not the trees. Not the grass. Nothing. She was clueless to where she was exactly. She figured she was somewhere along the border of North Dakota and Canada. At least, she presumed so, since that's where Sawyer Lake was located. She closed her eyes and tried to remember, but it was all dark in her mind, trapped inside like a lost, repressed memory.

The ropes numbed her hands and fingers, but she could still move her fingers. So she wiggled her fingers, but felt pain immediately stab down her forearms. Her wrists throbbed from the effort. Her joints ached.

Despite being stupefied, she remembered her name, and who she was, and her profession. She remembered her dog, and her neighbor. The neighbor was her friend, and watched the dog when needed.

She remembered her house, her books, her fake plants. Still, she couldn't recall how she got tied to the tree. The answers were there. They had to be. She just couldn't get to them. They were just out of reach, unattainable, blocked by her mind. Or there was an alternate possibility. Perhaps she couldn't recall it because she was unconscious for all of it.

Maybe she had done drugs the night before? Maybe she had gotten hit with the wrong kind? She'd done drugs in her youth, but that was more than a decade ago. And she'd drunk herself to black-out drunk before. But those days were also long gone because she'd been sober for seven years now, ten years if you don't count the month that she slipped up. None of that mattered now. She hadn't had a drop of alcohol. Still, what she was experiencing now felt like the after-effects of alcohol or some kind of drug.

Suddenly, the fear of the trees changed to a different fear. The new fear came as a question. *Maybe someone sedated her? Maybe they roofied her?* The thought crept up on her. Then the real terror set in. That had to be the answer. She'd been drugged and abducted and strung up to this tree. *But for what purpose?*

Stay calm, she told herself. She pushed the fears of this new realization down deep, as far deep as she could. She tried not to focus on it. Instead, she concentrated on the question that mattered. *Why?* Figuring out the answer to that might just get her out of this.

Whatever the answer, it wasn't good. Whoever roofied her and tied her to this tree was the enemy. No question. She'd been roofied and abducted against her will. The culprit behind it was her greatest threat. She had to figure this out. She had to survive.

Sudden cold wind whooshed across her naked body. Her skin goosebumped. She shivered.

Think, she told herself. *Don't get distracted.* Maybe if she could figure out some answers, then she could use her skills to get out of this. She strained her mind to come up with something. Answers. A plan. Something. But it was no use. Everything was all too fuzzy. So she focused on trying to recall the last thing she remembered.

She remembered driving into town, checking into the resort hotel near the lake, and settling into her room, the cheapest one the hotel offered. Which she had to take because the place was expensive and she was paying with her own money. Perhaps her boss would issue her a reimbursement after she got the whole story, or perhaps not.

The next morning, she started learning the town's layout. She asked around about the ins and outs of who's who to anyone who'd talk to her. That was several days ago. The exact number of days that she'd been there was also lost to her.

The locals were friendly. They'd given her straight answers. Then she started asking about the murder victim from long ago. He was the reason she was there. She was investigating his death, an unsolved cold case.

Once she started bringing *him* up, things changed. The air was different. Tensions rose. The tone shifted. The friendliness changed to unwelcomeness. Abruptly, the locals became tightlipped. Most people claimed they had no idea what she was talking about. But she felt they were lying. Part of her job was to spot lies when she heard them. She was good at it. Her line of work demanded that she be good at it.

Never heard of him, they'd say. Which didn't add up because she'd asked preface questions like: "How long have you lived in Sawyer Lake? Where were you born?" Or "Where are you from originally?"

She did this to weed out the locals who wouldn't know about the case. The murder was nearly seven years ago, after all. Outsiders or new citizens who hadn't lived there at the time wouldn't even know about it. The murder only got regional coverage on the news, not national or even statewide. Which was weird because of the brutality and sensationalism of the whole event. She'd studied all the FBI and state police files she could get her hands on. She knew the crime scene and the evidence. She knew all about the boy.

The murder victim was a fourteen-year-old boy. He was indigenous, from the North Dakota Mokani tribe. Their reservation was a part of Sawyer County, or rather, Sawyer County was a part of their reservation, depending on who you asked.

The naked woman remembered the Mokani Reservation. It was the last thing she passed on the only road in and out of Sawyer Lake.

Someone had brutally murdered the boy. His body was discovered deep in the woods by a group of hunters, totally by accident. Because they were armed, the police determined they had scared off the killer or killers.

The police discovered rope burns on the boy's body, like he'd been tied up for an extended period before he was murdered. The way he was killed was barbaric and primal. Someone had forced him into the woods, barely clothed, and then hunted him down over several miles. And shot him with hunting arrows. He ran through the forest until he collapsed. The hunters discovered his body face-down in a ditch.

When the story broke, panic ignited across the indigenous communities. The media barely covered the story. But the fear among locals and the Mokani People was that there was a serial killer out there. They feared he was targeting them. The reason for all the fear was three-fold.

First, several young indigenous people had gone missing over a period of months. None of them had ever been found. The dead boy sparked fears that all of them had been murdered. Second, the police found little evidence. Besides the dead boy and the tactical arrows, they found nothing at the scene. And third, the killer painted something on the boy, like a sick calling card. The boy was barely clothed. His torso was exposed. The killer had painted a target bullseye across the boy's chest and abdomen, small circles inside of larger circles. And they were in different colors. The center circles were the smallest. They were painted yellow. The next circles were red. The next were blue. And the largest, outside circles were black. It was just like the bullseye on a traditional shooting target board. Each color represented a better score.

The cops theorized that a twisted group of rednecks kidnapped, tracked, and hunted the boy, shooting arrows at him, like a sick game of target practice. Some police alluded that the whole thing was the action of outsiders trying to make the locals look bad.

During the naked woman's investigation, she discovered that the cops avoided answering questions that used the words *hate crime*. It might've been to keep panic at a minimum. But some in the community called it a cover-up.

Relations between the Mokani People and the town locals became tense for a period. The police never made an arrest. Eventually, the case went cold. Many in the Mokani tribe believed the serial killer theory over the racist rednecks theory. They believed a serial killer was still out there, waiting, biding his time until he could target more of them. The racist redneck theory wasn't much better. They could also return. Maybe they thought since they got away with it, they could just come back and do it again. *If the heat was gone, then why stop?*

The Mokani People stayed suspicious about the cops and the town locals for many years to come, and with good reason. Over the years, dozens of Mokani had gone missing. Young women and men vanished without a trace. The state media barely covered it, if at all.

Since no bodies were ever found, the cops chalked up the missing persons cases to being just a bunch of runaways. Young people run away all the time. Most of them never return. The young people were just more names tossed into the files of the lost and forgotten. And time rolled on.

The FBI investigated the murder of the local Mokani boy, but came up short. They kept the case open. That's where it remained to this day. There'd been no advance. The cold case sat in a file somewhere in a stack of unsolved cases.

The naked woman shook off thoughts of the case and returned to focusing on how she got there. And how she'd get out. She tried to recall the last thing she did. She remembered getting in her car and going to the grocery, getting supplies for a day trip to the Mokani Reservation.

Wait! Suddenly, a hazy memory sprung up in her mind, a detail. She remembered she had had no luck asking the townspeople about the dead boy. Eventually, she stumbled upon someone from the reservation who offered to help. *Who was it?* She remembered it was a man. She met him at a bar. She'd been asking about the boy. He told her he knew the exact spot where the boy had been shot, before he escaped and died.

The man offered to take her there that night. *What was his name?* She couldn't recall. *What did he look like?* She couldn't remember.

She'd met him when she was canvassing the locals for clues on what they knew about the case. He was odd, a bit flamboyantly dressed, and very full of himself, but he claimed to have answers. He invited her out to the parking lot, to his truck. They could talk in private if they sat in it. He claimed he wanted to be away from prying eyes. Reluctantly, she'd agreed. It seemed risky, but she'd been in riskier situations before. Her job was to get the scoop, the lead, and uncover the answers. Whatever it took to get the truth of the story. She'd investigated worse crimes in worse places. She figured she was safe enough. That was a grave mistake. She knew that now.

One minute, she was sitting in his front seat, talking with him. The next, she woke up here. She vaguely remembered his truck. She vaguely remembered his face. He must've drugged her.

She paused a beat, thought about it. It hit her. *Wait!* She remembered the struggle. He'd shoved a rag in her face and covered her mouth. There must've been something in the rag. He'd covered her mouth with it, and then, like a flick of a switch, she was out cold.

After that, she had no way of piecing together what happened from the truck to the tree. She was fairly certain she'd not been raped. But she had been undressed before being tied to the tree. The horror of what could've happened while she was naked and unconscious filled her mind. There could be pictures or video that could ruin her career. The trauma of what she might recall later could ruin her life. But she couldn't think about those things right now. Now she had to stay present and focus on getting free.

The naked woman again tried to move. She tried to buck and kick her feet, hoping the effort would loosen the ropes. But the effort was no good. Her feet were secured too tightly to the tree's trunk. She looked down at them. The same blue rope had been used all over her body. Like her clothes, her shoes were also gone.

The naked woman glanced up. Her eyes had adjusted better to the darkness, and she could see more clearly. In front of her, there was a huge open field of green needlegrass. Like the horizon, the grass rolled on for miles. At least, it appeared that way. It was hard to tell because hundreds of yards away, in front of her, the grass disappeared over rolling hills and into the darkness.

Mountains lingered all around her in the distance. She couldn't make out the exact details. They appeared as huge, shadowy figures. Between her and the farthest dark edges of the needlegrass, she saw more trees, below the mountains. There was no artificial light anywhere, which told her she was far from the nearest civilization.

Out of the darkness, across the open prairie, the first sign of life emerged from out of the trees. A pair of headlights appeared from the south. There was no road. The vehicle drove over the grass. It bucked and bounced across the prairie. She figured it was a truck—probably. She watched the headlights with frantic, desperate eyes. It could be her salvation. The vehicle's driver's side headlight flickered on and off like the bulb was going bad. The vehicle approached fast. Plumes of thick dust kicked up behind it. Like the ropes, the dust also appeared blue in the moonlight. The vehicle was loud. It sounded old, like something from the nineteen-seventies.

As the vehicle neared, she could make it out. It was an old white pickup. She didn't know the make and model, but she recognized the truck. She'd seen it before. Somewhere. The windows were tinted. The dark tint, the distance, and the night sky made it impossible to see the driver or if there were other occupants. She had no idea how many people were in it.

The truck sped and fishtailed over the open grass. Then it slowed as it drew closer. At the final thirty yards, the truck slowed to a crawl. She saw enough of it to know where she'd seen it before. She'd seen it on the Mokani Reservation. She'd seen it at the bar. And she'd seen it earlier that night. Her memories were fuzzy, but she recalled that much.

The white pickup truck had big black tires. It was old, but painted within the last few years to keep it looking current. Dirt and grime covered the fenders and the rims.

A large pair of longhorn horns jutted out of the front of the hood, like a macabre hood ornament. The truck stopped on the grass twenty yards away from her, but it didn't park. The brake lights lit the dust plumes behind them in a crimson red, creating an eeriness as the red lights mixed with the moonlit blue dust.

The transmission box cranked and clattered as the driver reversed the pickup. The truck backed up several yards and stopped. The passenger door creaked open, and a figure hopped out. It was a man, but she couldn't make out enough details to identify him.

She shouted, "Hey! I'm here! Help me!"

No response. He didn't even look in her direction. But she was sure he could hear her. She knew she was loud and within his earshot. At least, yelling should be within his earshot. Determined, she tried again.

"Hey!"

Nothing.

"Hello?"

No response. The man didn't look at her, or even in her direction. Instead, he spoke to someone inside the cab of the truck. He and the driver exchanged words. It sounded like the driver was yelling at the man.

The man stepped away from the truck, leaving the passenger door wide open. He sprinted off to the center of the grassy prairie, putting a large distance between him and the truck. He found a hill and stopped sprinting and stood on the hilltop. He looked east, and stayed there. He looked like he was searching for something far away. Then he turned back and stared directly at the naked woman on the tree.

She didn't call to him. She just watched, confused by what she had witnessed. *What the hell is he doing?* she thought.

The man on the hill used his hands and touched his index fingers and thumbs together, forming a square-shaped, boxy hole. He lifted the boxy hole up to eye level and held it out in front of his face. He stared through it at the woman on the tree. He looked like a movie cinematographer. It was like he was setting up a shot for a film.

Once he seemed satisfied with the shot, he lowered his hands and cupped them together. He placed them around his lips and called out through them, like with a bullhorn.

He shouted to the driver, "Move closer!"

The driver released the brakes and moved the truck closer to the woman on the tree. The driver stopped and glanced back at the cinematographer to get his approval. He repeated this process several times.

Each time, the cinematographer shouted, "More!" or "Closer!"

The driver inched the truck closer to the naked woman on the tree until it was less than twenty-five yards from her.

"Stop!" the cinematographer called out. The driver hit the brakes and the truck stopped there.

The cinematographer shouted, "Turn on the high beams!"

The driver switched the high beams on. The truck's headlights washed over the woman on the tree. Her face and chest remained in darkness, but her bottom half—her legs, feet, abdomen, waist, and nether regions—were in the light beams. All of it was on full display. Minus what the ropes covered.

The cinematographer grinned and shouted, "Move the truck back. Just a few feet!"

The driver reversed the truck, slowly, and angled the pickup so that the light beams inched up the woman's body. The high beams climbed slowly until they illuminated everything.

She grimaced and turned away because the lights were blinding. But it was critical that she saw what was happening. She turned back to the lights and tried to stare past them, at the driver. But the darkness inside the truck's cabin shrouded him, making his features impossible to discern because of the distance and the blackness.

The lights shone directly in her eyes. They were just too bright. She had to look away. But she didn't want to close her eyes and hope for the best, like a helpless victim. So, she looked down at herself. The light beam illuminated her torso. There was hardly any part of her naked body that was left up to the imagination. They could see it all clear as day.

Staring down at herself, she suddenly regretted it. Instantly, she knew what their intentions were because she was wrong about one thing. She wasn't completely naked. A better way to put it was that she was naked, but not uncovered. There was something on her skin. It covered her torso.

Horrified, she thought she knew who they were and what they planned to do. Immense terror exploded inside her. It consumed her faster than the nightmarish scene around her had done. The feeling was overwhelming, like being set on fire while pedestrians stood around and did nothing to help. The terror couldn't be ignored. There was no pretending.

The ropes were tied around her waist, her arms, her neck, and her legs. But they weren't across her abdomen and chest. Her breasts were exposed, but they were covered in paint. Her entire torso was covered in various paint colors. The designs were crude circles. Each circle was painted one inside the other. And each was a different color and a different size. They had painted a bullseye on her, like a target at a gun range. That's why she felt the fear. It was the answer to why she was there and who they were. Just like the kid who had been murdered seven years ago, now she was the target. She'd asked too many questions. Bad luck had put her in the path of the murderers.

The terror set in deeper than she thought possible. Panic exploded inside her. She couldn't fight it. No way could she stay calm. Not now. Not knowing the truth. She had come to Sawyer Lake and the Mokani Reservation to investigate a boy's death. Now she'd found the killers. And she was their next victim.

Abruptly, something echoed from the cinematographer. It was a familiar sound. A walkie talkie crackled in the cinematographer's hands. She stared in his direction, squinting her eyes to see him. He answered it. She couldn't hear the conversation, just the mumbling of words.

The cinematographer acknowledged something to the voice on the other line. Then he clicked off the walkie and returned to the truck. The driver left the pickup's engine running. He slipped the gear to neutral and engaged the emergency brake. Then he slid out and joined the cinematographer at the tailgate.

The driver lowered the tailgate, slid a drink cooler out from the bed, and opened it. The two men pulled out a couple of bottled beers, twisted off the caps, and walked to the front of the truck. They leaned against the grille, drank the beers, and watched the woman on the tree and waited, like they were waiting for a show.

She could barely see them past the headlights. Her heart raced. She squinted, trying to see more of the two men. Desperately, she stared at them.

She shouted to them. "Hey! What's happening?"

They said nothing to her. They responded, just not to her. She heard them. The cinematographer clicked the walkie and barked at the person on the other end.

The cinematographer said, "She's awake. Go when ready."

What does that mean? She thought. But she already knew.

The woman on the tree waited in agonizing terror. Frantically, she stared out across the open prairie, fearing what was to come. Then she heard it. A loud sound cracked across the plain. It was a sound that many people knew, and knew well. The sound was a rifle shot. It came from far away, in the distance, from out of the darkness. It echoed, loud and ominous.

The naked woman's eyes darted around, trying to locate it. She saw nothing. And nothing happened for several minutes after. No more gunshots. Instead, the cinematographer got on the radio and barked more orders. It sounded like he said, "To the left."

Just then, something else happened. It was something more alarming than the sound of a rifle shot. It was a loud crack. It happened on the tree to her left. She glanced over and saw the tree trunk splinter and explode like it had been hit by something with incredible velocity and force.

A split-second after the impact of the object, she heard another rifle shot. She looked out and forward, past the headlights, and past the pickup truck. She saw something. It was a flash of light. No. It was a muzzle flash. It was quick, like a blip. And it was far away. She couldn't judge the distance. Not accurately. But she guessed it was more than a hundred yards. It could've been more than two hundred yards. She figured it was less than four hundred, but more than two. But she really had no idea. She wasn't any kind of expert on guns or on measuring distance.

Another muzzle flash and another rifle shot followed. Between the muzzle flash and the echoing sound of the shot, there was another impact. This time it was against a huge branch that sprouted from the tree she was strung to. The branch was thick and long. It stretched up high above the ground. The impact struck the branch of her tree, only it was way too high to hit her.

Nothing happened for a long moment. The air was filled with terrifying silence. The woman's heart raced. Her adrenaline spiked hard, harder than it had before. And she knew why. She knew what the impacts were. They were bullets. Someone was sniping her, and the guys in the truck were watching, like voyeurs. This was sickly entertaining to them.

They drank from their beer bottles and chuckled at her, like the whole thing was a spectator sport.

The woman on the tree screamed in terror, over and over. But it was no use.

The adrenaline spike ignited her muscles. She fought against her bindings, against the bark of the tree. She wiggled her fingers and her toes. She tried to kick. She tried to buck. But nothing happened. The ropes were too tight. They were too big and thick. The struggle tired her in seconds. After, she felt exhausted and could barely move, barely put up any more fight. Even if she could, the only thing she could do was try to reason with them.

She shouted, "Wait!" But it didn't stop them. The cinematographer got back on the walkie. This time, she could hear him in the silence.

He said, "Lower."

"No! Please!" she called out.

No answer.

Several more minutes passed by, forcing the woman to wait for the inevitable, for her own execution. She stared up in the direction she'd seen the previous muzzle flash and waited in torment. Another gunshot flashed. It came from the same spot. It was the same shooter.

The bullet slammed into the tree, above her head. Tree bark splintered and cracked. Wood dust sprayed over her head. The rifle shot echoed across the landscape. The bullets were getting closer.

The onlookers laughed and cheered. They clinked their beers together and drank them down. They opened two more and repeated the process.

The sniper fired another round at the woman. It hit another branch of her tree. The bullet's impact vibrated through the bark, through the core of the tree, and through the trunk. She felt it in the back of her skull.

The sniper fired several more rounds at her—all spaced out, all missing—but coming closer and closer. The onlookers drank two more beers, watching and laughing.

The woman on the tree writhed and bucked and begged for her life. She wanted to escape, to free herself, drop to the ground, and take off running. It seemed impossible. It seemed unlikely. The boy had escaped them somehow. He'd taken arrows to his center mass and escaped. He'd gotten away, but only to die in the woods. He had been dealing with arrows. She was dealing with rifle bullets.

But could she escape? She didn't know. She figured two things. She'd found the boy's killers. And they were going to kill her next.

CHAPTER 2

The next morning, Jack Widow ordered a quad espresso—black, no cream, no sugar, and no nonsense—from a young woman in a string bikini in a coffee shop thirteen hundred miles west of the naked woman's tree.

Widow wasn't in the coffee shop for young women in bikinis. He was there for the coffee. But young women in bikinis were what he got. Bikinis were the uniforms they wore.

In front of him, the barista wore a string bikini and nothing else. Like his espresso, her bikini was also no-nonsense. It had little to it. There was string, it was a bikini, and that was that.

The only extra bit of clothing was a colorfully spotted nametag that was literally hanging on by a thread. The nametag read: *Samantha*. It dangled from a thin thread below her left breast, which was prominent. She wasn't shy about the display. She had no reason to be. The customers in the shop certainly didn't seem to mind. Of course, they were almost all men. There were some women there as well, but most of the patrons were men.

Widow glanced at the nametag. It was the only thing he could glance at that made him feel comfortable. Samantha stared at him with big brown eyes. Which made him divert his eyes. He looked straight ahead, checking the menu like he was deciding what to order, but he had already ordered. He simply didn't want to look anywhere else on Samantha's barely covered body. Not that he didn't like what he saw. He did. She was a beautiful woman. But Widow tried to behave like a gentleman. His mother had raised him that way. His mother was once a cop. She'd taught him honor and accountability. At least, she laid the foundation for those concepts. It was his sixteen years of military and NCIS service that cemented them in his character.

Ending up in a bikini coffee shop was his fault, as he was on a mission. The mission was coffee. The bikini baristas weren't his fault. It was all a dumb mistake. He hadn't expected them. All he had done was walk into the place, not knowing what it was exactly. He hadn't known it was a coffee bar with young women in bikinis. It was just his luck and his addiction to coffee. He entered the shop only because of the word *Coffee* on the sign above the front door. Like a Naval Strike Missile programmed to hit a specific target, Widow laser-focused on coffee, missing that the coffee shop was called *Trigger's Bikini Coffee Bar*. Widow should've known what it was. He could read fine.

He wasn't duped. The outside sign was clear and effective. It had a logo with a neon coffee mug and a bikini haphazardly draped over it like it was a shower rod. The whole thing was playful and suggestive. The sign was a work of art, in its own way.

Widow was a smart guy. *Smarter than the average bear*, his mom used to tell him. He didn't understand the reference. But that's what she'd said.

Right then, Widow felt pretty dumb, because for *smarter than the average bear*, he'd been so single-minded that he completely missed the sign's suggestiveness and went right for his target, the coffee.

Widow hadn't known it was a bikini coffee place. To his credit, this bikini coffee place was one-of-a-kind. At least, he'd never heard of one like it before. The coffee bar was unique because it had both outdoor and indoor seating. This was the first he'd come across. Normally, bikini baristas served coffee from the safety of a food truck or a side-of-the-road coffee hut, where there were walls and windows between them and the bikini-ogling customers. That made sense to Widow, because for every gentleman, there were certainly two or three guys who were less than respectful. He'd known restaurants—like the food chain *Hooters*—that had scantily clad women serving food, but this was a new experience for him.

At the counter, Widow tried diligently to keep eye contact with Samantha. Judging by her youthful appearance, he figured she was less than half his age. But he wasn't going to let a little awkwardness make him abandon his coffee mission. Nothing would come between him and his target.

Widow stood six-foot-four, and weighed two hundred and thirty-five pounds. Most of it was pure, stone-hard muscle. He had broad shoulders as hard as diabase rock. His legs were thick, like baobab tree trunks. His arms were thick, like the anchor chains on an *Arleigh Burke*-class naval destroyer.

Widow was in Port Gamble, about twenty-eight miles west of Seattle. It was fifty-five degrees outside, and in this area it was almost always either raining or about to rain. Which meant that fifty-five degrees on an early Washington day seemed a hell of a lot colder than it was on a Nevada morning, because of how everything felt wet and dreary outside.

Widow was wetter and colder than he should've been because he wore a Burnt Cognac Sheepskin Bomber Jacket. It wasn't waterproof, which was virtually required of coats sold and worn in the Pacific Northwest.

Widow's coat was faded and tattered and worn. He'd picked it up Idaho, not from a thrift store, but from a donation bin just outside a thrift store. A woman was donating it, with a bunch of other clothes, because her husband had passed away. That's the story she told Widow. He'd been about to step into the store to find something warm to wear when he saw her tossing it into the bin. They'd struck up a conversation, and she'd given it to him.

He offered to pay for it, but she wasn't having it. He expressed his condolences about the loss of her husband.

She'd said, "Don't worry about it. He was a cheating asshole, anyway."

Widow didn't respond to that. He didn't know the story or the circumstances. He did notice pain in her eyes, as well as a sense of relief.

Instead of prying or commenting, he mentioned a donut shop around the corner. He'd seen it after he stepped off the bus. He offered to buy her some donuts and coffee for the used jacket. She'd agreed, and that's how he paid for it.

That was nearly two weeks ago, and he still wore it. Her husband must've been a big guy too, because the jacket fit Widow like an old glove.

Under the jacket, he wore a navy plaid flannel shirt over a black t-shirt and blue jeans. Under the cuffs of the jeans, a pair of dog-eared boots stuck out. They had been the ugliest pair of boots on the store's shelf. But they were the only pair in his size. The ugly boots were more comfortable than they should've been for a pair so used and worn. The thrift store stuck little yellow tags on each item it sold. The tags had short, handwritten descriptions of the item. The ugly boots' tag read: *Broken in like a trusty Appaloosa.* There was no other commentary.

Widow guessed an Appaloosa was some kind of horse or donkey. Based on the thrift store's décor, the latter wouldn't have surprised him. But he bought the boots and loved them, almost as much as the jacket.

Widow bought a pair of cheap fabric gloves too, but they were stuffed in his back pocket. The last item he got from that same store was on his head. It was a black beanie hat. It was an impulse purchase. He almost didn't buy it. But he was glad he did. The cold, rainy weather of Port Gamble would've been murder on his ears.

Samantha, the bikini barista, stood under five-foot-two. Because of the height difference, Widow had to look down at her, which made him a little uneasy because he knew he'd see more of her intimate parts. It couldn't be helped.

Samantha looked up at Widow during the ordering and money exchange and said, "You're blushing."

Widow stayed quiet, but not because he had nothing to say. He said nothing because he was too embarrassed to speak. He paid for his espresso. She smiled and offered him his change. He waved it off for her to keep as a tip. She smiled, and said, "Thank you, mister."

Widow nodded. He found a wall toward the back of the store, six feet from the end of the counter where people picked up their orders. He leaned against the wall and waited. The wait wasn't long, and he held his espresso within minutes. He took it and headed to the door and walked back outside.

The bikini coffee shop was on a long and busy sidewalk that paralleled the coastline around Puget Sound. He was just north of the Hood Canal Floating Bridge. He'd spent the last few days aimlessly wandering around Bainbridge Island and Kitsap Peninsula. There was a major Navy base there. It was Naval Base Kitsap, the largest naval installation in the Pacific Northwest. It was created back in 2004. The US Navy amalgamated the former Naval Station Bremerton with Naval Submarine Base Bangor in order to merge the whole thing under one official umbrella.

Widow wasn't in the USN anymore or the SEALs or the NCIS, as he once had been. Now, he was a drifter, a loner. He liked to think of himself as a forever tourist. SEALs are unofficially known as violent nomads. That's what he was and what he always would be. He was a nomad. And, when the situation called for it, he was violent. The last time he'd been violent was a year ago. He'd stumbled into a situation where he became the protector of a young woman and her son. He'd ended up spending time with them in Mexico. That was a good time in his life. He'd made memories.

However, nomadic life isn't for the settling-down type. And Widow wasn't the settling-down type. Staying in one place made him too restless.

Still, Widow felt sentimental from time to time. That's why he was in Kitsap County. He was there because he felt nostalgic. Sometimes even a nomad gets homesick. Even though the Navy wasn't a place; it was a lifestyle, a career, and a sense of purpose. But for Widow, it was the only place he'd ever called home.

The last couple of days, he'd walked the coastline and stayed in motels as close as he could get to the water so that he could watch for docking ships and Navy boats. Even the uniformed sailors sitting around the tables at the bikini coffee shop reminded him of the good old days.

Being so close to Naval Base Kitsap made him feel like he was home. He'd also visited shipyards and museums and admired the large seafaring vessels that he loved. Ships and sailors and Marines weren't the only things he'd seen there. He'd seen orca pods breach the canals and waterways around the peninsula. Today, he'd made his way over to this location specifically because this was where he'd most likely see a submarine surface.

South of him was Bangor, the submarine component of Kitsap. That's where submarines docked for maintenance and where some were built. Or where they simply docked, so the crew could come ashore.

Widow walked out beyond the coffee shop, past a morning crowd that was building. He noticed most of the people walking into the coffee shop were sailors in and out of uniform. He knew the out-of-uniform sailors the same way an off-duty cop can spot another off-duty cop. There were some Marines as well. They were also in and out of uniform. Uniform or no uniform, the jarhead haircuts were a dead giveaway.

Widow located a good spot down by the water, just north of the bridge. He found an empty two-seat, metal table under a closed umbrella. He pulled a chair out and dumped himself down in it.

He sipped his espresso, turned to the water, and waited to see a submarine. He hoped it would satisfy his nostalgia, like seeing a classmate from high school thirty years later.

A submarine never came. But something came his way, something from the past. And maybe it should've stayed there.

CHAPTER 3

Just before eight in the morning, Widow finished his second quad espresso for the day. That was the one that hit the spot because he felt awake and alert and satisfied. He'd sat at the same metal table in the same spot for nearly two hours, people-watching and on the lookout for a submarine or any ships. He saw various Navy ships in the distance, passing farther onto the other side of the peninsula to Bremerton, presumably to dock. He saw many civilian ships and boats. Their destination was unknown to him, but he assumed they were headed to the port of Seattle.

So far, Widow had seen no submarines or whales breaching the surface. A bald eagle flew by and circled him for several minutes. It was fierce and majestic. He appreciated it. But that had been the highlight of his morning.

He'd seen passersby of all shapes and sizes. He'd heard a couple of foreign languages spoken between groups of tourists. And he'd seen most of the sailors and Marines leave. Most, if not all of them, had to be on base for their assigned jobs. The trains had to run on time, as one of his COs used to say. The saying was ironic, since he was the commander of one of the boats Widow had been stationed on, way back in the day.

The gray weather still lingered, but bright sunlight had pierced through some of it, making the sky look gray and blue and white all at the same time. There was no rain, but the air smelled wet. It could rain at any moment. It was best to always be *en garde*.

Widow tipped what was left of the espresso over his mouth one last time and swallowed the last drop. Afterward, he stared into the empty cup and contemplated ordering another, but twelve espresso shots in a single morning would be a lot, even for him. He decided to take a walk south along the shoreline until he couldn't go any farther, which he pictured would be the outer perimeter fencing that surrounded Bangor.

Widow stood up from his table, turned, and walked to a trashcan to toss the empty espresso cup. He passed a woman who was pushing a baby in a stroller, and a pair of bikini baristas on break. They were outside in the cold, but wore sweatpants and big, heavy coats. They were on a smoke break. One of them looked at Widow, and said, "That's him."

Widow kept walking, but stayed focused on them in his peripherals. And he noticed that the one who spoke was Samantha. He hadn't recognized her in clothes at first. He continued to the trashcan.

Samantha spoke to her coworker, but Widow could hear if he tuned out the surrounding sounds, which he did. She said, "I think he's cute."

The coworker said, "I don't know. He looks sketchy, dangerous, like you could end up on the six o'clock news because of him."

"No way. He's sweet. I'm telling you."

"So go talk to him."

Widow smiled to himself. It was flattering, but he wasn't planning on sticking around too much longer. He didn't look over. The temptation was there. Before he could indulge in it, he'd reached the trashcan, tossed his used espresso cup, and heard another voice speak to him from several feet behind him. It was a voice from the past.

A voice with a golden California accent said, "You can never cross the ocean unless you have the courage to lose sight of the shore."

Widow spun around, slow, and saw a man standing tall at around six feet. He had broad shoulders under a uniform: a sailor's ceremonial full dress whites, hat and all, like he was going to something fancy. In the Navy, that could be any number of events. The DoD loved to throw parties for various reasons. The whites were half-concealed under a coat, all-weather and double-breasted. The coat was open.

The guy's shoulder boards, ribbons, and medals were hidden beneath the coat. The guy was clean-shaven, with hair cut to match. Under the United States Navy Uniform Regulations NAVPERS 15665J, section 2201.1, the first section is for haircuts and styles. The first part covers men and the first line is: *Keep hair neat, clean and well groomed.*

The sailor in front of Widow had hit all the marks. His hair was cut right. It was gray with sprinkles of black in it. He had piercing blue eyes, which Widow remembered instantly.

Widow said, "That's Christopher Columbus."

The sailor nodded and grinned.

Widow said, "Any fool can carry on, but a wise man knows how to shorten sail in time."

The guy look stunned for a moment, and then said, "That's easy. It's Conrad."

Widow nodded. And then, the guy said, "Okay. What about this one? Smooth seas do not make skillful sailors."

Widow chuckled and said, "FDR, I'm out of the service, not dumb."

"Oh yeah, tough guy. Give me your best shot."

Widow paused a beat and said, "Okay. Smell the sea and feel the sky. Let your soul and spirit fly."

The sailor's grin crumbled, and he just stood there. His eyes looked up at the sky like he'd find the answers on the gray clouds. A puzzled look washed over his face.

Widow asked, "Stumped?"

"Hold on a second. I can get it."

Widow waited. The guy continued to search his memory for the answer, but found nothing. No answer. Finally, he said, "Fine. Who is it?"

"Van Morrison."

"Give me a break. No way!"

"It is. I swear."

"I thought you'd pull out Hemingway or something. You know? A man is never lost at sea?"

Widow said, "Well, I didn't."

"Okay. How about this one?"

"No. I already got you. No more."

"One more. Let me redeem myself."

"Fine. What you got?"

The sailor said, "Not all treasure is silver and gold, mate."

Widow stared at him dumbfounded. He glanced down at the concrete. It didn't ring a bell for him. He looked back up and glanced back over his shoulder at Samantha and her coworker on smoke break. They were no longer looking in his direction. They had moved on to other topics. He'd be lying if he said it didn't bum him out a little.

The sailor interrupted, "Come on, Widow. You gotta know this one. Everyone knows this one. My kids know this one."

Widow searched his brain, but couldn't come up with the right answer. So he took a guess. He said, "Emerson?"

The sailor palmed his face and shook his head and chuckled. He said, "That's embarrassing."

"Why? Who is it?"

"It's Captain Jack Sparrow."

Widow stayed quiet, but stared at the sailor. Questions lingered in his eyes.

The sailor said, "You never heard of Captain Jack?"

"Nope. What period was he in?"

"He's from those Disney movies?"

Widow stayed quiet.

The sailor said, "You know? Johnny Depp?"

Widow shrugged. The name sounded familiar, but he couldn't place it.

The sailor said, "Well, I guess I don't need to ask you if you've changed. You haven't, clearly. No kids I guess?"

"No kids."

The sailor smiled, walked to Widow, opened his arms and the two men hugged like old friends, which they were.

"Widow, it's great to see you again. I can't believe you're here."

"Reed Steslow, it's good to see you. It really is a small world. What rank are you now? Do I salute?" Widow asked, and he backed away from Steslow, grabbed his coat and opened the sailor's left coat flap to look at his rank. He saw it, and said, "Captain Steslow? You're supposed to button this up. You know? Regulations."

Steslow said, "You know me. I'm not a stickler for the rules, like you were."

"Is that why you're just a captain? What the hell have you been doing to move so slow? Probably spending all your time watching kids' movies?"

Steslow smiled, and said, "I've been busy getting married, having babies, and getting divorced, and raising kids. You know? Real-life drama."

Widow said, "Divorced? Sorry to hear that."

"Don't be. It was amicable. She's good with the kids. They're our priority. I get them whenever I'm back home."

"How much is that?"

"Not much. Not these days," Steslow said. He stepped back from Widow and looked him over. He said, "So, what about you?"

"What?"

"What the hell are you up to? You don't look military anymore. That hair alone would get you court-martialed."

Instinctively, Widow ran a hand through his hair. Not that bad. It was too long for the Navy, about four or five inches at the moment. He could use a trim, he supposed, but he'd wait for now. It wasn't a top priority.

Widow said nothing about his hair. He said, "I'm doing nothing."

"Not right now. I mean in life. What are you up to?"

"Nothing."

"Where do you work? Are you a private contractor? Working corporate security or investigations or something?"

"I told you. I'm doing nothing. I'm not contracting or working anywhere."

Steslow asked, "Are you retired?"

Widow shrugged, and said, "You could say that."

"Where are you living?"

"Nowhere."

Steslow frowned, and said, "Nowhere? Are you homeless?"

"Technically, yes."

"Where are you staying right now?"

"Last night I slept at a hostel in Seattle."

"Hostel?"

"I prefer motels. But Seattle has gotten expensive. So, I went on the cheap. It was alright."

Steslow's face went from happy to see an old friend to one of slight disappointment. He reached into his coat's inside pocket and pulled out his wallet. He opened it and took out a wad of hundred-dollar bills. It must've been a few thousand dollars. He peeled off a few of them and handed them to Widow.

Widow put a hand up and waved them away. He said, "Reed, I don't need money. I got money. I just didn't want to spend three hundred bucks for a motel room. That's all."

"I thought you said you were homeless?"

"Not like that. I don't have a home. I live wherever I am at the moment."

"You're a drifter?"

"Right."

"Isn't that homeless?"

Widow looked around. He saw Samantha and the other barista. They were getting up to go back to their shifts. He said, "Were you getting coffee?"

Steslow glanced at the bikini coffee shop and back at Widow. He said, "I was about to grab some to go."

"Want to grab a table?"

"Didn't you just finish your coffee already? I thought you threw it in the trash?"

Widow said, "That was an espresso, but I can get just plain coffee."

"Okay," Steslow said, and looked at his watch. "I can't stay. I got somewhere important to be."

"Important?"

"Yeah, but why don't you come along? Believe me, it's something you won't wanna miss. It's going to be something record-breaking."

"Record-breaking?"

"Yep. Trust me. You've got impeccable timing. You'll be sorry if you miss it. It'll go into the history books."

Widow paused and thought about his old friend's offer. Judging by Steslow's uniform, and the morning hours, the sailor had to be going somewhere special.

Steslow mistook Widow's silence as hesitation and he said, "What? You ain't got the time for us Navy folk anymore?"

Widow smiled, and said, "Navy folk I got lots of time for. But for you, I don't know."

"Come on, Widow."

Widow smiled, and said, "Just kidding. Of course, I'll go. It sounds like an offer I can't refuse."

Steslow smiled a hearty smile, nodded, and the two men went into the coffee shop, where Samantha was back behind the counter. She smiled when she saw Widow. The men ordered. Widow ordered a decaf coffee, at Samantha's suggestion, since he'd already been over-caffeinated from the eight shots of espresso. But Steslow ordered three coffees. When Widow asked who the other two were for, Steslow said to just wait. It would *blow Widow's socks off*. Those were Steslow's words.

Samantha put Steslow's coffees in a cup carrier for him. Steslow paid for his and Widow's, against Widow's will. Then they left the shop.

Outside, Widow followed Steslow out to the sidewalks along the water, and beyond to a sidewalk intersection. Steslow turned right and headed inland, away from the water and away from the floating bridge, dashing Widow's hopes of seeing a submarine. Whatever Steslow had planned, Widow was in too deep to back out now.

The two threaded through a crowd of women, and some men, all dressed in warm coats with yoga pants underneath. They stood outside of a yoga studio. They stood around talking, like classes had either just ended or they were waiting for them to begin.

Widow and Steslow made their way to a busy street. Steslow turned left onto a sidewalk. He gestured for Widow to follow. They walked toward a black Lincoln Navigator with tinted windows, which was parallel-parked on the side of the road in a space reserved for police and emergency vehicles. The vehicle's engine idled.

When they got about fifteen feet from the Navigator, the driver's side door swung open and another sailor stepped out. He was young, late twenties. He was a three-striper. He wore the blue camouflage-pattern uniform. One thing about him that set him apart from ordinary sailors walking around was that he was armed. He wore an M9 Beretta in a hip holster. He wasn't an ordinary sailor. He was a Master-at-Arms, the Navy's version of enlisted police and force protection. Not the Navy police or the NCIS, which were civilian forces. Of course, Widow recognized him for what he was immediately. Widow had worked hand-in-hand with them before.

He had aviator sunglasses on, blocking Widow from seeing his eyes.

The sailor closed his door, strode around the vehicle's nose, and greeted Widow and Steslow on the sidewalk. He took Steslow's coffee carrier, holding it one-handed, and walked to the passenger side rear door. He opened it for Steslow, referring to him as *sir*, like he was royalty or something.

Steslow gestured to Widow to get in. He said, "Get in. I'll sit up front."

Widow stood there on the sidewalk, dumbfounded for a moment. *What was Steslow doing now to have a personal escort from the naval police? And why was Steslow going to sit up front and not in the back on the other side?* Before Widow could ask him, Steslow herded him into the vehicle. Widow got in.

By the time Widow's butt hit the rear seat, he knew exactly why there was a police escort with a firearm. He knew exactly why Steslow had gotten three coffees. He knew exactly why all the secrecy. And he understood why Steslow wore his ceremonial dress.

Seated across from Widow, on the rear driver's side seat, sat a man in an expensive suit with a red tie. He looked very important, like some kind of politician. There was a US Navy pin on his jacket. It was gold and polished.

The man had a thinning crop of hair on his head and a clean-shaven face, even more clean-shaven than Steslow's. The man was short with a little belly. A pair of sunglasses covered his eyes. They weren't aviators, like his driver's. They were definitely expensive, as in the thousands of dollars—expensive.

Widow didn't recognize him, but he figured he was somebody important. The guy wasn't enlisted, and he wasn't an officer. He was civilian, but high up the food chain.

The driver opened the front passenger door, and Steslow got in. He slid into the seat. The driver closed the door behind him and walked around the hood and got in behind the wheel. He grabbed his coffee out of Steslow's cup carrier, put on his seatbelt, and pulled away from the curb, cutting off a car that was driving behind them. The other driver blasted his horn. The Navigator's driver flashed blue lights that were embedded in the grille and rear lights. It was just a quick blip of the lights, enough to let the other drivers know this was an official government vehicle. The car backed off.

Steslow turned in his seat and reached out the last coffee to the important man, who took it. Steslow turned to Widow and smiled. The important man slow-sipped from the spout on the coffee's plastic lid. It was too hot, so he backed off. He glanced at Steslow and asked, "Captain, who is our guest? And why is he here?"

"This is," Steslow said, and paused. He looked back at Widow. "Sorry, I don't know. What was your last rank?"

Widow said, "At my terminal leave, I was an O5."

Steslow said, "This is Commander Jack Widow."

The important man turned in his seat, passed his coffee from his right hand to his left, and offered his right to Widow to shake. Widow took it and shook it, and replied, "It's just Widow. No one calls me any of that other stuff. Not anymore."

The important man said, "What boat did you last command? A frigate? Or was it a destroyer?"

They stopped shaking hands, and Widow said, "How do you know I commanded a boat?"

"Well, you're far too tall to be a pilot and I can't imagine anyone from Medical Corps clearing you for an attack sub. The Navy would end up paying out the butt to cover your back problems at this age from always ducking down."

Widow said, "Actually, the upper limit for a pilot is six-five. I'm just under that. And I've been on subs before. It's not a big deal. But I commanded neither."

The important man arched an eyebrow behind his glasses. Before he could speak, Steslow said, "Widow was in the SEALs."

"Really?" the important man said, and looked at Widow with a look that said *of course*, like being told a riddle, getting the answer, and feeling dumb for not seeing it before.

Steslow said, "Widow, this is Adam Cress."

Widow nodded, but didn't recognize the name.

Steslow said, "He's the Secretary of the Navy."

CHAPTER 4

Cress's driver took them onto Washington State Route 104 briefly until it connected to State Route 3. They rode it the rest of the way for less than fourteen miles to the gates of Bremerton. The highway was surrounded by tall Douglas firs and various shrubs on all sides. The northbound lanes were separated from the southbound by elevation and a thick, grassy median. The highway wound mostly to the left.

Along the way, Widow and Cress talked. Cress showed interest in Widow and his current life. They did the usual small talk, which leads from introductions to résumés.

Cress began his career in the Navy before Widow's time and ended at Widow's three-year mark. He'd made it to Rear Admiral, a RDML, O7. Which was impressive. Then he became a congressman for the Lone Star State of Texas. He served two terms in Congress. The last president appointed him Secretary of the Navy, where he stayed on with the new administration. He remarked to Widow that he was surprised the new president kept him, since the predecessor was of the opposite party.

Widow responded diplomatically. He said, "They knew they had a good man at the helm. Why change it?"

Cress said, "Thank you. I appreciate the confidence. Especially coming from a SEAL."

"The only mistake I see from your leadership so far is keeping around this fossil," Widow joked, and nodded at Steslow, who half-turned and gazed at both men.

Steslow said, "Hey! At least I made Captain. You will forever be below me in rank."

Widow said, "I don't know. Maybe I'll re-up. Bet I could pass you in promotions within three months."

Steslow said, "You think so?"

Widow smirked.

Cress said, "Be careful, Reed. Your pal here looks like he can beat you in an arm-wrestling match at least."

Widow said nothing, but looked confusedly at Steslow, who said, "It's an inside joke."

Widow said, "Explain."

Cress said, "Oh, about two years ago, Steslow was up for promotion to Captain. And the night before, his shipmates took him out for a drink. Let's just say it got out of hand."

Widow said, "How's that?"

Steslow said, "I got too drunk and started arm-wrestling a group of Marines. One of them didn't take kindly to getting his ass kicked."

Widow asked, "You beat a jarhead in an arm-wrestling match? With those puny guns?"

"Hey, I was bigger back then. Not like you, but I was a good size. Anyway, there were some words and a tiny little bar fight."

Cress said, "Tell him about the next day."

Steslow sighed, and said, "The next day I missed my promotion ceremony."

Cress chuckled, and said, "It's worse than that. He missed it because he was in the brig."

Widow stared at Steslow, who turned a visible shade of red. The driver chuckled as well. Steslow shot him a glance, and said, "I still outrank you."

The driver kept it together and concentrated on the road.

Steslow sipped his coffee and turned back to Widow. He said, "It wasn't my finest hour."

Widow asked, "But you still got your promotion?"

Cress said, "It was nearly a year later. The charges were dropped, but the arrest is forever on his record."

Steslow faced forward, sipped his coffee, and stared out the window for a long second. Widow stayed quiet because he gauged that his old friend had more to say.

Cress interjected, and said, "That's how we met. We're both in recovery."

Steslow said, "It was a difficult period in my life. Lauren had left me and we battled over custody and all that. It was messy."

Widow nodded, but remained quiet.

Cress leaned forward in his seat, held his coffee in his right hand, and reached out with his left hand and put it on Steslow's shoulder. He seemed to genuinely care about the man.

Cress said, "Steslow's a good man."

Silence filled the vehicle.

Cress returned to his seated position and stared out the window, like he was suddenly either bored with the current conversation or deep in thought. Widow noticed some signals that Cress may have ADHD. He'd seen the symptoms before. In someone with ADHD, the mind has to constantly be engaged in the task at hand in order to maintain focus. If the afflicted person gets bored, they will zone out. At least, that was his observation of it. He hadn't had it himself.

The thought of bringing up his NCIS affiliations crossed his mind. But he decided not to disclose his involvement with Unit Ten, as he wasn't sure what Steslow's and the driver's clearance credentials were. He avoided talking specifics about past missions for the same reasons.

After a mile of silence, Widow asked, "So, where are we going?"

Steslow said, "We're going to Bangor Trident Base for a medal ceremony."

Without being asked, the driver glanced in the rearview mirror at the Secretary and interjected, "Five minutes ETA, Sir."

Cress said, "Thanks."

Widow asked, "Medal ceremony? That's why you're all dressed up. Who made the mistake of deciding you deserved a medal?"

Steslow said, "It's not for me."

Cress said, "That's why I'm here. There's a slew of overdue medals that need to be given out. But there's one special one that I wanted to give out. Plus, it's my job to hand this one out."

Widow said, "The Navy Cross. Who's getting it?"

Cress nodded.

Steslow said, "Did you ever meet a sailor named Lou Cosay?"

Widow said, "Never heard of him. What does he do?"

Steslow said, "He is a she. And she's an NCIS agent now, but she was a sailor. She's getting the Navy Cross for an old event. It's past due. I'm here as support. It's a surprise, really. She has no idea about it. She was getting a lesser medal."

Cress said, "Steslow recommended her. He fought hard. After I looked, I agreed.

Steslow said, "You're going to like her, Widow. She was a good sailor."

Cress said, "And she's a great agent. She's got lots of commendations."

Widow said, "Cosay sounds like she deserves the Navy Cross."

Cress said, "There's another reason it's special. She'll be the first Native American woman to get the Navy Cross."

Widow paused a beat, and said, "That can't be true? Is it?"

Steslow said, "It seems so."

Cress said, "We couldn't find a name. My assistant researched it and came up with no one. Not yet. Maybe recipients with Native ancestry, but no one who's fully Native."

"Sure. There was one. The name was," Widow said, and paused. He was sure there was a name on the tip of his tongue.

The cabin was silent for a moment.

Finally, Widow said, "What about that guy Pappy something?"

Cress said, "Gregory 'Pappy' Boyington was of Sioux descent. He was a Marine combat pilot during World War II."

Widow said, "Right. He was shot down by the Japanese and held prisoner for a year."

Cress said, "A year and a half. But he was the first Native American to get the Medal of Honor. We already looked at him. Of course."

Widow said, "And he got the Navy Cross, right?"

Cress said, "Maybe. I'm not sure about that, off the top of my head. Anyway, he's not a she. Cosay is. And she seems to be the first Native American woman to be awarded a Navy Cross. It's a great thing, and a good photo op."

Widow nodded, and said, "She sounds special."

"She's something special all right," Steslow said.

Widow glanced at him, but stayed quiet.

Steslow said, "What? I'm a free man now. And she's a good-looking woman."

Cress said, "No offense, Reed, but she's out of your league."

Steslow shrugged, and said, "We'll see."

Widow asked, "Does she even know you exist?"

Steslow glanced at him, and said, "Of course. We're friends. I've not seen her in years, but we keep in touch."

"Are you stationed here now?" Widow asked.

"No. My boat's getting worked on."

They went quiet after that because the driver said, "We're coming up on the Luoto Gate, Sir."

Cress nodded and sipped more of his coffee. He took out his cell-phone and began scrolling through something. Widow turned to the window and watched as they came up to a line at the entry gate. The driver switched on the blue lights again and drove through a special lane that was empty. They passed cars lined up for the visitor center, and cars lined up with sailors and Marines and other staff members trying to get to work on time.

A guard greeted them at the end of the lane. The driver buzzed the window down and the guard peeked in, just to make sure that the Secretary was actually in the vehicle. Then he waved them through the gate. Northwest Luoto Road turned into Trident Boulevard. They continued on. The driver ignored the speed limit, which was a big faux pas on any military base. But not for them. *Who was going to pull them over?* The driver was a Master-at-Arms. Plus, he was driving the US Secretary of the Navy.

They followed Trident Boulevard until it merged with Trigger Avenue, which took them north. The road looped and wound through the barracks, a skate park for the kids, a huge recreational complex, and heavily-forested areas. Finally, they slowed at a crowded parking lot to an official building complex named after a famous naval commander in the American Revolutionary War. It was called the John Paul Jones Building. It housed offices and ceremonial halls used for all kinds of naval events and ceremonies.

The driver pulled into the parking lot, and parked in a reserved space. Steslow was the first to get out, on his own. Widow also got out on his own. The Secretary waited for the driver to open his door.

Widow looked around at the faces of the people gathered outside the complex, and he realized just how important the event was. There were many people there. It appeared they were all there for the medal ceremony. There were families and friends of the medal recipients. There were public officials and commanding officers, along with local natives and representatives of various tribal nations. Various Native American political groups were in attendance. There was a woman there from the Bureau of Indian Affairs.

And the local and national press were there. There were vans marked with stations that Widow had never heard of, as well as two he had. Which meant they were a big deal if he'd heard of them because Widow didn't pay much attention to the news media.

Widow noticed another thing, standing there and examining everyone. He was underdressed. He stopped Steslow and asked, "Am I dressed okay for this?"

Steslow looked him over, as he had back at the bikini coffee shop, and said, "You look like a bum."

Widow stayed quiet.

Steslow smiled, and said, "You look fine. A little unconventional, but fine for this event. No one's going to care how you look, anyway. They're not here for you."

"I know that," Widow said. "I'm asking because I don't want to show disrespect to your friend and her accomplishment."

"Lou's not going to care about you or how you're dressed. Besides, it bodes well for me that I'm the better dressed of the two of us."

"Really?" Widow smiled, and said, "You afraid I'll get all your Cosay's attention? Can't say I blame you. You've not seen her in years. She probably forgot all about you."

Steslow said, "Funny. Now I know why I didn't miss you."

At that, the Secretary led the way past the reporters, who wanted to hassle him for comments for their newspapers or for a quick interview on-camera for their television audience. The driver was out in front of him before the first questions were asked. The civilians all left him alone. The driver pushed through the reporters to the front door, where a stiff-looking Vice Admiral waited for him at the top of a set of concrete steps. The Vice Admiral was standing in front of a grand entrance that had huge glass doors behind large concrete pillars.

The Vice Admiral was also in his full ceremonial uniform dress. He wore his hat, as he was supposed to when outside and in the presence of one of his few superiors. He saluted the Secretary, and they shook hands and chatted.

Widow followed behind and stopped at the bottom of the steps. Steslow stayed just behind the Secretary, beside the Master-at-Arms. The two men saluted the Vice Admiral and stayed that way like two chessboard figures stuck in a pose.

Widow didn't salute. He didn't do that stuff anymore and was quite proud of it. Maybe he was a little too proud now to even consider doing it out of a long-past sense of duty to the Navy. Despite that, he felt awkward just standing there like an idiot with nothing to do. He wondered if it had been such a good idea to come with them. Then a new concern dawned on him. He had forgotten the rest of his new coffee in the rear cup holder of the Secretary's Lincoln Navigator.

After a few minutes of pleasantries between the Secretary of the Navy and the Vice Admiral, the two men headed indoors to start the ceremony. The Secretary's Master-at-Arms escort stayed behind, and vanished into the crowd of other guards around the building, keeping close to the Navigator.

Widow followed Steslow into the building. The interior was as grand as the outside. The floors were polished tile, like the inside of a royal palace somewhere in the Middle East. The walls were white. A large double staircase led up into the balcony of a large convention hall, like the grand staircases of old French opera houses.

Widow had received medals before, but never at a fancy place like this. Most of his had been pinned on him either out at sea or in the back hallways of various Navy buildings, as if he were the Navy's dirty little secret.

He didn't resent it, not for a second. He had kept none of those medals, anyway. He'd left them in a footlocker at Unit Ten. Maybe they were still there.

Widow was impressed with Cosay, without even knowing her. To get this ceremony, she must be something special, just as Steslow described her. He couldn't believe that no other Native American woman had received the Navy Cross, but if the Secretary said they researched it, then he'd take him at his word.

Cress and the Vice Admiral went off to do the meet-and-greet thing with all the other attendees. They were pretty swarmed by various people in and out of uniforms. They had drinks and chatted it up and laughed, like at any social gathering. It wasn't Widow's thing. He and Steslow found their way into the convention hall, which was just as grand as the rest of the place. It had high ceilings, and crown moldings, and fancy track lighting. There was a crystal chandelier in the center of the room's ceiling. There were tables covered in white linens and navy blue napkins. The official US Navy seal was embedded in the middle of a tiled floor. The floor was white. It went up the center of the hall and ended at the bottom of a small stage. Tables lined both sides of the tiled floor. Navy blue carpet covered the floor of the table areas.

The stage was low and about a third of the width of the room. There was no backstage area. Drawn black curtains covered a wall. Short steps lined either side of the stage. At stage center was a lectern with another US Navy seal sculpted into the side facing the audience. A microphone rested in a cradle on the lectern.

Widow said, "This place is fancy."

Steslow said, "It looks like a wedding hall in an expensive hotel."

The two old friends were among the first into the hall. A few stragglers stood around in small groups of people. Several people were already seated at their tables. As they stood in the walkway between linen-covered tables, Widow asked, "See her?"

Steslow looked around the room, studying the people. First, he scanned one side and then turned and scanned the other. He shook his head, and said, "No. That's weird."

"She must be back out in the foyer somewhere."

"Nah, I checked. I didn't see her," Steslow said.

"Maybe she's being swarmed by the reporters, or someone from one of those Native groups."

"I hope not. It was supposed to be a surprise."

"Doubt she'll make it into the building without someone spoiling it for her. It's a big deal. You know?"

Steslow nodded, said nothing.

Widow nodded, and didn't bring it up again. The two men found a corner for last-minute guests. The section was closest to the entrance and down range from the stage.

"Guess this is where I post up," Widow said. "Think they're serving coffee?"

Steslow stared at him, and said, "Where's the one you had? You finish it?"

"Left it in the truck."

Steslow nodded, and pointed to a catering table on the back wall. A porter stood near it, preparing something Widow couldn't see from where was standing.

Just then, people started trickling in faster and faster. An officer in full dress whites got up on stage and began speaking. Steslow said, "It's starting. I got a seat up front at the Secretary's table. I'll see you after."

Widow nodded, headed to the catering table, and helped himself to another cup of coffee. He looked for a place to sit, but by the time he'd gotten around to it, all the guest chairs were occupied. So, he posted up on the back corner of the room, out of sight from the rest of the attendees.

The rest of the ceremony went by without a hitch. Medals were given out. Pictures were taken. Hands were shaken.

It was all pretty boring for Widow. He glanced at the exits more than once, contemplating taking one last coffee with him and leaving. The thing was, he wasn't officially registered to be on base. He hadn't stopped at the visitors' center to request a visitor's badge. He'd come in riding in the Secretary's vehicle. Therefore, if he wandered out and got stopped by the wrong Navy cop, then he might have a serious problem on his hands. He had to wait around. Steslow and the Secretary were his ride. He was tethered to them while he was on base.

Widow spent the last fifteen minutes of the medal ceremony thinking about Samantha, the bikini barista. She'd seemed to be attracted to him. He wasn't sure why. But he wasn't dumb enough to complain about it. She appeared to be in her early to mid-twenties. *Too young for him?* He had thought so. Then again, he had been with women ten and twenty years older than himself. Whatever. It was all just thoughts, anyway.

Now, he was here, and he wasn't going back.

The Vice Admiral took the stage and introduced Secretary Cress. Cress came up and shook his hand and took over the lectern. The Vice Admiral exited the stage and sat down, leaving the Secretary to do his thing.

Widow paid attention and sipped the last of another coffee.

Cress said, "Good morning everyone. I'm glad you could all come to honor today's medal recipients. Our real heroes. I'm not one for long speeches. And I think we'd all like to go to lunch soon so we can celebrate the real way, with a beer and a cheeseburger."

The sailors and Marines in the crowd all cheered.

Cress said, "First, let me tell you, we're here to honor a former sailor. She's a combat vet who served all over the world. I've never met her, not yet. But I've looked over her service record. She's served a prodigious career, with honor and dignity.

"She was on board various ships and stationed in Kuwait, where she took part in a mission where she helped rescue seven Marines pinned down by enemy fire. The after-action reports indicate she killed five Taliban in a firefight in that effort.

"And that's just one event. People who served with her have informed me she's tough as nails. A good sailor, and an even better American. Sadly, she's no longer with us."

Cress paused a dramatic beat. The crowd went silent.

Cress smiled, and said, "She spent nine years with us. And now she's no longer in the Navy, because, today, she is a Special Investigator for the Naval Criminal Investigative Service. She has been for the last six years. As a law enforcement agent, she's been involved in solving numerous cases, including a few high-profile ones. She's an essential part of the NCIS operations. We're proud of her accomplishments."

Many in the crowd sighed in relief. Others seemed unfazed by the humor. And some chuckled, probably fewer than Cress expected.

Cress continued, "She's got no idea that she's receiving this honor today. And boy does she deserve it. Frankly, it's overdue. I'm proud to announce that today, for the first time in the US Navy's history, a Native American woman will receive the Navy Cross. She's from the North Dakota Mokani tribe. I'm sure they're very proud of her. Please give a warm welcome to NCIS Agent Lomasi Cosay. Or as her friends call her, Lou."

Cress stared out into the crowd as they began cheering. Widow was leaning against the back wall, still, and still holding the same coffee. He stared around, along with the crowd of onlookers. No one got up. Widow glanced at Steslow, who was way down in the front. He was standing and clapping, staring back into the room. The lights may have blinded him a bit, since they were pointed in the stage's direction.

Several moments passed. More people rose from their seats and clapped. The applause roared through the small space. Widow glanced at different faces of Native American women. None were in uniform. And none of them backed away from their tables to make their way to the stage. Newspaper reporters' cameras flashed, snapping pictures. They captured the standing ovation and the fact that no one was standing up to accept the medal.

Steslow looked nervous. He'd said that she knew she was getting some kind of recognition. And that it was important that she be there.

Cress put a hand up over his brow and held it like a visor, blocking out the ceiling lights. He scanned the room. He said, "Lou, come on up. Don't be shy."

No one walked to the front. Cress continued to look out into the crowd, and then he glanced at the Vice Admiral. The crowd stopped cheering. Many of them returned to their seats. Eventually, they all did. They just sat in silence and waited.

The Vice Admiral shrugged. That wasn't a good enough response for Cress, who looked visibly annoyed. So the Vice Admiral got up out of his seat and walked up to the stage. Cress left the lectern and met him at the bottom of the stage. The two men spoke to each other. It was inaudible to Widow and the rest of the room.

The Vice Admiral signaled to someone out of Widow's view. Suddenly, the crowd started talking, like everyone was dumbfounded by the events unfolding in front of them. Widow heard one guy say, "Why would you ditch your own medal ceremony?"

The person the Vice Admiral signaled to turned out to be a female sailor. She approached him and he barked some order at her. She left him standing with Cress and walked the length of the tiled floor, past Widow.

Another sailor got up on stage and began talking to the audience, telling them to stay in their seats. And that there's a little mix-up. Just all standard crowd-control tactics for this kind of situation.

Widow got off the back wall and followed the female sailor out into the main hallway. By the time he got out there, she'd vanished. Widow looked around the hall. There was no one out there except for a patrolling Marine.

A second later, he heard a door thud closed. He looked in the sound's direction and saw two public bathroom doors, a men's and a women's. The female sailor came out of the women's, like she'd been in there checking to see if Cosay had stepped out to use the facilities. She wore her ceremonial dress whites. Widow stared at her shoulder boards, which signified that she was a Warrant Officer 1. She made eye contact with him and walked over, stopped and looked him up and down. She ignored the fact that he wore no visitor's badge. She asked, "Sir, you seen a woman out here? She's Native American. She's probably dressed in a uniform like mine."

Widow said, "I've not seen her, Chief."

The Warrant Officer nodded and reentered the auditorium, leaving Widow standing there alone and asking himself the same question that everyone was asking themselves. *Where is Lou Cosay?*

CHAPTER 5

More than twenty minutes passed before Steslow came out of the convention hall. Widow waited in the lobby after he finished his coffee and disposed of the cup. He stood near the entrance, figuring that Cress and Steslow would come back out soon enough.

Steslow saw him and went over to him. They met in the center of the foyer, under the grand staircase. Widow asked, "Where is she?"

Steslow shrugged, and said, "No one seems to know."

"She knew about this, right?"

"Yeah. Cress said her boss was informed two weeks ago. She should be here. I don't understand."

Widow asked, "Tried calling her?"

"Yeah. I keep getting her voicemail."

"When's the last time you spoke to her?"

Steslow said, "I talked to her several weeks ago. I've been at sea. But I texted her last week. She confirmed she was going to be here. She seemed excited about it. Of course, she didn't know it was for the Navy Cross medal. Still, she should be here. This isn't like her."

Cress and the Vice Admiral came out of the convention hall and into the lobby. The reporters surrounded them. Several Native American groups followed close behind. There were a few cameras on them. People talked over each other, trying to ask the same questions. They wanted to know where Cosay was and where the historical medal ceremony was that they were promised.

Steslow said, "Come on. Let's get to the truck before they stall us."

Widow nodded and the two men exited the building. In the parking lot, Cress's driver was back behind the wheel in the Navigator. The engine was running, warming up the interior. The Vice Admiral's officers got in between the Secretary and the reporters and other question-filled attendees, pushing them back so the two high-profile men could exit the building and enter the parking lot.

Cress joined the men at the Navigator. They got in. Cress ordered the driver to take them to NCIS headquarters. He replied, "Lights on?"

Cress said, "Yes. Get there."

Cress seemed frustrated. Not quite mad, but frustrated and embarrassed that he was stood up. And on stage, by the woman who was being honored. It didn't bother Widow. Cosay wasn't a sailor anymore. Although, being an NCIS agent, she was technically under Cress's authority, but not under his command. Not like Steslow or the Vice Admiral. She only had to answer to him if she wanted to. Maybe she didn't. Nothing said she had to be there. Maybe she thought the whole thing was stupid. A lot of former military didn't care about medals or glory. Many of the people Widow had served with only cared about getting to the next day alive. A piece of metal, hung on fabric, with a made-up name like Navy Cross or the Service Medal or even the Medal of

Honor meant little to those who fought everyday just to see their families again.

Widow thought nothing of it either way. To some, it was a great honor to be recognized. To others, it was unnecessary.

The Master-at-Arms swung the vehicle around the lot and back out onto Trigger Avenue. They followed the road back the way they had come and merged onto Trident Boulevard again. The Northwest Luoto Gate came into view. They drove through it, slowed and turned right, about seven hundred feet after the gate. The road was Sunfish Drive. The Master-at-Arms slowed the Navigator and turned into the parking lot of a three-story red brick building. Large windows lined the outer wall. A sign, posted between two poles out front, told them they were at the NCIS District Headquarters.

They parked in the lot and got out. The Master-at-Arms opened Cress's door for him and hopped out in front of them, and led the way up some steps and into the building through a set of double glass doors. The doors were tinted a heavy black. The Master-at-Arms led the way. He stopped at a security desk and explained to security who they were. Which needed little effort because everyone recognized Secretary Cress.

A few minutes later, they were inside the office of the Special Agent-in-Charge. He was a tall, lanky guy called Flory. He had some strands of hair on the top of his head, but not many. The hair on the sides did most of the heavy lifting. Flory was behind a metal desk in a corner of the office. The carpet had the NCIS seal sewn into a circle, like the seal in the White House's Oval Office. Flory stood as Cress entered his office, like a man waiting for the President. Which wasn't far off the mark.

Flory greeted Cress, and the two men shook hands. The Master-at-Arms closed the door behind them and posted up outside like a guard. Steslow and Cress sat in two leather armchairs facing the SAC's desk. Widow dumped himself down on a sofa behind them.

Flory remained standing until Cress was seated, and said, "What do I owe the pleasure of this visit, Mr. Secretary?"

He had asked the question, but Widow wasn't sure if he already knew or not. Cosay missed her medal ceremony only minutes ago. So he may not know yet. But there were a lot of people there. It struck Widow as unlikely that no one texted or called Flory to tell him, since she worked for him.

It seemed Cress thought it suspect that Flory hadn't heard yet, because he asked, "Have you not heard?"

"Heard what, sir?"

Cress glanced away, out the window. Then he said, "One of your agents was supposed to receive a medal this morning. We were just at the John Paul Jones Building. There was a crowd of people expecting it. I got up onstage, announced the medal, and called her up. She wasn't there. I had been informed that she would be there."

Flory leaned forward in his chair. He put his palms on the desktop in front of him. He looked confused—genuinely, like he was just as shocked as Cress. He said, "Wait. You're talking about Lou Cosay, right?"

Cress said, "Yes. She wasn't there. And I was left standing there looking like an idiot. Where the hell is she?"

Flory said, "Sir, I apologize. That's not like her. Let me see if I can get her in here. And we'll sort this out."

Cress nodded, glanced at Steslow, who stared on at Flory. Widow stayed quiet, but he wondered when they'd be back on the road. He didn't want to be there anymore. Especially, he didn't want to stick around and watch an NCIS agent get her ass chewed out for missing her own medal ceremony. He thought about excusing himself. He really didn't belong there. Maybe he should stand up and tell them he'd wait down by the security desk. Once he was there, he might convince someone to give him a ride out to Highway 3. Or he could walk to it. It was less than a mile away, after all.

But Widow didn't excuse himself. In the end, he stayed to watch it all play out.

Flory picked up a phone off the desk—a landline—and dialed a number. He listened, and waited as the phone rang and rang. Eventually, he hit a brick wall. There was no answer. He pushed the hook-switch on the phone's base and hung up the call. He looked at the other men in the room, and said, "Her voicemail."

Steslow rolled his eyes. Because he'd already tried calling her. Obviously, they'd thought of that before coming to the SAC's office. Widow couldn't see him roll his eyes, but he knew he had done it. He knew his old friend pretty well. Even though they'd only served together for a few months, those months can feel like an eternity in war.

Flory redialed the phone with a different number. Widow knew it was internal because Flory only used three digits. The phone rang, and he got someone else on the line. He ordered the person on the other end of the phone to come to his office. Without waiting for a response, he hung the phone up. Then he reassured Cress again that he would help find out where Cosay was and why she wasn't at the ceremony.

A few minutes later, there was a knock on the door. Flory told whoever it was to enter the room. The door opened. Widow and the others glanced at the door. A black man about Widow's age stood in the doorway. He was around six feet tall and a hundred and sixty pounds. He wore a suit and tie. There was an NCIS badge clipped to his belt.

The guy looked at Widow, Steslow, and then Cress. Surprise came over his face. He said, "Sir, you called me up here?"

"Gentlemen, this is Special Agent Darius Omar. Omar, this is the Secretary of the Navy, Adam Cress," Flory said, but didn't introduce Widow or Steslow.

Omar greeted the Secretary. He glanced at Steslow and at Widow and nodded to each of them. His eyes hung on Widow longer than the others. Which Widow took as a regular reaction by any agent who meets a guy that looks like him—hobo-like, not in any kind of identifying uniform, but present in the boss's office, like he was some kind of special operative from a different agency. Widow figured the guy might suspect CIA or DIA or something.

Omar entered the room and shut the door behind him. He turned to Flory, and asked, "What's this about, sir?"

Widow noticed the guy's fingers twitched a bit, like he was nervous. Which was understandable. It's not every day that an employee gets called to the big boss's office out of the blue. It's even more unusual when the Secretary of the Navy is present.

Flory said, "Agent Cosay's medal ceremony was this morning. Just now, in fact. You knew that."

It wasn't a question, but Omar responded with a nod anyway, and a "Yes, sir."

Flory said, "She didn't show up for it."

Widow watched Omar's fingers. They twitched even more. His shoulders slumped a bit, not a lot, but enough for Widow to notice. Agent Omar stood there, silent, staring at Flory. He didn't respond, not because he wondered if the SAC had more to say. He stayed silent because he knew something. Widow saw it in his stance and his posture.

Flory said, "So? Where is she?"

Omar said, "I don't know, sir."

Flory said, "She's your partner and you don't know where she is?"

Omar glanced at the floor, and back up at Flory. He said, "Sorry. I don't."

Flory said, "She was supposed to be at this medal ceremony today. The Secretary of the Navy is here to give her the medal. And she was a no-show."

Omar stood there in the silence. He had no answers to give. Widow could see that. But he suspected the guy knew something. And he was keeping it to himself.

Cress interjected, and said, "Agent Omar, what's going on? There was a room full of people who came to see Cosay get this medal. There were reporters there. Some had video cameras. Now I'm going to end up on the news, calling out for Agent Cosay and no one answers for her. So, what gives? Where is she?"

Flory stared daggers at Omar, like he'd better answer or his job would be on the line.

Omar said nothing.

"Omar," Widow interjected.

Omar turned to look at him. Both Steslow and Cress turned in their armchairs and stared at Widow. Flory looked over at him. Widow sat up on the sofa, rested his hands across his lap. Calmly, he asked, "When's the last time you saw Lou?"

Omar stayed silent.

Cress said, "Answer him, agent."

Omar said, "She called me late Wednesday night and begged me to cover for her. She said she had to take care of something important. And she didn't come in the next morning or Friday. That's the last time I spoke to her. I've called her and texted her. I get no response."

Flory said, "Today's Monday. She's been out of touch since last week?"

"Yes. I'm sorry I didn't speak up before. She..." Omar said, and paused a beat. "I promised I wouldn't."

Cress asked, "You promised Agent Cosay?"

Omar said, "Yes. Lou made me promise to cover for her. She sounded desperate, like it was urgent. So I did. That's why I said nothing. But I didn't know she was going to miss the ceremony." He looked at the Secretary, and said, "I swear, Sir. She was supposed to make it. She told me she just needed a few days."

"That explains your silence," Flory turned to Cress. "Agent Omar is loyal to a fault."

Cress waved the explanation off, and said, "It's fine. But where is she now?"

Omar said, "I really don't know, sir."

Widow asked, "Where was she going? Why did she ask you to cover for her?"

Omar said, "That I don't know. She said it was something personal. She didn't want to go into it. I owed her. She's saved my ass more times than I can count. So, I promised."

Flory asked, "What about your caseload?"

"We got a couple of cases. I'm handling them," Omar said.

The room fell silent for a long, perplexing moment. Out of the five men, it was Steslow who broke the silence. He said, "We have to find her."

Reluctantly, Cress said, "Actually, we don't."

Steslow turned to him, and asked, "What do you mean?"

"Why do we have to find her?" Cress asked.

Steslow said, "Sir, you heard Omar. She's vanished. She's gone AWOL. She missed one of the most important events in her career. That's totally out of character for her."

Cress said, "Captain…"

Steslow interrupted, "We got to look for her at least. She's an NCIS agent. She might need our help."

Cress said, "She's not AWOL. Cosay's an NCIS agent, not a sailor. Not anymore. She's a civilian now. Civilians up and leave, abandoning their jobs all the time."

Flory said, "Sir, it is very unlike her."

Cress thought for a moment. Steslow gritted his teeth, like he wanted to say more. Cosay wasn't under Cress's command, not anymore. But Steslow was. He had to hold his tongue, even though the two of them were friendly.

Omar had to be careful what he said because he didn't want to lose his job. He was already on the line for covering for a missing agent. If it turned out that Cosay was playing hooky somewhere, like lying on a beach down in Mexico or something, then it was Omar who would take the heat. Cosay would be fired, for sure, and Omar would probably be right after her. Embarrassing a Secretary of a military branch like that was simply unforgivable. Part of their power was dictated by their public perception. And the perception couldn't be that you could walk all over them. That would diminish their ability to command.

Flory wouldn't stand up to Cress on this either, for the same reason as Omar; he had his career to think about.

However, Widow wasn't under anyone's command. So he said, "We shouldn't jump to conclusions. Mr. Secretary, perhaps we should check up on her."

Flory said, "We could send a Navy police unit to do a welfare check at her house."

Widow said, "I think it would be best if we go look ourselves. We can just ring her doorbell. If she answers, then we know she's okay."

Steslow glanced at Widow, nodded, and said, "Yes. That's a good idea."

Cress took a breath, calming himself. He said, "Yes. You're right. We should. I apologize, gentlemen. I'm just annoyed at being embarrassed like that."

Widow said, "Maybe she's got a good explanation. Let's find out."

Steslow said, "Lou is a good agent. She deserves the benefit of the doubt."

"I agree," Cress said, and he turned to Flory. "You're coming with us. And you as well, Agent Omar."

Flory and Omar both nodded along, like they had no choice. Which they didn't.

The four men rose from their seats, joined Omar at the door, and exited Flory's office. On the way to the elevator, Cress asked Flory, "Got her address?"

Omar said, "I know where she lives."

Flory said, "Omar and I will ride together. You guys can follow us there."

They rode the elevator down to the lobby, passed through the lobby, passed the security desk, and exited the building. Flory left them standing at the front of the parking lot. He went into the lot and pulled around with his personal vehicle, which was an electric SUV. Widow wasn't familiar with the maker. He had ridden in a few electric vehicles. There were more and more of them on the road. He had no opinion of them. He figured they were probably the wave of the future.

Flory pulled up alongside them. Omar got in on the passenger side. The other men got into the Secretary's Navigator, with the Master-at-Arms. Moments later, they were back on Northwest Luoto Road, and out the main gate.

CHAPTER 6

Seventeen minutes later, the two vehicles and five men were thirteen miles south of the NCIS District Headquarters on Sunfish Drive. They came off Highway 310, and hooked onto a peninsula called Rocky Point. The waterways, lush green surroundings, and hilly roads made it an idyllic neighborhood to live in. There were lots of trees with both green and red leaves because of the beginning of the autumn season.

The weather was pretty nice for Washington State. The temperature had warmed a bit, helped by the morning sun finally breaking through the gray clouds. Locals took advantage of the sunshine. Several of the neighbors walked their dogs. A group of women walked together. Two of them pushed baby strollers. Trash cans lined the street for collection. They saw one of Cosay's neighbors pulling his cans in already. The trash pickup had happened earlier in the morning.

"She lives around that loop," Omar said to Flory. He peeked at his phone, where a GPS map app guided him to Cosay's address.

Flory nodded and took them slow around the loop. Cress's Navigator followed. The blue lights were off. Traffic in the neighborhood was light. But everyone they passed stopped and stared at them as if they were strangers entering a small town.

Both vehicles rounded the loop and stopped in front of a mailbox. Flory waited for the Navigator to pull up behind him, and then he turned into Cosay's driveway. Cress's driver pulled up to the mouth of the driveway, in front of the mailbox, and put the Navigator in park. He got out and opened the door for Cress. Widow and Steslow got out on their own. They met Cress at the bottom of the driveway and walked up to meet Omar and Flory near the house.

The house sat on about a third of an acre of land. The driveway was longer than most, but shorter than others on the street. Some houses they passed had driveways so long that the houses were barely visible from the road.

Cosay's land had a few trees, but it wasn't covered in them like the neighbors with the longer driveways. The front yard was longer than the back. But the backyard ended in a small pebble beach. Beyond it was a body of water called Oyster Bay.

The house was a small, one-story affair. It looked to be two bedrooms and around twelve hundred square feet at the most. Large bay windows lined the front side of the house. There was a detached garage to the right of the house, at the end of the driveway. There was no car in the driveway other than Flory's.

Widow gazed around the place. It was quiet and cozy, with a great lot that was on the water. Cosay didn't have a boat dock, but one could be put in. Widow figured the bay opened to a canal and he could get out to the ocean, if he lived there. It was a great spot. He could picture himself living in a little house like that on the water, near the Navy he knew, but far away enough to enjoy a life. It was a good place for an NCIS agent.

The men huddled at the rear of Flory's electric SUV. Widow stayed back out of the group. He scanned the yard and the house. The windows were big, and the shutters were closed from the inside. They were plantation shutters. The place looked dark. There was no sound coming from inside the house.

A dog barked frantically across the street. Widow glanced in its direction. The barking came from the yard of a neighbor's house.

It was a small house, like Cosay's, but it wasn't on the water. The others stayed where they were, talking like they were brainstorming a game plan.

Widow took several steps back towards the road. He stopped halfway and stared at the house with the barking dog. There was movement in one of the windows. A curtain opened, like someone was checking them out. Then it closed swiftly.

Widow turned and went to join the others. By then, Steslow and Omar had led the way up a walkway to Cosay's porch and her front door. Shrubs with flowers lined the sidewalk. They were watered and cared for. The grass was well-maintained also.

Steslow was the first to the front door. He rang the doorbell. It chimed. They all heard it from the porch. Widow stayed the farthest back. Cress and Flory stood on the steps to the porch. There was no answer.

Widow studied the windows. There was no movement. He glanced around the outside of the house.

Steslow called out to Cosay. He shouted, "Hey, Lou! Are you here? It's Reed!"

They listened. No answer.

Steslow tried the doorknob. It was locked. He turned to Omar. They backed away and walked the porch. Each man cupped his hands and tried to peer into the windows.

Flory said, "Guys, can't do that."

Steslow asked, "Why not? She might be in danger."

Flory said, "It's not legal. Not unless we have probable cause that she's in there and needs our help."

Omar said nothing. Steslow frowned. He came off the porch and passed the others and went over to Widow. He said, "Door's locked. She's not here."

Widow said, "Seems that way."

"What do we do now?" Steslow asked.

Widow looked at the garage, and said, "Let's see if we can look into the garage." And Widow passed his old friend and the others and headed to the detached garage. Steslow followed.

The garage was a two-car garage. The door was automatic. Widow tried to push it up and open, but it wouldn't come up. Then, he walked around it until he found a window. He cupped his hands and stared in.

Omar, Flory, and Cress joined Steslow and Widow at the garage. Flory repeated, "Can't be looking in her windows, guys."

Widow ignored him. He came back from the window, and said, "There's no car in there. She's probably gone."

Steslow glanced at Flory, who shook his head in disapproval. Steslow ignored him and looked through the window after Widow.

Widow left the garage and met Omar in front of Flory's electric SUV's trunk. He asked, "She have a boyfriend? Or a partner that you know of?"

"I don't know about anyone like that in her life. She's pretty dedicated to her job," Omar said.

"She must've done something else in her free time?" Widow asked.

Omar shrugged, and said, "I really wouldn't know."

Steslow joined them, and asked, "She ever mention me? Reed Steslow?"

Omar shook his head, and said, "Sorry."

Steslow asked, "How do you know she didn't have a boyfriend?"

"I think I'd know. She had no one," Omar said.

Flory studied the front of the house one last time, and said, "There're no signs of break-ins or forced entry. So, nothing much we can do. Not legally."

Widow looked at Omar, and asked, "You guys were partners. Would you say you're pretty close?"

"We're partners on the job. I'd say we were friends, sure," Omar answered.

Widow asked, "Any chance she gave you a spare key? If she gave you a spare, that would be considered permission by her to enter."

Omar shook his head, and said, "She'd never give me a spare key. I doubt she'd give anyone a spare key."

"Why you say that?" Steslow asked.

Omar said, "She really keeps her personal life private. She has as long as I've known her."

The backyard was behind a short chain-link fence. Widow went over to it. He put his hands on the top bar, and said, "There're no signs of forced entry at the front. What about the backyard?"

Flory said, "There's a fence."

"It's got a gate," Widow said, keeping his hands on the top bar.

Flory said, "Doesn't matter."

Steslow said, "There's a lock on it. We could jump it."

Flory shook his head, and said, "We can't go past it without cause or permission."

Steslow said, "You're a real pain-in-the-ass, Flory."

Widow didn't look back at them. He pulled down on the fence, squatted, and hopped over it without touching the fence with his feet. He landed on the other side, in the backyard. He said to Flory, "*You* can't go past it."

Steslow didn't look back at the others, either. He followed suit and hopped the fence. The others stayed behind. Before Flory could object again, Cress said, "Make it quick, boys."

Steslow nodded. He and Widow walked around the house, out of sight of the others. Widow inspected the backyard, while Steslow peered through the rear windows. The backyard was all grass, with a small deck on the back of the house. The yard ended at the water's edge, just past the fence. Widow scoped the exterior of the house for security cameras. He saw none. He joined Steslow in peeking at the windows. But he wasn't looking inside for signs of life. He studied the glass for security sensors, the kind that alert the security system's base that a window's been opened or broken. He saw none.

They moved from window to window, stopping only at the back-door, which was a slider. Both men peeked in and saw nothing out of the ordinary, nothing alarming.

Steslow asked, "See anything?"

Widow said, "There's no security system."

"Yeah?"

"This's a nice neighborhood, but it's not gated. And Cosay lives alone."

"Yeah?"

"So, a woman who is a "looker" as you described her to me before, living alone, would have a security system unless…"

"Unless what?" Steslow asked.

"Unless she has a dog."

Widow returned to the slider and peered in again. This time he spent all his time gazing into the kitchen.

Steslow asked, "What are you looking for?"

Widow stayed quiet and kept searching until he saw it. He said, "There." And he pointed. Steslow joined him at the slider and looked in the direction Widow pointed.

Widow said, "There's two empty dog bowls on the floor."

Steslow said, "It could be for a cat."

Widow moved away from the slider and started inspecting the outside wall. He moved patio furniture out of the way, until he found what he was looking for.

Steslow said, "What?"

Widow pointed at a large square hole cut out of the bottom of the wall. Plastic flaps hung on the outside of the wall. Widow said, "Doggie door."

Steslow looked at it, and said, "Looks like it's for a large dog."

Widow nodded, and said, "She has a dog, but where is he?"

"Maybe she took him with her."

"Maybe."

They finished checking every window and the slider doors. They saw a clean living room, a tidy kitchen, and two bedrooms. Both beds were neatly made. There were no signs of anything else worth checking out.

The two men gave up, hopped back over the fence, and returned to the others. Widow went to Omar, and asked, "Did you know she had a dog?"

"I told you. I've never been to her house. She was private, like I said," Omar said.

Widow said, "I didn't ask you if you'd been here. I asked if you knew about her dog."

Omar just shrugged and said, "I don't know about a dog."

Flory said, "I guess we should return to my office."

The men returned to their vehicles. They were about to reenter them, when the neighbor's dog barked again. Widow paused at the rear door to the Navigator. He looked across the street at the neighbor's house. He looked back at Steslow, and said, "We should check with the neighbor. Maybe that's Cosay's dog."

Widow didn't wait. He left the Navigator and walked over to the neighbor's house. There was a single minivan parked in the driveway. There was a sticker in the back window with two kids, a baby, and two parents. It was like one of those *Baby on Board* stickers.

He saw the curtain move in the same window as earlier, like someone was watching him through it. He walked up a long walkway to the front door. The dog barked furiously from the backyard. He saw it at the neighbor's back fence. It looked at him and barked again. It was a large dog, some kind of mutt. There was boxer in there, but the rest of it, Widow couldn't figure. It had one blue eye and one brown. Even though it barked, it seemed excited to see him, like they were old friends.

Widow stepped up to the front door, stood on the welcome mat, and rang the doorbell. A moment later, he heard shuffling behind the door. He glanced back over his shoulder. Steslow and Omar both stood behind him on the walkway. Cress and Flory were back on the street. Flory had reversed his electric SUV and parked it behind the Navigator. He stood there with his arms folded across his chest.

The neighbor's front door opened a little, and a woman peered out. She asked, "Can I help you?"

"Good morning, ma'am. We're here looking for your neighbor across the street," Widow said, and pointed at Cosay's house.

The woman glanced around behind Widow at the other men. Then she asked, "Who are you?"

Widow glanced back at Omar, who was already on it, like he read Widow's mind. Omar stepped forward, grabbed his badge off his belt, and showed it to the woman. He said, "We're with the NCIS, ma'am. Agent Cosay is my partner. We're just looking for her."

The woman stared at the badge through the crack in the door. Then she said, "Hold on." She shut the door, and they heard the chain come off the lock. The door reopened, and the woman stepped out. She was younger than Widow had thought. She looked to be about Samantha's age, only completely different. Samantha was young and vibrant. This woman looked aged and worn, like life had taken her for a ride and never let go. She wore a housecoat and slippers. Her hair was a mess of curly and straight hair, like she was in the middle of straightening it or curling it. She had tanned skin, and some early wrinkles, probably from smoking. She smelled like a smoker.

She came out onto the porch. Widow backed away several feet to give her room. Steslow and Omar followed suit and backed farther down the walkway.

The woman closed the door behind her. Widow heard a baby whimper one time inside the house. A television played somewhere inside as well.

The woman stared at Widow. She ignored the other men. She just kept on looking up at Widow, like he was the only man in her front yard. She said, "What happened to Lou?"

Widow said, "Nothing's happened. We're just looking for her, that's all."

Omar said, "She's not been to work in a few days."

The woman said, "She left here on Wednesday night."

Widow asked, "Do you know where she went? Or why she left so abruptly?"

"No. She didn't tell me anything. She never really does. But I'm watching her dog for her. That's him in the backyard."

Widow nodded, and asked, "Does he bark a lot?"

"Not when he's back at his own house. He's a good dog. He's just anxious that Lou left him like that," the woman said.

Widow asked, "Does she normally leave him with you?"

"No. Never," she said.

Widow asked, "How long has she lived across the street?"

The woman said, "She's been there like six or seven years. She's a good neighbor. I like her a lot. It's especially reassuring having her around."

Widow asked, "Why do you say that?"

"Because she's a cop, like you guys. Or an agent or whatever. Law enforcement," she said.

Widow thought about Cosay not having any security on her house, and asked, "Is crime high here?"

"Oh no. This is a very safe area. I just mean that it's nice to have her around because of my husband," she said.

Steslow asked, "What's wrong with your husband?"

She glanced at him, and at his ceremonial dress whites. She said, "My ex-husband. He's a Marine, like you. Only he wasn't in very long. I never saw him dressed like that."

Steslow said, "I'm in the Navy, not the Marine Corps."

The woman said, "Whatever. I got a restraining order against the bastard. That's one reason I'm hoping she'll return soon. He never tries to come around when she's there. The police won't do anything hardly. Her dog helps keep him away, I think."

Widow didn't ask how Cosay helped with her ex-husband. He imagined she did it the same way that he would've done it—with a one-on-one conversation and a little brute force. He liked Cosay already.

The woman glanced at Omar and then at Widow. She said, "He looks like an NCIS agent. But not you. Are you undercover or something?"

"I'm retired. Just here to help, ma'am," Widow said. It was an incongruous reply because the guys he stood with thought he was lying to her. She thought he was telling the truth. Only she thought he meant he had been an agent like Omar, like Cosay. An agent who worked the cases out in public. And he was the only one who knew that it was a truth. He had been in the NCIS, only as a part of the secret Unit Ten.

After another couple of minutes of talking with her, it became apparent that she knew nothing else that could help them. Widow was the first to thank her for her time. He left the porch and walked back to the Navigator. Steslow followed him. Omar stayed behind and gave her his business card, in case she saw Cosay or thought of anything else. He thanked her and returned to the vehicles with the others.

Cress, Steslow, and Flory stood on the street, facing the neighbor's house. Widow and Omar stood with their backs to her house. The Master-at-Arms stayed in the Navigator. Omar said, "She's confirmed what we already thought. Cosay left late Wednesday night. She left her dog with this neighbor."

Flory asked, "Did she say where Lou went?"

Omar shook his head.

Widow said, "Wherever she went, whatever was her reason, she didn't want anyone to know."

Steslow said, "We should keep looking for her. You guys can track her cellphone."

Flory shook his head, and said, "We need a warrant for that."

Widow said, "Or probable cause."

Flory said, "We ain't got either."

With a look of concern on his face, Steslow said, "We got probable cause. She missed a super important event. And you don't know where she is."

Flory said, "That's out of character, but it's not probable cause."

Steslow said, "We gotta do something."

Flory turned to Cress, and said, "Agent Cosay is a private citizen now. Technically, all I can do is reprimand her for abandoning her job. Unless she's got a good reason, I'll have to fire her. But if you want me to escalate this to a missing agent, that would be different. We could call it an agent in distress and start searching for her. That would give me a reason to legally track her phone."

Cress nodded, and said nothing. A long moment passed.

Steslow said, "Sir, we have to find her. She could be in danger."

Cress glanced at Steslow.

Steslow said, "We should look for her, Mr. Secretary."

Cress sighed, releasing a deep breath. He said, "Agent Cosay has done this nation a service. We owe her for that. However, Flory's right. She's not in the service anymore. She's a civilian working in law enforcement. It's a job. People abandon their jobs without a word every day. There's not much I can do."

Steslow said, "Come on. I'm telling you this isn't like her."

Omar said, "He's right, Mr. Secretary. Cosay has always been by-the-book."

Cress glanced at Omar, and said, "I understand your concerns. We all want her to be safe. We all want to find her. But Cosay told you she was leaving. She asked you to cover for her. She gave her dog to her neighbor to watch for her. And she left in a hurry, middle of the night, and on her own volition. None of that says that she's in peril. It appears she knew she wouldn't be here for the ceremony. I'm sorry, Reed. I can't authorize a massive search for a civilian employee. Not under these circumstances. Now, if things change or she shows up needing our help, that'll be different."

Widow said, "This doesn't seem right to me. Why would she work so hard, have a stellar Navy and NCIS record, and just vanish? Just stand you up like this?"

Steslow said, "And skip out on a Navy Cross."

Cress said, "Mr. Widow, we all agree on that. Again, we have no recourse. We've already come out here to check on her. If she doesn't want to be found, then she doesn't want to be found. She's a citizen now. She can jump ship if she wants." Suddenly, a low beeping sound emitted from under the Secretary's jacket sleeve. He swept his sleeve back to reveal an expensive watch. He stared at it and pressed a button to cancel the noise. He said, "I've got to get going. There're other things going on in my day than Ms. Cosay."

Cress glanced at Steslow, saw the disappointment on his face, and then looked at Flory. He said, "You guys keep trying to reach her. If she turns up, call me and let me know."

Flory said, "Yes, sir."

And with that, Cress left them standing there and returned to the Navigator. His driver got out before Cress reached the vehicle and opened the rear passenger door for him. Cress stopped before getting in. He turned back to the men, and said, "Steslow, Widow, let's get going. I'm already late."

Flory glanced at Omar and gestured for them to leave as well. The two NCIS agents turned and walked away, back to Flory's electric SUV.

Steslow and Widow remained on the street. Steslow said, "I have to return to port. I've got a ship to look after."

Widow asked, "When are you shipping back out?"

"Supposed to be the day after tomorrow."

Widow stayed quiet. Cress called out to them again to come along. Steslow looked at Widow, and said, "Come on. We'll take you back to base. You can hang around with me for the day."

Silence. Widow didn't respond. He just kept staring at Cosay's house.

Finally, Steslow said, "Widow?"

Widow said, "I'm not going back."

"What're you going to do?"

Widow looked at Steslow, and said, "Someone should look out for her. She's one of us. It looks like it's gotta be me." Then, he put a hand out for Steslow to shake.

Steslow took it and shook it. He asked, "Are you sure?"

"Yes."

"What will you do? How will you get back to town?"

"Don't worry about me. I'll figure it out."

Steslow glanced at Cress, who waited impatiently. Steslow said, "Okay. Call me with updates. Or if you need anything." Like Omar, Steslow dug into his pockets and pulled out a business card. He handed it to Widow.

Widow took it, looked at it, memorized the number, and pocketed it. Then he said, "I'll need background and closest relative information on Cosay. Can you get that for me?"

Steslow said, "If I can't, I think her partner will. I'm sure he'll help. Do you have a phone? I've not seen you play with one this whole morning."

"No phone. I don't have one," Widow said. "I just need an address. I'll call you in an hour."

They shook hands one last time. Steslow returned to the Navigator. He climbed in. The Navigator k-turned in the middle of the street, and drove away. Flory and Omar followed in the electric SUV.

Widow was left there, in the middle of the street, with nothing but questions.

CHAPTER 7

E arlier, the gray clouds seemed to have cleared up, leaving a sunny day. That changed quickly. It started drizzling as soon as Widow saw Flory's electric SUV's brake lights turn the corner and vanish from sight. The light rain didn't bother Widow as much as the cold, wet wind that came with it. He pulled his beanie out of his back pocket, where he had stuffed it earlier, and pulled it over his head. He covered his ears with it. Then he returned to the neighbor's house. The dog saw him coming up the driveway and barked again.

He reached the front door and rang the doorbell. A moment later, the woman opened it again. She saw him and undid the chain latch as before. Then she opened the door all the way and came out onto the porch. The baby was silent, but Widow heard other little kids. It sounded like they were fighting over whose turn it was to play a video game.

The neighbor said, "You're back." She glanced behind Widow, at the street. "What happened to your partners?"

"They left me behind. I'm going to continue investigating without them," he said. "I just wondered if you had a spare key to Lou's house?"

The woman stared up at Widow. She said, "If I did, why would I give it to you?"

Widow asked, "What's your name?"

"Thatcher, like that English lady. Only I'm not related to her."

"It's a good name. She was Prime Minister of the UK for eleven years."

Thatcher said, "No she wasn't. She was Prime Minister of England. Not the UK."

Widow paused a beat. His instinct was to correct her. But he'd been told a few times over the years that it was annoying when he did that. His mom used to say: *No one likes a know-it-all.* And he needed her to like him, if he was going to get that spare key. So, he said, "Oh right. Stupid me. What's your first name?"

Thatcher changed her posture, straightened up, and looked up at Widow. The question had caught her off-guard. She asked, "Why you wanna know that? Are you asking for personal reasons? Is that why you stuck around?"

Widow smiled, and said, "I appreciate you watching Lou's dog and being so neighborly. I think that makes your name worth knowing."

Thatcher said, "My name is Claudia."

"Well, Claudia Thatcher. My name is Jack Widow. You can just call me Widow. Everyone does."

"Okay, Widow. It's nice to meet you."

Widow asked, "Are you single?"

"I told you my husband is an ex. There's no one else in my life. No man."

Widow nodded, and asked, "So, Lou must've trusted you?"

Thatcher said, "I suppose so."

"You guys must be pretty close."

"Lou's not really close with anyone. But we're friends."

Widow said, "Being that you're both single women living in proximity, and that Lou is an NCIS agent, and she trusted you enough to watch her dog, I presume that she also gave you a spare key to her house. And you probably gave yours to her. Who better to safeguard your spare key than an armed federal agent?"

Thatcher's smile faded. She was onto Widow. She said, "You're not into me. You're just trying to get me to give you her spare key."

"So, you have one?"

"Yeah, she gave me one."

Widow said, "Well, you know it can be both things."

"What things?"

"I can be interested in you and also want to help my friend."

Thatcher's smile returned. She said, "Really?"

"Listen, I'm on the clock right now. I gotta do what I can to find Cosay and make sure she's safe. Think you can help me out? It'd be great if I can get that key."

Thatcher looked at Widow, and then to the sky, like she was on the fence about it.

Widow said, "Look, she might be in trouble. I can help her."

"How is going into her house going to help her?"

"There could be clues in there."

"I don't know."

Widow said, "Think about Lou. She's not answering our calls. She was supposed to receive the Navy Cross this morning and didn't show up. Does that sound like her to you?"

Thatcher asked, "What's a Navy Cross?"

"It's the highest medal she can get in the Navy."

"Like the Medal of Honor?"

"It's under the Medal of Honor."

"I thought you said the Navy Cross was the highest?"

Widow said, "The Medal of Honor is open to all branches of the military. The Navy Cross is exclusive to sailors."

Thatcher nodded. A child's voice called out to her from inside the darkness of the house. It was a boy. He shouted, "Mom!"

Thatcher shouted back, "Hold on! I'm coming!" Then she looked at Widow, and reluctantly said, "Wait here."

Thatcher went back into the house and shut the door behind her. Widow heard the deadbolt lock. He stayed on the porch and waited. Several minutes passed. He started to doubt himself. He started to think that he'd taken the wrong approach. But he waited.

Several more minutes passed. Now he'd waited longer than he normally would've. He shrugged and started to walk away. As he neared the middle of Thatcher's walkway, the front door opened behind him. He spun around and saw Thatcher. She had changed out of her housecoat and into a pair of jeans, a top, and a warm coat. Her hair was up in a ball cap. She walked to the end of the porch, but stopped before she got into the drizzle. She reached her arm out and opened her hand. A set of keys dangled from her fingers. She called out, "Here they are. You still want them?"

Widow came back up the walkway. He stopped at the bottom step. Even with her standing on the porch, three steps above the ground, he was taller. She kept holding the keys out towards him. He reached up, slow, and put his palm under the keys for her to drop them. She said, "I'm trusting you."

"I'll return them to you."

She nodded, smiled, and let them drop into his hand. He took them, turned, and walked to Cosay's house. The dog stopped barking, but stayed at the fence, in the light rain, and watched.

Thatcher said, "Maybe after you can stay for a drink?"

Widow kept walking. He didn't respond. He left her yard, crossed the street, but stopped at the end of Cosay's driveway. The drizzle began coming down a little harder. Widow looked to the sky. The gray clouds had taken over sixty-five percent of the sky. It looked like it was only going to get worse. He turned back to see if Thatcher was still watching him. She wasn't. She'd already gone back inside her house, probably to deal with her kids. She was a single mom, running a hectic ship. He could empathize.

Widow definitely respected her for it. He respected all single moms who go it alone. But he certainly didn't envy them. He wouldn't trade his life for anyone else's.

Widow turned to Cosay's mailbox. He opened it and found several letters and one small package. He checked the package first. It was from Amazon. He ignored it and checked the letters. They were all bills or just commercial solicitations. There was nothing of interest. He returned the mail to the mailbox and headed up the driveway.

Widow knocked hard on the front door and waited, in case someone had been hiding inside. He didn't want to get shot. There was no answer. He used the spare key and opened the door and stepped in past the threshold. There was an inside rug and a bench against the wall with shoes neatly lined up.

Immediately, Widow noticed an empty spot, probably where her boots normally rested. He figured it was the ones on Cosay's feet, wherever she was. He thought about taking his off, but he wasn't staying long.

The house was neat and tidy. There wasn't much to see. It was pretty standard and pretty simple. Potted plants were strategically placed around the house. Bookshelves lined various walls. And they were stuffed with books.

There was the foyer, a short hallway, a living room with a wood-burning stove, a small but efficient kitchen, a single bathroom, and two bedrooms. The beds were made. The bathroom was clean. The laundry was folded. There was a pleasant smell in the air, like candles had been burned. The house had tile floors in the hallway, foyer and kitchen. The rest were carpet. And it was all clean and maintained. There were no dishes in the sink.

The entire house was decorated in Native American art and décor. There was a large hand-sewn quilt thrown over a sofa. It looked like the warmest blanket Widow had ever seen. A lot of time and love had gone into it.

Widow found Cosay's bedroom and looked it over. He knew it was hers because the other bedroom was generic and unlived-in. Hers was decorated with more Native artwork and keepsakes. Also, there were photos of Cosay and the various men and women she had served with.

Widow stopped on one photo because he recognized two things in it. The photo was framed and hung on a wall filled with other photos and framed Navy memorabilia. This photo wasn't the largest, and it wasn't the smallest. On the spectrum of Cosay's Navy photos, this one sat right in the middle. But it was in color. Many of them were black and white. Widow wasn't sure why. Maybe it was because they looked better in black and white.

The photo was taken from a drone, he figured. It was angled downward at the flight deck of a ship. There were several members of a crew posing for it. They stood in formation near several parked jets. The crew looked happy and friendly. They were all smiling and hugging each other. It was a personal photo, not an official one for the Navy. The crew was too playful for it to be officially sanctioned by the Navy.

At the middle spot, Cosay stood next to a man. The man had his arm draped around her. But not romantically. They appeared to be good friends, comrades. The man outranked her.

The two things Widow recognized were the man and the ship. The man was Steslow. And the ship was the USS *Bataan*, a *Wasp*-class amphibious assault ship, named for a World War II event called the Battle of Bataan in the Philippines.

Cosay and Steslow looked friendly in the photo. Widow glanced at the photo and then back at Cosay's bed. She had displayed the photo in such a way that she could look at it from her bed. *Interesting*, he thought. Steslow would like to know that. But Widow wasn't going to tell him. He was in Cosay's private space. And he'd respect that.

Naval ribbons and accolades were displayed with pride all over the room and the house. She appeared to be proud of her accomplishments, which told him she definitely would've been at the medal ceremony. Something had happened. He felt it in his gut before, but now he had confirmation. The signs were all there. Whatever happened didn't mean she was in trouble. *Maybe there was a death in the family?*

Widow looked around the room and under the bed. He stopped to look at the photos more closely. He found Cosay in many of them. In some of the ones on the end of the wall, she was no longer in a Navy uniform. The rest of the photos were from her NCIS years. They were recent.

Widow took a mental picture of the most recent one to remember what she looked like. And Steslow wasn't kidding with his description of her. She was a looker. She was thin, not muscular, but toned. Next to Steslow, she appeared short. It was hard to gauge from a photograph. But Widow knew how tall Steslow was. Therefore, he estimated Cosay to be around five feet five inches, which might be right, unless she had lifts in her shoes.

Cosay had narrow, dark brown eyes, like pools of darkness. Her eyebrows were pronounced. Her bone structure made her look chiseled from stone. Her skin appeared dark and ivory-smooth.

Steslow said he came to Kitsap because his boat needed work. But it was obvious he really wanted to see her get the medal. Mostly because of his sincere respect for her. Still, it was hard to ignore her particular kind of beauty. Widow knew Steslow well enough to know it was both.

Widow left the photos and the Navy memorabilia and moved on to the important stuff. Which was searching through her drawers and closet for clues. Before he took another step, he spoke out loud.

Widow said, "Okay, Lou. I'm going to look through your stuff. Forgive me."

Widow started in Cosay's closet. He found clothes neatly hung on hangers. He found a couple of old uniforms hung up and covered in dry cleaner's plastic. He found more shoes lined in a neat row on the closet floor. Then he found something he was looking for. He found a case for a gun. It was made of black rubber and plastic. There was a lock, but it was off the case. He pulled the case out, set it on the floor, and opened it. The gun that had rested in it was gone. And so were two magazines.

She'd taken her service weapon with her. Which wasn't unexpected. It could've meant that she went somewhere where she expected trouble.

Widow closed the gun case and returned it to the closet. Then he searched further and found a three-piece luggage set. Only it was missing one bag. He knew it was a three-piece set because the luggage stood up on spinner wheels, nice and neat in a row, lined up on the back wall of the closet. And there were large and medium checked bags. But there was an empty spot at the far left of the set. It was where a carry-on bag would fit. She had apparently packed and taken the most efficient bag for the trip. She'd left late Wednesday night. So, she had the clothes she was wearing, plus maybe three or four full outfits packed into the carry-on.

There were random spaces in between her hanging clothes, where empty hangers dangled in the closet. This suggested she had picked out a few things, and in a hurry.

Widow backed out of the closet and checked a chest of drawers. He found her underwear drawer first. He blushed, but inspected it. He didn't linger, but he had to move things around to get a complete picture of what she took.

There was a space on one pile, like two or three pairs of underwear were missing. And there was one more item of interest.

There was an empty gun holster. It was a small, low-ride holster. It probably could fit a SIG P938, which is a great concealed carry firearm for a woman. It's got a low profile, but fires nine-millimeter bullets. It'll hold six rounds in the magazine plus one in the chamber.

Widow knew that her service weapon was probably the SIG Sauer P229R, which was the weapon prescribed to NCIS since 2019. And it was a fine gun.

So, Cosay had taken both her service weapon and her backup weapon. She'd left behind the holster, which didn't necessarily mean anything. Maybe she had more than one holster.

At least she was armed, he thought, and he closed her underwear drawer. He searched the other drawers and found nothing out of the ordinary. He noticed that she'd left behind her warm-weather clothes and her bikinis. He knew that because the drawers were neat, but jam-packed. Nothing had been taken from them. And in the closet, the clothes that were missing had been hanging between winter clothes. As neat and organized as Cosay was, it was fair to assume that she grouped her clothing by season. Therefore, she'd gone somewhere cold.

The last thing Widow noted was that, along with her guns, she'd also taken all of her ammo with her. He found no boxes of ammunition. No left-behind magazines.

He already knew that she'd driven her personal vehicle some-where. Maybe she'd parked it in airport parking before boarding a plane. He couldn't be sure. Not without combing the local airport parking lots. Which he wasn't going to do.

Widow left Cosay's bedroom and headed to the living room. But first he stopped and checked the bathroom. The one thing of note was that her toothbrush was missing.

Widow moved on to the living room. Nestled in the back corner of the living room, next to a television on a console with a Wi-Fi router, was a corner desk with a PC on it. The Wi-Fi router had numerous lights on the front. The lights blinked and shone red and green colors, like the internet was active, despite no one using it.

On the desktop, there was a wireless keyboard and mouse, and more photographs. These looked to be of Cosay's family. They were old photos because she was young in them. Widow recognized her face. She appeared to be a child in some and a teenage girl in the others. There was an older woman in some. She must've been Cosay's mother. They looked alike. There was a young boy, younger than Cosay. He looked similar to her as well. *Perhaps a younger brother?* Widow wondered.

There was also a very young girl, who must've been a sister. In several of the pictures, they were on different parts of a farm. There was only one man in only one of the photos. He could've been her father. He appeared stoic, like he was there, but not quite happy and not quite sad. He was just a man in the photos, nothing more and nothing less.

Widow tapped the keys on the keyboard, and the PC came to life. A wallpaper popped up, of rolling grassland and trees. It looked like an American landscape, but it could just be generic. It didn't automatically point him in any direction. It might've been a real place from Cosay's past. Or it might not.

Widow couldn't get past the wallpaper screen because the PC required a password. He wasn't going to get it by guessing. Cosay was a former sailor and a trained NCIS agent. She wasn't going to use her dog's name or her birthday as her password.

Widow left the PC and went into the kitchen. It looked like a normal kitchen. But one thing was noteworthy. There was old coffee still lingering in a pot, on the warming plate in the coffee machine. The coffee machine was turned off. It had a safety mechanism that switched it off automatically after a pre-programmed period of time.

The old coffee told Widow that Cosay had left in a hurry. He closed his eyes and imagined her in the kitchen, after work last Wednesday. She made coffee at night. *Why?* Widow knew why he would make coffee any time of day. But he wasn't most people.

Widow opened his eyes, and pulled out the pot and smelled the old coffee. He stuck his finger in and dabbed a little on his fingertip. Then he licked it off his finger and grimaced. He returned the carafe to the warming plate and opened the machine's lid. He took out the filter basket and stared at the used grinds inside. He sniffed them like a wild animal. And he grimaced again. Not because the coffee was old and smelled bad.

He grimaced and spoke one word, out loud. Widow said, "Decaf." And returned the filter basket to the machine.

Cosay was drinking decaf, probably loved coffee, like a lot of cops did. Since it was nighttime, she made decaf. Which was a poor substitute for the real deal to Widow. But he couldn't judge her for it. Decaf coffee was always better than no coffee.

Widow looked into the sink and realized that he missed one dish that she hadn't cleaned. There was a coffee mug in the sink. It was empty. She'd poured it out. Something happened while she was standing in the kitchen, drinking her decaf coffee. He checked the trashcan. Inside was trash and nothing else of interest.

Widow checked the kitchen countertops and saw a house phone, not that far from the coffeepot. There was no answering machine. The phone was cordless and fairly new. He picked it up out of the cradle and looked it over. It had a little digital window on it that lit up when he took the phone out of its cradle. He inspected the options. It had a call log. Widow went through it, checking the calls and the times.

On the log for Wednesday, he saw outgoing calls to a 959 area code and to a 701 area code. Widow scrolled down the list. The first call that night, after Cosay would've been off work, came in from a 212 number. That was followed by two outgoing calls to the 959 number, and one call to the 701 number.

Widow started with the first, which was the incoming call from 212. He figured that was the number that set off a chain of events that led to Cosay leaving in such a hurry. He also knew 212 was New York City. The other two area codes, he didn't recognize.

Widow dialed the 212 number. New York City was three hours ahead. Widow glanced at a clock on the stove. It was thirteen minutes to eleven in the morning. So it would be thirteen minutes to two in the afternoon in Manhattan.

The phone rang and rang until finally a female voice answered. She said, "*Shedding Light*. How can I direct your call?"

Widow asked, "*Shedding Light*? What's that?"

The woman didn't answer. She just repeated, "*Shedding Light*. How can I help you?"

"What is *Shedding Light*?"

"Sir, are you trying to reach someone in particular?"

"I got a call from here. Just trying to figure out who you are?"

The woman said, "This is *Shedding Light* Network. We're a family of true crime podcasts and a YouTube channel."

"What do you do exactly?"

"We investigate and present a weekly show about various unsolved crimes around the nation."

Widow asked, "So, like investigative journalism?"

"Pretty much. Do you have a story to report?"

"No story. Just trying to figure out who called."

The woman said, "It could've been anyone from the staff. Unless you know who it was, I don't know where to transfer you."

Widow stayed quiet. The phone went silent for a long moment.

The woman got impatient, and said, "We're very busy here. Is there anything else I can help you with?"

"No. I suppose not. Thanks for your time."

The woman hung the phone up before Widow could finish the sentence. He stared at the phone's call log again. Next he redialed the 959 number. It rang four times until finally a voice came over the line. It said, "This is Cassie Fray. Leave a detailed message." It was a voicemail. Widow hung the phone up and checked back with the call log. He redialed the last number on the log, the 701 number. It rang twice and someone answered. A male voice said, "Sawyer County Sheriff's Office."

A sheriff's office, Widow thought.

The voice said, "Hello?"

"Yes. Ah," Widow said, and paused a beat. He wasn't exactly sure what to tell the guy. He wasn't expecting that Cosay had called a sheriff's office. "What office is this?"

"Sheriff's Office. Is there something I can help you with?"

"Where're you located?"

"We're on Gertrude and Elm. Do you need help?"

Widow said, "What's the name of the city?"

"Sir, is this a prank?"

"I'm calling from out of state."

The guy asked, "Why?"

"I missed a call from this number. I'm just trying to figure out who from."

"We're in Sawyer Lake."

"Sawyer Lake? What state?"

The guy said, "North Dakota. We're just south of the Canadian border. We're just off Route 5."

"Thank you."

"Anything else I can help you with?"

Widow paused a beat. He hesitated to ask his next question. But he did anyway. He asked, "You know anyone named Cosay?"

The guy took a long pause. Then he said, "There's an Indian family on the reservation named Cosay. But I don't know them."

Widow nodded along even though the guy couldn't see him. *There was a family on the Indian reservation named Cosay.* That's gotta be the connection he needed. There were pictures of Lou on a farm that could've been on a reservation. *Maybe she returned home for a family issue?*

Widow asked, "Is the reservation in Sawyer County?"

"Yes. And I'm not paid for geographical questions. If you want to ask questions, dial information on your phone, sir. You got a crime to report?"

Widow said, "I just want to know if it is in your jurisdiction?"

"Look, it's in our county, and technically we go out there from time to time, depending on the crime. But they got their own police force—the tribal police."

"Right. What's the name of the tribe again?"

"They're called the Mokani. That's it with the questions. I've got important things to do, sir."

"Wait. Let me ask you one more question. Ever heard of a woman named Cassie Fray?"

"Nope. Gotta go now. Goodbye."

"Thanks for your time," Widow said, and hung the phone up.

Widow studied the phone numbers again and memorized them. Then he walked back out of the house, locking it back up, and headed over to Thatcher's house. He didn't want to engage in further conversation with her, so he put the spare key on her front door mat and rang the doorbell. Once she moved to the door, he walked away. The dog barked at him as he walked back down the drive, down the street, and into the rain.

CHAPTER 8

Two miles north of Rocky Point, Widow stopped in a gas station to ask about a payphone. The clerk looked at him like he was crazy. He commented, "Who has payphones anymore?"

Widow ignored the question and asked about the closest bus terminal. The clerk directed him just a couple of streets over. It wasn't a terminal, just a bus stop.

Widow made it to the stop just in time to see a bus pulling away. The driver stopped for him. Widow boarded and rode for over an hour until the bus came to a station. He got out, and found a payphone inside the station. They only had the one phone, and it appeared to be on its last legs.

Widow sank some quarters into it and dialed Steslow's number from his business card. The phone rang. Steslow answered, "Hello?"

"Reed, it's Widow."

"Widow, did you find out anything?"

"Maybe. I got a look inside Cosay's house. There were some phone calls on Wednesday night, before she left. I think whatever the callers told her made her drop everything and leave in a hurry."

"Who called her?"

"I don't know, but you can check out some names for me. Maybe we can build a picture of what's going on."

Steslow said, "Okay. Give me the names."

"The first one is *Shedding Light*. It's some kind of podcast. They must be successful because they have a Manhattan number, and it sounded like an office. Also, they had numerous people working there because the secretary couldn't figure out who'd called Cosay from there."

"*Shedding Light*. Okay, who else?"

"Cosay called a cellphone twice and in rapid succession afterward."

"Who answered?"

"I'm not sure if anyone answered. When I call it, I get voicemail. The name is Cassie Fray."

Steslow said, "Cassie Fray. Okay. What else?"

"Finally, she called a sheriff's office in a place called Sawyer Lake."

"Hmm. That's gotta be something. I got her file from Omar, like you asked."

Widow stayed quiet.

Steslow said, "Lou grew up near Sawyer Lake. So, that's the connection with the sheriff's office. I guess. She grew up on the North Dakota Mokani Indian Reservation, which is in Sawyer County."

"Okay. Anything else?"

"Yes. There's something that I didn't know. Omar acted surprised about it as well. About seven years ago, Lou's younger brother was murdered. She quit the Navy right after."

Widow thought of the photos on Cosay's home desk. There was a photo of her with a boy, who could've been her brother. *Was it him?* Widow wondered.

Steslow continued, "He was only fourteen. The case was never solved. Apparently, it was a big deal, and yet, not taken seriously enough. The short of it, from what I read, the locals feared a serial killer, and the cops said they had it all under control. Even though it went cold and has stayed that way ever since. I'm not sure about the FBI."

"FBI? Why would they be involved?"

"Because Indian reservations fall under their jurisdiction. Crimes like murder would get their attention."

"Was the boy murdered on the reservation?"

"That I don't know. Possibly. Someone shot him full of arrows."

Widow arched an eyebrow, and said, "Arrows?"

"Yeah, and it gets worse. Or it gets weirder."

Widow waited, said nothing.

Steslow said, "The boy had a target painted on his torso."

"A target?"

"Yeah, like body paint. There were different colored circles like at the shooting range or on a dartboard."

Widow said, "That's bizarre."

"I'll say. Lou probably has some severe PTSD from it."

"What else?"

Steslow told Widow all he knew from the FBI and police files— how the boy was found deep in the woods by a couple of hunters, that they apparently scared off the shooter, and the boy's miraculous escape.

After he laid Cosay's brother's murder out, Steslow asked, "You think this has something to do with why Lou vanished?"

"Could be. You got an address for her family in Sawyer Lake?"

"Yes," Steslow said, and he recited the address to Widow.

Widow asked, "Reed, how long before you ship out? In case I need you."

"I'm still onshore for a couple of days."

"Good. I'll call you if I need you."

Steslow said, "Okay. Thanks, Widow."

Widow hung the phone up, approached the bus station clerk, and bought a bus ticket to the closest destination he could get to Sawyer Lake, which was Bismarck, North Dakota.

CHAPTER 9

Bismarck was less than an eighteen hour drive from Kitsap County, but that was by car. It took Widow closer to twenty-five hours. He rode Greyhound. Buses don't work the same way as cars. He had to ride three different buses, which meant three different routes and three different stops. He felt lucky that was all it took and no longer. Traveling by bus cross-country wasn't the most efficient way to travel. But it was cheap, and it got him there.

Along the way, Widow slept a full eight hours. It just wasn't consecutive because of the stops. When he arrived in Bismarck, the local time was just before four-thirty in the evening. Asking locals where Sawyer Lake was seemed hard. Most people had heard of it, and simply replied it was north. But no one seemed to have been there. Eventually, Widow found a truck stop that sold what the kids today would call old-fashioned maps. Which were *old-fashioned* because they were printed on paper. The clerk at the truck stop made him buy one before he could open it. So he bought it, along with a bottled water and, on an impulse, he bought a new toothbrush, toothpaste, a razor, and shaving cream. It was getting dark early because it was October. He figured it would take him a while to find a ride to Sawyer Lake. He might have to settle in somewhere for the night. And he hadn't shaved in a while. He hadn't brushed his teeth since he lost his last toothbrush somewhere back in Washington State. He remembered brushing his teeth on the morning he ran into Steslow, but couldn't remember when he saw his toothbrush after that. The new toothbrush wasn't foldable, like he preferred. Instead, it was two pieces. The bristle end came off and stuffed inside the handle to protect the bristles from brushing along any other surface when not in use. Also, it seemed not very durable. But it would do for now. He put his new belongings in a plastic bag, rolled them all up, and shoved it all into his inside coat pocket.

Widow tried for over an hour to get a ride to Sawyer Lake from people at the truck stop who were headed north. He even offered to pay for their gas. It was becoming frustrating.

Finally, he got lucky. He saw an elderly man with his granddaughter gassing up a pickup truck, hauling a horse trailer on the back. There was a horse inside. The granddaughter was in her late thirties. She'd heard Widow asking for rides and offered to drop him off in Antler, before the border with Canada. They were headed back to Winnipeg, where they had a ranch just outside the city. The grandfather was wary of giving Widow a ride, but once Widow paid for the gas, which was a lot of money, the old guy acted like Widow was his best friend in the world.

Of course, the grandfather's one rule was that Widow had to ride in the truck's bed. Which he did without complaint. But the wind and temperature nearly gave him a cold. He stayed bundled up with a Native American quilt the granddaughter offered him. They kept it in the truck because she got cold all the time. It reminded Widow of the one in Cosay's house.

He stayed as warm as he could with it for the three-hour ride to the border. On the outskirts of Antler, North Dakota, they let him out at another truck stop, the last before crossing into Canada. Widow thanked them. Before they left him, he asked the time. It was five minutes to nine at night.

Widow decided to get a motel room before heading into Sawyer Lake. He grabbed a room at a rundown motel with a sign tacked onto the motel sign that claimed the place was *recently renovated*.

Which really just meant it had a fresh coat of paint and a couple of other upgrades. But the room was warm and clean.

Widow showered, shaved, and brushed his teeth. Afterward, he filled the bathtub with hot water and soap from a bottle of shampoo. He scrubbed his shirts, socks and underwear clean, rinsed them, wrung them out, and hung them up over the shower rod. Then he took his jeans and spot-cleaned them. They were fairly okay. He shook them out to help them get dry. Then he went into the room, lifted the mattress, and checked that the top of the box spring and the bottom of the mattress were clean. Usually they were. People hardly ever lifted these motel mattresses.

Satisfied, Widow laid the jeans out over the box spring and dropped the mattress down over the pants so they would be good and flattened out by morning. It was the best thing next to ironing or steaming them out.

Widow turned down the bed, got in. It seemed too early to sleep just yet. He thought about watching the TV that was on the wall across from the foot of the bed. He sat up and searched for the remote. Usually, these places had it velcroed to the nightstand. This place didn't. He opened the drawer to see if it was in there. It was, but so was something better than television. There were two books in the drawer. The first was the Bible, a book he'd seen in thousands of motels. The other must've been left behind by a previous tenant. It was a fiction book by an author named Blake Crouch. The book was called *Dark Matter*. It sounded good to Widow. He read until he fell asleep.

CHAPTER 10

I n the morning, Widow drank the rest of his bottled water. Then he dressed and left the motel, leaving the book, half-read, along with the razor and shaving cream and toothpaste. The book was pretty good, but Widow wanted to respect the donor's intention. Another reader had left it in that drawer for the next person. So he would do the same, paying it forward. He could pick up the same title later on from a bookstore if he saw one on his travels.

Widow kept the road map folded in his back pocket with his tattered old passport. His new toothbrush, encased within itself, was stuffed into his front pocket, next to his loose cash and bank card.

Widow walked a short bit. Light snowfall peppered the ground. He got a ride from a long-haul trucker, who was headed in the right direction, which was east. The trucker's destination remained unknown to Widow. The guy wasn't a great conversationalist, which was fine with Widow, but also unusual. In Widow's experience, most truckers who picked him up wanted conversation to kill the loneliness and boredom. They wanted to be entertained by a stranger. They wanted to live vicariously through others. This guy seemed to just want to have someone around, without too much talking, just a warm body in the passenger seat.

The trucker drove Widow fifty-five minutes east and dropped him off on the shoulder of Highway 43, in the middle of nowhere, without questions. The trucker gave him a look that seemed to say: *I hope you know where you're going*. But he never said it. He never remarked on Widow's choice of destination.

The truck pulled away, kicking up mud and melting snow. Widow watched him until he was gone from sight. Second thoughts about getting himself involved crossed his mind for a moment. But that little voice in his head, the one that plagued him from time to time, said: *Do the right thing*. It was his mother's voice. She'd died years ago, in a hospital bed from a gunshot wound to her head. She'd held Widow's hand. And her last words were: *Do the right thing*. And now, he couldn't help it. He was bound to it, like a family curse to do good deeds. If Cosay was in danger, then he needed to step in. She was a sister-in-arms. Judging by her accomplishments, she was also a kindred spirit. He couldn't just look the other way. Not until he could confirm she was safe.

Widow looked around. All that was around was a large, rundown house to the south. It looked like no one lived there, but there was a vicious-looking dog in the yard. It barked at him differently than Cosay's dog had. Her dog had barked in a more friendly, vying-for-attention kind of way. This dog barked like he wanted Widow to be his next meal.

Widow checked the highway's oncoming traffic. There was none. So he crossed over the lanes to a thin two-lane road, heading north, with signs indicating that Sawyer Lake lay ahead, as did the Mokani Indian Reservation. Beyond the street signs, two competing signs were posted in empty fields, each advertising men running for sheriff. One was *Reelect Sheriff Vedely,* and the other was *Elect Henry Braaten*. The picture of Braaten had him in a deputy's uniform. He had a car salesman's smile, all white teeth. The two men worked in the same department. One was the sheriff, and the other wanted to be the sheriff.

Interesting, Widow thought. It must be awkward to work for the guy while competing to get his job.

Not far past the two signs was another one that read: *No Border Crossing.* Which meant that going this direction was not a way to get into Canada, at least not legally.

Widow walked for three miles before he came to a fork in the road. If he stayed heading straight, he would end up in the town of Sawyer Lake. If he took the left road, it'd take him to the reservation. Sawyer Lake's entrance looked more appealing. Signs were posted, welcoming visitors with tourist information about activities on and around the lake. They included ice skating, fishing and ice fishing, skiing, and hunting. The sign also clarified that activities related to ice, snow, and hunting were all closed at the moment. October was cold, but not cold enough to freeze the lake or cover the mountains in enough snow for skiing. Hunting was closed because of something to do with migration patterns of a bird.

Since Widow had no reason to go to Sawyer Lake, not yet, he started his search for Cosay on the reservation. It was better to check in with her family first before going off-script, like interacting with the sheriff's office. Odds were, her family was most likely to know her whereabouts.

The main road in was lined with fences on both sides. Most of the roads were paved. But dozens of dirt roads split from the main road. Most ran either north or south. As he walked, Widow scanned for street signs. Some had them. Some didn't. He kept looking anyway, hoping to find the right one. So far, he had had no luck.

Long, winding gravel driveways sprouted off here and there from the various roads. Old metal mailboxes mounted on posts were at the end of most of the driveways. Widow scanned each for the Cosay name or for the right number combination, or even for numbers close to the ones for Cosay's family. He had no luck.

Power lines trailed along one edge of the main road, occasionally branching off into different lines, following other roads. The reservation was mostly farmland. Beyond the fences, grassy fields rolled on for as far as the eye could see. Beyond them, there were large farms, teeming with life. Farmers were winding down for the end of the season, preparing for winter. Large Native families tended to their livestock and chores. Most houses, farms, and roads seemed old and used and lived-in, but they were well-maintained. Many of the farmhouses appeared to have been remodeled in parts, like the families had lived there for generations, and each generation updated things as they saw necessary. Old barns had new roofs. New farming equipment existed side-by-side with old equipment. Old machinery butted heads with new technologies. Old fencing lined up with new. Generations of old faded away, while new generations paved the road to the future.

Farmland wasn't all there was. Thick wooded areas perched on the horizon to the northwest. Large, rugged mountains climbed the sky behind them. Sawyer County was quite something. The population wasn't huge. The Indian reservation seemed to have been largely forgotten, as well as the farmlands and rolling hills. There was the town of Sawyer Lake, which Widow hadn't seen yet. Of course, there was a lake, which he also hadn't seen yet. And there looked to be a large national park to the north.

Widow walked on for three more miles, not seeing much other than cows grazing in the fields. Several vehicles passed him, going both deeper in and farther out of the reservation. A few of them circled back around by going up various roads and swinging back by him. This was probably to get a second look at the outsider. He stuck out like a sore thumb. No one stopped for him, but they all slowed to look at him. He saw mostly indigenous faces of all ages. There were some mixed white faces as well. The one thing they all had in common was living this laid-back, country lifestyle. They all had pickup trucks or SUVs, no cars, not that he'd seen. Definitely no electric cars like Flory's.

No cars, but there were motorcycles. Two guys rode motorcycles right past him once. They rode together, side-by-side, like gang members. No helmets, but their faces were wrapped up in ski masks to keep them warm. The bikes were expensive-looking, and well-maintained, like all they did was ride around on them and work on them. Widow didn't know if they were Harley Davidsons or what.

What Widow knew was that he'd had his fill of motorcycle gangs. He didn't want to scuffle with any more of them. He'd had enough from a run-in he'd experienced last year with a motorcycle club. The two bikers glanced back at him as they rode past. He simply waved at them, hoping they wouldn't see him as any kind of threat. It must've worked because they kept on rolling.

The locals weren't the only residents to take an interest in him. A murder of black crows followed Widow for the last mile. He saw them on several fence posts. He was pretty sure they were the same birds each time. In fact, he was positive one of them was the same because it had white streaks on its talons. The streaks weren't natural. Somehow, the crow had gotten white paint on its feet, like it landed on a freshly painted post before the paint had dried. The paint would be there until rain came along and washed it away.

The white-paint-taloned crow made eye contact and cawed at him twice. It behaved like it knew him, like they were old friends or old enemies.

After passing several more winding dirt roads, Widow found the first public buildings. There were only two. That told Widow he hadn't found the reservation's main drag yet, just an offshoot. He presumed the main drag was on a different street.

On the corner there was a church, which was all wood and white paint. There were no stained-glass windows, like in many churches. If it weren't for a cross in the front yard, and a sign, Widow wouldn't have known it was a church. The church was called *Independence Mound Church*. Not very descriptive. Widow wasn't sure what kind of church it was. He figured it was a nondenominational Christian church, as the religions of indige-nous Americans varied significantly. Many were some sort of Christian, and many were not. Many stuck with the spirituality of their ancestors.

The second building was across and down the street a short ways. But it stood within view of the church. Widow skipped the church and headed down the street to the other building. It was a bar. Seeing a church and a bar on the same street, in proximity to each other, struck Widow as both an American thing and a Southern thing.

The bar was one story, built from wood, painted a light blue color. A rusted corrugated-tin roof protected the inside from the outside. It was the kind of thing that dinged and echoed when it rained. A wooden railing lined a long front porch. The entrance was a pair of glass doors. One was propped open. Country music blasted from a jukebox somewhere within the bowels of the place. An ice machine hummed on one side of the building. The parking lot was gravel. It wasn't full, but it had vehicles parked in it.

Widow was a little surprised there were as many people there as there appeared to be. He figured some vehicles were still there from the night before. And that some of the people were there having a drink before returning to their farms for the rest of the day's plowing and harvesting. There was a neon sign posted on the wall with the bar's name on it. It was on. Plus, another neon sign was lit up. It indicated that the bar was open for business.

The bar's name was *The Ranchman*.

Two motorcycles were parked in the lot. They could've been the same ones that passed Widow on the road. They looked the same, but he couldn't tell for sure. The other vehicles were mostly modern-day pickup trucks. There was one panel van. It was old and generic. An economy car was parked in a space under a light pole. It stuck out to him because it was a tiny hatch-back car. It was bright blue. It kind of resembled a blueberry. Snow caked the roof, windshield, and tire treads. It'd been left there a while, like someone got too drunk to drive home, left the car, and hadn't come back for it yet. A tow warning sign was posted not too far away from it. Widow wondered when the bar owner would make good on the threat.

Widow climbed the steps to the long porch and entered the bar. The lights were low; even in the daytime, the place was dimly lit. It was smoky. Ugly red tile lined the floor. Various Native artifacts and artwork hung on the walls. There was an old-timey cigar store Indian statue in one corner, which was used as a coat rack.

There was a small stage in another corner. There were a couple of empty stools on it and some old musical instruments piled up. No one was onstage. A jukebox was playing behind a single pool table near the back wall. Two guys were shooting pool. And three of their friends watched from high-top tables. They all drank beer from the bottle.

As Widow entered, low voices rumbled. The bar's occupants were ninety percent men. The rest were women, and half of them worked the bar. There were a couple of waitresses, a female bartender, a male bartender, and a cook, also male.

Some customers drank liquor and ate lunch, maybe on their lunch breaks from whatever farm job they had. The rest of the customers just drank liquor. One guy was half passed out on his table, drunk. Everyone else seemed to be having a good time.

Whereas Widow had seen a few mixed white faces on the road, his was the only white face in the bar. He really stuck out like a sore thumb.

Widow stepped past the bar's threshold, and the rumbling voices lowered to murmuring whispers. Eyes turned to him. They hung there on him for a long second. And the whispers continued. Another moment passed, and everything slowly went back to normal bar chatter. Most of the patrons returned to their drinks and their conversations and forgot about the newcomer.

Widow headed for the bar and took a seat. He picked a spot in front of the female bartender. She greeted him with a warm smile. There was no hesitation in her. She treated him like any other customer. He ordered coffee. She nodded and stepped away to get it. But she never came back with it. Instead, the male bartender stepped up, and said, "Can I help you?"

The guy was older than the rest of the staff. He was heavier in the midsection, but tall, like a stretched-out teardrop. He had thick, short hair and gray sideburns. His hair was jet black on top.

Widow said, "I ordered already."

"I know. What I mean is, are you lost, friend?"

"Nope," Widow said, paused, and glanced at the bar. Across from him, behind the bartender and shelves of liquor, a large mirror hung on the wall. He glanced in it and saw several of the customers turn their heads and stare at him again. He asked, "Are you going to serve me?"

"Sure. It's just that we don't get a lot of outsiders here," the bartender said reluctantly, and stepped away. He came back with the coffee and set it down on the bar in front of Widow.

Widow smiled, grasped it, and took a sip. He said, "Not bad."

"So?"

"So, what?"

"You didn't answer my question. Are you lost or something?"

"Why?"

The bartender said, "I've never seen you in here before."

"What about them?" Widow nodded at the rest of the bar. "You seen all of them before?"

"Yes. I own the place. I've seen everyone. I know everyone. They live here. No one comes here that's not from here," he said, and paused a beat. He glanced up at the ceiling, like a memory just struck him. "Well, not usually."

Widow sipped the coffee, and said, "So, what? Are you going to tell me to keep on going? That I'm not welcome here or something?"

"Would you listen?"

Widow's eyebrow arched. He shook his head.

The bar owner said, "I didn't think so. You sound like you've heard that before?"

"I've heard it a time or two."

"We like tourists here. I wish we had more. It's just that most of them never end up here. Not at my bar. That's all."

Widow asked, "Where do they end up?"

"To the north."

"How? The road that brought me in was to the southeast."

"That's the road in. No one comes here that way. Not tourists. They usually come from Sawyer Lake. They come by boat. There's a little main drag to the north on the reservation. It's a place to stop, have lunch, stock up on fishing supplies, etc."

Widow nodded and said nothing.

The bar owner placed two big hands on the bar's lip. He leaned forward, stared at Widow, and said, "Some locals may not like seeing you. You know they've got a four-hundred-year-old chip on their shoulder about white men taking our land and all?"

"Bullshit."

"What?"

"That's not why you're saying that. Why do you want me to leave so badly?"

The bar owner glanced past Widow at a few guys off to the back of the bar, the ones playing pool. Widow saw them in the mirror. Two of them wore leather bomber jackets. They had tattoos, like him. They may have been the guys that passed him on the road with the motorcycles. And they may not have been. Either way, they were the guys who owned the pair of motorcycles parked outside. That was obvious.

The bar owner said, "I just don't want any trouble. I want nothing to happen to you, is all. Some of our more colorful citizens just don't like outsiders. So whatever your purpose is here, I'd be done with it and move on."

Widow took a big, long pull of his coffee, and said, "I'm looking for someone."

"Yeah? You a cop or something?" the bar owner looked Widow up and down. "You don't look like a cop. You look more like an out-of-work linebacker."

Widow glanced at himself in the bar mirror. He was clean-shaven, showered, wearing clean clothes, and the stylish coat given to him by the widow he met back in Washington State. Suddenly, he realized he probably shouldn't have cleaned up before he came out here. Even though his clothes were second-hand, with them being clean, and with the stylish coat, he could pass for someone who was more well-to-do than he really was. It was a terrible cover story for him. He should've thought it out better.

The bar owner asked, "Who you looking for?"

A guy who seemed nervous and edgy walked over to the bar from the pool game. He stood a few feet from Widow's left. He stepped close to the bar, and picked up two handfuls of freshly opened beers from the female bartender. He was close enough to hear Widow's conversation.

"I'm looking for a woman," Widow said.

Before Widow could say another word, the bar owner interrupted him. He said, "Saw her a few nights ago. But I'm sorry to be the one to tell you this. She left here with another man. So, if you're out here searching for her, I'd say she's not your girlfriend anymore."

The skittish guy scooped up the beers, and scurried away, fast, like a baby crab running from a predator.

Widow said, "I'm not looking for my girlfriend."

"She's your wife? Then I'm really sorry. She left here a few nights back with a guy you don't want to be messing with. Not that you couldn't take him in a fight. You look capable," the bar owner said, and leaned in closer. He whispered, "But he comes with a crew. And they're bad news. Some of them are behind you, at the pool table."

Widow glanced at the bar mirror, saw the group at the pool table. He looked back at the bar owner, and said, "I think you're confused."

"I don't think so. Like I told you. We don't get a lot of white faces here. I remember her. Listen, if it makes you feel better, I'm going to have her car towed."

"What?"

"It's been sitting in my lot since she left. I'm not running a long-term parking lot here. I already called the tow truck," the bar owner said, and glanced at his watch. "It's been a day or two, though. So, if you find her and make up and get her away from the guy she left with, then I'd get her and get that car by tonight, before it's towed. Then I'd get the hell out of here, and never look back."

Frustrated, Widow said, "I got no idea what you're talking about. I'm not here looking for a white woman."

"No? Then what woman are you here looking for?"

"A woman who grew up here. She's Mokani. Maybe you heard of her? Her name's Cosay. People call her *Lou*."

The bar owner went silent, like he'd heard the name of a ghost.

"Do you know her?"

"Lomasi is the name folks here knew her as—Lomasi Cosay. Yeah, I knew her in passing. But you won't find her here. She don't live here no more. She left years ago. I don't remember how many. And she won't be back either. Not unless it's for a funeral."

A funeral was the last time Cosay was in Sawyer Lake. Widow figured that from what Steslow had already told him. She'd come back when her brother died, and joined the NCIS shortly after that.

Widow recited the Cosay family address that Steslow had given him, and asked, "Know where it is? I've had no luck locating it. The roads here aren't marked well."

The bar owner glanced behind Widow to the guys playing pool again. Widow watched in the bar mirror. They were watching, pool sticks in hand. There were the two bikers and a few others. One guy seemed more interested than the others. He was skittish, shifting from one foot to the other. He had no drink in his hands. No pool stick. But he was holding something. It looked like a cellphone. He held it out in front of him, arms stretched out. He pointed it in Widow's direction, like a guy trying to find the wind's direction with his thumb.

The guy wasn't reading a text or conversing with anyone on his phone. He was simply aiming it at Widow.

The bar owner noticed as well. He said, "Listen, I think you should finish your coffee and go, friend."

"What's that guy doing?"

The bar owner glanced back at the bar mirror behind him, like he just realized that Widow was using it to see the guys at the pool table. He said, "He probably took your picture."

"Why?"

The bar owner didn't answer that. The skittish guy lowered his phone and slid it into his pocket. Then he said something inaudible to the group of people at the pool table. He turned and high-stepped out the front of the bar, like he had to be some-where urgently.

The bar owner said, "Please, friend. You gotta get going."

"Who was that?"

"That was trouble. Please, go. For both our sakes."

Widow stared at the bar owner's eyes. He didn't want to cause the guy trouble. He was just a small business owner, trying to run his bar in a small community that he'd have to face long after

Widow was out of the picture. So Widow said, "Tell me where Cosay's family lives and I'll get out of your hair."

The bar owner told him where to go and pointed in the direction. Widow thanked him and asked if he could have another coffee, but to go. The bar owner glanced at the entrance, like he was expecting someone to enter. Then he poured Widow a fresh coffee into a Styrofoam cup with a lid. The cup wasn't meant for coffee. It was meant for sodas, so it was double the size of a normal coffee to-go cup, like what Starbucks would call a *grande*. Widow paid him, thanked him, got up, and walked out.

Outside, Widow felt uneasy, like he wasn't alone walking out of the bar. He stepped out onto the porch, turned right, and came out into the parking lot. Standing dead center in the lot was the skittish guy, the one who snapped Widow's picture on his phone and high-tailed it out of the bar afterward.

The skittish guy stood on the gravel, shivering. He was short and scrawny. He wore a cowboy hat. His clothes looked more worn and tattered than Widow's passport.

Widow didn't know if the skittish guy shivered because he was cold, or scared, or just because he was so skittish, like it was his nature. He was quivering the way a pine needle would be in a stiff breeze.

Skittish or not, the guy held his hand up to Widow. His palm was open. The skittish guy spoke in the best authoritative voice he could muster, which was the same as that of a titmouse. The guy said, "I can't let you leave, mister."

Widow stared down at the guy. He was brave, no doubt about it. He was stupid, too. No doubt about that either. Widow was six-four, two hundred and thirty-five pounds. And he was all muscle and combat experience. There was more lethality in Widow's ice-blue stare than in the skittish guy's entire imagination.

Widow said, "What?"

"I can't let you go anywhere. Not yet."

Widow saw a third reason the guy shivered so noticeably. When he spoke, Widow saw his gums and teeth. The guy was a meth addict—either now, or in the past, or both. He had lost some of his teeth. And the ones that stayed behind were yellow, and not looking so good. His grin looked like a mouth full of holes and candy corn, instead of human teeth. His gums were rotten. There were holes in them, like someone used them for target practice with a tiny gun.

"I don't know who you are, but I'm going to leave," Widow said, and walked toward the road, past the guy.

The skittish guy scrambled around in front of him, stopped, but stayed back several yards. He put his hand up again, like a bridge troll demanding Widow pay the toll.

Widow smirked, and said, "Step aside, while you still can walk. I'm not going to ask again."

The skittish guy paused a long beat. Fear crept across his face. He shook more violently, which Widow didn't think possible. The skittish guy glanced around at the parking lot, nervously, like he was looking for some imaginary force to step in and help him.

Widow started to wonder if the guy was out of his mind. It was a real possibility. He didn't want to hurt a weak meth head who probably had screws loose. But he had someplace to be. So he shook off any concerns, and walked right toward the guy, not past him like before. He shoved the guy aside. Not hard, just enough to get his point across. It didn't work.

The skittish guy shouted, "Stop, mister! I'll stop you if I have to!"

You and what army? Widow thought rhetorically.

Right then, even though the question had been in Widow's mind and no one had heard it, the question was answered. Behind Widow, five guys stepped out of the bar, onto the porch, and down the steps into the parking lot. Two of them were the motorcycle guys, the same two who owned the bikes in the lot. The other three guys had been playing pool with them.

The skittish guy shouted, "Stay where you are, mister!" There was a sudden burst of courage in his voice. Now that he saw his comrades had come out of the bar to join the fight, he felt better equipped to face off against Widow.

Widow stopped walking towards the skittish guy and glanced behind him. He saw the five new guys coming up to him. He turned his back on the skittish guy and faced the new ones. The five new guys circled around him. The skittish guy said, "Stay here. I'm not going to tell you again." Widow's own words spat back at him.

The five new guys fanned out around Widow. Some flanking him. Widow stared at one of the bikers, not because he seemed to be the leader, but because he was the biggest one of them. And the large biker spoke. He said, "Better listen to him, friend."

The second biker said, "He told you to wait."

A third guy said, "Stay put, Nakai."

Widow had no idea what the word meant. In context, he assumed it was a Native American word, probably Mokani. And it was probably a derogatory slang word, like they were calling him *white man*, only with a negative inflection.

The skittish guy said, "You'll wait for Billy!"

Widow looked around him casually. He kept his hands by his sides, visible and relaxed. The only thing of note was the coffee in his hand. He asked, "Who's Billy?"

Another guy said, "Billy's the guy who tells you when you can leave."

Just then, as if on cue, a vehicle came plowing down the road from the west, behind the skittish guy. Widow watched it. It was a pickup truck. The truck was all white. It was a wide-body truck. The tires were big. The thing was old, like a classic collector's edition. It was a country truck. There was a set of large steer's horns stuck on the front like a hood ornament. Widow looked past the driver at a shape he knew well. Racked on the rear window of the truck was a sniper rifle.

The pickup bounced over the road and the gravel and into the parking lot. The driver slammed on the brakes, booting up snow and gravel. A plume of dust kicked up behind it. The truck stopped behind the skittish guy. The driver thumped the emergency brake, shot the door open, and hopped out of the truck.

The driver of the truck was Native, like the rest of them. He wore a cowboy hat, blue jeans, and a western cowhide leather jacket with fringe and beads. A bolo tie hung from his neck, covering the top buttons of his collared shirt. Flashy cowboy boots tied the whole outfit together.

He had long black hair, pulled back. A patchy mustache grew above his upper lip. He walked up behind the skittish guy and moved him aside like a gate to an animal pen. He stepped between Widow and the others. He looked Widow up and down, and asked, "Who are you?"

Widow saw no way past them, not without running, and he never ran. He wouldn't get away, anyway. He was on foot, in the cold. They had vehicles. And they were from here. Therefore, they'd be more acquainted with the reservation. Plus, they'd be more acclimated to the cold weather than he was.

Widow said, "Guys, I got no idea why you're trying to engage with me, but I'm not here for trouble. I'm just looking for someone. That's all."

The skittish guy spoke to the guy in the bolo tie. He said, "He was asking at the bar for a woman."

The bolo tie guy said, "Nakai, my name is Billy. Like Billy the Kid. And that's what people around here call me. Know why?"

Widow stared him down, stayed quiet.

Billy flapped open his coat to reveal a gun holstered at his hip. And it wasn't just any firearm. It was an Old West style revolver, like a Colt Single Action Army Revolver, aka the Peacemaker. The guy pulled it and twirled it around his fingers like an Old West gunfighter from a bad movie. He flipped it and swung it. And then he re-holstered it. It was all fast. It looked all professional, like the guy had practiced it for years, behind a barn somewhere. Widow almost retorted as much, but he only wanted to get on his way. He really didn't want to fight seven guys he had just met. Not on only one cup of coffee.

Billy the Kid holstered the gun, and kept walking to Widow. He stopped two yards away, just out of Widow's reach. Billy said, "I'm a good shot with it, too. That's why they call me Billy the Kid."

Widow nearly rolled his eyes at the presentation, the comment, and just the thought that this guy had ever fired a gun in a real firefight in his whole life.

Billy the Kid put his hands up in front of him, and squared them like a camera. He stared at Widow through the hole, like he was blocking a scene in a movie. He said, "I can see shooting you. Easy. A big target like you. You'd be so easy to hit. It'd take one snap of the wrist." Billy dropped both hands to his sides. He flicked his wrist, brandished the Peacemaker from the holster, and aimed it at Widow. It was a quick series of motions. He was fast with it. "Then all I'd have to do is pull the trigger, and BOOM! You'd be dead."

Widow didn't flinch, which was what Billy had intended. Instead, he said, "Why did you have to pull a gun on me? It all could've been resolved friendly-like."

Billy stared at him. His eye was over the Peacemaker's sights. He seemed disappointed that Widow wasn't affected by him or his gun or his threats.

"It's cowardly to pull a gun on an unarmed man. Especially when you outnumber me seven to one. What is that, seven guns against one unarmed man? What about the rest of you? You gonna pull your guns out on me, too?" Widow said, and glanced around at each of them. He tried to make fast eye contact, but he was also scanning with his peripheral vision to see which of them moved their hands toward potentially concealed firearms. He knew that his mentioning it would make most untrained men reach for theirs. Even if they weren't going to pull them. They would move to their guns. It was instinct, basic human behavior. Widow employed the same tactics of a trained prizefighter going up against his deadly opponent in the ring. He looked for a twitch of an elbow, a jerk of a shoulder, or a head tilt toward their guns. He saw two of them react in such a way. The bikers. The other three guys were just backup or in the gang. They weren't much of a threat. Not by the looks of them. They were farmhands, moonlighting for Billy. They could probably throw a punch or two, but that was about it, Widow thought.

The skittish guy wasn't armed. Even if he were, he'd be the first to tuck tail and run when things got dicey.

Widow believed in first reaction, or be the first to act. React first. Move. Shoot. Communicate. However, Widow also hated wasting good coffee. Luckily for him, *The Ranchman* could pour him a second to-go cup if he wanted it. And their coffee was good, but not that good. So, he reacted first.

Widow didn't know Billy from Adam. He'd never met Billy, never seen Billy, and never heard of Billy. But Widow saw the truck, the bullhorns, the outfit, the bolo tie, and the pristine Old West gun. And he knew an egomaniac when he saw one. This guy romanticized his own image. Widow had known officers like that in his time. He even knew admirals like that, men with overblown egos, who needed to be taken down a peg. Billy was cosplaying himself to be some sort of local crime boss, an outlaw. And maybe that act worked around the reservation. He certainly had his guys convinced. But not Widow.

Widow stared at Billy, and asked, "Is that a prop gun? And that thing you did with your hands, what're you, one of those dandy boys who work on shitty westerns? You the guy that gets shot? Falls off a horse?"

At the same time that Widow was talking, he popped the lid on the to-go coffee with his thumb.

Billy's fragile ego couldn't take it. He turned a shade of red, and said, "You don't think it's real?"

Widow stayed quiet, stayed relaxed, but readied himself for action.

And as if on cue, Billy played right into his hands. Billy stepped back, pointed the Peacemaker into the air, and fired it, thinking he was showing the gun worked fine. But he wasn't. What he was doing was twofold. First, he moved the danger away from Widow by redirecting the line of fire. And second, he gave Widow the diversion he needed to draw everyone's attention away.

Billy fired the gun. It boomed and echoed over the parking lot, the road, and an empty field of tall, rolling grass next to the bar.

Widow seized the moment and exploded into action. Widow thumbed the lid of the to-go cup the rest of the way off and launched the steaming hot coffee at Billy's face. The skittish guy and one of the farmhands stood so close to Billy that they also got the fiery liquid in their faces. Which was a bonus for Widow.

Widow snatched the Peacemaker out of Billy's hand and snapped the hammer back. It clicked as it locked into place, ready to fire. A split-second later, Widow head-butted Billy full on in the face. The guy's nose cracked. Billy toppled over like a guy kicked off a building. Blood gushed out of his broken nose faster than Widow was moving.

Widow danced right and kicked the next farmhand square in the nuts. He crumbled and writhed in agony faster than Billy had. Then, Widow spun around and pointed the Peacemaker at the three remaining guys, which were the two huge bikers and the last farmhand.

Behind Widow, the skittish guy was screaming obscenities as he grappled with the sting of hot coffee in his eyes. Billy held two palms to his face, trying to stop the bleeding. The one farmhand also screamed from the intense heat of the coffee on his face. The farmhand that Widow had kicked in the nuts had his mouth hung open, but couldn't muster a sound out of his voice box. He was in too much pain in his nether regions.

Widow saw that the one farmhand with the coffee to the face was getting antsy. So he stepped in and put a stop to any ideas the guy was getting by dancing toward him and kicking him full on in the nuts. The farmhand folded over, grabbed his groin, and fell flat on his face.

Widow shoved the Peacemaker in the face of one of the bikers. The biker was going for his gun, but froze when he saw the gun's barrel.

Widow said, "Hands up. All of you."

The three standing men raised their hands, collectively.

Widow said, "Now, slow, and one at a time. I point this gun at you. That means it's your turn. Follow me so far?"

All three nodded. Just then, the bar patrons stumbled out of *The Ranchman*. Some gathered on the porch. Some of the braver ones made it out into the parking lot. The staff came out after. The bar owner pushed through the crowd, to the front of the line. He stopped and watched, but said nothing. He didn't intervene, as many small business owners might. No one got on their phones to dial 911.

The locals weren't friendly to cops. Even the tribal police had a hard time dealing with the locals. So, Widow continued with his self-defense.

Widow pointed the Peacemaker at the nearest biker, and said, "Remember, slowly, take your gun out. Pinch it using your index finger and thumb. You touch the trigger and I'll put a hole in you."

Reluctantly, the biker did as he was instructed. He pulled out a Glock, keeping his finger away from the trigger.

Widow gestured toward a field of tall grass and snow near the bar. He said, "Throw it in there. And I mean throw it far. I'm talking outfield range. You understand baseball?"

The biker said, "Of course, I know baseball."

Widow said, "Good. Now throw it."

The biker reared back and heaved the Glock high in the air. It wasn't outfield range, but it was far enough. The gun vanished into the tall grass.

Widow pointed the Peacemaker at the second biker, and told him to do the same thing. The guy repeated the process. It was another good throw and his gun vanished into the tall grass. His throw wasn't outfield either, but it was better than the first guy's. It was more like second base.

"Good. Now, I got a dilemma, fellas. See, I can't have you following me. But I can't trust you to say you won't. So, I'm going to give you a choice," Widow said, and pointed the gun at them. He moved it from one face to the other. He stopped on the last farmhand. "Okay, you. Bullet or nuts?"

"What?"

Widow asked, "Those are the outcomes for the answer you give me. Understand?"

"What?" the farmhand repeated.

Widow asked, "Point out your truck?"

"What?" the farmhand repeated, like a talking doll stuck on a phrase.

"Which truck did you come in? Which is yours?"

Billy said, "Don't tell him nothing."

Widow didn't face Billy. He mule-kicked him in the face. Billy's nose broke again. The broken parts broke into more parts.

Widow asked, "Which truck? Point them all out."

The farmhand pointed at an SUV in the lot, and said, "We all came in that. It's mine."

Widow said, "Good choice. You chose the bullet."

The farmhand raised his hand in front of his face, like Widow was going to shoot him. But Widow didn't shoot him. Instead, he spun, pointed the Peacemaker at the SUV's front tires, aimed, and squeezed the trigger in rapid succession. The gunshots boomed. Some onlookers ducked and gasped. The two bullets hit one front tire apiece. The tires exploded and air gusted out, deflating the tires.

Widow spun to the motorcycles next, aimed, and squeezed the trigger. Once. Twice. He shot out the front tires of both motorcycles. The gunshots boomed, and the tires exploded.

One of the bikers stepped forward like he was going to charge at Widow. But Widow spun to him next, pointed the Peacemaker at him, aiming right between his eyes. The biker froze.

Widow said, "Five shots fired, one left. Do you want it?"

The biker's face was flushed with rage at what Widow had done to his bike. But he shook his head, and said, "No."

"Good," Widow said, and he leaned to the left and glanced at the bar owner. "Hey, I spilled my coffee. Would you bring me another one?"

The bar owner glanced at a waitress. She hopped to it.

Widow glanced at Billy, who wasn't looking good. He was sitting upright, which was a good sign, but his nose was bad. He might need facial reconstructive surgery. Widow wasn't sure. He wasn't a doctor.

Widow glanced at Billy's truck, and saw the sniper rifle again. Then he looked down at Billy, and said, "Hey. Get your keys out of your pocket."

Billy replied, but it was mostly garbled and nasally because of his nose. He said, "What for?"

Widow said, "Get them!"

Billy slowly fished the keys out of his pocket.

"Toss them to me. And Billy, I better catch them."

Billy tossed them to Widow, who caught them. He said, "Thank you. And Billy, consider yourself lucky."

"Lucky? How? You broke my nose," he said, at least that's what Widow made of it.

Widow said, "Normally, a guy points a gun at me. I break his hand so I don't have to worry about him shooting me anytime soon. You don't want me to break yours? Do you?"

Billy said nothing. The waitress came back out, pushed through the crowd of spectators, and scurried over to Widow. She handed him the coffee in a to-go cup. A napkin was tied around the cup. He took the cup with his free hand, kept the Peacemaker slowly sweeping from man to man.

The waitress whispered to Widow. "My number is on the napkin. Call me."

He glanced at her. She smiled and giggled and ran back to join the crowd.

Widow took the coffee, the Peacemaker, and Billy's keys, and headed to the truck. He set the coffee on the hood. It turned out he didn't need the keys because the door was unlocked. He climbed inside, set the Peacemaker on the dash, and grabbed the sniper rifle off the window rack. He came back out with both guns.

The rifle was a bolt-action rifle. Widow stuffed the Peacemaker into his waistband, raised the rifle, squeezed the trigger slowly. Unlocking the bolt, he pulled it out of the gun. He tossed the rifle into the truck's bed. Then he reared back and threw the bolt as hard and far as he could into the tall grass. That was an outfield throw. He repeated the process with Billy's keys, so Billy couldn't follow him. Then he left. The crowd watched him go. He waited until he was several minutes away from them and had made sure no one followed him, and then he emptied the last bullet out of the Peacemaker and threw the empty weapon into one quiet field and the bullet into another.

CHAPTER 11

T he murder of crows was back. The white-paint-taloned one was also back. He flew over Widow's head and landed on a fence post. The post was a part of the farm that Widow was searching for.

Widow followed the bar owner's directions to the Cosay farm. He turned down winding dirt roads and walked for another hour, for three miles, until he found it. He downed the rest of his to-go coffee and crushed the cup and pocketed it. When he came across a trash bin, he'd dump it.

The Cosay farm was run down. Many of the neighboring farms were run down, but this one was one of the worst that still had people living on it. It needed a lot of work. The grass was overgrown, and that was the grass that was alive. The livestock was depleted. And the animals they had didn't look to be in prime condition. They were fed and taken care of, but they weren't like the ones on the other, more prosperous farms on the reservation.

The Cosay farm was large and unkempt, but it had a lot of potential. Widow walked up the road to it. He approached a black, rusted mailbox at the end of a gravel driveway. As he walked, he noticed a dark SUV parked across the road. It sat on the grass, just off the shoulder. The windows were tinted. Snow and mud were caked all over the vehicle like it had driven through a lot of bad weather.

Widow walked closer, trying to see if someone was in the vehicle. Which there was. Someone sat in the driver's seat. He knew that because the moment he appeared in their rearview mirror, the brake lights came on and the engine started and the SUV peeled away. He picked up speed and jogged to the mailbox. He stopped and tried to get the license plate, but he couldn't. The SUV was too far away by the time he was in sight of the plate. It wasn't North Dakota. He knew that. North Dakota plates are bright blue at the top for the bright blue sky. This plate was white at the top. He didn't see enough of it beyond that to know where it came from. It could've been a Washington State plate. *Did someone follow him here? Or was it Lou Cosay herself? But if it was her, why would she take off like that when she saw him?*

They'd never met before.

Widow pondered these questions briefly, and shook them off. He turned to the mailbox to check the address. The numbers matched, and it said *Cosay Family Farm* on the box. The letters were old and faded, but they were there.

Widow walked up the driveway, following it up a hill and down the other side, where it wound farther into the property. There were more fence posts. On one, he read a warning sign that read: *Private Property*, and another that threatened that *Violators will be shot on sight*. It was too late to turn back now. So, he kept going.

He saw a couple of horses frolicking in the distance. The crows followed him, but stayed high above, circling more like vultures than crows. Off to the north, the left side of the driveway, Widow saw a small cemetery. It must've been a family plot. He came to a footpath that veered off toward the cemetery.

A broken-down tractor was in one of the fields, covered in overgrown grass. Widow continued on. As he neared the farmhouse, he saw a bedraggled old greenhouse, and a barn on one side, and another building he figured was stables. He saw more horses.

There were pens on the other side of the barn. He wasn't sure if there were animals there or not.

He walked up the final leg of the driveway to the farmhouse. It was two stories, painted white with brown trim. The paint was chipped in various places, but still hanging on to life. There was a brick chimney. Someone was burning a fire in it. Threadlike plumes of smoke puffed out the top. A large porch took up the front of the house, with steps at the bottom.

Two vehicles were parked on the side of the driveway. Both were old single-cab pickup trucks. One older than the other by about ten years. And they were both older than twenty years. They were a little beat up, but probably ran fine.

Widow stopped in the driveway. He called out. "Is anyone here?"

He waited. No answer. He said, "Hello? Anyone here? Lou Cosay?"

Suddenly, an animal answered him. It was a Catahoula Leopard dog. It came running out from behind the house. It stopped three yards in front of Widow and barked ferociously.

"Whoa! Easy, boy!" Widow said.

Just then, the front door to the house opened up and an old Native American man stepped out. He was wrapped up in warm layers: a coat, a sweater, and long johns underneath. He wore heavy boots. He stepped out onto the porch and down the steps towards Widow. He stopped at the bottom. That's when he revealed a double-barreled shotgun from under his coat. He raised it and aimed directly at Widow.

Widow raised his hands, and said, "Keep calm with that gun, sir. I'm not here for any trouble." Suddenly, he wished he would've kept Billy's Peacemaker. Simultaneously, part of him wished he would've stayed in Port Gamble.

The old man's face was hardened, like he'd lived a rough life. He said, "Whatever you selling, we don't want!"

"Sir, I'm not selling anything."

The old man took three giant steps forward. The dog kept barking. The old man barked at the dog in a language Widow didn't understand. He presumed it was Mokani. The dog stopped barking and sat on its haunches and stared at Widow.

The old man took a good look at Widow, and said, "You're a long way from your world, Nakai. You lost?"

"I'm not lost. I'm looking for someone."

The old man said, "You can't read too well, Nakai? There're signs posted back the way you came."

"My name is Jack Widow. I'm with the NCIS," Widow lied, technically. He kept his hands out and open and visible to the old man. "I'm looking for someone named Lou Cosay."

The old man paused a beat. His eyes sunk into sadness. He glanced out over the barn and the stables and the field, like old memories he'd tried to outrun all came flooding back over him. Within seconds, he relived an entire lifetime.

A single tear streamed down his face. That hardened look he had in his face softened. He said, "She ain't here. She ain't been here in years. Now leave."

"It's important that I find her. Do you know if anyone else in your household has seen or heard from her?"

The old guy's face hardened again. He wiped the tear from his eye, fast, and returned his hand to the shotgun. He pointed it directly at Widow's center mass, and said, "I said we ain't seen her in years. Her business is her business now."

"Sir, again, I'm sorry for bothering you. I just really need to find her."

"Son, did you see the family cemetery back there?" The old man said, fighting back more tears. Widow nodded, but the old man didn't wait for it. "That's where our family is buried. Has been for generations of Cosays. So they're all here, on my farm. They're all accounted for. The living and the dead. My only daughter is in the house. My son is buried in the cemetery. My wife. She's out there too." He paused, took a breath, and said, "Lomasi went and lived in your world, the white world. She left us. She's not one of us no more."

Widow asked, "She is your daughter, though? Right?"

"Son, I'm giving you to the count of ten, then I'm shooting you where you stand."

"Do you have any idea where I might find her?"

"Nine. Eight."

Widow said, "Sir, she's missing. I'm just trying to make sure she's not in danger. Don't you want her to be safe?"

Old man Cosay said, "Six."

Widow shrugged, turned around, and left the Cosay farm. The murder of crows followed with him.

CHAPTER 12

idow walked over a mile, but north this time, towards the Canadian-American border. The bar owner at *The Ranchman* had said the reservation's main drag was in that direction. So Widow figured he could locate it and turn east to the town. Maybe folks were nicer there. And maybe he could get a ride. He doubted they had public transportation.

The air was cold, but the sky was big. Puffy white clouds loomed overhead. Still, there was plenty of sunlight to keep the temperature warm. Widow passed lively farms and derelict farms. All had the same long driveways. All had the same old mailboxes. At one of the derelict farms, the mailbox had bullet holes in it.

Something funny had happened since Widow's encounter with Billy and his friends. They'd kept their word and not followed him or sent out a hunting party for him. Which Widow was glad about. He expected that he'd scared them enough that they knew he wasn't to be messed with. But what he didn't foresee was how fast word of his presence had spread around the reservation. The locals must've heard to avoid the big stranger walking around because in the last twenty-five minutes, he'd seen four different vehicles drive toward him, like normal. Then they would slow, stop, and look at him. And they'd immediately turn around and go back the way they came.

Widow walked north to the end of another road and stopped. He saw an intersection coming up. It was a simple four-way stop—two roads intersecting, four stop signs. Like the mailbox at the derelict farm, two of the four stop signs had various-sized bullet holes through them.

Widow looked all four ways. No one was coming. He knew going west would take him farther into the reservation. He'd probably end up at that huge forest to the northwest. He could either go straight, which wasn't true north, but north-ish. Or he could go east, toward Sawyer Lake, the town.

Before he could make a decision, he heard a motor coming up behind him. It was loud, but not like a motorcycle or a damaged engine. It was loud in the way of old trucks. And that's what it was—an old truck. The truck looked familiar. Widow watched it. It drove straight towards him, not fast, but over the speed limit. Which wasn't all that unusual because almost everyone drove over the limit in rural areas.

He stepped off the road, near the stop sign. He stayed back from the road a good four yards, giving the driver space and making it up to him if he wanted to pick Widow up or not. No pressure.

Whether or not giving Widow a ride, the driver was going to stop because of the four-way stop. Widow doubted he'd offer to pick him up, since the whole reservation seemed to have already heard to steer clear of the stranger who'd broken Billy's nose. Maybe the driver would stop and give him a ride anyway? Billy and his guys were bullies. Anyone with eyes could see that. There had to be a large portion of the community who'd heard about what happened, and cheered. Forcing obedience through fear isn't the same as earning respect. Groups that lead by fear get taken out at the first opportunity. Leaders who earn respect get far more done.

As the truck got closer, he recognized it. It was the older of the two trucks he'd seen on the Cosay farm. The driver played pop music. The bass thumped the metal and rattled the windows. The Cosay truck slowed to a stop at the intersection. The driver was a young woman. She had makeup on to make herself look older. She had long, jet black hair, good bone structure and good facial features. Which, like the truck, also looked familiar to Widow. She wore a thick brown coat with a sweater underneath.

The girl stopped the truck just in front of him. She unbuckled her seatbelt, turned the music off, scooched across the front bench, leaned over, and cranked the window halfway down. She asked, "You need a ride?"

Hesitantly, Widow asked, "How old are you?

"I'm old enough."

"Old enough to what? Drink, or just drive?"

"I'm twenty-one."

Widow stared at her with disbelief in his face.

"Okay, I'm nineteen. Get in. I'll take you to town. That's where you're going, right? To Sawyer Lake?" She unlocked the passenger door and clicked the handle, popping it open. She gave it a hearty shove. The door squeaked open, bounced off its hinge and started to slam shut. But Widow caught it midway and held it there.

He asked, "Isn't it a little risky for a young woman like you to be picking up random men off the side of the road?"

"You're not random. I drove here just to pick you up."

"What do you mean?"

"You're looking for Lou, right?"

Suddenly, like lightning striking him, it dawned on Widow. That's where he knew her from. That's why she was so familiar. She looked just like Lou Cosay, only she was younger. But they looked very similar, like clones conjured fifteen years apart. He asked, "You're her sister?"

"Yeah. Get in."

Widow got in, shut the door, and buckled his seatbelt. The interior of the truck was warm. The heater worked well. No question about that. The younger Cosay buckled her seatbelt and drove past the sign, north.

"I heard about what happened at *The Ranchman*," she said.

"Word travels fast around here?"

"Of course it does. I think everyone knows by now."

"Your dad didn't seem to know. Or did he?"

She said, "He wouldn't know. He's not in the loop. My dad is…" she said, and paused a long beat. "He's a complicated man. He's very traditional. Like many people around here. He's stuck on the old ways, a very proud man."

"Nothing wrong with that."

She said nothing to that.

Widow said, "I'm Jack Widow. So, you know where Lou is?"

"My name's Aponi. If you saw it spelled out you'd want to say *a pony* but it's pronounced ah-POWN-iy."

"Aponi?"

"That's right. It means butterfly. But don't worry; I'm young, but I'm not fragile."

The truck she drove was a standard. She sped up and shifted like a professional racecar driver. Which made Widow sense she was telling the truth. She may have been named after a butterfly, but she was no delicate flower. Which probably ran in her family. Her sister was tough as nails. Her father seemed ornery, but tough.

Widow said, "Why are you giving me a ride?"

"I'm headed into town anyway. I gotta be at work. I work nights," she said, and tapped her shifting hand on a uniform that was folded and resting on the middle of the bench between them. There was a name badge on the top with her picture on it. It dangled from a lanyard.

"Okay, but you said you were looking to pick me up?"

They came to the end of that road. It ended at a fork. To the left, Widow saw the main drag of the reservation. It was right there, about a quarter of a mile from them. There was another bar and another church. There were tourist traps and Mokani temples and souvenir stores and grocery stores. There were other stores and buildings along the drag that Widow couldn't make out. Dead ahead of them was the coastline. The lake was huge, a lot bigger than Widow had pictured it to be. At the moment, it was calm, with slow-moving ripples. There were piers, and docked boats, and locals fishing and drinking beer. There were signs that warned against fishing without a license.

Aponi didn't answer him and she didn't go left. She turned right and sped up. They drove on for another couple of miles in silence. Widow had questions, but he still waited for her to speak. She didn't. So, he asked again, "Why did you want to pick me up?"

She sat upright in her seat and stared forward. She said, "Wait. Scoot down."

"Why?" he asked, and looked forward, out the windshield. But he saw why. It was because of a truck that was headed straight towards them, driving down the other lane, headed back to the main drag.

Aponi said, "Tribal police. They might be looking for you. You made quite the scene at *The Ranchman*."

Widow asked, "Won't they suspect you might give me a ride?"

"Why?"

"*The Ranchman's* owner gave me directions to your farm. He'll know I went there."

She said, "Nah, he won't say nothing. The people around here hate cops more than Billy and his idiot crew. Believe me. They're more likely to lie for you than to give you up."

Widow nodded, unbuckled his seatbelt, and sank down into the footwell as best he could. Old trucks are big and typically have a lot more foot room than new ones. But he still could only get part of himself down there. His head stuck out over the dashboard. He had to cram himself down and fold over the seat. He asked, "How far away are they?"

"Coming up on us now."

"Turn your music back on. They'll find it suspicious that you're not playing it."

She switched it on quickly. Widow stuffed his fingers into his ears. The speakers were loud and thumped, vibrating Widow's bones. She kept driving, looking straight ahead. Widow knew when the tribal police truck passed because Aponi stared in the rearview mirror, like she was watching them until they were gone from sight.

She drove on for another long minute, and then switched off the music. He unplugged his ears. She said, "It's safe now."

Widow climbed back up onto the seat, re-buckled his seatbelt, and stared straight ahead. A moment later, they drove out of the reservation and into Sawyer Lake's township. It was obvious because there were more election signs for the sheriff. And the roads were even and blacktopped.

Widow looked out over the lake. It was just as vast here as it was back on the reservation. He realized that he'd been partially wrong about the forest and the mountains. They weren't just to the northwest of the lake. They circled around to the Canadian side and then back around to the northeast border of Sawyer Lake. The trees were huge, even from where he sat. The mountains were big and looming.

The lake was pristine and majestic. It reminded him of Lake Tahoe or even a Great Lake, Lake Ontario, perhaps, only Sawyer Lake was nowhere as big as one of those. It looked big, which it was by lake standards if you take the Great Lakes out of the equation.

They drove on, taking the main road through the town and along the shoreline, until it forked into two directions. One was straight ahead. And the other veered left into a small peninsula. The road to the left was a service drive. It entered a small but sprawling resort. There was a large sign out front that read: *Sawyer Lake and Ski Resort*. Widow didn't know where the skiing was, exactly. It certainly wasn't on the property. There must've been a second site farther down the lake that led up one of the mountains. Perhaps there was a shuttle that took guests up there during the winter.

Aponi turned into the service drive. They drove through an unmanned security gate. There was a guard hut, but no guards posted. The large entry gate was wide open.

Widow asked, "What's the point of a security gate with no security?"

Aponi said, "It's manned during peak seasons."

"When's that?"

"We're really busy in the summer. And pretty busy in the winter. Right now, the whole town's dead. Hunting just closed. It's too early for ice skating or ice fishing. And you need more snow than this for skiing."

Widow asked, "Okay. Follow-up question. Why're we here?"

"This is where I work. I do the front desk at night."

"Okay, but why am I here? You could've dropped me off anywhere."

She pulled the truck up a winding drive, passing a lush garden and a large wood-carved statue of a grizzly bear. It was what kids and families took their pictures in front of. Past that was the main building. It wasn't huge, but it was impressive. It looked like a big lodge. There were lots of windows and grand front steps to the main entrance. And the rest was wood with large timber pillars holding up a thick roof. It was hard to gauge how many stories the place had because the main lobby had forty-foot ceilings.

There was a valet section that was closed. Guest parking was out front of that. Aponi drove them to the left. She parked at the water's edge of a second parking lot. It must've been designated for employees. Most of the guest parking was completely empty. There was a handful of vehicles in the employee side of the lot. She parked, slipped the truck into neutral, and kicked the emergency brake into place. She left the engine running and the heat on.

Aponi turned to face Widow. He looked back at her. She said, "Why're you looking for Lou?"

"Do you know where she is?"

"No. But tell me why you're looking for her. Maybe we can help each other."

Widow said, "Not sure I should share with you. No offense, but you're still a teenager. Whatever is going on might be a little mature for you."

"I'm not a kid. If my sister's in trouble, I can help. I might know something."

"Do you?"

"Tell me why you're here. Who are you? So I can decide if I can trust you."

Widow thought about it for a moment. Then he told her as much as he thought she needed to know. He told her he went to Lou's award ceremony as a guest of a mutual friend. And that it was strange for her to miss it. And about her skipping out on work.

"So what? You came here out of the kindness of your heart?"

"I'm just concerned. I used to be one of her."

"What's that mean?"

"I served. Like her."

"You were NCIS? Or Navy?"

"Both," he said.

"Okay, so what do you do now? You a cop or private investigator or something?"

"Neither. I do nothing. I just wander around."

"What? Like a drifter?"

"Yeah."

She said, "You're a Nakai."

"What's that? People've called me that all day."

"It's a Mokani word. It just means a man who wanders."

Widow nodded, and said, "Okay. Your turn. What do you know?"

Aponi sighed, dug into a small purse tucked in the seat next to her, and came out with a vape pen. She puffed it. Her exhalations smelled like strawberries. She said, "My father doesn't talk to my sister anymore. Not since my mother's funeral. Do you know about my brother?"

"He was murdered."

"Yeah, do you know the details?"

"Why don't you tell me."

Aponi puffed again, and said, "I was nearly thirteen. My brother, Mika, was fourteen. He and my father got into it one night. It was an August night. They got into an argument. My sister was in the Navy. She was thinking of reenlisting. She'd already been in several years. She loved it. My father was against her leaving the reservation, against her leaving our people."

She glanced ahead out the truck's windshield at the lake, and said, "Whatever that means." Aponi puffed again, exhaled the strawberry vape. "My father is traditional."

Widow stayed quiet.

Aponi said, "He wasn't always like the way he is now. The night Mika disappeared, my father waited up all night for him. When he didn't return, the next day a lot of the men of the reservation went out hunting for him. But he wasn't on the reservation. Some hunters ran into him out there." She pointed straight ahead at the thick forest and mountains across the lake from where they were parked.

"Mika was found dead. Someone had shot him full of arrows," She said, puffed again, and wiped tears from her eyes. "They abducted him, stripped him of most of his clothes, beat him, and painted him with those circles like on a target. Then they took him out into the woods and hunted him like an animal. They caught him and shot him full of arrows."

Widow asked, "What about the hunters that found him?"

"No. They were a couple of out-of-towners. They found him like that. It was a pair of fathers with their sons. They were cleared."

Widow nodded.

"My sister was crushed. She loved Mika. We were all crushed. But the person who was hit the hardest was my mom. Mika was her little angel. They'd always been so close. She went to his funeral with the rest of us. Half the reservation was there. Everyone was up in arms about what happened to Mika," Aponi said, and puffed again. "At first, Lou stayed with us, in her old room at our house. A week went by. The cops were useless. We told them it was an obvious hate crime. I mean they killed him with arrows. They didn't want to hear it. They just called it a murder," Aponi said, and then fell silent, puffing more of her vape pen.

Widow asked, "What happened?"

"At first, there was a lot of uproar and much to-do by the cops and the state police. My mother kept working with her plants. She used to have a little greenhouse. She loved working in there. She acted like it was the only thing that mattered. Her way of grieving I guess. My father went out with hunting parties to find clues, etc. But really they were just getting drunk in the woods. My sister stayed and tried to hold us all together. She debated going back to the Navy. They would've let her out, I believe. She was at the end of her contract."

Widow said, "They would've given her an honorable discharge. No question."

Aponi nodded, and said, "A month passed, and there were no arrests. One day, my mother lost it. She cried like no one I'd ever seen before. My sister consoled her for hours. My father went out and got drunk with his buddies, which I guess was his way of grieving. And that night we all went to bed. The next day my mom hung herself in her greenhouse."

Widow stayed quiet. He wanted to speak, but didn't know what to say.

Aponi said, "My sister stayed for her funeral too. My father and her had it out. It was like World War III that night at my house. He shunned her. Told her never to come back. He blamed all of it on her. He told her that if she hadn't left in the first place, our brother would be alive. My mother would be alive. My sister enrolled in the NCIS and left. And she never returned." She looked at Widow. He stared back at her. Widow was a beast of a man, but in that moment, she saw tenderness in his eyes.

Aponi said, "I keep in touch with her through social media, mostly. But we text too. About a year ago, she mentioned she was working with someone and they might be closer to finding a lead on who's responsible for Mika's murder. And then, a couple of weeks ago, she told me she was going dark for a while. Those were her words. She told me to be patient and stay out of it. But I had no idea what *it* was. She stopped responding to me. But with you here, and her secrecy, it's gotta be related to who killed my brother. Maybe she's found them? She could be in trouble, like you feared. She was consumed by Mika's murder. She might do something stupid, or get herself killed. I gotta ask you: can you help her?"

"I'm here to find her. I'll make sure she's safe."

"But can you help her?"

"If she needs my help, then I'll help her."

"I can pay you. I don't have much. But…"

Widow stared at her, blankly.

She said, "Like a private investigator."

"I don't need your money. I'll do it for Mika and Lou. Don't worry about it."

"Okay. Where to now?"

Widow glanced out the window at the sky. Then he looked at the clock on her old car stereo. Time had lapsed from late afternoon to early evening hours. He said, "I need to think about my next move here. Plus, I'm tired and hungry. Think I'll find something to eat and probably find a motel around here, and take a nap."

"I can get you a discount here. It's the nicest hotel in town. You could get a room with a great view. The lake is pretty. Especially at night."

Widow turned in his seat and glanced at the resort, and said, "I don't know. Looks out of my price range, even with your discount."

"Not this time of year. The prices are already low. My discount takes fifty percent off. And you're going to pay that anywhere around here anyway."

Widow nodded, and said, "Okay. Sounds like a deal."

Aponi vaped one last time, returned the vape pen to her purse, shut off the engine, and grabbed her uniform off the seat. They got out of the truck and headed inside. Aponi dressed as they walked. She slipped her uniform shirt over her sweater. Widow had to hold her coat and purse for her.

At the lobby, she left him to go clock in. She gave him instructions to wait until she was behind the front desk. She pointed out a restaurant inside the resort. Widow sat at the bar, got a coffee and a burger and fries. Which were good, but overpriced. Afterward, he checked into the hotel. Aponi served him and discounted his room. The discount was pretty good. The off-season rates were not. But he didn't complain. He yawned as she checked him in on the computer. The hotel had a guest registry book. She asked him to sign it. He put the name Jason Dessen.

Aponi asked, "Jason Dessen?"

"He's the lead character in this book I'm reading."

"You don't like to use your real name?"

"I never do. If I can help it. That's one reason I usually avoid places like this, because you guys require a credit card."

She paused, and asked, "You don't have a credit card?"

"Got a bank card. But I'm not leaving it with you."

"I'll just use my card. Try not to break stuff in your room."

Widow smiled.

Aponi checked him into his room and gave him a keycard. Widow thanked her and wished her a good shift. He went to his room, turned down the bed, took his clothes off, and bundled up under the covers. He was asleep within seconds.

* * *

A FEW HOURS after Widow checked into the resort, Aponi got cut early from her shift. She was happy about it. So she skipped to her truck in the parking lot. She got in, fired it up, and headed out of the lot and onto the main drag.

Near her parked truck, a dark SUV with plates from another state cranked its engine. The driver watched the nineteen-year-old skip through the parking lot and get into her truck. The driver was a professional, trained in surveillance and reconnaissance tactics by the federal government. The driver knew how to tail somebody and how to do it without being seen.

The dark SUV drove slowly out of the parking lot and turned in the same direction as Aponi did. The driver stayed far back enough to not be noticed. Several other vehicles came between them. But that was okay. The driver knew where Aponi was going anyway. No way to lose her. Especially since the girl had no idea she was being followed.

* * *

MOMENTS AFTER APONI'S stalker followed her out of the resort's parking lot, Widow woke up. He looked out the window over Sawyer Lake and thought he would get some coffee and maybe check out the local nightlife. He dressed, trashed the to-go cup from his last coffee, left the gas station map on a table, grabbed his keycard, and headed out the door. He headed down to the lobby. His first stop was the hotel bar. There were a few customers this time and more staff. He got another coffee in another to-go cup from the bar and stopped at the front desk on his way out to check in with Aponi. She wasn't there. The guy behind the counter told him she'd gone home early. He asked if there was anything he could do for Widow. Widow declined the offer. The desk guy said that Aponi would be back the next night.

Widow left the resort, walking into an uneventful, quiet night out.

CHAPTER 13

Many of the reservation's roads were dark at night. There were street lights up on some of the telephone poles. But a lot of them burnt out over the years and were never replaced. Getting things fixed on the reservation took an act of Congress. The metaphor wasn't far from the truth, and Aponi knew it.

She drove home the same way that she drove to work, only she didn't drive straight home. Her father would be up and he'd be drinking. He wasn't an abusive man or anything like that. She just didn't want to see him in that condition. He didn't get drunk every night. But when he did, it was always the same. He'd get drunk and walk around the property, talking to himself. He'd always end up in her mom's greenhouse. She could hear him talking to her like she was still there. Usually by the end of the night, he'd be so drunk he'd fall asleep in the cemetery, next to her mom's headstone.

Sometimes, he'd go out and get drunk at *The Ranchman*. At least on those nights, he was with his drinking buddies. He was sad and pathetic when he was drunk. It wasn't every night he behaved this way. It was usually whenever he got triggered. And Widow on his property, asking him about Lou, would trigger him. And she just didn't want to see it. She drove around the reservation for an hour.

She went down the long roads, past quiet farms. She liked to drive. Quiet roads on a quiet night were special to her.

Eventually, she pulled the truck off the road and followed an old trail onto an abandoned property. High, rolling grass surrounded her. The property was on one of the highest hills on the reservation. She parked the truck, left the headlights on and the engine running. She got out of the truck and sat on the hood, and took out a half-empty bottle of whiskey. Aponi wasn't big on drinking her sorrows away, not like her dad, but sometimes it helped her feel better.

She texted her friends to join her. But no one showed up. Not so far. One girl said she would try. They all knew where to go. She doubted any would come since the night was cold and some of them had work in the morning. Two of them were still in high school. They would've showed up for sure otherwise. If it were Friday or Saturday night, they would've been there with her.

Aponi knew she could text one of the guys she knew. Any of them would show up. A night out at the meeting place, alcohol, and Aponi alone? The temptation would be too great for any of her guy friends to resist. If she'd asked one of them to come hang out with her, they'd expect sex from her. She wasn't about to do that. Not that she didn't like her guy friends. It's just that she grew up with them. And they never treated her that way before, not when they were children. Now, that's all the boys wanted. She missed the old days. She liked boys. That wasn't the issue. She just didn't like the reservation boys *that* way. Tonight, Aponi just wanted someone to talk to, someone who'd listen and understand her pain. She was one of the last of a dying tribe, and one of the last of her family.

She sat on the hood, took a few swigs from the bottle, and stared out over the only place she'd ever called home, the reservation.

Aponi drank another long swig. Then she capped the bottle. She didn't want to get intoxicated, just a small buzz. She set the bottle on the truck hood next to her, scanned the horizon from left to right, and spoke out loud. She said, "Lou, where are you?"

Startlingly, a mechanical sound, like the whine of a shifting gear, pierced the quiet. Aponi glanced back over her shoulder, over her truck's roof, at the road behind her. She saw a dark figure moving up the road toward her. It was large and dark. It moved fast. It was larger than a buffalo, but smaller than an elephant. The moving object got closer to the abandoned lot. It bounced up over a hill on the road. And she knew it was a vehicle with the headlights off.

Aponi sat up straight and watched it. The vehicle was a large, black SUV. *Keep going, whoever you are*, she thought. The SUV's headlights flared on and switched to high beams. The SUV sped up, barreling down the empty road. She hoped it would pass her by. But it didn't. The SUV slowed ahead of the trail. Then it turned onto the trail and drove up to the abandoned property, to where she was parked. The high beams washed over her and her truck. She threw a hand up to block them out. They were blinding. The black SUV stopped behind her truck. Then her heart sank because a blue strobe light flashed on from the SUV's light bar. It was a police vehicle. But not tribal police because they only had trucks and none of them were black. It was a deputy from Sawyer Lake. It had to be. But this wasn't their jurisdiction. *Why was he out here? Why was he stopping to talk to her?*

The deputy switched off the light bar and then stepped out of the dark SUV and strolled out in front of it. He stayed inside one of his high beams, making his features impossible to identify. Sawyer Lake had the sheriff, and at least three deputies that she knew of. Some of them were less savory than others. One of them had a reputation. That one was called Atland. Over the years, there had been rumors involving him, and local female residents complaining about sexual harassment. No official complaints were ever filed. At least, nothing was ever done about it.

Without looking away from the deputy, Aponi grabbed the whiskey bottle and slipped it into her purse. She was under the drinking age and didn't want to get caught with it.

The deputy stopped behind her truck. He stayed inside the high beams' light. He spoke loudly enough for her to hear him, but too softly for her to recognize his voice. She hadn't interacted with any of Sawyer Lake's cops before. She wouldn't have recognized any of their voices anyway.

He said, "Little Aponi Cosay. What're you doing way out here? And all by yourself, too. Are you by yourself?"

Not sure what to say, she didn't answer.

"I'm talking to you, little Aponi," the deputy said.

"I don't have to answer you. This is reservation land. You got no jurisdiction here."

"Now, Aponi, I'm not here to harass you. I'm just having a friendly conversation with you. Understand something. Jurisdiction or not, it's illegal for a nineteen-year-old girl to drink or possess alcohol in the state of North Dakota. I know you got a bottle of something with you. I can smell it from here."

Aponi didn't respond. She didn't move from her perch on the truck's hood. She just froze.

The deputy raised his voice. Sternly, he said, "I *can* arrest you for that. It don't matter where we are."

"No you can't!"

"Sure I can. I can detain you and call the tribal police on my radio. They can book you."

Aponi said nothing.

The deputy said, "I can put handcuffs on you. And I can frisk you, until I find that liquor you got. You know what frisk means, little Aponi?"

Trembling, Aponi clutched her purse. She didn't own a gun, like her sister had begged her to get. She had a canister of pepper spray. But she was too afraid to pull it out. He was a deputy, out of his jurisdiction, but an official officer of the law. And what was she going to do? Threaten him with pepper spray? He had a gun on his hip. And his hand rested on it right then. She asked, "What do you want?"

"I want you to come on back here. I got a question for you."

Scared, that little voice in the back of her mind told her to scream. It told her to run. She did neither. She said, "Just ask me from there."

"It's a private type of conversation. Come on back here to me."

Aponi wished she'd gotten one of her friends to come out, even one of the guys. Having no choice, she reached into her purse and took out the pepper spray, held it tight in her hand. She slid off the truck, and slowly walked back around her truck and toward him.

"That's it. Come on, now."

She walked to him, taking slow steps. The wind gusted around them. The walk back to him seemed to slip into slow motion. Everything slowed down. She gripped the pepper spray. Her feet felt heavy. She concentrated on putting one in front of the other, again and again. Then she remembered that pepper spray, like a gun, needed to be aimed. She gazed up at the deputy, trying to focus on his face, trying to find his eyes, but she couldn't see any detail at all. The high beams were too blinding, and the night was too dark.

She kept walking.

With his non-gun hand, he gestured her to come to him. He said, "Come on. Closer. I just wanna ask you some questions about that man you were seen with."

She froze, and asked, "What about him?"

"Closer. All the way back to me now."

She continued to walk to him. *Now*, she thought. If she didn't attack him first, he could overpower her. He could handcuff her. Then she'd be powerless and he could do whatever he wanted to her. She was getting in the recommended pepper spray range. It was now or never. She had to use it now, the voice in her head told her.

Just then, across from the abandoned lot, a car engine kicked on and another pair of headlights lit them both up. Both Aponi and the deputy turned to look at it.

Where did this new car come from? Was it parked there the whole time? Watching me? Aponi thought.

The driver of the other vehicle left the headlights on and pointed at them both. They heard a car door open and shut. The driver got out of the vehicle and stepped out onto the road. They heard the footsteps.

The deputy shouted, "Who is that? Who's there?"

The driver stopped in front of the vehicle's lights, like the deputy had. Aponi couldn't see the driver's face or much of the driver's outline. The driver shouted back, "Everything okay? Y'all need help?"

"We're fine here," the deputy said. He squinted his eyes to see this new stranger. But he couldn't. He could use his flashlight, but they were standing too far away. He was certain that whoever it was couldn't see him either.

The driver said, "Sorry, Deputy. I thought you needed help because you don't have your blue lights on. I didn't know you were a cop. I just saw two vehicles sitting there in the dark with only your vehicle's lights on. I thought you'd broken down or something."

"No, no. Everything's fine here. You can go on about your business."

"That's okay. I think I'll stick around. It doesn't bother me."

The deputy watched the shadow figure. He saw it move quickly, like it was taking something out of a pocket. But he couldn't see the hands. He wasn't sure if there was a firearm or not. He started to feel angry. He said, "I told you to go on about your business."

The driver said nothing.

Frustrated, the deputy said, "This is official police business." He pulled his service weapon from the holster and pointed it at the shadowy figure. "I'm not going to warn you again, whoever you are. I want you out of here! Now! Get in your vehicle and drive on!"

"Actually, Deputy, it just dawned on me she's right. You don't have jurisdiction here."

The deputy said nothing. He was running scenarios through his head. He could shoot at the shadowy figure, but would he hit the guy? And if he shot the driver, then what would he do about Aponi? He was told to find out about the drifter. But at what cost? How far was he authorized to go? Two murders might be too far. He weighed his options. He was thinking of letting them both go, of just driving away. But the driver had pushed him too far. The driver pointed in the distance, and said, "See that ridge line past that farm way over there, about as far as you can see from here?"

Both the deputy and Aponi looked in that direction. "That's the border for Sawyer Lake and the reservation. And the reservation is under Mokani tribal police jurisdiction. And you ain't tribal police."

The deputy took a step forward, gun in hand, and said, "You just walked into this at the wrong time. Whoever you are. Now you're pissing me off."

Silence. None of them said a word for a long moment. Aponi felt the tension, and she was afraid. She thought she could die tonight. Between this corrupt deputy and this new shadowy person, one of them could kill her.

Just then, a pair of blue lights flashed in the distance. It was another police vehicle headed right for them. It dipped and bounced along the roads. The deputy froze, stared at the blue lights. They were coming on fast.

The shadowy driver said, "That's Mokani tribal police right there. I know. I called them already. See, this is their jurisdiction. They'll be very interested in asking you some questions, like, *What are you doing here, and why are you harassing one of our citizens?* And she's so young too."

The deputy grimaced, holstered his gun, and backed away, slowly. He'd been beat. And he knew it. He said, "I hope we meet again, stranger."

"We might."

The deputy returned to his SUV, climbed in, and shut the door. A few seconds later he drove away, back to Sawyer Lake.

Aponi's heart raced. She watched the deputy drive away. She never got a look at his face. She saw the Sawyer County Sheriff logo on the truck and got part of the license plate. But what good would that do her? They shared vehicles. Even then, what would Sheriff Vedely do about it? It might've been him, for all she knew.

Aponi made sure not to take her eyes off the deputy until he was gone from sight. She slipped the pepper spray into her pocket, stepped to the rear of her truck, and took a deep breath. She looked out one more time to make sure he wasn't turning around and coming back for her. Then she sighed in relief. She turned back to the stranger from the other SUV. She walked back around her truck, toward the road, and shouted, "Thank you for helping me."

No answer. The stranger's SUV's headlights were off again. Aponi looked harder at where they had been, at where the shadowy stranger had been standing. But there was nothing there. No SUV. No stranger. They were gone. She turned around and looked up and down the trail. Then she saw the SUV's taillights heading off the opposite way. Within moments, the shadowy stranger's taillights were also gone from sight.

Minutes later, the Mokani tribal police pulled up on the trail in front of her. She threw the liquor bottle off into the darkness as far and as hard as she could. It must've hit a rock or an old structure, because it shattered into pieces. The sound echoed over the rolling grass for a second.

The tribal police said they were called to the scene by an anonymous caller. They asked if Aponi was okay. She told them she was. Then they inquired about what happened. She told them nothing. Although she'd feared for her life around whichever deputy that was, Mokani don't trust cops. And she was Mokani.

CHAPTER 14

Billy, or Billy the Kid, as he preferred to be known, walked out of the Sawyer County hospital. His face was all wrapped up in bandages. His nose had been badly broken. The doctors and nurses had to stitch it up and put it back together with staples. The doctors told him he'd be left with wicked scars. Perhaps he could have it repaired with plastic surgeries. For now, they did the best they could, stapled him up, and gave him a bottle of painkillers. He took them, but they were a joke to him. He had better stuff at home.

By the time Billy got discharged from the Sawyer County Hospital Emergency Room, the skittish guy and the two bikers had spent all afternoon searching for his truck keys, the Peacemaker that he loved so much, and the man who took it. They never found the man or the gun.

The skittish guy met Billy at the entrance to the hospital. He stood there, alone, shivering even though he was bundled up in a ratty coat over a thrift-store sweater. Only it hadn't been bought from a thrift store. The guy stole it from the church's clothes donation bins. He figured they'd have given it to him anyway.

The skittish guy held his arms open, offering Billy a welcoming embrace. Billy looked angry, even through the thick face bandages. The skittish guy had been Billy's sidekick for years, since they were teenagers. He knew when his boss was upset.

Billy ignored the hug attempt and held his hand out, palm open. He said, "Keys?"

The skittish guy dug Billy's keys out of his pocket and dropped them in Billy's hand. He said, "We filled the tank and washed your truck for you."

Billy didn't look pleased. It was the bare minimum he expected from his guys. The skittish guy decided it was best to start with the good news. He said, "We found your rifle. But not the bolt. Not yet. But we can replace the bolt, right?"

Billy didn't answer him. He just stared at him.

The skittish guy said, "Look on the bright side. Jasper and Elliot got it real bad. Their doctors say they'll be lucky to have kids again. And right now, they can't even walk. At least you can walk, right?"

Billy looked at him, and spoke. It strained him to talk. The words came out all nasally. He said, "Where's my truck?"

The skittish guy pointed at it. He'd parked it far from the entrance. Billy stared at it. He could barely see any of the details. He wasn't wearing his glasses. He kept them in the truck's console. He only needed them to drive, and to shoot far away. Normally, he wore contacts for this. But they got knocked out back at *The Ranchman*'s parking lot by the Nakai that busted his nose.

Billy asked, "Why did you park it all the way over there?"

The skittish guy didn't answer the question. He just apologized for it. They threaded through the parked cars, crossed three empty aisles, and stopped in front of Billy's truck. The truck was parked at the end of the lot, which backed up to a forest of trees. The skittish guy looked around nervously.

Billy sensed it, and asked, "What's wrong with you?"

"Nothing."

"Okay, well get in. Let's go."

The skittish guy said, "Nah, boss. You go ahead. I'll meet you at the house. I got...ah...thing I gotta take care of first."

"Okay. Whatever," Billy said, and he got into the truck. He shut his door, looked down at the ignition switch, slid the keys in, and fired it up. The truck came to life. Country-western music hummed over the speakers. Billy glanced up and saw that the skittish guy was gone. He had taken off fast. Billy leaned forward, squinted his eyes, and scanned the parking lot for him. He saw no one.

He dug in the console for his glasses, found them, and put them on. Suddenly, his passenger side door squeaked open and a large man climbed in. At first, he thought it was the Nakai who had busted his nose, but it wasn't. It was a different white guy, standing at six feet tall. The guy was big in the shoulders and arms. It looked like his skin had been stuffed with bowling balls. His head was completely bald, shaved smooth—another resemblance to a bowling ball. Not a stitch of hair stuck up there. The bottom half of his face was covered by a thick beard. He sat in the passenger seat, put one huge arm up and across the top of the bench. The man closed the door and rested his other arm on his lap. He made himself at home in Billy's truck, Billy's second-most prized possession next to the Peacemaker gun the Nakai stole.

No one treated Billy's truck like this, not unless he invited them. And Billy never invited this guy. He didn't even recognize him. Billy said, "Excuse me, pal! This ain't your ride!"

The bald man turned his head, slowly, and stared Billy in the eyes. It was the second gaze today that sent shivers down his spine. The first was from the Nakai that broke his nose. In that moment, Billy wasn't sure which was more terrifying.

The bald man said, "He wants to see you."

Billy asked, "Who wants to see me?"

The bald man said, "Vedely."

Billy swallowed, and said, "Okay. Where we going?"

"His house."

That wasn't the place that Billy wanted to go. But he knew better than to argue. He shifted gears and drove the truck out of the lot. It never dawned on him that the skittish guy had betrayed him, not until it was too late.

* * *

BILLY AND THE bald guy drove away from the hospital and turned north, through Sawyer Lake's downtown. They passed through the business area and passed the local Sheriff's Office, where Sheriff Vedely's name and photo were on a sign outside. Billy glanced at it as they passed. They drove past the Sawyer Lake Resort and turned right on the fork, at the entrance to the resort. They drove northeast, along the lake, through winding roads into the forested area. They passed huge mansions and houses. That was the part of town where millionaire Midwesterners kept their summer homes. Many of them were lit up, but silent, because the rich occupants were somewhere warm for the coming winter.

They drove until the road wound into a single lane. They came to the last drivable point in America and stopped at a large iron rod gate. They were surrounded by trees on one side and the lake on the other. Billy looked up at a state-of-the-art security camera high on a tree. He knew it wasn't the only one. There were probably a half-dozen or more stuck around the entrance to the last house on the street. This property had tons of secret security measures all around it. First off, it was twenty acres away from the nearest neighbor. And the nearest neighbor's house was vacant during this time of year, like the rest.

The bald man rolled his window down, leaned out, and pointed a tiny remote that was encased in hard black plastic. He clicked a button and a security camera on the side of the gate clicked to life. It rotated automatically and angled itself so that the lens pointed directly at the truck and the two men. A split-second later, a machine pulley system activated and the iron gate cranked open. The bald man returned to a seated position, and said, "Go."

Billy did as he was instructed. The men drove through the gate and into the dark abyss of the property. Billy glanced in the side mirror. The iron gate closed behind them.

They followed the long drive. A canopy of leaves covered the driveway. Little moonlight seeped through them. But there were dim lights stuck on stakes in the ground along the sides of the road at various intervals. They reminded Billy of airport runway lights at night.

He didn't need to drive slowly because he'd been to the house before. He hated coming out here. Vedely was a scary man, scarier than the bald man, scarier than the Nakai who busted his nose.

When Billy looked into Vedely's eyes, he saw darkness. Vedely was like the incarnation of the Miniwashitu, a local monster from Mokani folklore. It's a red devil in a distorted bison body, standing on two legs. The legend was told to him by his great-aunt when he was a kid. It was his tribe's version of the bogey-man. The thing gave him nightmares as a child. He slept with the light on until he was in his double digits. But nothing scared him as much as Vedely.

They came to a large clearing, where the trees had been cut down to keep distance between the house and any unwanted invaders. Vedely was a well-read, educated man. When Billy asked about cutting down the trees once, Vedely explained that Macbeth's mistake was having the forest too close to his castle.

Billy had no idea what he was talking about. That was six years ago. He hadn't seen Mr. Vedely since. But he still did work for him. It was just all done through text message and email.

Why Vedely wanted to see him was a mystery that he really didn't want to solve.

The house was like an enormous cabin built on the lake. It boasted the best views in all of Sawyer Lake. It was built out of oak and thick gray stone. There was a four-car garage to the left, and a sprawling house to the right. The house had two chimneys. One of them was smoking. And it was the one from the back of the house. Billy had been in that room before. Enormous floor-to-ceiling windows covered the front. The house, and the twenty acres around it, would've run a buyer around twenty-five million dollars somewhere like Lake Tahoe. But here, it was probably valued closer to ten. Still, it was a lot of money for a kid that grew up here in Sawyer Lake. Mr. Vedely had done well for himself.

An American flag flew high from a flagpole about thirty feet from the house's front door. "Park there," the bald man said, and pointed at a space next to a black SUV. Billy parked the truck. The bald man reached over and held his palm open, and said, "Keys." Reluctantly, Billy dropped the keys into his hand. They got out of the truck.

Billy walked around the tail and stopped. The bald man stood there in front of him, not budging. He said, "Stick your arms out. I'm going to frisk you."

"Really? Come on, man. I just got out of the hospital. I'm tired. I don't have any weapons."

The bald man moved the flap of his coat to reveal a holstered gun. It was just a quick action, like a fast show-and-tell. Billy got the message and put his hands out. The bald guy stepped close to him, towering over him both physically and metaphorically. So Billy complied. The bald man frisked him fast. Satisfied, he gestured for Billy to lead the way. The bald man knew that Billy already knew where to go.

Billy entered the house, stopped in the grand foyer, and kicked his boots off. He set them neatly by the others against the wall. Then he walked into the house. The floors and ceiling were all dark wood. Large pillars jutted between the floors and ceilings throughout the house.

Billy walked through a large, empty living room, a huge kitchen, and down a hallway. Deer, elk, and moose antlers hung from both the ceilings and walls throughout the house. There was a large game room off to his right, from where he heard voices and the sounds of someone breaking the first shot of a billiards game. He glanced into the room and saw more of Vedely's guys, drinking and playing pool. One stared back at him. His gaze was as intimidating as the bald man's.

Billy pressed on through the dark bowels of the house until he came to the end of the line. There was another huge den. He entered it. A roaring fire crackled in a ceiling-high rock wall fireplace. A dim lamp on a large mahogany desk lit up the far corner of the room. The fire from the fireplace lit up two large armchairs in front of it. Mr. Vedely sat in one of them, reading a book.

The bald man stepped in behind Billy, and stayed there like a guard dog waiting for a command. Vedely kept reading his book. Billy stood there for a long moment, and then he spoke to break the silence. He asked, "When did you get back in town, Mr. Vedely?"

Vedely said nothing. He shot his index finger up to shush Billy. He read a little longer, and slow-turned the page of his book. Billy glanced at the cover, but the book was hardbound and had no book jacket. It could've been anything.

A long moment passed, and Vedely closed the book, making an audible smack, like dropping a heavy Bible on a table. He got up from his chair, strolled over to a tall bookcase, and slid the book back into its place on the shelf. He turned to Billy, and said, "Billy, you don't look so good."

Billy snorted, "I had a little accident is all."

Vedely nodded, and said, "Follow me." Vedely turned, walked back through the den, and slid open a thick glass slider door. He stepped through it, leaving the door open. Billy paused, not because he didn't know he was expected to follow, but because he didn't want to follow. He wanted to run. Maybe he could lose them in the forests behind the house?

The back of the property bumped up against an enormous, forgotten national forest. The forest spilled over into Canada, where the mountains were. Then it circled around the Canada side of the lake, and looped back around to the Mokani Indian Reservation side of the lake. He'd just been on that side a week ago. He and his guys had been there at night. He prayed Vedely didn't know about that.

The bald man shoved Billy through the slider and out onto an enormous rock terrace. The thing jutted out one floor over the backyard below. Expensive patio furniture was placed across it, along with tall outdoor heaters. The heaters were all dormant. There were no other people on the terrace. The backyard below was so dark, Billy couldn't see either grass or snow. All he could make out was the thick forest of trees to the north and lights from a boathouse on the lake to the west.

Vedely stepped to the edge of the terrace. He put his hands on a heavy metal railing and leaned against it. He gazed out over his magnificent night views. The moonlight bounced off half his face. He was as tall as the bald man, but far easier to look at. He had a thick coif of gray hair. He was clean-shaven maybe a day ago. Tonight, there was gray stubble on his face. He smelled of expensive cologne. His shoes looked like they cost the price of Billy's truck when it was new. He wore a dark suit, no overcoat, and no tie.

Vedely said, "Billy, this is Paul Harvey. Harvey isn't new to me, but he's new to you. So, let me explain his role in my company. He was one of my personal trainees. Now, he's important to my organization. He's like my right-hand man, if you will. Harvey, be polite and say hello to Billy."

Billy turned to the bald man named Harvey and offered his hand for Harvey to shake. Instead of shaking his hand, Harvey threw a left haymaker at Billy. It caught Billy completely off guard. Harvey had huge fists and a lot of upper body muscle. He could've killed Billy if he'd wanted to. But that's not what he did. He threw the haymaker, connecting to Billy's right cheek and knocking him clean off his feet.

Billy spun backwards and landed on the terrace's hard rock floor. He landed on his stomach. Harvey didn't hit Billy's nose, but the pain below it ignited the nose to agony anyway.

Billy spat blood out of his mouth. He laid there on the floor and held his mouth. Two of his teeth were loosened from the attack. He looked up at Vedely, and asked, "Why did you do that for?"

Vedely stepped away from the railing and stared down at Billy. He said, "You're paid to do a job for me. Your job is to scout new targets for us. To vet them. It's important that this job is done properly. Otherwise, people ask questions. And we don't want questions."

"Mr. Vedely, I don't understand. What did I do wrong?"

"Billy, I'm going to ask you some questions. If you lie to me, we're going to kill you. Understand?"

"Yes, sir."

"Good," Vedely said, and nodded at Harvey. Harvey bent down and scooped Billy up, hauling him to his feet. Harvey faced him, brushed his clothes off, and straightened his tie.

Vedely looked around the sky, and said, "You know what? It's a nice night. Let's take a walk."

Billy said, "I left my boots."

"Don't worry about that. Pick a pair of those," Vedely said, and pointed out some slip-on shoes. Billy shoved his feet into a pair closest to his shoe size, and smiled.

Vedely nodded, led the way along the terrace, and down heavy wooden stairs to the grass below. Billy walked behind Vedely, against his will, because he could sense Harvey close behind him.

They followed a thick walkway, paved with more gray stone. It was well lit. It led them through the backyard, to the west, back to the lake. At the end of the walkway, there was a stone boathouse and a fishing pier with two speedboats docked at the end.

Billy's fear was that they would get on one of the boats. But Vedely didn't ask him to do that. Instead, they walked to the end of the pier.

Vedely stood there, staring out over the lake. Then he shifted his gaze upward and stared at the night sky, like he was stargazing. Billy stood there in silence because of what happened minutes ago when he interrupted Vedely.

Finally, Vedely turned to face Billy. He said, "What were we doing?"

Billy said, "You wanted to ask me some questions, Mr. Vedely."

"Oh yeah," Vedely said. "You should've told us about the girl. Instead, you had to show off. You made a lot of mistakes, Billy. Too many. It can't be overlooked."

Suddenly, Harvey jerked a black sack over Billy's head. Vedely exploded and struck a flurry of punches into Billy's stomach, neck and face. Vedely hit him so hard that Billy passed out in a matter of seconds.

Billy collapsed to the pier. Blood trickled out from under the black bag.

Vedely glanced at Harvey, and said, "Help me get him in the boat." The two men grabbed Billy's limp body; one got the feet, and the other the head. They lifted him and tossed him into one of the speedboats. Moments later, the three men were in the boat. They sped out to the center of the lake, the deepest point. Three men boated out there, in the middle of the night.

An hour later, two men came back. Vedely ordered Harvey to return Billy's truck to the hospital parking lot, and park it where he had found it.

CHAPTER 15

Widow woke in his hotel room the next morning. The night before, he'd found his way into a country-western dive bar and ended up listening to live music, which was just a couple of guys with acoustic guitars. . He'd struck up two different conversations throughout the night. The first was with an older Canadian couple who were celebrating their twenty-fifth anniversary. They stopped in Sawyer Lake for the night because that's where they'd met.

By this time in the morning, they'd be headed south to San Diego, where they'd cross over into Mexico. They drove it by themselves. It was a yearly ritual. In Mexico, they rented the same beach villa every year. It was called Balandra Beach in Baja California Sur. They had pictures on their phones, and showed them to Widow. Some dated back to when pictures were first stored on phones.

The second person Widow spoke with was a woman who'd lived in Sawyer Lake her whole life. She was a little drunk when they started talking. The tequila smell was strong on her breath. She was in her late forties and single. She mentioned it more than once. Widow chatted with her a while. When he asked about the murder of Mika Cosay, she blew off the topic and turned her attention to another guy sitting alone at a table. She excused herself, said she'd be back, but never returned.

The bartender knew nothing about Mika Cosay's murder. She'd only lived and worked there for three years. Widow sat and enjoyed the last set from the musicians, which was a long rendition of a Johnny Cash song. Then he paid his tab and headed back to the resort.

Widow had purchased a travel kit from the resort's front desk the night before. He bought it from the same guy he saw when he left, Aponi's replacement. The travel kit had miniature versions of things travelers might need: toothpaste, toothbrush, shaving gel, a single disposable razor, floss, and a tiny bottle of mouthwash. He used the toothpaste with his two-day-old toothbrush and left the new one in the kit.

Widow picked up the hotel room's phone, dialed nine to get an outside line, and dialed Steslow's phone number from memory. Steslow answered, sounding sleepy, and Widow said, "Hey. It's me."

"Widow?"

"Yeah, I got nothing yet." Widow said, realizing the time difference. He was two hours ahead. For Widow, it was seven in the morning. "Sorry, if I woke you."

"Nah, it's okay. I'm getting up in thirty minutes, anyhow."

"Are you shipping out?"

"I'm supposed to, but I asked Cress to pull some strings to keep me here another day or two. Hopefully, you'll locate Lou by then."

"He did that for you?"

"Actually, he did it for you."

"Me?"

Steslow yawned, and said, "Yeah. He looked into you. I think he was intrigued by you. He wouldn't give me details, but whatever you did in the SEALs must've been some high-level impressive stuff because he said to tell you that if you need any support, he'll help in any way he can. He told me to give you his personal number." Steslow recited the number to Widow from the contact list in his phone.

Widow memorized it. He ignored the SEAL comment. Steslow knew nothing about Unit Ten, which was the way they liked it. Widow asked, "Has anyone heard from Lou?"

"No, but I found out about *Shedding Light*. It's a media company that mainly has a couple of true crime shows. They're podcasts and YouTube channels. Their flagship show features weekly stories of unsolved cases. And one of their investigative journalists and podcasters is that woman, Cassie Fray. And Widow, she's really something. Hang on a second," Steslow said, and he set the phone down on a bedside table. Widow heard him yawn again, and imagined Steslow got up out of bed, stretched, threw a robe on, picked up the phone, and moved to a desk with a laptop on it.

After a long moment, Steslow said, "I'm back." He explained who Fray was. It sounded like he was reading her bio from a website. "Cassie Fray is an award-winning journalist and author. She's written a few books here. One of them was on the New York Times Bestsellers List for like an afternoon... Yada yada. Fray broke a story about an African warlord and some kind of mess in West Africa. So she seems like the real deal. And the *Shedding Light* podcast is pretty good. I listened to an episode yesterday about a serial killer out of California. It was entertaining, and enlightening. The owners of the network are Bret and Susie Prawat. I tried to speak to Bret, but he was too busy to take my call. Or he wouldn't take my call. He does the hands-on thing. His official title is Co-founder and Executive Producer, according to their website. Susie is also listed as Co-founder, but in her day job, she's a lawyer. And that's all I got so far. You learn anything new?"

"I learned that people here really like their trucks."

"What's that supposed to mean?"

"Nothing. Dumb joke. I'll call you if I find her. Tell the Secretary thanks for helping."

Steslow suggested Widow try calling Fray again. Then he said goodbye, and Widow clicked the phone's receiver button, hanging up. Afterward, he dialed Cassie Fray's phone number. He waited. It rang. And he got the same voicemail as he got the day he was in Cosay's house. He hung the phone up.

Widow took a shower, but didn't shave, and left his room with only his money, bank card, passport, room keycard, and the old toothbrush in his pockets. He wore the same clothes, the only ones he had. Today he'd keep an eye out for new underwear, and new clean socks wouldn't hurt either.

Widow walked out of the resort, past the front desk, which had two females working behind it. A patrolling security guard on a golf cart waved a friendly hello at him. Outside, the sky was gray, like back on the Kitsap Peninsula. But it wasn't raining. Which Widow was grateful for. He found getting rides from strangers in the rain was harder than one would think. When someone sees a guy on the side of the road in the rain, one instinctively thinks to help get him out of the rain. But then the prospect of a stranger getting one's car interior all wet sinks in. And people back out.

Widow left the resort, heading toward the town. And the moment he set foot on the pavement at the fork in the road, he saw a black police SUV idling, facing the direction he walked.

Widow walked the shoulder and stepped out onto the street so he could walk around the police SUV. The moment he stepped past the driver's side door, the sheriff's deputy strobed his blue lights. The driver's side window was rolled all the way down. The deputy hung an arm out of it. He looked at Widow, square in the face, and said, "Dessen. Get in. Sheriff Vedely would like a word with you."

Widow stopped half on the street, turned and stared back at the deputy. He asked, "Me?"

"You're Jason Dessen, right?"

Widow slowly nodded. That was the name he'd checked in under at the resort. He asked, "Why me?"

"I don't know. I was instructed to pick you up and bring you in."

"Bring me in? For what?"

"I don't know. I was told to get you. So I'm here picking you up."

Widow looked over the SUV's hood at the lakeshore. Locals on a pier turned to look at him. He glanced around and saw trucks passing by. Some occupants stared at him. Others minded their own business. He asked, "Am I under arrest?"

The deputy said, "You don't see me getting out, pulling my gun, and throwing the cuffs on you. Do you?"

"No."

"Then you don't got nothing to worry about. He just wants to meet you and talk."

Widow said, "So, I don't have to come with you then?"

"You don't have to, but I wouldn't advise resisting."

Widow thought for a long second, and then he shrugged, walked to rear of the SUV, like he was going to hop in the back, which was normally the protocol for every police interaction he'd ever had involving him riding in their cars.

The deputy said, "Not back there. You can climb in the front with me."

Widow had his hand on the rear door's handle. He froze, dropped his hand, and walked around the hood of the SUV. He climbed in on the passenger side and reached down, grabbed the adjustment bar, and racked the seat all the way back. He buckled his seatbelt, making sure the deputy heard the click. He also did it so he could have a reason to look at the deputy. The guy's name was Atland. He was a white guy with thinning red hair. The top was more bald than thin. The hair the guy had wrapped around his head from one sideburn, looping around the back to the other sideburn. Nothing much was left on the top but fine hairs. He had broad shoulders like he lifted weights, but it looked like he only worked out his upper body. His waistline was heavy and neglected.

Atland's sidearm was a Glock 22, pretty standard across the United States. Widow had seen it in the holsters of law enforcement agents more times than he could remember. It was a good choice.

Atland switched off the blue lights and drove away from the shoulder. Police chatter rumbled low over a radio mounted on his dash.

They drove for ten minutes in complete silence. Atland took Widow into downtown Sawyer Lake. Widow saw the dive bar he was at the night before. And he saw a bookstore on a corner, next to a *Dunkin Donuts*. Both places became his next destinations of choice. If he got out of this sheriff meeting thing. In his experience, police meetings can be brief, or they can last hours. It all depended on what they wanted to see him about.

They turned another corner, heading south. Widow saw a dark SUV that looked familiar. He could've sworn it was the same one he saw yesterday, parked outside the fence on the Cosays' road. The vehicle's windows were all tinted. The windshield was also tinted. It was probably illegal, but Atland seemed not to notice or care. He was on a mission from the top, to bring Widow to see his boss.

They arrived at the sheriff's station, which was on another corner, next to the fire station. Atland pulled into the lot, parked the SUV out front, and got out. In front of the hood, he said, "Let's go, Dessen."

Widow nodded, and got out. He followed Atland through black glass doors and into a sheriff's office with a reception desk at the front and a large bullpen behind a barrier. There was a receptionist at the desk, answering calls. She smiled at Atland, but didn't smile at Widow.

Atland led Widow through the barrier and into the bullpen, which was a lot of empty desks. Atland's footfalls were heavy. A thief would hear him sneaking up a driveway at a hundred yards. There was another deputy there, standing in the Sheriff's office doorway. He turned around when he heard Atland stomping his boots.

Atland introduced Widow to the deputy, but Widow already knew his name. Atland said, "Dessen, this is Deputy Braaten."

Braaten didn't offer his hand to shake, but he wasn't unpleasant either. He said, "Hello." And nothing else.

Widow said, "Saw your pictures on those election signs."

"Did you? Are you a voting member of our public?"

Atland said, "Dessen is a guest at the resort."

Braaten nodded.

They walked into the sheriff's office. Atland said, "This is Sheriff Vedely. This is the guy, boss."

Sheriff Vedely sat in a desk chair on wheels, behind a wood desk. His whole office was all wood—wood bookcase, wood tables— even the desk lamp was in a wood casing.

Vedely was around five-foot-ten inches tall. He was thin, with a head full of graying hair. A matching mustache covered his upper lip. He wore reading glasses and typed away on a desktop computer. He looked up at Widow, and said, "Mr. Dessen. Come in, please. Have a seat."

Widow dumped himself down on a chair facing Sheriff Vedely. He sensed the two deputies standing behind him—Braaten filling up the doorway, and Atland leaning in the corner adjacent. Widow asked, "So, what's this about?"

"I'm Sheriff Vedely. I've been Sheriff here for five years. In that time, I've never heard of what I heard of this morning."

Widow said, "Which is what?"

"I heard a stranger wandered onto the Mokani reservation and assaulted seven of our citizens. I heard you beat them up, fired a gun at them, and put several of them in the hospital."

Widow shrugged, and asked, "What guys? "

Sheriff Vedely said, "You know what guys. In the parking lot of *The Ranchman*. Was that you?"

"Is that part of your jurisdiction?"

"It's the tribal police's, but they like us to back them up when necessary. And the hospital is my jurisdiction. Yesterday, several of them checked themselves in. We've got assault and battery and the illegal discharge of a firearm at civilians. And you took the gun from Billy Tabaaha, one of our more popular citizens."

Widow stayed quiet.

Sheriff Vedely said, "You sent three men to the hospital. Two of them will probably need help from doctors if they ever want to have children. But the real trouble is with Billy. You broke his nose so badly, he'll likely need reconstructive surgery."

Widow said, "Any of them pressing charges?"

"No. Six of them refuse to identify their attacker. The tribal police interviewed the bar staff, the owner, and the customers, and none of them recollect seeing a thing. But the real trouble is with what's happened to Billy," Sheriff Vedely said.

Widow asked, "Is he pressing charges?"

Sheriff Vedely said, "He disappeared last night. We know Billy really well around here. And like him or not, he's a citizen. Last night, he left the hospital and never returned. No one's seen him since the doctors discharged him."

"Sounds like this Billy-person picked a fight with the wrong guy. Maybe his guardian angels talked him into starting a new life somewhere else," Widow said.

"Billy loves three things in this world, Mr. Dessen. He loves attention, his truck, and his momma. And nothing else matters very much to him. I can't speak for attention, but never in a million years would he abandon his truck or his momma. And that truck has been parked in the hospital lot since yesterday — all night and all morning. It's still there now. Billy never leaves that truck unattended. And his momma says he didn't come home at all."

Widow said, "I got no idea about any of that. I was in my hotel room."

Sheriff Vedely said, "All night?"

"I stepped out for a few hours. And I was back by midnight."

"Can anyone corroborate that?"

Widow said, "I stopped at a dive bar. They played live music. The bartender in there will probably remember me. Then I returned to my room. The front desk guy will know that. There's not a lot of patrons there right now."

"Yeah, it's the off-season. But when you were back in your room, can anyone confirm that part?"

Widow paused a beat, glanced back over his shoulder at the two deputies. He looked back at Sheriff Vedely, and asked, "Am I under arrest?"

"Not yet. We're just talking here. I'm just looking for one of my citizens. Trying to see if you know anything about it."

Widow made a decision. He might regret it later, if he needed their help, but his mind was made up. He stood up from the chair. The two deputies stopped leaning and perked up. Atland put his hand on his gun's butt. Widow said, "Then I'm not answering questions."

"Why? Cause you're guilty? You know where Billy is?"

Widow stayed quiet.

Atland said, "The Sheriff asked you a question."

Widow said, "You guys don't listen too well. I told you. I'm not answering questions."

Widow turned, his hands at his sides, and started to leave. He stopped at the door. Both Atland and Braaten stood in his way, like two armed bouncers at a nightclub.

Sheriff Vedely asked, "Where you going?"

Widow glanced back at Sheriff Vedely over his shoulder, and said, "That's another question. I told you. I'm not answering any more questions. You can arrest me or turn me loose."

The two deputies stood their ground. They didn't budge.

Widow stared at them, kept his eyes on theirs, but his peripherals on Atland's gun hand. He seemed the most careless, like he'd grab his weapon and shoot first, ask questions later. Widow said, "Move."

From behind Widow, Sheriff Vedely said, "Let him go."

Reluctantly, the two deputies stepped aside and let him pass. Widow walked out of the station, and back towards where he'd seen the bookstore and the donut shop.

CHAPTER 16

From the inside of a black SUV parked down the street, they watched Widow walk out of the sheriff's station. He walked out of the station almost as fast as he'd entered. The deputy had taken him in. They saw it happen. Presumably, Sheriff Vedely interrogated him. But now they watched him leave.

Harvey glanced at his rearview mirror to see his passenger. They both wore dark sunglasses, even though gray skies loomed overhead. Harvey asked, "What do you think?"

Vedely said, "Not sure."

Just then, Vedely's phone buzzed. It was a text message. He checked it, and said, "Our man in Quantico says Jason Dessen isn't his name. It's not a real name."

"Alias?"

"Gotta be."

"Did they check to see if the Sheriff checked his ID? You know? Maybe the cops entered it into the system."

"Let's just ask them directly," Vedely said, and pointed out the SUV's windshield at one of the deputies. He walked out of the sheriff's office, towards his police vehicle.

The deputy pulled the handle on the driver's side door, opened it, and was about to hop in, but then he glanced to the right, down the street, and saw a pair of headlights flashing at him.

Damnit, he thought. He shut his door and looked back at the sheriff's station to make sure no one was watching him. He checked around the parking lot. No one was looking at him. He shut the door and jogged away down the street. He stopped at the black SUV, and leaned into the open driver's side window.

Harvey waved him to the rear door. He nodded and stepped back to it and opened it. He peered in and saw Vedely sitting on the other side.

Vedely said, "Get in."

The deputy slid into the backseat and closed the door.

Harvey spun around from the driver's seat, stared at the deputy, and put his hand out, open-palmed, like he was waiting for his change back.

Vedely said, "Give him your gun."

The deputy pulled his Glock 22. He held it in his hand a long second. Then, hesitantly, he reversed it and handed it to Harvey, who took it, and spun back around to face the road and the sheriff's station.

Vedely asked, "What's the stranger's name?"

The deputy looked at him, and back at Harvey, who watched him from the rearview mirror. He looked confused. He said, "Jason Dessen."

Vedely said, "No. It's not. We already checked it with the FBI."

"That's the name he gave us."

"Did you guys check his ID?"

The deputy paused a beat, stared at his empty hands. Then, he said, "We had no reason to charge him."

Vedely said, "I didn't ask if you charged him. I asked did you check his ID?"

The deputy said nothing.

Vedely shouted, "What's his name?!"

"I don't know. I thought it was Dessen."

Vedely furrowed his brow, and rubbed his forehead, like he had a sudden migraine. He said, "Okay. Get out." He waved the deputy away, like he was a servant.

The deputy looked at Harvey, and asked, "Can I have my gun back?"

Harvey stared at him through the rearview mirror. Only his eyes were visible. He said, "Get out first."

The deputy nodded, glanced at Vedely, but knew better than to say any more. He got out of the vehicle and closed the door. He stood outside, like a child waiting for instructions. Harvey didn't hand him back the Glock through the driver's window. Instead, he opened his door and got out. He stuffed the Glock into his pocket and stepped up to the deputy. He put one huge hand on the deputy's shoulder, grabbed it hard. His hands were heavy, like big stones.

The deputy asked, "What is this?"

Harvey exploded at the hips. His shoulders dropped and his other hand balled into a fist and he slammed it into the deputy's stomach—a serious gut punch. The deputy folded over, like a folding chair. His face turned pink and his eyes bulged, like they were going to pop out of the sockets. He looked like a drunk man about to puke. Which he did. Right there, in broad daylight, right down the street from the sheriff's station.

Harvey patted him on the back, and said, "Okay. You're okay. Breathe now. It's all good."

The deputy couldn't breathe. He could barely even hear what Harvey was saying because his eardrums nearly popped from the pressure. His voice was gone. The wind, along with everything else, had been completely knocked out of him. He hacked again.

A group of passersby crossed the street from one block over to another. They stared at the deputy and what was happening. Harvey stared back at them, and shouted, "What you looking at?"

Each of them looked away. They returned to talking to each other. None of them mentioned what they'd seen. And they never would. The citizens of Sawyer County knew better.

The driver's side rear window of the SUV buzzed down. The deputy was still folded over. Harvey's stone hand slid up to the back of the deputy's neck. Vedely stuck his head partially out of the window. He said, "Our whole operation is at stake here. Billy brought unwanted attention on us. I know that's not your fault. But I pay you to keep me in the know. Next time, use your head. When I call, you better have answers for me."

Trying to catch his breath, the deputy spat the words out. He said, "Yes. Of course."

"Good. Clean yourself up. You got a town to police. Go out there and represent us like a good sheriff's deputy," Vedely said, and buzzed the window back up.

Harvey released his grip on the deputy. He took out the Glock 22, ejected the magazine and the chambered bullet. He tossed all of it onto the street. The loose bullet rolled under the SUV. Harvey stepped around to the front of the deputy, who was still bent over, ready to puke again.

Harvey said nothing. He just climbed back into the black SUV, and drove away, leaving the deputy with the knowledge of which Vedely was his real boss.

CHAPTER 17

Widow grabbed donuts and coffee from *Dunkin*, ate them, and ended up walking the aisles of the bookstore next door, with a coffee in hand. The store allowed drinks with lids, food as well, but food was only allowed at a designated corner filled with tables. The tables were half-filled with customers. Several read books in silence. And others clicked away on their laptop keyboards. Remote workers, Widow figured. That was all the rage these days. He figured that if things ever got bad for him, money-wise, he could apply his skills online somehow. Of course, he'd have to invest in a laptop. He would need something to carry the laptop around in. Which meant buying a rucksack. If he started a remote business, he'd need reliable internet. Public Wi-Fi wasn't always available. It wasn't always reliable, either. So he'd have to invest in some kind of portable internet. Satellite, maybe? He'd probably need a phone, which meant signing contracts, and paying for expensive devices, and buying warranties. Running a business also required various insurances, because even remote businesses have some kind of exposure.

With all that, there also the tax obligation, which meant accountants and forms. That was his nightmare—living static, being stationary, tethered someplace for eternity, being stuck.

He shook off the thoughts and walked the aisles, sipping his coffee, enjoying his freedom of movement and freedom from attachments. He walked down the aisles in the non-fiction section, under true crimes. He'd already found a paperback edition of *Dark Matter*, the book that had been left at the hotel near Antler.

He stopped when he found the shelf he was searching for. And flipped through the various books until he found the one he was looking for. He pulled it out. It was a hardback book about a true crime that took place in California. The author was Cassie Fray, *New York Times Bestseller*, according to the top front of the dust jacket.

Widow skimmed the back of the book. He got the gist of the case it was on. He opened the dust jacket and stared at Cassie Fray's author bio and photo. The bio was a highlight reel of her accomplishments. She went to the State University of New York for her undergraduate in journalism. Then she got a master's degree from NYU. She had three books out. One about a warlord in Africa, and another on a mayoral campaign *involving more crimes than a mafia family*. That's what the dust jacket claimed. Fray was a talented investigative journalist, a woman who knew how to find answers. So why was Cosay calling Fray? Gotta have something to do with her murdered brother.

Aponi had described the aftermath of the situation as dismal, in so many words. Maybe Fray was doing a podcast episode about the murder? Or maybe she wanted to write another *New York Times* bestseller?

The picture they used of Fray was flattering. She looked classy, like a woman in an old eighties movie. She resembled actress Morgan Fairchild, only decades younger. They probably used special filters on her.

Widow noted the mention of *Shedding Light* in the list of her current endeavors. He cracked the book open, and flipped to the copyright page. It read that it was published in association with *Shedding Light Networks*. Which meant they co-produced the book. If it was a

New York Times bestseller, that meant they probably made a pretty penny for it. Which would explain why they would grant Ms. Fray a lot of leeway on what cases she wanted to go after.

Widow shelved the book, headed to the front of the store, and purchased the copy of *Dark Matter*, giving him one more thing to carry.

* * *

THE DRIVER KNEW that Aponi Cosay wasn't working the morning shift. She worked nights only. And no one else would recognize the driver, making it safe to just go in and ask what room the stranger was staying in.

The driver parked the dark SUV out in the resort's side parking lot, the bigger one. The driver parked in the same parking space that Aponi and Widow had the night before.

The driver parked, locked the SUV, and strolled across the parking lot, avoiding unwanted attention. A security guard glanced in the driver's direction, but didn't linger.

The driver entered the resort and went to the front desk.

The woman behind the desk asked, "Yes, can I help you?"

The driver asked, "I'm here to visit a friend. I need to know his room number?"

"What's his name?"

"Jack Widow."

The woman tapped the keys of desktop computer. Then she looked back at the driver. She said, "I don't see anyone with that name."

"No one?"

"I'm sorry."

The driver described Widow to the woman behind the counter. The driver said, "He's a big, scary guy, the kind of guy you wouldn't want to run into in a dark alley."

The woman behind the desk said, "Sure, I know who you're talking about, but he's been nothing but pleasant with me. And we only got a handful of guests right now. It's the slow season. You know?"

"What room's he staying in?"

The woman behind the desk sighed, and said, "I can't give out that information. It's different if you have his name. But if you don't, then I have to assume you're not a friend of his?"

"I gave you his name. It's Jack Widow."

The woman behind the desk stared at the computer screen again, in case she'd seen the name wrong. She said, "That's not the name I got. Maybe you're looking for someone else? Maybe the guy you're looking for is down the street at one of the smaller hotels?"

"He's here," said the driver.

The woman behind the desk said, "I can't just give out information without his consent."

The driver looked frustrated, and was considering pulling out a law enforcement badge. That would get things rolling in the right direction. But the driver really wanted to stay off the radar. Especially since Aponi worked there. And the driver didn't want Aponi to suspect anything. The driver didn't want her to know about this visit to Sawyer Lake. If the driver pulled a badge out, certainly the woman behind the desk would tell another coworker, and the rumor mill would start up. Eventually, it would blow the driver's element of surprise.

The driver thanked the woman for her help, turned around, and left to cruise the town, searching for Widow.

Viewing the details of Jason Dessen's check-in, the woman behind the desk saw that the credit card put down as a deposit for his room didn't have his name on it. It didn't have the name *Widow*, either. The credit card belonged to one her coworkers, a night shift girl named Aponi Cosay. The woman behind the desk couldn't imagine why. But it wasn't her business. Come to think of it, the driver reminded her of Aponi.

* * *

IN THE LATE AFTERNOON, Widow flipped the last page of his new book. He set it on the table, and inspected his coffee. There was a drop at the bottom of the cup. He'd had two refills already, but he contemplated getting another. But he didn't. He downed the last of this one and trashed the cup. He stuffed the paperback in his inside coat pocket and left the bookstore.

Standing on the curb outside, he gazed up at the sky. The sun was an hour from its daily sunset protocols. Some would say he'd wasted the whole day lounging around, reading a book and drinking coffee. To Widow, it sounded like the perfect day. He'd had no new leads on Cosay anyway.

Widow turned right at the corner and headed north to the lake. When in doubt, go scouting. He walked through the downtown area, back to the lake, and west along the shoreline, where Aponi had driven him back from the reservation. While scouting the town, he saw several more of those election signs for Sheriff Vedely and Deputy Braaten. He passed a line of senior citizens heading into an all-you-can-eat buffet for dinner, early for what he'd call dinner time. Four competing kids' teams played baseball at a large park with two regulation-size baseball diamonds. There were two batting cages, where boys practiced hitting a ball spat at them by a cannon on the other end of the cage. Their fathers stood outside the cages, criticizing them about their form or praising them for it.

Widow counted at least two banks, one local and one a branch of a large chain. He saw three churches in the town. He saw a school, a couple of self-serve car washes, gas stations, a hardware store, and more hunting, bait, and tackle stores than he could remember ever seeing in a town that size. It was overkill. One bait shop had a bar in the basement.

Widow reached the top of a rise, and looked from west to south. He saw the tops of roofs. The sun glimmered through sparse, gray clouds, like it was the answer to the town's gloom. The sun would begin its descent soon into the setting phase, leaving Sawyer Lake with clouds and darkness and cold air.

In the corner of his eye, Widow saw something. It was the flash of a familiar vehicle. The vehicle drove through a busy intersection three blocks away from him. The windows were tinted, but he saw movement from the driver's side window. It was a burst of action from the driver, like a double-take. The vehicle was passing through the intersection, going one way, but something to the left caught the driver's attention. The driver slammed on the brakes, stopping midway through the intersection. Horns from other vehicles blared. Angry drivers yelled at the offender. It stayed there in the middle of the intersection for a long moment, like the driver was trying to focus on Widow, to make sure that he was the one the driver was looking for. Without knowing the driver's intentions, Widow felt like a target.

The vehicle was a dark SUV. It was too far away for Widow to read the rear plate again, same as at the Cosay farm. But it wasn't North Dakota. He was still sure of that. The dark SUV stayed there in the middle of the intersection, in the middle of the angry drivers. It didn't budge. It was practically parked, but the brake lights were lit up.

More angry horns shrieked, drawing the attention of every pedestrian on the sidewalks. The driver released the brakes and drove the rest of the way through the intersection, completing the transaction that had been started. The SUV went through the intersection. Then it sped up, squealed into a 180 slide, and reversed course back in Widow's direction. The vehicle returned to the same stoplight and turned right, onto the road where Widow walked.

He watched it for a second. He couldn't make out the driver's features, but he felt the driver's eyes staring right back at him.

The closer the SUV got, the more he was positive it was the one he'd seen before. It was the same dark SUV he'd seen at the Cosay farm, like it was staking out the place, waiting for Lou to show herself. Whoever it was, it probably was no friend to Lou, which meant the driver wasn't a friend to Widow, either. And now, the SUV was barreling towards him. Not good.

The SUV was a mid-sized vehicle, not a big one like a Chevy Tahoe or a Ford Expedition. And the brand was foreign, like a Land Rover or a Toyota. Not being one of the larger vehicles cut down on the number of passengers that Widow would have to potentially deal with. A mid-sized SUV could comfortably hold five people. Sure, there could've been eight or nine or maybe even ten guys crammed into it, but not likely.

However many people were in it, the SUV was almost certainly the same one that drove away from Widow at the Cosay farm. Maybe there'd only been one or two guys sitting in it, staking out the farm. Maybe they'd heard about what Widow did to the seven guys at *The Ranchman* bar so they ran, thinking they needed more firepower. Or maybe they were law enforcement, which he found doubtful. *Who were they and why would they be looking for him?*

Widow didn't want to wait around and find out. If they were some kind of law enforcement agency, they hadn't identified themselves to him yet. Which meant he was free to evade them at any cost. It's not considered resisting arrest when they've not distinguished themselves from any other group of guys chasing Widow around.

Widow walked on. The sidewalk had pedestrians on it, but not a huge number of people. Sawyer Lake wasn't Times Square, but the end of business hours approached. And people were getting off work, going on to wherever it was they went afterwards.

Widow walked through a dilapidated shopping mall, with two empty storefronts in it, a barber shop with no customers, and a gun store with several customers. He came to another intersection, looked left, looked right. To the right was the lake and the road that paralleled it. It had steady traffic on it, but the traffic kept moving. Going that way wouldn't slow the SUV down or give him the chance to lose them. Which wasn't what he wanted to do. Right then, the occupants were an unknown quantity, an x-factor. *Who were they? What were their intentions?* He needed to know.

Widow came to the corner of another intersection and turned left, behind the building, into an alley. He ran to the next road and stopped. He saw an opportunity. Right in front of him was an abandoned parking lot with a run-down old tire shop. It looked completely abandoned and forgotten about, like it had blended into the fabric of the town over many years, and now, no one remembered it.

The building used to be painted white. But the white had peeled away to reveal a green color. An old sign crumbled above the entrance. The doors to enter were completely boarded up. The windows were all boarded up except for one spot. On the far right corner of the building, at the last of a set of boarded-up windows, there was a window with one board that half-dangled, and the other half was broken off and splintered on the cracked pavement below. It was the spot where meth heads, or homeless people, or local teenagers, or whoever, had broken in to get out of the viewing range of the public. Most large, abandoned buildings had such an entry point.

Widow stepped back into the alley, glanced back, and saw the SUV slow at the corner and stop, like the driver was searching for him. He stayed where he was, waiting for the driver to notice him. The driver must have because the SUV backed up, turned in to the deserted alley, and sped toward him.

Widow froze and stared at it, pretending to be dumbfounded, pretending to be worried. But he wasn't. Then he walked out of the driver's view, and ran to the opening on the tire shop. He waited until the SUV was in the empty parking lot. He didn't wait long. The dark SUV sped out of the alley and skidded into the lot. Widow would've made eye contact with the driver if the windshield hadn't been so tinted. The way it was tinted, he could only make out the driver's outline.

Widow waved at the SUV, turned, grabbed the dangling half of the board on the last window, and ripped it all the way off. Otherwise he wouldn't have fit through the window. Whoever used it previously had apparently been only a third of his bulk. He flung the broken board behind him, kicked in another loose piece, and used his boot to kick away large shards of glass. He made the entry hole big and wide so he could climb through it, but also to make it obvious to his pursuers.

Inside, Widow glanced around. The interior was dark, but navigable. Plenty of holes in the roof allowed for sunbeams to pierce through. The problem was that the sun was setting, and the sky was already grayish, making visibility low. The floors were all concrete. The tire shop was laid out like a big box. It was huge and echoey. The ceilings were high. There was one L-shaped area with a hallway, office, lobby, and unisex restroom. The rest of the place was wide open, where three garage doors opened up to three auto bays. Most of the tires and tools and machinery had long since been scavenged or stolen.

Outside, the dark SUV skidded to a stop near the windows. One car door opened, and nothing else. There was only one occupant, one pursuer. That was the driver.

Widow walked away from the window and into the large emptiness of the garage area. He hoped to find a weapon. Garages usually have plenty of tools that made good blunt force weapons. He was certain the driver would be armed with a gun. He wasn't going to find something in there that would give him an advantage or make them even, but any weapon was better than nothing. Never bring a knife to a gunfight, unless a knife is all you have.

Widow searched everywhere, as fast as he could move. He had a little head start. He sifted through piles of flat tires and dusty, old metal shelves. All he found were empty boxes and corroded auto parts. One box was filled with something small and crawly. He figured some eight-legged arachnid had made it home.

Widow struck out at every turn. Then he heard the boards squeaking and a body ramming through the hole he left. The driver entered the tire shop, hit the ground, and rolled away. *Smart*, he thought. Otherwise, if he'd been armed and simply laid in wait for the driver to enter, he could've just shot the guy.

Widow crouched, shrinking his profile, in case the guy had a gun. He looked back, past a concrete corner and over a stack of old broken-down boxes and shreds of rubber tires, at the light from the window. He saw the driver's silhouette. The guy was small, slim, and lightweight, making him a harder target to hit. His face was in shadow, making identification impossible for now.

The one thing that was identifiable was the gun outstretched in the guy's hands. He pointed it in five of the positions on a clock face, from nine o'clock back to one. The driver seemed professionally trained.

Widow tried to stay quiet. He was big, making him an easy target, but he was also trained and had natural talent. He knew how to be stealthy and quiet. And his eyes had already adjusted to the dark shadows inside the tire shop, giving him precious seconds.

Widow crept to his left, staying along the wall and keeping the biggest distance between himself and that gun barrel. He used the fingers on his left hand to gently brush against the concrete wall, guiding him along. He snuck to the opposite end of that one hallway.

Then, his one advantage of seeing better in the dark was scuttled by the driver. The driver clicked on a small tactical flashlight. He lined the beam up with the gun's line of fire and started sweeping and clearing the tire shop.

Widow was as low as he could go without jeopardizing his ability to run if he needed to. He kept moving. The driver had two choices—left or right. If he went left, he'd follow Widow's first choice and enter the garage. Right, and he'd end up going down the dark hallway, and possibly shooting Widow up close.

The driver chose the garage. Widow waited until the guy was fully committed to the choice. Then Widow watched as the flashlight beam scanned across the first of the three garage bays. He was too far away for the beam to light him up. Widow hopped into the open doorway of the one end of the hallway, and crept to the restroom. He figured the office was empty. And he'd already seen the lobby from his entry point. He'd searched the large garage area and found nothing he could use. When businesses close and move out all their inventory and furniture, they usually leave behind the toilets. This business had been no different.

Widow lifted the tank off the toilet. He figured it would be as good weapon as any. One good whack with a toilet lid could kill the driver. He wasn't planning to do that. It was more of a last resort. Between getting shot and killing the driver with the toilet bowl lid, he preferred the latter over the former.

But the toilet bowl lid idea wasn't a good one because the lid broke in half in his hand. Apparently it'd already been broken into two halves and someone stacked it back the way they found it.

Widow picked up the toilet bowl lid, making a low scraping sound. That's when the two halves came apart in his hands. He dropped one. The whole thing was like watching slow motion. The porcelain dropped to the concrete and shattered. The noise echoed across the tire shop. Widow turned and darted out of the bathroom. He heard the driver's footfalls coming towards him from the doorway where he'd entered the hallway. The driver's flashlight beam bounced and shook as he ran.

Widow hugged the opposite wall, prepared to hit the guy as he turned the corner. But Widow felt the wall with his free hand. It was just a thin layer of drywall. Parts of it were busted through. He saw there weren't many studs inside. The wall was barely held up. It was only meant to be a cheap partition.

The driver's footfalls got closer. Widow realized this was not a good plan. He spun around and crept back in the lobby's direction and entry point. He didn't look back. At the opposite corner, he waited. He knew the driver was professionally trained. And he knew the guy would check his blind spots first, which would be where Widow stood. The driver stopped running and threw his back up against the opposite side of the thin wall, but didn't lean on it.

Widow knew all the ways to enter a hostile area. He knew the various scenarios that law enforcement agents are trained for. Instinctively, his brain flipped through them, like someone thumbing through a Rolodex. The driver had already forecasted his entry style when he came through the window after Widow. And he reinforced it when he ran toward the sound of the toilet lid breaking on the floor.

Therefore, Widow already knew how he'd clear the hallway. And that's exactly what the driver did. He leapt into the hallway, and quick-pointed his gun at every angle and every shadow. The second he entered, Widow rotated out and around the other side, back into the garage. He took a deep breath, held it, and waited.

The driver moved slowly and stealthily, but footsteps on concrete could still be heard in the complete silence. The driver checked the bathroom, saw the shattered toilet lid half, and came back out, pointing his gun down the hallway. The driver had to figure that now Widow had half of a toilet lid as a weapon. It wasn't whole, but could still do a lot of damage as a blunt weapon. Plus, now it had a sharp edge. A lot of civilians don't know this, but there are professional knives made of ceramics instead of steel. Ceramics cut just as fine as steel edges and they don't set off metal detectors. The toilet lid wasn't ceramic, but porcelain was just as deadly.

The driver shined his flashlight on the ground and saw Widow's footprints in the dust. He followed them, stopping to check the office, which was clear. Then he resumed following Widow's footprints until they turned right at the end of the hallway. About two-thirds of the way down the hallway, the driver stopped when he heard a loud crash behind him. He spun around, pointed the gun at the sound, and saw that the other half of the toilet lid had been thrown against the back wall of the garage. Pieces of it had clattered into the hallway.

Stupid, he thought. He couldn't believe Widow thought he was dumb enough to fall for a distraction like that. He didn't go for it.

He knew if Widow tried to draw him back toward that end of the hallway, then Widow was on the other end.

The driver continued to follow Widow's footprints, but he never made it to the end. Suddenly, the thin drywall behind him exploded into dust, and paint chips, and huge arms. Widow burst through the drywall and bear-hugged the driver. He lifted the driver off the ground and slammed him back through the drywall and into the garage.

Widow hoped the shock and awe of his attack would cause the driver to drop his gun. But it didn't. Widow slammed him through the wall and threw him to the floor. The driver slammed into the concrete, chest first. But the gun stayed in his hand. However, the flashlight clattered away, spinning and rolling. It finally rolled into a pothole and stopped. The light beam fell between them.

The driver scrambled to his feet, spun back around, and pointed the gun at Widow. Only he'd been too late because Widow was right on top of him.

The gun came up and Widow swatted it out of the driver's hands. The gun went flying, and clattered away past the flashlight.

Widow didn't go after it. And he didn't wait for the driver to get his bearings.

Widow charged the driver like a bull. But the driver was small and agile and it was dark. Widow threw two fast jabs and a cross, overkill in his book. He could kill someone with the driver's small frame with one or maybe two jabs, if he threw them hard enough. But he didn't kill the driver with any of them. He didn't even land any of them. He'd completely missed. The driver had dodged each swing and landed two quick body blows under Widow's swings.

The blows were so fast, Widow didn't even know he'd been hit until after he finished his last swing. He backed away, stunned. The driver danced back, but in the dark. Now Widow wasn't sure about the driver's body's details. The driver was dressed all in black from head to toe. And he was so small that in the dark, Widow couldn't really watch his feet and shoulders, which he normally did to anticipate his opponent's next move.

The driver danced towards him. He threw a flurry of jabs in Widow's direction. Widow danced right, danced left. He blocked two jabs to his jaw, but took another body blow. The driver was no amateur street fighter. He was good. Widow couldn't remember fighting too many opponents this skilled before, not outside of the Navy. The driver was fast, too. But his punches weren't powerful. Sure, they would've knocked out the skittish guy he'd encountered at *The Ranchman.* But not a man of Widow's size. The other factor was that the driver was short and Widow was tall, forcing the driver to punch upwards at an uncomfortable angle. However, a thought occurred to Widow. He was grateful the driver hadn't pulled a knife or a blade. If he had, Widow would've already lost. Those body blows were targeted to cause the most damage. They didn't faze Widow that much because they were targeted for an opponent of average size. Widow wasn't average. And he was covered in dense natural muscle, which protected him from punches of lesser power. The driver went in again, only this time Widow was ready. He side-stepped the first jab, but he did it right in front of the flashlight beam. The beam shone directly into the driver's eyes. Widow danced back in and swung a powerful right hook. His massive fist slammed into the driver's chest plate, knocking him into the darkness and onto his butt. The guy tried to scream or shout or say something, but he couldn't. The massive blow knocked the wind out of him.

It bought Widow some time. His first instinct was to go for the driver's lost gun. But he'd have to find it in the dark. He could take the flashlight, find it, and use it. But that would also require searching. The inside of the tire shop was so echoey, that gun could've clattered anywhere, and Widow couldn't narrow down the search area by the sound it had made.

Widow's next instinct was to pick up the flashlight and strike the driver with it. But the flashlight wasn't that big or heavy looking. So, he chose his third instinct.

Widow scrambled over to the driver and stood over him. The guy was clawing at his chest, like he couldn't breathe or speak. His face was still in shadow. But Widow saw the guy had long, black hair, like Billy the Kid had, only longer.

Like a hulk in the dark, Widow knelt, grabbed the driver's belt, and dragged him back into the flashlight beam. He got behind him and put the driver in a sleeper hold. It was time for the driver to take a nap, until Widow could figure out who he was.

Widow had the guy in a wicked sleeper hold. The driver knew the immediate danger, balled up his fists, and whaled away on Widow's arm, like a hammer swing, only in reverse.

The pounding fists hurt this time, much worse than the body blows. Widow squeezed his arm tighter and tighter, trying to put the guy to sleep. The driver's long black hair covered his face. The guy's reverse hammer-swings began slowing, like he was running out of energy. Which he was because he'd be asleep in seconds.

Then the guy did something Widow didn't anticipate, which was another dumb mistake. Only Widow made it. The guy came out with another gun. He'd had a backup gun in an ankle holster.

Instantly, Widow released his grip around the driver's neck and grabbed at the gun. The driver raised the gun above his chest, trying to angle it at Widow's face. Widow clamped both hands over the gun, forcing it to aim away from them. The driver took advantage of the opportunity and hammer-fisted Widow again, only he did it into Widow's groin.

The pain was instant. An explosion of searing pain shot through Widow's thighs. He released his grip on the driver's gun hand. It was natural. Any man would've done the same.

The driver rolled away, across the concrete, putting distance between them. He came up on his feet, but facing away from Widow. He spun around fast and aimed the backup gun at where Widow had been grabbing his groin. But Widow wasn't there. He'd scrambled to the other side.

Widow clamped his hand over the driver's weapon again, wrenched it out of the driver's hand, and stepped into the light. His face was red and flushed. He looked like a version of the Hulk right at the beginning of his transformation.

Widow's groin hurt, and that earlier flurry of body blows left him stinging, like an after-effect, but he wasn't about to get shot. He shoved the backup gun back into the driver's face. He barked a command at the driver, only his voice was off. It was shrill, and the octave was all wrong. He had been hit in the nuts, after all.

Widow said, "Step into the light."

The driver held his hands up, surrendering. He stepped into the flashlight's beam slowly. First, Widow saw his hands. They were empty. Then he saw the top of the driver's head, the thick black hair. Strands of it covered the driver's face, but as he stepped into the light, Widow realized he wasn't a *he*. He was a *she*.

Widow glanced at the driver's backup gun, in his own hand. It was a SIG P938, like the one that could fit an ankle holster he'd seen three days ago in Washington. He'd seen it in someone's house.

Widow lowered the backup gun halfway, a sign of faith. The driver lowered her hands slowly down to her chest. She cupped her breast. The touch alone made her wince in pain. She said, "You hit me in the boobs!"

Still with his voice in a higher octave than normal, Widow asked, "Lou Cosay?"

Cosay stepped closer to him and closer into the light. She stared up at him. Her lip bled. Her hair was disheveled. She was also red and flushed, probably as much as he was. Strangely, she cracked a smile, like she had enjoyed the combat. She said, "Jack Widow."

CHAPTER 18

Twenty minutes later the sun descended in the west, over the reservation and into the heavy trees. Orange light sparkled off the lake. Fishing boats returned to their respective docks for the night. The locals were coming back in. The bait shops were closing up.

Widow and Cosay sat in the front of her dark gray Range Rover, icing their bruised areas. Cosay wore a navy blue puffer coat, black slacks, and thick hiking shoes. Her hair was long and black. Her ears were pierced in several places, possibly against NCIS regulations, but she might've had religious waivers. Widow wasn't sure either way. She had a small tribal tattoo peeking out from the top of a black knit V-neck sweater. Her tattoo had minimal colors. It wove up from her collarbone. It was exposed to Widow when she shoved a hand-sized icepack under her sweater, one-handed from the bottom. It pushed her sweater outward.

Widow pressed down on his own icepack, over his groin, and over his jeans. It felt cold, but soothing. They had bought the ice from the bait shop twenty yards in front of them. They were parked in the lot of Sawyer Lake's main boat dock.

Getting the icepacks took some deliberation between them. Cosay was trying to stay under the radar. So far no one who knew her had seen her. She wanted to keep it that way as long as she could, until she achieved her goals. Therefore, she didn't want to risk going into a place where she might get recognized. The reservation and the town locals shared the boat docks. Anyone might recognize her.

Widow didn't want to go get the ice because he was still having a hard time walking straight. Which gave him great sympathy for the farmhands he had fought in *The Ranchman's* parking lot. Cosay got him good, but she hadn't used her full punching potential because she wasn't trying to incapacitate Widow. Plus, she was small, so although the extent of her power was good, it was limited. Widow was a big guy. He had overwhelming power in his strikes and kicks. And he hadn't held back when he kicked the farmhands in the nuts.

The realization made him feel a little bad. Was he justified? Absolutely. He had no doubt about that. Did they deserve his full force? Maybe not. But the US Navy spent two million dollars training him to be a hammer. When you're a hammer, everything looks like a nail.

In the end, they flipped a quarter from the loose change in the Range Rover's cup holder. Widow lost the coin flip. He slow-walked to the bait shop, trying to look normal to passersby. In the store, he had to stand in line behind a pair of old guys who were shooting the shit with the store owner, another old guy. All Widow wanted was to get the bags of ice and get back inside Cosay's SUV. The standing wasn't agonizing, but it didn't feel great either. He tried not to draw attention to himself, which proved difficult because of the faces he kept making.

Finally, the old guys wrapped up their conversation and Widow bought the ice. He had to shovel it into a couple of small bags. He brought it to Cosay's vehicle. Now they sat in silence, icing their bruises.

They sat facing the bait shop. The lake was directly behind it, with a couple dozen boats either docked or docking. There were also two boat launches. And both were busy with locals and non-locals picking up their boats, getting them on their trailers, and hauling them away. It was busy enough that Widow wondered why the resort was so slow. It made sense that the locals didn't go there because they were local. They didn't need to do the tourist thing. Perhaps the non-locals weren't tourists, but just avid fishermen who lived within driving distance of the lake. He noticed some Canadian plates. There wasn't a border crossing in Sawyer County, but there was in Minot to the southwest, and whatever city was to the east. The Canadian plates also told Widow that there was no official town establishment on the Canadian side of Sawyer Lake. If there had been, then why would they drive around to the US side?

After ten long minutes, they finally spoke. Widow broke the silence. He said, "You know who I am."

"Yes. I know who you are."

"How?"

Cosay pushed the icepack into her breasts, and leaned forward against the steering wheel, giving her more pressure. She said, "My partner, Omar. He told me you were coming."

Omar? Widow thought. Cosay read his face, and said, "You didn't think he'd tell me? Of course he told me."

"He said he had no idea where you were. He said it to Steslow and Flory. He said it to Adam Cress."

She paused a beat, and asked, "He lied to the Secretary of the Navy for me?"

Widow nodded, and said, "He's a good partner."

"He's the best partner I ever had."

"So, all that stuff he told us about not knowing your personal life and never being to your house before, that was all a lie?"

"Of course it was. Omar is practically my best friend. He's been in my house a hundred times."

Widow asked, "He tell you about Steslow?"

"I knew about Reed and the medal already. I don't know why the Secretary is so involved."

"Omar didn't tell you everything. Then again, I don't think he knew," Widow said, remembering Agent Omar's surprise that the Secretary of the Navy was in Flory's office on Monday.

"Knew what?"

"Secretary Adam Cress was there at the ceremony to give you the Navy Cross."

Cosay's eyes widened. She said, "What? Really?"

Widow nodded, and said, "It was supposed to be a surprise. Something you did back in the day involving a gunfight. Supposedly, you saved lives."

"The Navy Cross?" she asked again, dumbfounded and humbled, like she didn't deserve it.

"The Navy Cross can be awarded to any member of the Navy, or Marines, who distinguishes himself in action by extraordinary heroism but not justifying an award of the Medal of Honor."

"Or herself," Cosay said.

"Of course."

"Also, you left out the Coast Guard. They also can receive a Navy Cross."

Widow stayed quiet.

Cosay said, "A Navy Cross. Wow. It's amazing. Flattering. But what I did for it was years and years ago. Why now?"

Widow shrugged, and said, "You know how these things go. It can take years. Some people don't get it until after they're dead."

"Omar told me about you. I didn't believe it, at first. Why would you come all this way, go through all this, just to find me?"

Widow stayed quiet, because it was a rhetorical question.

Cosay said, "I saw you yesterday at my family farm, then I saw you with my sister. And here you are."

"Were you really going to shoot me?"

"I didn't want to."

"But you were going to?"

"Were you going to choke me out?"

"It was a sleeper hold. I was trying to incapacitate you, until I saw your face."

Cosay said, "You threw some big punches at me. You could've killed me with one of those."

"No. You would've ended up in the hospital for a few months. Tops."

"In the hospital?"

Widow shrugged, playfully, and said, "Yeah. Maybe you'd be drinking through a straw for a year."

"Is that right?"

"Honestly, I thought you were a man."

She came back off the steering wheel, turned, and stared at him. She opened her coat, like she was showing him her figure, and asked, "Do I look like a man to you?"

Not even close, Widow thought. He said, "Of course not. But you chased me with your car and then with a gun. I never saw your face until later. How was I supposed to know?"

"I was chasing you so I could talk to you. That's all."

"Why the gun?"

"I didn't know if you were for real."

"I'm real. I'm sitting right here."

She closed her coat, and said, "I didn't know if you were serious about finding me. Like why would you come all the way out here for me? What do you care? Did you do this for Reed?"

"Partially. He couldn't come himself. Although I'm sure he would've, if he knew you were in danger. But also I did it for myself. I wanted to know why you skipped such an important event. I never heard of a sailor skipping out on the Navy Cross before."

Cosay said, "I think you're lying."

Widow stared at her, blankly. His groin wasn't agonizing anymore. Now, it was just throbbing and numb. He asked, "How so?"

"I think those things are true, but that's not really why you're here. You came because you wanted to protect me."

"Protect you? I just met you."

"Omar looked you up. He told me your files are classified beyond classified, like it would take a direct order from the President just to look at them."

"I was a SEAL for sixteen years."

"True, but NCIS investigates SEALs from time to time. He should've been able to access some information without a warrant. The thing about yours is, he said he doubted a warrant would've even got him in. So, what's up with that?"

"I did some things," Widow said, and he left it at that.

"Whatever. I think you can't help it. I think you came here to save me if I were in any danger."

"I doubt you need saving," Widow said, and lifted the icepack. He showed it to her, like it was court evidence. "Maybe I came to help you? Call it a sense of duty. If you like."

"Help me? Do you know what I'm doing here?"

"I know it's got something to do with a podcaster named Fray."

She looked at him, surprised. She asked, "How did you know that?"

"Like you said, my file is more classified than most. I have my ways."

"You were in my house? You checked my outgoing calls?"

Widow said, "It's how I knew it was you back at the tire shop. I made the connection when I saw your backup gun, that SIG P938.

"My backup gun?" she asked, and narrowed her eyes.

"That and your shampoo. It's girlish," Widow said, and smiled.

She narrowed her eyes, and asked, "Did you go through my underwear drawer?"

"That's a likely place for people to keep valuable things, like a backup gun."

Cosay paused a long moment, like she was calculating how to feel about Widow going through her stuff. Dismissively, she said, "Whatever, just count yourself lucky. You've already gotten closer to me than most men do."

Widow pressed the icepack back on his groin, and said, "Yeah, but I paid a price for it."

Cosay said nothing to that. Instead, she turned in her seat and leaned back over the center console. She held her chest with one hand, to keep her breasts from brushing against the console and stinging. Widow stared forward, out the windshield. A flock of marbled godwits flew across the lake. Cosay dug around behind her seat with her free hand, and came back up with a small ruck-sack. She sat back in the driver's seat, unzipped the bag, and pulled a blue folder out. She said, "Fray is an investigative jour-nalist. She's damn good too."

"I saw her book today."

"So, you know she's the real deal. When she first emailed me, I didn't believe her. I didn't believe she was who she said she was.

And I didn't believe she could help with my brother's case. I assume you know what happened to him?"

"I do."

"What do you know about it? Tell me."

"Mika was murdered six-plus years ago. It went unsolved."

"You know about the paint?"

Widow nodded slowly.

"Do you know about the arrows?"

"Yes."

"Fray came to me about a year ago. We began a dialogue," Cosay said, and handed Widow the blue folder. He took it and opened it. It was a thick folder, stacked with foreign police reports of murder cases and photographs of dead bodies. The files were divided into tabs with various colors. He flipped through the first section, skimming over it. It was a lot of dead people. "She'd been doing an investigation into murders of missing people in Somalia. She found there were missing villagers in rural areas—men, women, and children. A large group of them vanished without a trace. The locals found some of them in a mass grave. Most of them had been shot."

"With arrows?"

She didn't answer that. Instead, she said, "7.62-millimeter NATO rounds."

"They were sniped?"

Cosay nodded, and said, "And 5.56-millimeter NATO rounds. Which are used in the M4A1. Plus, nine-millimeter parabellums. All weapons and ammunition used by NATO special forces."

"And the US military. Somalia is a dangerous place. What's that got to do with your brother?"

"Fray worked hard on this. She did a ton of research and investigation. She found more. Flip the page," Cosay said, and pointed at the first tab, separating the first section.

Widow flipped to it and saw more foreign police reports and more photographs of dead people piled on top of each other. They were photographed in mass graves. It was hard to pick out the various limbs and body parts. The police report wasn't in English. It was in French. Widow flipped back to the last police reports. They were in Arabic, one of Somalia's two official languages. He said, "The second one is written in French."

"It's Burkina Faso. Notice anything?"

Widow glanced at the photographs, and the police report, which he couldn't read, but he recognized the short parts, written in English. He read them out loud. "7.62- and 5.56-millimeter NATO rounds, and nine-millimeter parabellums. And what's this word?" Widow paused, and flipped to the Somalia police report, read the same word in Arabic, which was السهام. He struggled to pronounce it, but he got it right. He said, "Alsiham and Flèches?"

"Pretty good. The words mean arrows. But look at the next tab."

Widow thumbed to the next tab. It was the same as the others— dead bodies, the same ammunition, but a third country. The police reports were in Spanish, easier for Widow to read. He said, "Venezuela?"

"And the other tabs are more countries and more deaths. Know what they all have in common?"

"The dead people?"

"These are all the world's most corrupt countries. Some of them are in war zones. And the murder victims are all undesirables."

Widow said, "They're people no one notices."

"They're dead people no one misses. And here," Cosay said, and leaned across the console, pressing herself into his arm. She grabbed the files from him and flipped to the last tab, and handed it back to him. She pointed at another photograph of a dead man. He was Arabic, dehydrated, but young and athletic. "This guy got away, like my brother, and look at him."

Widow looked, and said, "He's covered in body paint and it's circles, like on a target."

"Like my brother. Someone is going around the world, kidnapping undesirables, and using them for target practice, or hunting them. And some of them were stabbed to death. They're also knifing them in close-quarter combat. Some of them were tortured to death."

"It's the same M.O. everywhere?"

"Yes. They've killed dozens, and that's just what Fray has compiled over the last year."

"Who's doing this?"

Cosay shrugged, and said, "I don't know. That's why I need to find Fray."

"Where is she?"

"Here, somewhere. She came here. She was here last week, and now she's gone dark."

"How do you know she just didn't leave?"

"Because of this," Cosay said, and took her phone out. She thumbed through the various screens, stopped on her voicemails, and put it on speaker. She clicked play.

A voice spoke over the speaker. It was Fray's voice, the same one Widow had heard on Fray's phone's voicemail. She said, "Lou, I think I found something. It might be them. It all leads back to Sawyer Lake. Your brother was the first. I don't want to say more over the phone. I'm flying to Minot today and renting a car. I'm going to drive to Sawyer Lake and do more digging. I'll call you when I have more." Fray paused, and said, "I hope we can bust these guys."

The voicemail ended there.

"What's it mean?" Widow asked.

"These murders all lead back here. I'm not sure about the rest. Fray is here. I just don't know where. We got to find her."

"This is big. International borders, murder, and government corruption. Whoever these guys are, they're talented, armed, and well-financed, probably connected too. Why are you here in the dark? Why all the secrecy? Why not call the FBI? You're an NCIS Agent. They'd listen to you."

Cosay paused a long beat, and moved back to her seat, leaving the files in Widow's hands. She stared out the windshield, and then back at Widow. She said, "After my brother was buried, my father hit the bottle, hard. That's how he dealt with it. But my mother couldn't take it. She lived for a month after, pretending it was all a lie. And then she killed herself. The day we buried her, I promised her I'd find the bastards who did this, and I'd kill them."

Widow stayed quiet.

Cosay turned back to him. Faint tears streamed out of her eyes. Suddenly, she looked like her father looked when Widow saw him with tears in his eyes. She said, "I intend to keep that promise. Widow, I'm not here to arrest anybody."

"That's why you came back without telling anyone."

"I'm going to find the men who killed my brother. And I'm going to kill them," Cosay said, staring into Widow's eyes like she was staring into his soul. "Widow, will you help me find and kill them?"

CHAPTER 19

The western horizon swallowed up the sun. Darkness washed over the sky, dragging stars with it. The clouds lingered, but left giant gaps for the stars to flicker through. Cold air gusted off the lake. The fishermen and lake-goers packed up and left, but didn't look at them. No one recognized Cosay. She sat there, staring at Widow. He didn't answer her question.

Cosay took a breath, wiped the tears from her face, and said, "I have to kill them, Widow. Whoever killed Mika. They hunted him down like an animal. Killed my mother. Destroyed my father, ruined my family. They have to die." She was passionate, resolved, and almost pleading with him. She'd thought about this for over six years. And she couldn't do it alone, not if she was going up against a force. She needed his help.

Widow stayed quiet.

Cosay repeated, "Will you help me?"

"Let's take it one step at a time."

"I know you've killed before. I can see it in you. I've killed before too. You know? In combat. I can do it."

Widow reached across the seat, left-handed, squeezed her shoulder tenderly, and said, "Let's find Fray, first. We need to know what we're up against. Okay?"

Cosay nodded, laid a hand on his, and asked, "Where do we start?"

"What's Fray's last known location?"

"She's here somewhere. I think she has a room at the resort, where you're staying."

"How did you know where I'm staying?"

She stared at him sideways through a head-tilt, and said, "Please. I'm an investigator."

"You figured it out because you checked everywhere else already?"

"I did. I used my badge on ninety percent of the motels and hotels in the area. They all thought I was doing an official investigation. So it was easy enough. I wasn't worried about getting recognized in the town. And I knew she wouldn't stay on the reservation. Looking for her, I realized I didn't see you in any of those places. Also, I saw my sister driving you. She works at the resort, so it made sense that's where you'd stay. But how come your name isn't on the registry?"

Widow said, "You checked on me? Aren't you worried about Aponi seeing you?"

"I went in the morning and asked about you. Aponi is nineteen. She doesn't wake up before noon."

"I used the name Jason Dessen."

"Who's Jason Dessen?"

"Nobody. It's made up," Widow said, and reached into his inside jacket pocket. He jerked the book out, and showed it to her. "It's a character from this book I read."

"Okay. At least you're not using dead presidents. That would be lame."

Widow shrugged, and said, "I went through them already. I used sports figures too. Now I use book characters."

Cosay rolled her eyes, dropped her icepack into the cup holder, and buckled her seatbelt. She said, "Okay. Let's go."

Widow removed his icepack, but quickly put it back.

Cosay said, "It still hurt?"

"Just do me a favor and try not to run over any potholes."

She smiled, and said, "I guess it's true that women have a higher threshold for pain than men."

"So they say," Widow said, and buckled his seatbelt.

Seconds later, they were back on the road, headed to the resort.

CHAPTER 20

At the Sawyer Lake Resort, Cosay pulled into the same parking lot she had parked in just hours earlier. She stopped the Range Rover and looked out the windshield. She said, "Aponi is here already."

Aponi's truck was parked on the far side of the parking lot, same as when she'd brought Widow there. He said, "If she's working the front desk, I don't think you'll be able to get past her."

Cosay continued on and swung around the lot, but parked in guest parking, facing away from the resort. She said, "It doesn't matter. You go alone. Ask Aponi which room Fray is in. That'll be the easy part because they give that out if you just have her name. The hard part is how will you get access to her room?"

"I'll figure something out."

"You'll have to finagle my sister. You're not her type and you're too old for her. You could charm her, but do you even have any charm?"

"Thanks."

"You've got that brooding thing, but she doesn't like that."

"I got this. Don't worry."

Cosay shrugged.

Widow got out, held the door open, faced her, and said, "I'll call you from her room." He shut the door.

"What, don't you need my phone number?" Cosay called out through the closed window.

Widow put a finger to his temple, tapped it, and said, "Is it the same one Steslow has?"

Cosay nodded.

"Then I already got it," Widow said, and left her parked. He walked to the resort and up the steps and into the lobby. Aponi stood behind the front desk in her uniform. A security guard leaned on the counter. He was an older guy, maybe late sixties. Widow could tell by his posture, and hers, that he was flirting with her and she wasn't flirting back. She nodded continuously, like she was agreeing with him, just to speed him along.

Widow walked up to the counter, in full view. The guard stopped leaning, and stared up at him. The guard was about five-foot-six, but he probably told his buddies he was five-ten.

Aponi looked excited to see him. The guard faced Widow, looked him up and back down. Behind him, Aponi looked at Widow, and mouthed the words *help me*.

"Aponi, I need your help with something," Widow said, and clamped his hands down on the counter, spreading his fingers wide. The old security guard stared at them. Widow spread them wide so that the security guard would see them. He was peacocking, an act that the birds of the same name do for many reasons. One of those reasons was to intimidate predators.

The guard stared at Widow's hands, which looked to have the same dimensions as heavy weightlifter plates. Part of the guard's job was to protect employees and property. Technically, he should've stuck around to make sure that Aponi was safe from the large hotel guest. But he didn't want to stick around. Even though he knew they kept firearms in a padlocked locker upstairs in the security station. And he had the key for it.

However, staring at Widow, he wasn't sure if the calibers were large enough. He decided to check the second part of his protection directive, the property.

"I'm going to patrol," he said, and walked away. Halfway down the hall he turned back, and said, "Aponi, call me on the radio if you need me."

She smiled a wide, sarcastic smile at him. And he was gone.

Aponi turned to Widow, and said, "Thank you. He doesn't normally work nights. As you can see, I hate working with him."

"If he bothers you, why not tell your boss?"

"I have. They won't do anything."

"Want me to talk with him?"

"What're you, my big brother now?"

Widow shrugged, and said, "Just a suggestion."

"I'm sorry. I'm just frustrated. So how are you today? Did you make any progress?"

"I'm getting somewhere. In fact, I need your help."

Aponi got very excited at the sound of that, like a bored small-town girl being offered an adventure. She asked, "What is it? Did you find my sister?"

"Hold on. All good things to those who wait. An investigation takes patience and double and triple checking. Which is what I'm doing. I need to find a reporter who checked into this hotel."

Aponi said, "Okay. Who are we looking for?"

Widow gave her Fray's name, and she looked her up on the computer. She found her name, and said, "That's weird."

"What is?"

"She's checked in and never checked out, but I've not seen her. Not this whole last week."

"What room is she in?"

Aponi told him the room number.

Widow said, "This is very important to your sister's case. I need to get into Fray's room. Can you let me in?"

"Why don't you just knock on her door?"

Widow thought for a moment. He could make up a lie to give to Aponi, but he decided the truth was easier. He said, "Your sister is here because she's searching for Fray. They were working on something and Fray vanished. No one knows where she is. Not her producer. No one. And she's not answering her phone. Call her room for yourself and see."

So, Aponi did. She dialed the room. It rang and rang. No one answered. Then she tried again. No answer. She still looked on the fence about it. Widow gave her Fray's personal phone number and told her to call her direct. Which she did, then she moved the phone from her ear and said, "Voicemail."

"That's because she's missing. She has been ever since last Wednesday. Check your records. When did she check in?"

Aponi checked the records, and said, "Ms. Fray checked in about a week ago."

Widow told her to google Fray's name. Which she did. He said, "See her face. Have you seen her?"

"I saw her when she came in. I remember her. I checked her in."

"Have you seen her since?"

"No. Do you think she's dead in there?"

Widow said, "I doubt it. Dead people decompose and smell really bad. Someone would've noticed her by now. Do your maids ever go into the room?"

"Ms. Fray has an open-ended stay, so not necessarily. Some people do that when they don't know when they're leaving. We just keep charging their card till they check out," Aponi said, and paused. She keyed in something into her screen. She stared at some piece of information. "It looks like she's not had any room service. And she's got a lot of missed messages."

"Can you retrieve the messages?"

"I can't access them. They're on a server. She can access them direct from the landline in her room."

"Can you see the numbers?"

"Yes."

Widow recited the 212 number from memory, and asked, "Is this the number that left her messages?"

"Yes. Most of them are from that number. How did you know?"

"It's her producer's phone number. Fray came here to work on a story with your sister."

Aponi stared at the screen. Her jaw dropped.

Widow asked, "What?"

Aponi pointed at the screen. She said, "That's my sister's phone number."

"We gotta get into that room and have a look."

Aponi stared at the computer screen, at her sister's phone number. She looked conflicted. She held this pose for a long minute, staying silent, working it all out in her mind. She knew she wasn't supposed to let Widow into a guest's room. He wasn't a cop. There were protocols in place. Only security could enter a room, and only with probable cause. But she couldn't let the guard enter. He was a creepy nitwit. Finally, she said, "Okay. But I'm going with you."

Widow didn't argue. She left him standing there alone for a moment, while she grabbed a backup keycard for Fray's room from out of a back office. She returned and put a plastic sign up on the counter next to a landline. The sign read: *Attendant on break, will return soon. You can wait, or dial 1111 on the phone for service.*

They left the front desk. They followed the path the creepy old security guard had taken. Aponi said he wouldn't come back the same way. Therefore, he wouldn't get nosy and start asking them questions.

Five minutes later, they were on Fray's floor and at her door. A *Do Not Disturb* sign hung on the doorknob. Aponi knocked several times, announcing her presence. No answer. She used the backup keycard to open the door. She pushed it open. The lights were off. She flipped them on.

Widow put a hand in front of her, and said, "Let me go first."

He led them into a corner suite. It was twice the size of Widow's room. There was a tile shower, large bathroom, a walk-in closet, a king bed, a brick fireplace, and a large balcony beyond a set of French doors.

Widow and Aponi walked all the way in. The heavy door automatically closed behind them. Fray's room was freezing cold. Aponi grabbed at her button-up sweater and pulled it closed. She said, "Brrr. She left the balcony doors wide open."

A draft gusted in, slapping them both across the face with cold air. Aponi moved to the French doors, closed and locked them. Beyond her was a magnificent view of the lake, facing northwest. Before the doors shut, Widow heard the calm swooshing of the water. He said, "She's not been here in days. No one has."

Aponi stayed near the French doors, took out her vape pen, and puffed it. Like before, her exhalations smelled of strawberries. Widow checked the room. Everything looked tidy and clean.

Widow searched the room, which didn't take long, because there wasn't a single personal item of Fray's in the suite anywhere. Not a toothbrush. Not a comb. No makeup. Not a stitch of clothing. Not a loose thread. Nothing. It was like no one had ever been there before.

Aponi asked, "Where's her luggage? Where's her stuff? I don't understand. If she's here or was here, then wouldn't there be something left?"

Widow went into the bathroom, checking the closet on his way. Both were empty. He stopped at the vanity mirror, crouched and inspected the countertops, and then the faucets. He moved to the toilet, inspected the flusher, and finally he inspected the shower handles and the drain plug.

Widow backed away, checked the trashcan, and then stopped and stared at the mirror. He came out, and looked at Aponi.

"What?" she asked.

"There's been no maid service?"

"No. I told you. The room is rented out. Maid service was turned down for the duration. Plus, she's got the *Do Not Disturb* sign on the knob. No way would one of the maids come in. I know them all."

Widow said, "Someone's sanitized this suite."

"Sanitized??"

"Never mind. She's not here. You should go back to work."

"What about you? What about Fray? What about my sister?"

"I'm on it. Don't worry. Just keep doing your job. We have to appear like it's business as usual."

Aponi nodded, and they left the room. They went back to the front desk. Widow left, and returned to Cosay in the parking lot. He got inside her Range Rover. She asked, "Well?"

"Empty. And someone sanitized Fray's room. Someone professional."

"Are you serious?"

"Not one of her belongings was left behind. Not even pocket lint. And her fingerprints weren't on anything. Not the toilet flusher, not the handles in the sink or shower—nowhere. Your sister knows nothing about it. But the security here is a joke. Someone could've come in anytime pretty much and used her key to get in and search her suite. They took everything and erased any evidence of her even being there. I wouldn't be surprised if even a forensics team couldn't find her DNA."

Cosay asked, "So what do we do?"

Widow paused a long beat. He stared out the window at the lake, then the parked cars. He said, "Wait." He got back out of her SUV.

"What?"

"Be right back," Widow said, shut her door, and ran back inside, and back to Aponi at the front desk.

She said, "You're back quick."

"Can you go into Fray's registration for me again?"

"Sure," Aponi said, and she typed into her computer. "Got it. What am I looking for?"

"Is Fray's car registered? What was it?"

"Yes. It's a Chevy Bolt. Color blue."

"What kind of car is that?"

"It's a tiny economy car. Why?"

"Thank you. I'll see you later," Widow said, and left her again. He ran back out into the parking lot, and hopped back into Cosay's Range Rover.

"What was that about?"

"I know where Fray's car is. She flew in from New York and rented a car. I saw it yesterday. It's parked at *The Ranchman* bar on the reservation."

Cosay asked, "Are you sure? How do you know it was hers?"

"She registered a Chevy Bolt. Which is a tiny car. People here don't drive tiny cars. They've all got trucks and SUVs. I saw an economy car, left in the parking lot at *The Ranchman*. It's covered in snow, like it's been there for days. And the owner complained about it to me. He said: *She better come back for it.* Or something to that effect. I bet he saw Fray in there."

"Then let's go," Cosay said, and she backed out of her spot and drove them to the reservation.

CHAPTER 21

They drove up to *The Ranchman* bar at a quarter past seven in the evening. The parking lot was two-thirds full. It was both *Happy Hour* and nearly peak bar hours, when most bars do most of their prime business. And it was a Thursday night, less than a week since Widow first heard Lou Cosay's name. Now he worked alongside her. Life was full of strange events.

They parked in the lot where Widow had seen Fray's car, only it wasn't there. Cosay asked, "Are you sure you saw it?"

Widow ignored her and got out. Cosay put the Range Rover in park and she got out. Live music boomed from inside the bar. Sounds of clinking glasses, and cheery people talking cheery things, echoed from the bar.

Widow walked to the spot where Fray's car had been. There was a Chevy parked there, but it was a truck, not a tiny blue car. Cosay walked through the Range Rover's headlights and joined him. She asked, "Where was it parked?"

"Right here."

"So if it was here, then where is it now?"

Widow sidestepped, and looked behind the truck. He saw the *No Long-Term Parking Violators Will Be Towed* sign. He pointed at it, and said, "They towed it."

Cosay stared at it and said nothing. Bar music thumped beside them. The live band had stopped for a break, and house music played over the bar's speakers. It was louder than the daytime jukebox music Widow heard the day before.

Widow spoke loudly. He asked, "Do you know where the tow truck company is?"

"No. I've not been here in more than six years," Cosay said, glanced at the sign, and then at her watch. "We could call the number and ask. They're probably still open. Maybe they're twenty-four hours. Some of those places are."

"Forget it. They'll haggle you over price, thinking it's your car. They might hang up on you and let you sweat it out till tomorrow, when you're more inclined to pay a higher price to get your car back."

"So what now?"

"The bar owner will know. Come on."

"Widow, I'm trying to stay under the radar here."

"What does it matter now? You were going to get seen, eventually. Let's cut to the chase here."

She stared up at him, and swallowed hard. A fear came over her, like she had demons to battle and she wasn't ready to face them. He suddenly felt bad for pushing. He grabbed her by the shoulders, and said, "I'm sorry. I know you came here to get retribution. I understand that. Believe me. I'll help you. Really, I will. But Fray is missing. She's a civilian. We took oaths long ago to protect civilians. She's probably in real danger here. This differs from before. Before, you suspected she was missing, but you didn't know about her hotel room. You didn't know someone sanitized it. And I didn't know who she was. But, Lou, put two and two together. Those murders she's investigating overseas. Whoever's been doing this is serious. This has gone way too far. I'm not a cop, but I think you should consider how far you want to go before we should reach out for help."

A single tear welled up in her eye. She said, "You're right. Let's go a little farther. Right now we have nothing concrete, just the instincts of a drifter, and a broken sister wanting revenge. Can we do that? Can we go a little farther? The moment we get evidence that Fray's alive and in trouble or anyone's life's at risk, then we'll go to the cops."

"You sure?"

"Yes. The very second we confirm she's alive and in danger or if anyone else is in danger, we can go to the cops."

"Okay," Widow said. "I'm going inside to ask the owner about the tow truck company. Just wait for me out here."

Widow turned and entered the building. Low blue lights illuminated the bar. The crowd was thicker than on his previous visit, a lot thicker. Some people looked at him and some didn't. He threaded his way through people and tables until he reached the bar. There was a crowd at the bar. People stood in disjointed groups of three and four to order their drinks.

Widow waited for nearly ten minutes until he changed tactics. He moved to the end of the bar, to the service well, a spot designated for the waitresses only. A female bartender asked him to return to the bar. He asked for the name of the towing company they used. She called someone to get the owner out of the back office.

Widow waited until the bar owner came out. Which he did, and immediately froze when he saw Widow. He slowly approached Widow, behind the lines of customers. They met in the walkway. The bar owner appeared half scared and half angry. He looked up at Widow, and said, "You need to leave!"

"I just want the name of the towing company you used to tow that woman's car."

"You're not welcome here. Please go."

Widow said, "Give me the name of the company that towed the woman's car that was parked outside yesterday, and I'll go."

"What woman?"

"You know what woman. I don't have time for games. Just give me the name of the towing company and I'll leave."

The bar owner looked around, like he was anxious about who might see Widow. Suddenly, Widow knew why. The skittish guy and the two bikers were in the crowd, and this time they were with a larger group of guys. There were three times as many bikers. The skittish guy remained as one. But the farmhands outnumbered Widow and the bikers two to one. They hadn't seen him yet. So, he repeated his question to the bar owner. "Tell me the tow truck company's name and I'll leave."

The music's bass thumped and rattled in his ears. The bar owner glanced around nervously. He started to answer Widow, but it was too late. The skittish guy saw Widow. He ran up on the little stage, knocking over the guitar player, who was just about to play again. The skittish guy grabbed the microphone and spoke into it. He said, "That's the asshole who beat up Billy!"

The crowd of happy bar-goers stared at Widow, like his last visit, only now he was outnumbered by a lot more people, and in crowded quarters. And half of them were large men who were drunk or buzzed. Widow wasn't near the entrance. He was closer to the middle of the room. They could surround him easily. In the low lighting, it was hard to tell who was friend and who was foe, whereas they all knew each other. He was the outsider. For all he knew, Billy was beloved by many of them.

One of them shouted, "Where's Billy?"

Another said, "What've you done with him?"

Widow began to back away, backing towards the door slowly. He didn't want to turn his back on the threats he recognized—the bikers, the farmhands, and the skittish guy. He kept his head on a swivel, checking every face that looked at him. He scanned them like that scene in *Terminator*, where the machine walked into a bar and scanned everyone for threats and for a good pair of leather biker clothes that fit Arnold.

Widow knew he could take on a bunch of them. He already had. But not in a tight room full of thirty hostiles in the dark. Not in hand-to-hand combat, when he was certain there were several guns in the room.

The bar owner turned to the crowd, and put his hands up in the air, like a musical conductor without his baton. He said, "Okay, guys. He was just leaving. Please. Don't start anything inside the bar." He begged and pleaded with them, but it was hopeless. Most of them weren't present when Widow destroyed Billy's face, but they'd all heard about it. The rumor mill had already circulated the story. The crowd's mood turned from local angst into mob rage. It all happened right in front of him.

The crowd fell silent. The music stopped. The bar owner got pushed away. And the crowd seemed to breathe in and breathe out, like a bull gearing up to rush him.

Suddenly, blue police lights flashed from the parking lot. The single blip of a police siren followed. The crowd stared at the front door. Everyone looked except Billy's crew. They maintained eye contact with Widow.

A moment later, the front door opened wide, and Cosay stepped in. She held her service weapon down, but in full view. She held her badge out and up for everyone to see it clearly. She had a gold shield on a badge holder with a black leather back—no chain. She shouted, "Federal Agent!"

Cosay was a small woman, but right then she seemed like a giant. Her presence was felt. Her cop voice would've made the biggest men fold. Widow already knew that none of the men in the room would want to fight her. He'd been on the losing end of that battle himself.

While the crowd was distracted, Widow scooted to the bar owner, grabbed his arm, and jerked him through the crowd and toward the door, to Cosay. He struggled at first. But Cosay called him by name, and told him to come out. He stopped struggling and followed Widow into the parking lot.

Cosay waited till Widow and the bar owner had passed her in the doorway, then she stared at the mob and said, "Stay in the bar! Don't interfere with a police investigation! Interfering with a federal agent is a crime! I better not see anyone follow us!"

In the parking lot, Widow escorted the bar owner over to where Fray's car had been parked. They stopped in front of the truck parked there now, and Cosay's Range Rover. Blue lights strobed from the Range Rover's front grille and rear end.

Cosay came out after them. She kept her eyes on the bar's entrance, pocketed her badge, and holstered her SIG Sauer but kept a hand near it. Then she joined Widow and the bar owner at her vehicle. The bar owner stood between them. He stared up at Widow, fear in his eyes. He stared at Cosay, and his fear turned to surprise. He asked, "Lomasi?"

"Agent Cosay," she said. "What tow company did you call to take the car that was parked here?"

The bar owner asked, "Am I in some kind of trouble? Don't I need a lawyer or something?"

"The tow company? I'm not going to ask again. He will!" she said, and gestured at Widow. The bar owner glanced back at Widow. Widow clamped a hand down on the bar owner's shoulder. Cosay watched the bar. She figured they only had seconds before Billy's crew got brave and rushed out.

The bar owner told them the company he called. Cosay looked at Widow and said, "We should go now."

Widow nodded, and looked at the bar owner. He said, "Forget about what we asked you."

The bar owner nodded. He understood. Widow removed his hand from the guy's shoulder. The bar owner walked away, returning to his bar.

Cosay and Widow started to get back into the Range Rover. Widow opened the passenger door, while Cosay skirted around the grille and stopped cold just in front of the driver's side wheel well. She stared in the bar's direction. Widow followed her gaze to an old Native man standing in the parking lot, just in front of the bar. He wore a ball cap. The bar owner walked past him without making eye contact with the old man.

The old man's face was hardened. There was a lot of pain there. His eyes had teared up so badly, it surprised Widow he could see straight. The old man stared at Cosay. She froze in place. They stood about twenty yards apart. The old man reached up and took his ball cap off. He took two giant steps forward, and paused, like he'd changed his mind. He spoke in a language that Widow only recognized because he'd heard the same old man speak it the day before. It was Mokani.

The old man stopped talking in Mokani. He stared at Cosay, and asked, "Lomasi?"

She said, "Daddy?"

The old man was her father. Aponi had said he shunned Lou. She hadn't seen him in over six years, not since they buried her brother and then her mother. Aponi had said he blamed Lou.

Lou Cosay took a step towards her father, and stopped. His face went from sadness to anger. He said nothing. He just turned around, faced away from her, and didn't move. He turned his back on her, like a dishonoring. He stayed like that as long as she could see him.

Cosay's shoulders sank, like her father had rejected her, which he had. Widow figured turning his back meant something in their culture, and it wasn't good. She was cast out.

Defeated, Cosay turned around, and slowly got back into the Range Rover. Widow followed. He asked, "You alright?"

Cosay said nothing. She killed the blue lights and got them back on the road.

Trying to change the mood, Widow said, "I didn't know NCIS had Range Rovers."

Deflated, but still resolute, Cosay said, "It's my personal vehicle. They installed the light package for me. Not everyone gets it. But when you been there as long as I have and you produce arrests that stick, they provide perks."

A few minutes later, they saw a tribal police truck barreling down the road, back toward *The Ranchman*. Its emergency lights strobed.

Widow asked, "What happens if we run into them?"

"Let's avoid them. They're pretty useless."

CHAPTER 22

They drove to the tow truck company, to the south, just on the border of Sawyer Lake and the reservation. It was located more on the Sawyer Lake side than the reservation side. On the way, Cosay explained to Widow that she had a friend in the sheriff's office. She concluded it best to involve him. It would cut down on any bullshit the tow truck owner would give them. And she anticipated that there would be bullshit.

She also decided that since she had already been seen, protecting her anonymity was futile at this point. So, she looked up the number from some kind of NCIS database on her phone. And she texted the deputy she knew from before. Back when she was a teenager, the reservation's high school was still being built. She had to spend two years going to the one in Sawyer Lake. She had made some friends. And he was one of them. She hadn't spoken to him in fifteen years, but she thought he could help. And she thought he *would* help.

As they drove, Widow asked, "If you've not seen him in fifteen years, how do you know he's a deputy?"

"I didn't say I haven't seen him. I said we've not spoken. I've seen him every day since I've been here. He's right there," she said, took one hand off the wheel, and pointed at one of the *Elect Sheriff* posters. It was a picture of Deputy Braaten's face.

"Your friend is running for sheriff against the current sheriff. The guy who's his boss?"

She nodded.

Widow said, "I had a little meeting with the local sheriff and his deputies, including your old friend. They seemed averse to helping us at all. What makes you think it will be different now? He may not be the kid you knew in high school."

"We need help, Widow," she said, and ten minutes later they stood in front of the tow truck company's lot, which was a large complex with tall chain-link fences and barbed wire and corrugated steel on the buildings. Widow scanned the part of the lot they could see, but didn't see the little blueberry Chevy Bolt.

There were a couple of tow trucks and two personal trucks parked in their parking lot. There was a large sign on the fence with a phone number to call to get one's car out from the impound. The impound was the huge parking lot behind the locked fence. And getting a car out, Widow was sure, came with a hefty fee.

The entrance to the main office was a big red door, next to a large bay window. The window had no shades or curtains behind it. And the office was lit up brightly. They could see two office workers inside. One was a modest woman in her late fifties with big beehive hair, dyed blond. The other was a man in his early sixties who also had dyed hair. Only his dyed hair was the most obvious toupee Widow had ever seen. It was dyed jet black. And had an Elvis swoosh cut that probably never changed.

Widow and Cosay stayed outside, leaning on the grille of her Range Rover, waiting for Braaten to show up. He'd responded to her text almost immediately, like he'd been waiting for it for fifteen years. She explained to him all he needed to know, which was she was a federal agent now and was working a case and needed local law enforcement's help. He responded pleasantly and said he was on his way.

On the big bay window, the tow truck company's hours were posted. It closed at eight o'clock on weeknights. And it neared that time now. The two people inside kept coming to the window and staring out at them.

The tow truck company's name was plastered on the side of the corrugated steel siding of the building in huge Old West style letters, like in an old cowboy show. It was called Ray-Ray's Towing.

Widow glanced at Cosay, and said, "It's gotta be getting close to eight."

She looked at her watch, and said, "Five minutes."

"Think we should go in? Before they close?"

Cosay didn't answer. She stared at her watch and then her phone screen. Braaten had said nothing in a while. She debated on just trying without him.

Widow said, "We should just try. You don't know how they'll respond. Maybe they'll respect an NCIS badge. Maybe they won't even inspect it."

"I've done this a thousand times, Widow. Rural folks tend not to get all cooperative for Feds, even if you got an FBI badge. Folks out here especially. I know these people, don't forget. The only two types of Feds they respond to are DEA and Border Patrol."

Just then, Ray-Ray's entry door creaked open and the older man stepped out. He ducked down a bit, like his toupee might hit the doorframe and get knocked clean off his head. He came out, and said, "Hi folks. We're closing up. Ah, I noticed you sitting out here. Could I help you with something?"

Cosay pushed off the grille, pulled her badge out, showed it to the guy, and said, "I'm a Federal agent. This is my partner. I need to look inside one of the cars you've got back there."

The guy went to scratch his head, but he did it weird. He plunged his fatty index finger into the hair and then jolted it slowly. His whole toupee moved with it. Then he waddled closer to Cosay, staying a good distance from Widow. He leaned in and stared at her badge. He asked, "Is that real?"

She made a face at Widow. He stayed quiet.

Is that hair real? Cosay thought, but she said, "Yes. It's real."

The old man stared at the badge, like he was memorizing her badge number. He said, "NCIS? What's that?"

Cosay said, "Naval Criminal Investigative Service."

"Doesn't that mean you have jurisdiction on the water, like on Navy bases?"

She said nothing.

The old guy said, "We ain't got no Navy base here. I don't think you got the right to be bothering us."

Widow pushed off the Range Rover's grille, and stepped closer to the old man. The old guy skipped a step away. His hair jiggled like *Jell-O*. Widow said, "There's a lake."

"That doesn't count," the old guy said. He glanced at his wrist-watch, and said, "Oh, look. We're closing. You'll have to come back tomorrow." He turned to go back to the door.

Just then a Sawyer County sheriff's patrol SUV pulled up into the lot and circled around and parked near the front door. The old guy stayed where he was. Suddenly, he trembled with excite-ment. He said, "Oh goodie. Now, you'll have to explain your-selves." He turned to Cosay. "Impersonating an officer is a capital offense."

The guy didn't understand what a capital offense was. He barely seemed to have a grasp on basic law to begin with. Widow rolled his eyes.

The patrol vehicle stopped in the lot and the deputy from the election posters, the one Widow had met earlier, stepped out. He walked around his vehicle, stopped out front of his headlights, and greeted them. He pulled his uniform coat in tight and made a gesture like it was cold outside. He said, "Ray-Ray, are you helping our guests here?"

The old guy was Ray-Ray, the owner of the tow truck company. Ray-Ray asked, "Guests? We don't know these people."

"Ray-Ray, this is Federal agent and local superstar, Lou Cosay. Are you playing nice?"

Ray-Ray said nothing.

Cosay said, "He was just about to help us."

"Good," Braaten said, and winked at Cosay. No one saw it but Widow.

Begrudgingly, Ray-Ray turned to Widow and asked, "What can I help you with?"

Widow thought about redirecting the guy to help Cosay. She was the actual NCIS agent, after all. But for the sake of time and avoiding long-winded explanations, he simply responded. He said, "We're looking for a blue Chevy Bolt. You towed it from *The Ranchman*?"

Ray-Ray said, "Yes. It's here. Meet me at the gate. I'll go around and unlock it." Then he waddled back inside the big door. Widow watched him through the window. He and the lady appeared to have a short argument. Widow figured they were married, and probably business partners. He was the face of the operation and she handled the back end. Small businesses are the American way.

Braaten walked to Cosay and hugged her. She seemed averse to it, but it was too late. His arms were already around her. He squeezed her once, backed away, but kept his hands on her biceps. He asked, "What're you doing here? I've not heard from you in like ten years and you text me out of the blue."

"Fifteen years," Cosay said. "And I need your help with this one thing. We're investigating a case."

"Oh?" Braaten said, and looked at Widow. "What kind of case? How come you didn't call our office? That's usually how it's done."

Cosay stood motionless. She weighed the options of telling him the truth or lying to him. She didn't know who to trust. And Mokani people don't trust cops automatically, she'd told Widow. So, he answered for her. He said, "We're investigating a missing person."

"Okay. That's serious business. We could've helped earlier. How come no one reached out to us?" Braaten asked.

Cosay smiled at him, lowered her voice to a whisper, and said, "You know, we just don't trust that sheriff. That's why I'm so glad you're running."

Braaten settled back on his feet and smiled at her. He said, "You might just be blowing smoke up my butt, little Lou Cosay, but it works."

Widow rolled his eyes again.

Cosay stepped away from Braaten for a moment, stepped to the cargo door of the Range Rover, popped it, and grabbed something from inside. She slid the object into her jacket, concealing it from view. She closed the cargo door, and rejoined Widow and Braaten.

A moment later, Ray-Ray appeared on the other side of the gate. He unlocked a padlock and shoved the gate all the way open, which was large enough to drive the tow trucks and their hauls through. He said, "Right this way." And led them down a row of cars and trucks. Some new. Some long-since abandoned.

Widow saw the Chevy Bolt as they rounded a corner. He pointed it out, and they headed toward it. Ray-Ray said, "If you're reckoning on getting inside it, I don't know how you'll accomplish that. I ain't got the keys. Only the owner will have those."

They stopped at the Chevy Bolt. Cosay glanced at Widow. He looked it over. He wished he'd memorized the plate he saw at the bar, but he hadn't. He turned to Ray-Ray, and asked, "This is the car from *The Ranchman* bar's parking lot?"

"I suppose," Ray-Ray said.

Cosay took out the object she had hidden inside her jacket. It was a Slim Jim tool. She went around to the driver's side of the car and started to work to open the door.

Widow thought Braaten would object, but he didn't. Widow knew Ray-Ray would object, and he did. He put a fatty finger in the air, and said, "Hold on a minute little missy! If there's damage to the car, the owner can sue me for it."

Braaten put a hand on Ray-Ray's shoulder, redirected and walked him away from Cosay while she attempted to break into the Chevy Bolt. Braaten gave him reassurances and complimented him on helping an important investigation, and so on. *It was professional-level ass kissing*, Widow thought. Braaten was a good diplomat and a good politician. He might get that Sheriff position. Out of the two choices, given Widow's short experience with both men, he'd choose Braaten. If he knew nothing else about either of them.

Cosay got the door open, and said, "Bingo. Got it."

Widow said, "Pop the hatch door. I'll check back here."

Cosay popped it and Widow opened it up and dug around. He found a first aid box, with a couple of flares, bandages, and a flashlight. There was a sleeping bag, and winter gear, and not much else. There was nothing to identify that this was Fray's rental car.

Widow came back out of the rear cargo space and looked at Cosay over the backseat. She said, "I got a tablet." She held up an electronic tablet in a pink case. "I see nothing else of interest. Except this." She held up an envelope with a long document inside that looked like divorce papers. "It's the car rental agreement. And Fray signed it."

The backseat was empty, but Cosay searched it anyway, leaving the tablet and the car rental agreement on the car's roof. Satisfied that she'd searched everything, she came back out of the car. She said, "That's it."

"At least now we have some proof that she was here and is definitely missing."

Cosay tried the tablet. She laid it across the Chevy's roof, and tapped the screen, and said, "Shit! Password protected. We need to get into this. There could be GPS. It could be attached to her phone."

"There could be a lot of clues in it. Her notes are probably in there or backed up in there. So, how can we get in?"

Cosay said nothing for a long minute, like she was thinking. Then she said, "Minot Air Force Base has got the 5th Security Forces Squadron. I've worked with them before. They got the right guys and the software. I bet they can bust into this in under an hour. And we can get some answers."

"Minot is an hour drive southwest, and that's just one way. You're looking at three hours minimum."

She looked at her watch, and said, "I better go now. I'll call ahead and make sure one of the right guys is there."

"Okay, let's go."

"Not you. I don't think I can get you in."

"You can get me on base."

Cosay said, "Sure, but not into their police department. You should stay here. I might need you here. Go back to the hotel. Get some rest. I'll call your room when I know something. I promise. I'm not going this alone. Not now."

"Okay."

CHAPTER 23

Cosay thanked Braaten for his help, and Ray-Ray for his. She left Widow there. Braaten agreed to give Widow a ride back to the resort.

The two men rode back in silence, which made Widow feel awkward, only he didn't know why. Halfway through the ride he broke the quiet. He said, "Saw your election signs. How's that going?"

Braaten stared out the windshield at the road, and said, "It's going okay. Not sure I can win, though."

"Why not?"

"Sheriff Vedely's got a famous family name."

"I never heard of it."

"It's famous around Sawyer County. His great-great-great-grand-father was one of the town's original founders."

"That's a lot of greats," Widow said.

"Not even sure if I got the right amount in there. Anyway, the name is known."

"What about Braaten?"

"I'm second generation here. My daddy moved here for the fishing and he used to work the oil fields in Canada," Braaten said, and turned the wheel so they could turn onto another road.

"Are you Canadian?"

"My family is. We're mixed up in both countries. What about you? What's your story?"

"My story isn't very interesting," Widow said. "Once upon a time I was somebody. Now, I'm nobody."

"What's your real name?"

Widow stared at him, and asked, "You checked up on me?"

Braaten said, "Well, I know it's not Dessen. I want to be Sheriff. I searched for a Jason Dessen, couldn't find one, at least not with a criminal record. And no offense, but a guy like you has got a record."

"Jack Widow is my real name."

"What're you doing with Lou?"

"I'm helping her with this missing persons case."

Braaten asked, "Why though?"

Widow didn't want to get into the whole rigmarole of running into Steslow and the medal ceremony and his insatiable need to right wrongs, so he lied, "I'm a private investigator. Our cases merged. I'm looking for the same person she is. We're just helping each other out."

"Private investigator?" Braaten asked, and glanced at Widow through a side-eye. "What state are you licensed in?"

Widow lied, "Washington."

Braaten said nothing. The sheriff's SUV went quiet again. Widow looked ahead, and recognized the next road they turned onto. The lake was to the north, and the resort was coming up on the left. A moment later, they'd turned into the resort, and Braaten pulled right up through the valet lane and into the drop-off and pick-up lane. There was no valet working. A sign posted by the curb said so. The off-season.

Braaten craned his head and stared at Widow. He said, "Can I give you some friendly advice?"

Widow turned back to him, and nodded.

"I'd go back and tell your client Sawyer Lake is a dead end. You should check out tomorrow and go somewhere else. Lou Cosay is a lot of trouble. Trouble you don't want, friend. It's only advice. I'm just saying that she's got a black mark on her, in this town," Braaten said, and turned back to the steering wheel.

Widow stayed quiet. He didn't know what to think of Braaten's so-called advice. He got out of the SUV and walked into the resort, never looking back at Braaten. But he heard Braaten pull away and take off.

Widow entered the resort and walked past the security guard from earlier. The old guy stared at him as he passed. The guard was on patrol, going out onto the exterior of the property.

Widow stopped at the front desk, and saw Aponi. She sat behind the desk in the back office, on a stool. She was alone, scrolling through her phone. The screen lit up her face. She saw him and jumped off the stool and pocketed the phone. She scrambled to the front desk, and took her post, like she was a sailor being busted by her CO.

She said, "Oh hi. Did you find out anything about Ms. Fray?"

Widow stopped in front of the counter and smiled at her. He said, "Nothing so far."

"What about my sister?"

"I'm working on it. Trust me."

Aponi smiled, and said, "I do. I'm glad you're here."

Widow looked down the hall and at the bar. He said, "So, it's pretty dead around here."

"Yeah, it's the…"

"Off-season. Yeah. I keep hearing that."

"It's true," she said, and she tapped on the computer's keyboard, waited, and read something on the screen. "Yep. We don't have any reservations for tonight. There's a wedding next week. But this coming weekend looks like a ghost town. Which is good for me. I can catch up on some stuff."

"Like what? Playing on your phone?"

"You caught me," Aponi said, and smiled. "It's a problem with my generation. I know. I've heard it a million times."

"What are you doing on there, anyway? Social media and all that?"

Aponi pulled her phone out of her pocket, leaned over the counter, and lined herself up close to him so he could see her phone. She cleared the lock screen. It resumed on the app she had been using. She showed it to him by swiping up on the screen. Widow watched the screen.

It showed various strangers from around the world doing short videos. Some danced. Some talked about real estate, others about dating online. There were countless videos of dogs and cats doing funny things.

"What the hell are we watching?"

"It's called *metronome*. It's an app for short videos. The algorithm knows what I like. It studies your viewing habits or something and then it shows you videos it thinks you'll enjoy."

Widow said, "This is what you're into?"

"There's not much else to do in this boring town. Plus, I can't do much else while I'm sitting here bored."

"Your boss lets you play on your phone?"

"As long as no customers are around, they don't mind. I got three different bosses."

Widow nodded, and asked, "Can you read books?"

"I could, but books are…," she said, and trailed off.

"Books are what? Boring?"

"They're for old people."

"Old people? I'm barely forty."

Aponi smiled, and said, "That's old now."

"Ouch."

"I'm sorry," she said, smiling and joking.

Widow said, "You really should give a book a try. You might like it. Certainly, it's better than wasting time on that app. You'll rot your brain doing that."

"I never read a book that interested me. They're all old, like text-books, or that stuff with dragons. I'm not really into all that."

Widow glanced at her phone's screen. Standby mode kicked in because the phone sensed inactivity from the user. Her lock screen came up. It was a picture of her sister, Lou, and that vicious-looking Catahoula Leopard dog from her farm. Only both Lou and the dog looked ten years younger. Lou smiled from ear-to-ear. *Happier times*, he thought.

Aponi would've been nine years old, and her brother would've been ten, at a year older than she was. He didn't mention the picture. He read the time off her lock screen as well. It was nearing nine-thirty in the evening. Minot was an hour southwest. Cosay said it would take the airmen in the 5th Security Forces Squadron less than an hour to crack Fray's tablet. They'd use some kind of software they had available to them. Widow wasn't a hacker. He didn't know what software they were going to use. And he was certain he wouldn't understand it if they explained it to him, even if they used small words.

"I better get to my room. I'm expecting some calls," Widow said, and turned to walk away.

"Are they about my sister?"

"Yep. I'm all over it. Stop worrying," he said, and made it halfway down the hall to the elevators.

Aponi shouted, "Hey!"

Widow stopped, and turned back.

Aponi fast-walked to him, carrying a circular metal can with a lid over it. It was decorated in tribal symbols. She said, "Later on I'm going to eat some frybread. Want to join me?"

"Frybread? What's that?"

Aponi popped the lid off the metal can, and held it under the can. Inside the can, there was aluminum foil bundled tight around something. She reached in and tore back a corner. An alluring, bread-like smell wafted out into the air. She held the can up towards him.

Widow peeked in and saw a flaky and fluffy round bread, like a fried pancake. It looked great. Suddenly, he realized how hungry he was. He sniffed the air, like a wild animal getting the scent of its prey. He said, "Wow! That smells good."

"It's so delicious. It's Mokani, but it's Navajo originally. I think."

"Did you bake it?" Widow asked, and reached in to tear off a sliver, without thinking. It was an instinctive move.

Aponi pulled the can back. "Not now!" she said, and closed the lid.

"Sorry. It just smells so good. I couldn't help myself," Widow said, and retracted his hand apologetically. He was just as surprised as she was.

"I baked with my mom when she was alive. She was much better than I am. My dad doesn't do any of that. But sometimes, I like to bake her recipes and let the smell linger in the air around the house. I think he likes it," Aponi said, and looked down briefly. "I'm going to eat it in like two hours. Maybe two and a half. Want to join me outside in my truck?"

"Outside? In this cold? Why not just eat it in here?"

"Cause the security guard will take his break at the same time and sit next to me in the break room. I gotta eat in the truck. But the heat works great. Please, join me? You'll be saving me."

"Okay. In two hours?"

"Yes," Aponi said, smiled, and turned to walk away. She called back, "I'll call your room."

"Sounds good. See ya later," Widow said, got on the elevator, and rode it up to his room.

In his room, Widow cranked the shower on to hot, and let it run to let the water heat. Then he undressed to his birthday suit, parking his boots by the door, leaving his socks rolled up and stuffed into one boot. He folded his jeans and left them on a table, next to his folded shirts, beanie, and underwear. He brushed his teeth over the bathroom sink. The shower steam fogged the mirror. He wiped one big streak across it, looked at himself, and spat the last of the toothpaste out of his mouth. He washed his toothbrush in the sink, and recapped it into itself.

Widow showered, going delicately around his groin where Cosay had kicked him. Which turned out to be unnecessary because it didn't hurt anymore. There was no swelling. There was no bruising. *Good as new*, he thought, relieved.

An hour later, he lay in bed, under the covers, dry and naked, rereading the same book he'd finished earlier in the day. He started at the beginning, thinking it would pass the time, and just kept going. Widow reread a lot of books over his life. There was something special about a book that can be read over and over again. It was like visiting an old friend. Widow thought of it as comfort reading. Instead of comfort food, he reread certain books. He read until he fell asleep.

CHAPTER 24

Widow napped for an hour and woke up from a dream about Lou and him, together on a tropical beach. It was all subconscious. Dreams are dreams. People can't help what they dream. However, he'd never tell her about the dream, for fear she would get offended and fight him in a round two match. And he never wanted to experience that again—not ever.

The dream was hot and steamy and best forgotten. Cosay had zero interest in Widow. At least, that's what he thought. Plus, Steslow had a thing for her. And Steslow had been a good friend to Widow over the years. That put Cosay in the no-touching zone. She was off limits. He figured the dream stemmed from her being a sort of forbidden fruit, like a cup of coffee after last call. It was best to leave it at that.

On the other hand, *All's fair in love and war*, as John Lyly said in some old boring book Widow had forgotten and didn't care to research. He didn't want to betray Steslow. Not because it was morally wrong. Cosay was a single woman, as far as he knew. And she and Steslow weren't dating, or courting, or anything beyond friendship. In reality, Cosay was fair game. But even if Widow ignored his loyalty to his friend, was Cosay interested? Probably not, he figured.

Widow purged the thoughts from his mind, and promised himself he wasn't going to step on his friendship with Steslow—end of story. And promises are meant to be kept.

Widow thought about Cosay's promise to kill the men responsible for her dead brother. *Will you help me?* she had asked him. Cosay had made a kill promise to her dead mother.

Widow could relate to Cosay's kill promise. He thought of his own dead mother. Someone had murdered her. And Widow did what he had to do. But he also remembered what his mother had said to him. On her deathbed, she'd said: *I raised you to do the right thing.* Was helping Cosay kill someone *the right thing*? It was a gray area. Widow had killed before. He'd be lying to himself if he claimed that part of his motivation wasn't dipped in vengeance for whatever crimes had been committed by the unlucky evil bastards that crossed his path.

The bedside lamp was the only light switched on in Widow's room. He rubbed his eyes, knocking the Blake Crouch book off his chest, where it had fallen as he'd dozed off to sleep. He sat up, grabbed the book, set it on the bedside table, and swiveled his legs off the bed, planting his feet on the floor. He got up, and stretched out long and hard, like a brown bear breaking from a winter-long hibernation.

Widow walked over to the window, and looked out over the end of the parking lot and the lake. His room didn't have a magnificent balcony like Fray's had. He glanced at the small digital clock window on his room's phone. He watched the time change from eleven-twenty-nine pm to eleven-thirty pm.

Aponi hadn't called his room about that frybread yet. Which was disappointing, because now he was pretty hungry and would take her up on the offer. He supposed she'd call when she was ready. Perhaps the hotel got busier than she thought it would.

Lou Cosay would've been at the Minot Air Base an hour ago. Certainly she would've called ahead about having one of the computer guys from 5th Security Forces Squadron meet her there, ready and alert. Widow figured that if she'd cracked Fray's password, then she would've called him by now.

He thought about Fray and her password. Suddenly he realized —feeling stupid for not thinking about it earlier—that Fray's producer probably had the password, or he'd have the same files. At the very least, he'd know more details about Fray.

New York City was Eastern Standard Time, making it one hour ahead of Sawyer Lake, or twelve-thirty am. Would there be anyone in the office who could help him? Almost certainly the answer was no. That didn't mean it wasn't worth a shot. There might've been an answering service for after-hours callers, like a doctor or a bail bondsman would have. Maybe they received sensitive news tips after hours, or from all parts of the world, which might be the kind of thing that required constant monitoring. The news media was all about getting the scoop early. Being the first to put it on air, or in print, was the name of the game. Sometimes this meant without even fact-checking correctly. In today's digital—all-consuming, all right now, all the time— world, getting the likes and the clicks were more important than accuracy. Clicks are king. What was that term Widow heard someone use once? *Clickbait*.

Widow wasn't going to discard the idea, thinking it was bad, not without knowing it was bad. So he picked up the phone and dialed the *Shedding Light* number from memory. It rang only once, which took him off-guard. The line paused. There was a second of dead air, and it rang again, with a different tone this time, like the line was programmed by computer to redirect after hours to another phone number. The phone rang twice more, and a woman answered. She was in hysterics, like she'd been crying all night.

"Hello?" she asked.

Widow wasn't expecting an answer. On the spot, he figured he'd tell a felonious white lie to see if he could get some answers. He said, "Ma'am, I'm sorry to call so late. I'm glad you picked up. My name is Jack Widow. I'm a federal agent with the NCIS. Is there any chance you could give me the number of your Executive Producer? I believe his name is Prawat?"

The woman on the line sobbed nearly uncontrollably, like she'd just received some terrible news. She could barely get the words out. They were garbled and broken apart by her sniffles, but she was understandable. She said, "This is Susie Prawat."

"Is this a bad time, Ms. Prawat?"

She paused for a lamenting beat, and said, "Yes. But it'll be a bad time for a long time. How can I help you?"

Confused, Widow asked, "Ma'am, maybe you should put your husband on? He's the one I need to speak with." He remembered Steslow told him that both Susie and Bret Prawat were cofounders and co-owners of *Shedding Light*, but Bret handled the workload full-time. Therefore, he would be in the know. Widow's best chance at cracking Fray's password, or getting what was on her tablet, would lie with him. Susie may not be able to help.

"This is his personal phone. Did you call the office? Because it redirects at night to this number. In case there's an important tip or news event. My husband worked too much. But he loved his job," she said disjointedly, and began crying openly, over the line.

She wasn't making sense. Widow figured he needed to coerce her to hand the phone to Bret, who would hopefully be more put-together. Widow figured they'd probably been just as worried about Fray as anyone else. Whenever dealing with someone in a frantic state, a tactic police used to shake them back to reality was to use keywords, something that overrode their delirium. Here, Widow used Fray's name. He asked, "Ma'am, can I speak with Mr. Prawat? It's urgent. It's about journalist Cassie Fray."

Susie Prawat paused for another sorrowful beat. Something Widow was unaware of really bothered her. He could hear pain in her voice, in her breathing. He could almost hear her tears. He felt bad for pushing her in this moment of whatever was going on with her personally. But he needed that password. She asked, "Who did you say you were?"

"Jack Widow. Naval Criminal Investigative Service."

"Naval?"

"Yes ma'am. It's like the FBI, but for cases involving the Navy, Marines, and Coast Guard."

"You're investigating Bret? Why?"

Now, Widow was confused. He said, "No, ma'am. I'm working on finding Cassie Fray. That's why I need to speak to your husband."

Susie Prawat said, "You can't speak to him, Agent Widow. My Bret's dead. He was murdered tonight. NYPD just dropped me off at our home, an hour ago. I'm still processing everything." She paused again. The lawyer side of her fought to take hold of her emotions. "I really shouldn't be talking to any federal agents right now. You should probably talk to the police. This is Bret's after-hours phone for work. I forgot to give it to them."

Bret Prawat was murdered? Stunned, Widow said, "I'm terribly sorry, ma'am."

"Thank you. Maybe I should get my daughter. She's in better shape to talk than I am."

"Actually, ma'am, this is time-sensitive, and no one else will know about Fray like you. I'm really sorry. But your answers could be crucial to our investigation."

Susie Prawat said nothing.

Widow said, "It's really important, Susie. Is that okay? Can you give me just a couple more minutes?"

"I guess so. Is Cassie in danger?"

Widow didn't want to answer truthfully, because truthfully, he suspected Fray was in danger, and it was grave. He said, "I don't want to give away details just yet. It's important to our investigation."

"Okay. How can I help?"

"I know it's hard, but I need to ask you about Bret's murder. Is that okay?"

"I'll try."

"Do the cops know what happened?"

Susie Prawat took a deep breath, fought back more tears, acted brave, and said, "He stayed late tonight, after everyone left. Some guy entered the office and killed him. We only rent one half of one floor of a commercial building. So, anyone could access the floor. The guy just walked right in through our door. He shot my Bret and robbed us."

Widow asked, "Do the police have any leads?"

"There's cameras on the entrance to the building. They stopped working, for some reason. I might sue the building's owners for that. I don't know yet. It's all so sudden. Nobody saw anything. Why would anyone do this? There's gotta be better places to rob."

"What was taken?"

"Bret's computers, and one of the other office computers. But they left his wallet, which had money in it. I think that's weird. The cops said nothing about it. Don't you think that's weird? It's like they were only after our computers."

"Does Cassie Fray have an office there?"

"She does. It's the second biggest, next to Bret's. She's our highest paid employee, except for the on-air talent. But she makes more than some of them. She's got a lot of awards and then there's her bestselling book. A private office was in her contract."

Widow asked, "Ma'am, I'm sorry to keep asking questions. But was anything of Cassie Fray's taken?"

"Her office was the second one ransacked. The killer took her desktop," Susie Prawat said, paused a beat. "Do you think this guy killed my husband over Cassie Fray?"

"I really can't comment. But you've been a big help. Thank you."

"Wait! Who did you say you were again? So I can tell the police. They'll want to connect with you. I'm sure."

"Don't worry about that. We'll contact them."

"Okay."

"Get some rest, ma'am. I'm sorry for your loss," Widow said, and hung the phone up. The conversation brought him back to the days when he was assigned to death notification, where he had to inform widowed women that their husbands weren't coming back to them alive. Back then, he'd been a freshly minted officer, right out of Annapolis.

Widow didn't put the phone back in its cradle. Instead, he called Cosay. The phone rang twice, and she answered it. He heard wind gusting in the background like she was driving fast.

"Widow?"

"It's me. I got something. I called Fray's producer, thinking maybe he could give us the password, or he knew something about what she had."

Cosay interrupted him, and said, "We already got into her tablet."

"Lou, they killed him."

"What?"

"Someone entered his office after hours and shot him. They also stole his and Fray's computers."

Cosay said nothing.

Widow said, "We should inform the NYPD and the FBI. This is getting serious. More people could die."

"I know. You're right. And we will. Soon. I promise."

Widow didn't push her. He knew she'd made a promise already that outweighed everything else. And he wasn't a cop anymore.

Cosay said, "The guys at Minot cracked Fray's password. I already showed you the police and crime scene reports from all over the world. What's new is she got a name. According to her notes, she linked the murders to a private paramilitary group called Gray Ghosts."

"Gray Ghosts? Sounds like something out of a bad TV show."

"That's the name of it. She hit a dead end with the company. Names for representatives are literally like ghosts. But that's as far as the public goes. I'm not the public. Omar dug a little and found the Gray Ghosts have Pentagon contracts."

"That's not surprising. The Pentagon loves to hire mercenaries to do black ops things for them so they can deny it later."

"Right, like Blackwater shit. According to some of Fray's research, Gray Ghosts have outside affiliations as well."

Widow asked, "You mean they have contracts for other countries?"

"Countries, warlords, dictators; they even got contracts with drug dealers. This is according to Fray. The Pentagon doesn't know this. If it's true."

"That's treason right there."

"Right. If we can prove it."

Fray must've gotten their attention. Hope she's still alive, Widow thought. He asked, "So who's behind them? Got any names?"

"Yes. The Gray Ghosts were founded by, operated by, and owned by a guy I went to high school with. I never knew him. His name is Vedely."

Suddenly, the numerous posters Widow'd seen all over Sawyer Lake flicked through his mind. Re-elect Sheriff Derrick Vedely. Some of them had his face on it, in his uniform. He smiled, but unlike Braaten, he didn't have those pearly whites like a car salesman's smile. Widow asked, "Sheriff Vedely?"

"Not him. His younger brother, Alton. He left Sawyer Lake before I did. He was an asshole when we were in school. And I didn't know him, just his reputation. Omar sent me his file. I looked over it. He joined the Marines like twenty years ago. Like you, he ended up in the SEALs, and after that a lot of his file's redacted. Also like you. Ever heard of him?"

"There are thousands of SEALs. We don't all know each other. What else?"

"After the SEALs, there's a lot more on him. It's all redacted. Except that he started Gray Ghosts."

"Anything else?"

"The Gray Ghosts also do a bunch of training of special forces overseas now. But get this. Some locations aren't redacted. So I compared them with Fray's composite of the undesirables with the targets painted on them and the police reports."

Widow said, "Let me guess? They line up?"

"Yes. Alton Vedely started Gray Ghosts. They sell their services all over the world. And to keep his men's skills sharp, they do terrible things."

Widow said, "Bad men do bad things.

"They practice their skills on real people."

"Undesirables."

Cosay said, "And Alton Vedely started it all in Sawyer Lake. They tricked my brother somehow, used him, and they hunted and killed him. And so many others."

Widow stayed quiet.

Tearfully, Cosay said, "Mika was one of their first victims."

"They're not going to get away with it. We won't let them."

Cosay said nothing.

Widow asked, "What about the sheriff? How much does he know? Is he involved?"

"We have to assume so."

"Okay. Come get me. We'll take care of it."

Cosay said, "I already left Minot. Headed your way now."

Widow disconnected the call, and hung the phone back into its cradle. He got up, got dressed, and stuffed his beanie into his back pocket. Then he pocketed his toothbrush, passport, bank card, and hotel room keycard, and walked out the door.

CHAPTER 25

Widow rode the elevator down to the ground level, got out, and walked the hallway to the exit. He froze at the front desk. There was no one there. No Aponi. No security guard. No one. He circled the counter to get a better view of the back office. Maybe Aponi was back there? He leaned against the counter, and glanced into the back office. There was no sign of anyone.

"Hello?" Widow called out.

No answer.

"Aponi?"

No response.

"I'll take some of that frybread?"

No reply.

He listened hard. There was nothing to hear but the whir of cooling fans on the computer, the hum of a heater vent high above, and the whistle of wind from outside the window glass.

Widow glanced around. There was no sign of security or Aponi or anyone else. Not anywhere. He was completely alone. There were security cameras up on the corners of the walls. He skirted around the counter to an opening and stepped behind it. A security monitor for the cameras was under the counter, on a shelf, out of view of the public.

Widow looked at the screen. But there was nothing to see, because the cameras were all disconnected or damaged. Or maybe there was an issue with the connection? All the camera feeds showed static. Which was odd, but Widow didn't know if they simply were offline, or going through a monthly reboot to the system, or if the owners were too cheap to run them during off-season. Or all of the above.

Widow glanced at the sign that informed guests to use the phone on the counter to call in case the attendant is away from the desk. But he didn't use it.

He glanced at the clock on the wall. It was getting close to midnight. Cosay was on her way. He wasn't sure what her ETA was. It could be close to an hour, or sooner. It depended on when she left Minot, and how fast she drove. Her Range Rover was equipped with blue lights embedded in the grille and in the rear lights. She could've been flooring it back. If she pulled into the parking lot, she might run into Aponi. Lou seemed adamant about keeping Aponi out of all this for now.

Widow figured he'd better head to the parking lot to wait. Aponi was probably sitting in her truck, on her break, and eating that frybread. She'd said she'd call his room when she went out there, so he could join her. Maybe she'd changed her mind? Or maybe she'd forgotten?

Widow walked out into a light snow, and pulled his coat together. He yanked out his beanie and pulled it over his head. Bright sodium lights up on poles lit his surroundings. The parking lot was quiet and empty. A handful of vehicles were parked in the lots. He presumed some of them were employees. Aponi's truck was one. She'd parked it in the back corner, under a light, and right at the edge of a concrete wall, with Sawyer Lake beyond.

Widow headed over towards her. He stepped off the curb and cut through the visitor parking lot and over to Aponi's truck. It faced away from him. Through the back window, he couldn't see anyone inside. But she had to be in there, because the headlights and rear lights were on. He saw the low white-blue lights from the cluster panel on the dash. They shone in the interior.

As he got halfway through the lot, he saw exhaust drifting from her tailpipe. The engine was on. It idled and hummed. Aponi's music blared from inside the vehicle.

Widow walked on a direct path up to the tailgate of the truck, then he skirted left until he was at a wide berth from where he started. He didn't want to scare her by coming up directly behind her. She'd probably not be looking at the rearview mirror, and wouldn't see him until he was knocking on her window.

From about twenty yards away, Widow saw tire tracks in the snow. He stopped and tracked them with his eyes. The tire tracks were for a big SUV or truck. They were recent because they hadn't been snowed over yet. The vehicle had entered the resort, swung around the valet area, bypassed guest parking, and driven into employee parking. At ten yards, Widow saw that the vehicle had stopped right behind Aponi's truck. By the time Widow stood in line with the truck's rear tire tracks, he saw two sets of footprints in the snow. The pattern looked like two people aggressively dancing in the snow.

At Aponi's driver's side window, he knew the footprints weren't two people dancing. It was two people struggling.

Widow reached her door. There was a snowy boot print on the door panel, like someone kicked the door shut. It looked like a man's size twelve shoe.

There was more. Aponi's frybread was thrown on the ground, metal can and all. The lid was off and flakes of bread were everywhere. Another one of those men's size twelve boot prints had stomped over half the bread.

Widow grabbed the handle and jerked the door open. Aponi's pop music boomed out into the quiet. Heat blasted from the air vents. Her purse rested on the passenger seat. And her phone was upside down in the footwell, like someone had ripped her from her seat, forcing her to drop the phone.

Widow popped back out from inside the truck. He left the door open and looked around. "Aponi?" he called out. But he knew it was no use. Someone had snatched her away. He ran along the tire tracks back out of the parking lot, onto the service drive, and out to the main road. The tire tracks went left and vanished into the darkness, toward a grove of trees and lush, expensive houses.

Widow turned, ran back up the service drive, and returned to Aponi's truck. He opened the door and climbed inside. He grabbed her phone and tried to dial Lou's number with it, but the phone was locked. All he could do was dial nine-one-one, which he was considering doing. He struggled with it. He didn't want to interfere with Lou's plans, but this was a missing nineteen-year-old girl. She was potentially taken, and potentially in danger. Plus, she was Lou's sister.

He could take Aponi's truck and follow the tire tracks in the snow. However, that was a long shot. They were already fading away in the snow near her truck.

Before he could decide, the decision was made for him. Blue lights flooded the trees and the entrance to the resort. They bounced off the snow and buildings, as a sheriff's SUV drove up the service drive.

Widow dropped Aponi's phone in her cup holder, killed the ignition, left the keys next to the phone, and hopped out of the truck. He stepped out five yards and waved his arms above his head, big and obvious, like an aircraft marshaller guiding a plane to a gate, only without the big orange marshalling wands.

The sheriff's SUV turned towards him and drove into the parking lot and pulled up in front of him. The driver hopped out and circled the truck's nose. It was Braaten. He stopped in front of his SUV, and said, "Hey, Widow. What's going on?"

"It's Aponi. Someone took her," Widow said, and explained how he came outside after finding no sign of her, and what he'd found. Then he showed Braaten the tire tracks and the footprints. Then, Widow asked, "Wait. Why're you here?"

"Someone dialed 911. A girl. She sounded in distress. Something happened, and the call dropped," Braaten said. "I didn't know it was Aponi. But we check every call like that."

Just then, another set of police lights illuminated the sky and the trees and the service drive. Another SUV barreled up the service drive, turned into the parking lot, and stopped on the other side of Widow, giving him serious déjà vu from all the times he'd been arrested or suspected in the past.

Widow at a crime scene, with no witnesses, and no one around but himself. Bad luck followed him. Trouble came after. The second sheriff's SUV was driven by Sheriff Vedely himself. Both Braaten and Widow saw him.

Widow's first thoughts were of what Lou found. Alton Vedely was behind Gray Ghosts. Was Sheriff Vedely compromised? Widow didn't know the answer. For now, he'd have to play along, but keep his guard up. He looked at Braaten, and asked, "Did you tell him anything? Does he know about Lou?"

Braaten said, "I didn't tell him yet. Lou's not even told me what's going on. We all got the call from the station. I can't help that. But you and Lou can't keep him in the dark anymore. Not if Aponi's been taken. Her life's more important than whatever Lou's up to."

Sheriff Vedely stepped out of the SUV, his hand on the butt of his gun. He walked up to the men and stared at Widow suspiciously, never breaking eye contact. Sheriff Vedely spoke, but his mustache concealed his lip movements. He asked, "Did you call us?"

Braaten said, "No. It was Aponi Cosay."

Sheriff Vedely asked, "What's the situation here? Where is she?"

Braaten said, "He thinks she's been abducted against her will."

"He does? Why's that? Did you see it happen?" Sheriff Vedely asked.

Braaten looked at Widow, and said, "Tell him."

Widow explained about coming down to the lobby and seeing no one there, the tracks, finding Aponi's truck running, her music blaring, and her phone abandoned inside. He explained the scuffle footprints in the snow, and showed them to Sheriff Vedely. He mentioned nothing of Cosay, or Fray, or the Gray Ghosts, or the Sheriff's brother. As far as Widow was concerned, this was an emergency. Information was need-to-know. And Sheriff Vedely didn't need to know, not everything. Not yet.

After Widow finished, Sheriff Vedely said, "Those tracks could be anything. They mean nothing, not conclusive."

Widow stared at him dumbfounded. He said, "I just told you Aponi is missing. I can show you which direction they went. If we leave now, we can follow them."

"Who's they?" Sheriff Vedely asked, staring at Widow with deep skepticism in his eyes.

"Are you not listening to me? Whoever took her!" Widow said.

Sheriff Vedely glanced at Braaten, who said, "I think he's telling the truth."

Sheriff Vedely said, "You would."

Widow repeated, "Vedely, are you listening to me? The snow is falling. If we leave now, we can track them. Every second we wait is another second that the tracks could be covered up."

Sheriff Vedely put a hand up to Widow, and said, "One step at a time. If Aponi was taken, like you said, then we'll find her."

"Like I said?" Widow said, shocked. "I'm not lying to you!"

Just then, two more deputies pulled up, lights flashing. They circled the parking lot, and parked in a way that cut Widow off from going anywhere on foot. The only way he was getting past them was if he spun around and dove into the lake and swam to Canada.

The other two deputies parked and hopped out of their SUVs. One of them was Deputy Atland. The other one, Widow had never seen before. None of them drew their firearms, but all of them kept their gun hands a second away from quick-drawing. *How fast were these country boys?* Widow wondered. He didn't want to find out. But if he was going to make a run for it, then this was his last chance.

While contemplating his chance to escape, Widow missed his chance to escape, because Sheriff Vedely drew his weapon after all. He raised it and pointed it at Widow's chest, and said, "Atland, cuff Mr. Dessen."

The unknown deputy drew his firearm and pointed it at Widow. Atland pulled out a pair of handcuffs, approached Widow, and said, "With pleasure."

Braaten didn't pull his gun. Instead, he said, "This is a mistake, Derrick. We should go look for Aponi."

"I'm still the sheriff, Henry. Do as I tell you. Take out your weapon, until we secure the suspect," Sheriff Vedely said. Braaten took his firearm out, and pointed it at Widow, but slightly off from his center mass, which Widow noticed.

Widow kept his hands free, and palms out for them to see. He kept himself as unthreatening as possible. He didn't want to give them a reason to shoot. Atland approached him with a grin on his face. He grabbed Widow by the forearm, cuffed his wrist, and tried to spin Widow around so he could cuff him from behind. Widow didn't budge, not an inch, not a hair.

Atland said, "Turn around!"

Widow turned around, and Atland cuffed him. Sheriff Vedely holstered his gun, and directed the others to do the same. They did. Sheriff Vedely said, "Stick him in your truck."

Atland jerked Widow back over to his SUV. Only Widow didn't budge again, not until Atland barked at him to walk. Widow walked. Atland opened the rear of his SUV, and guided Widow inside.

Widow shouted at Sheriff Vedely, "You're making a mistake! Aponi is in danger!" Atland slammed the door on him, muffling the last sentence.

Sheriff Vedely glanced at Braaten, gestured at the resort's entrance, and said, "Go inside and see if the girl is in there."

Braaten nodded and ran to the entrance to the resort, opened the door, and went inside.

Sheriff Vedely turned to the deputy Widow didn't know, and ordered him to follow the tracks Widow was talking about back out to the main road, and see which direction they headed. The unknown deputy headed back to his SUV. The Sheriff barked at him, "Not with your truck! You'll contaminate the tracks. Go on foot. Go!"

The deputy did as he was told and jogged down to the main street, staying off the tire tracks. Widow watched the guy until he was gone from sight.

Sheriff Vedely inspected the boot prints on the ground. Widow turned and watched him. The Sheriff sidestepped around them, like he was trying not to ruin them. He went to Aponi's truck, opened the driver's side door all the way, and peered in. He looked around at things for several seconds, before dipping back out. He backed away, shut the door, and stared at the footprints again. He scratched his head, and stuffed his hands into his coat. Widow glanced at the resort's entrance. Braaten came back out and jogged back toward them.

The Sheriff pulled a handkerchief out of his coat, knelt out of Widow's line of sight, and came back up with something. He held it with the handkerchief covering his hand, preventing his fingerprints from touching it.

At least he was doing something right, Widow thought.

Sheriff Vedely approached the hood of his SUV, and set the hand-kerchief and whatever he picked up onto the hood. He stepped out into the parking lot and put a hand on his hip, scratched his head again, and waited for Braaten.

Braaten reached him. Widow scooted his butt over against the door, slid down as best he could, and planted his ear on the window glass so he could hear what they were saying.

Braaten said, "Vedely, I think he's telling the truth. There's no one inside. No sign of Aponi."

Sheriff Vedely asked, "No sign of security?"

Braaten shook his head.

Sheriff Vedely asked, "Are we sure she even worked tonight?"

Braaten pointed at Aponi's truck, and said, "That's her truck. No doubt about it."

The Sheriff nodded, and said nothing. He just scratched his head again, like it was a bad habit.

The unknown deputy jogged back up the service drive from the exit side and over to the men. He stopped in front of Braaten and Vedely. Atland stayed off to the side, like he had nothing to add to the conversation, which he didn't.

The unknown deputy stopped and panted to catch his breath, like he had run little in years. Once he caught his breath, he pointed at the exit lane to the resort, then at the main road, and then in the direction of the wood hills and huge lakefront houses. He said, "There're tire tracks, boss. They head into Lake Hills."

Lake Hills must've been the name of the rich people area. That's what Widow called it. They were the areas where the houses were overpriced, gated, and secretive. Every small town with a pristine land feature—like a lake, a river, or mountains—has one. The super-rich like their privacy.

Sheriff Vedely glanced back at Widow. Braaten said, "He's telling the truth, Derrick. We should go now. We can still track her."

Vedely said nothing. He just continued to scratch his head and look around, like he was looking for an alternative option.

Widow hadn't thrown Vedely into the Gray Ghosts category, not yet. There's a big difference between a guy who's become inept from being sheriff for so long, and a straight up cold-blooded killer, like one of the Gray Ghosts, like the sheriff's brother.

Suddenly, Sheriff Vedely and his deputies all froze because another vehicle turned into the resort. It drove in slowly at first. Then it turned and sped over towards them. Blue lights flashed from the grille. It was Lou Cosay in her Range Rover. She drove straight over to them, put her Range Rover in park, and hopped out. The engine idled behind her. Her door stayed open. She marched straight to them.

Sheriff Vedely stared at her, like he was seeing someone from ancient history. He asked, "Lou Cosay?"

She pulled her badge out, and showed it to all of them, except for Braaten. She pointed at Widow, and said, "Get him out of there! Now!"

Atland hopped to it, like she was his new commanding officer. But Sheriff Vedely put a hand up, and said, "Hold it!" Atland froze halfway over to Widow. Sheriff Vedely snatched Lou's badge right out of her hand, and stared at it. Widow was surprised she didn't shoot him, or worse, fight him in hand-to-hand combat. Suddenly, Widow's groin ached, but it was phantom pains. Which he realized was his body warning him to stay on Cosay's good side.

Braaten stepped in between the Sheriff and Cosay. He put a hand on the badge, but didn't snatch it back for her. He said, "Derrick, it's real. She's a Fed."

Satisfied, Sheriff Vedely handed it back to her, and said, "Sorry, Lou. It took me off guard, is all."

"Let Widow go!" she said, like a pit bull.

Confused, Sheriff Vedely said, "Who?"

"Him!" she said, and pointed at Widow.

Sheriff Vedely slowly nodded, realizing that they didn't know his real name. Or Cosay didn't. Vedely didn't give the order to release Widow. So, Atland did nothing. He continued to stand there, waiting for Vedely to give the order.

Braaten stepped in first. He pushed past them, and walked to Widow, and opened the door. He showed Widow his handcuff key. Widow stepped out and spun around. Braaten unlocked the cuffs and turned back to the others. No one protested. Widow took the cuffs off and threw them at Atland, who caught them against his chest.

Cosay turned to Widow, walked over to him, and asked, "You okay?"

"Yeah."

"What's going on?" she asked.

Widow looked down at her, and said, "They took Aponi."

Unimaginable terror washed over Cosay's face as realization set in. She couldn't speak. Panic paralyzed her. A thousand fears invaded her mind all at once. It was happening all over again. Another family member had been taken by the Gray Ghosts. They were efficient, cold-blooded killers, and they had her little sister, the only sibling she had left.

Widow saw he was losing her to the terror. He reached out to her, grabbed her shoulders, and said, "It wasn't long ago. We can track them. But we gotta go now."

Cosay snapped out of it, and composed herself. She was as tough as they came. *No wonder they wanted to give her a medal*, Widow thought.

Cosay nodded, and turned to Vedely. She walked to him, looked him in the eye, and said, "We have to get my sister back!"

"I was just about to get on that. We were just looking over the scene," Sheriff Vedely explained.

Cosay wasn't having it. She said, "Skip it. Your brother took her."

"Alton?" Sheriff Vedely said. Genuine shock came across his face. "What the hell are you talking about? He's not even here. He's not been back to Sawyer Lake in years."

Cosay said, "Oh he's here. Or he's pulling the strings."

Widow said, "Listen to her, Sheriff."

Braaten said, "Derrick, something is going on. Listen to her."

Sheriff Vedely said, "I told you Alton isn't here!"

Widow asked, "Where is he?"

Sheriff Vedely said, "I don't know! He's got a house here, but he lives in Europe."

Cosay asked, "Where in Europe?"

"I don't know. Alton's got a few houses. Look, we're not close. I've not seen him in years," Sheriff Vedely said, and paused a sorrowful beat, like painful memories were creeping up on him. "Since our father died. I'm not even sure Alton's alive."

Widow asked, "He's got a few houses?"

Sheriff Vedely said, "He's done well for himself. So what? That doesn't mean he kidnapped your sister!"

Widow asked, "What do you think he does for a living?"

Sheriff Vedely said, "Investment banking."

Widow asked, "What does that mean?"

Sheriff Vedely said, "I don't know. Didn't go to college. Okay? I don't understand all that stuff. That's why he went off and did things with his life. And I stayed behind."

Cosay struggled to stay calm. She kept thinking about her sister. They were wasting time. But she needed answers, and Sheriff Vedely had them. She said, "Your brother isn't in investment banking. He owns Gray Ghosts."

Sheriff Vedely said, "No, he doesn't! He owns a company called The Týr Fund. It's his hedge fund. He started it years ago with his SEAL buddies."

Cosay said, "No, Derrick." She started to believe he knew nothing. Alton might've kept him in the dark. Which would make sense. Why would Alton tell his brother that he owned a multi-million dollar private military business, one that hunted and murdered real people as part of their training? And why leave his brother behind to be sheriff of Sawyer Lake? It was plausible.

Widow asked, "Hedge fund?"

Sheriff Vedely said, "Yes. Why?"

"Alton and his SEAL buddies run it alone?"

"Yeah." Sheriff Vedely said.

Widow said, "And it's called The Týr Fund?"

"Yes. So?" Sheriff Vedely said.

Widow said, "Sheriff, Týr is Norse. It's the name of the God of War."

Sheriff Vedely said, "So? That doesn't mean it's not legit. Lots of businesses use names like that."

Widow said, "A bunch of SEALs started a successful hedge fund together? With no outside help?"

"Yes! What's wrong with that?" Sheriff Vedely asked.

Widow said, "Nothing's wrong with it. I'm a SEAL. I know SEALs. A lot go on to be successful at business. SEALs are dangerous people. They're also honorable men. But the Wall Street world that you're thinking of requires a different kind of dangerous person. Honor has no place there. Plus, a bunch of SEALs together, running a successful hedge fund on their own? Not likely."

Cosay said, "Your brother isn't a hedge fund banker. He runs a private military company. They sell their services all over the world. I got the proof."

Vedely looked at Cosay. He looked like a man who had been living a lie, and just realized it. His bubble burst right before their eyes.

He glanced at Braaten, who shrugged. Vedely asked, "Like the Pentagon? That doesn't sound bad. Alton's a patriot."

Widow said, "Gray Ghosts aren't patriots. They're soldiers of fortune."

Vedely looked at him blankly. Cosay said, "Your brother's a mercenary."

Widow said, "They've killed people for money."

Cosay stepped away. She went to the Range Rover, stepped on the step bar, bent over the seat, and reached in. She came back out with that blue folder she'd shown Widow, with all the overseas police reports and crime photos. She went over to Vedely and handed it to him.

He opened it and stared in disbelief. She pieced it all together for him—Fray, why she was there, all of it. She left out her kill promise, and the part about her being here on her own, without NCIS support and approval. She told him that Widow was her partner in this investigation. He was undercover, trying to flush the Gray Ghosts out of the dark.

After she explained it, she said, "The Gray Ghosts practice their skills on innocent people. They've done it all over the world. And they started nearly seven years ago. Here, with my brother."

Vedely stared down at the tracks. Snow fell softly, like feathers falling from the sky. There were no tears in his eyes, but Vedely looked genuinely disturbed.

Cosay said, "Derrick, we have to go! My sister's life is on the line! I need your help!"

Vedely stared up at her, and spoke. His voice cracked. The words were slow and painful to get out. He said, "Okay. If he's here, he'll be at his house in Lake Hills. I'll take you." Vedely paused a beat. "If he's guilty of what you say, then we can arrest him."

Widow knew arresting him wasn't going to be good enough for Cosay. But she wasn't going to risk her sister's life over a promise. Tonight, they could arrest Alton Vedely for his crimes. Tomorrow, Cosay could figure out her next moves.

Widow and Cosay got in her Range Rover. The deputies got in their SUVs. And Vedely led the charge in his vehicle. Sirens were off. But blue lights flashed. They charged into Lake Hills, and to Alton Vedely's house.

Widow couldn't help but think they were headed into an ambush. He hoped he was wrong.

CHAPTER 26

At the fork, they followed the tracks northwest, along the lakeshore. The resort faded from view in Cosay's driver's side mirror. The water was on the left, and dense trees, winding driveways, and huge houses were on the right, sprawled out for many acres. Widow marveled at the affluent, hidden estates, the acreage, the hills, and the land as he rode with Cosay up into Lake Hills. They were the second to last vehicle in a convoy of flashing blue lights and reinforced SUVs. Five SUVs. Five heavy vehicles. The Range Rover weighed roughly seventy-five hundred pounds. But with the police package of reinforced steel it was closer to eight thousand. The sheriff's SUVs were probably the same. All of it combined totaled twenty tons of reinforced steel. Four armed police. One armed federal agent. And Widow.

Behind Cosay and Widow, Braaten pulled up the rear. Atland was third in line. The unknown deputy was second. And Vedely led the charge. They drove fast, skidding here and there, kicking up snow and dirt. Moonlight crept in through the clouds in the sky. Starlight gleamed behind that.

Widow felt that old rush, like right before closing a long investigation. It was the feeling of going in for the bad guys with all the legal I's dotted, T's crossed, and X's slashed. It was the takedown rush. It was that sensation of a job well done, of putting evil men behind bars, of justice done. They were about to slap handcuffs on Alton Vedely and his guys. That's if they were even there. And if Alton's brother, Sheriff Vedely, allowed it.

Widow glanced at Cosay. She was in the fight. Her senses were sharp. Her determination was focused. On the outside, she appeared cool, calm, and collected—a professional. Still, Widow wondered how she was dealing with it on the inside.

Widow spoke. He had to talk loud, like he was in the back of a Black Hawk helicopter trying to speak over the rotor noise. He asked, "How are you doing with this?"

"I want to get my sister back."

The Range Rover bucked and hopped over a hump in the road. So did all the other SUVs. But everyone stayed on track. Widow said, "What about what you said before?"

"What?"

"About killing them? About killing Vedely?"

Cosay glanced at Widow. She wasn't angry with him, or troubled that he asked the question. Her face was neutral. She was there, in the moment, doing what was needed. She said, "The only thing that matters is rescuing Aponi. If we get Alton and his guys in custody, then I'll have to live with it."

Silence fell briefly between them. Cosay smirked, and said, "Who knows? Maybe he'll do something stupid. Suspects get shot all the time for doing stupid things."

He asked, "Think Vedely is really in the dark about his brother?"

Cosay turned the wheel, taking the Range Rover around another bend. She said, "Not sure. I guess we'll find out." She paused ten seconds, and asked, "You think this is a trap?"

"I'd feel better if we were going in with DEVGRU."

"With what?"

"SEAL Team 6," he said, which was sort of true. SEAL Team 6 was dissolved in 1987, and renamed Naval Special Warfare Development Group, the classified-beyond-classified SEAL Ops team. Widow's home away from Unit Ten, back in the day. Dissolved or not, the name SEAL Team 6 stuck.

"Well, we don't have SEALs. We got what we got. And we can't wait for NCIS or the state police. It'll take them hours, if not days, to mobilize. Don't forget, civilians need warrants and due process."

"So do we. To an extent," Widow said. "But we got probable cause."

"Yeah, but we'd have to go up the chain for all that. Some bureaucrat, sitting in the middle tier, will want to go through the motions. Meanwhile, my sister could be dead and the Gray Ghosts could be in the wind. You heard what Sheriff Vedely said. His brother's got houses all over the world. And that's just what he knows," Cosay said.

Widow nodded. She was right. And really he knew all that already, but he had wanted to test her state of mind. Like dry firing a new firearm he found in the field, Widow needed to know Cosay was also reliable. He figured she was, but he believed in *trust, but verify*, when possible.

Widow said, "We should call Steslow."

"Why?"

"He should know what's happening. He's in touch with the Secretary of the Navy. They can send in the cavalry. We might need it."

Cosay said, "No. We can handle this. If we tell Reed, he won't wait. He'll call the Secretary, who will send in NCIS units. This whole thing will get out of my control. I'll miss my chance to kill Alton."

Widow said, "Things are already out of our control."

"Please, Widow. Let's wait. We'll call him the first sign of danger. I promise."

Another promise from Cosay, and Widow stayed quiet. He was on the fence. So, he just let it go, for now.

They drove through more scenic vistas on the left and beautiful properties on the right, until the road snaked into a single lane. At the end, their convoy came to an abrupt stop. Braaten tracked off to Cosay's side and stopped. Atland stayed in line, and so did the deputy whose name Widow didn't know.

Cosay said, "What now?" She stared forward.

Widow stayed quiet, and leaned right to see around the two SUVs in front of them, to get a look at why Sheriff Vedely stopped them. The strobing police lights, and the darkness, and the thick trees to the right made it impossible to tell.

A long, edgy moment passed. Cosay undid her seatbelt, jerked her hips up off her seat, and reached for her SIG Sauer P229R. She drew it and set it into the cup holder, butt up, so she could grab it quick.

Widow asked, "Can I have your other gun?"

Cosay glanced at him, then reached down, moved the cuff of her pants leg away and pulled out her backup SIG. She handed it to him. But he never got to take it because someone knocked hard on the passenger side window, next to Widow's head.

It was Sheriff Vedely. He shouted, "Roll down the window."

Cosay kept her backup SIG in her hand. Widow lowered his hand and faced Vedely. Cosay buzzed the window down. Sheriff Vedely said, "Don't give him that."

Cosay said, "He should be armed."

"No! You're a Fed, fine. I don't believe you about him," Sheriff Vedely said, and gestured for Cosay to follow him. "Get out. Come with me." And he walked away, like she was already behind him. Like it was a done deal.

Cosay shrugged at Widow, holstered both weapons, and slid out of the Range Rover. She walked up the line of vehicles from her side. Widow didn't wait. He got out on his side and walked up past the convoy, following Vedely. The other deputies joined them. They stopped out front of Vedely's SUV.

There was a huge iron gate blocking the entrance to the last driveway in Lake Hills. On both sides of the gate, there was a high brick wall. It wrapped around the front of the property and vanished into the trees on the east and stopped at rocky cliffs that dropped off into Sawyer Lake.

The wall and the gate were both impressive, but that's not what caught Widow's eye. It was the security cameras. He spotted the one over the gate, another on a tree, and four more hidden in the trees, beyond the first one.

Sheriff Vedely, his deputies, and Cosay huddled in front of his headlights. They argued for nearly ten minutes. It was Vedely's jurisdiction, but Cosay outranked him technically, although they weren't in the military.

Widow stayed close enough to hear them, but far enough away to be considered out of the huddle. He didn't want to irritate Vedely. He considered himself lucky to not be in handcuffs in the back of Atland's SUV anymore.

Sheriff Vedely pointed down at the road in front of the iron gates. Snow continued to fall, but the canopy from the tree overhang kept a lot of it from hitting the ground. Where the road met the mouth of this driveway, the snow was light. But there were visible tire tracks. That's what they stared at.

Widow maneuvered so he could see them too. He saw tracks that looked similar to the ones from the resort, the tracks left by whoever took Aponi. But there were multiple tire tracks. Some only had one line. *Motorcycles*, he thought. Billy's guys were here.

Sheriff Vedely said, "No one's supposed to be here. But as you can see, someone's here."

Cosay said, "It looks like multiple people are here."

Atland said, "Boss, shouldn't we call in the state police?"

The deputy that Widow didn't know said, "We need more guys."

Cosay said, "We can't wait! My sister's life is on the line!"

Sheriff Vedely waved her off, and said, "No outsiders! We're going in. We can handle this on our own."

Although Widow was on Cosay's side, he spoke up and said, "Things could get dicey. These guys could be better trained than you think. And they know we're coming."

Sheriff Vedely said, "They don't know yet."

And it dawned on Widow that he was the only one who saw all the cameras. Sheriff Vedely only saw the one camera above the gate, which was pointed downward so it could pick up visitors who stopped directly in front of the gate. That's why Sheriff Vedely stopped far enough away to be out of the line of sight.

Braaten asked, "How are we going to get in?"

Sheriff Vedely glanced at the gate, looked it up and down, and at the hinges. He said, "We'll ram through it."

Cosay stepped past the others, joined him, and Widow followed. She studied the gate as well, looking for weak points. Widow looked around, spotted the various cameras around the perimeter again. He didn't know if anyone was watching, or not. He was certain there were motion sensors. Therefore, whether anyone was watching, they were still being recorded. The video feed was being stored on an app or a server somewhere.

The others talked about what to do next. But Widow heard something. It was faint, like a muffled humming sound. He looked straight up into the sky above them. Sheriff Vedely argued with Braaten about how to go about getting in. Cosay joined in the discussion.

Widow interrupted them. He said, "Vedely, you got a flashlight?"

Sheriff Vedely said, "Of course. Why?"

Widow glanced at him, and pointed up, and said, "Shine it up there, seven o'clock from the moon."

Sheriff Vedely glanced up, found the moon, and looked where Widow was telling him to. They all did. Sheriff Vedely said, "Atland, shine your light up there."

Atland said, "Okay, boss." Then he took a MagLite off his belt and clicked it on and shone it at the right position. Everyone gasped in surprise, except Braaten and Widow.

Braaten asked, "What the hell is that?"

Widow closed one eye, so he could focus better on an object floating a hundred feet above them. He said, "Looks like an expensive spy drone. Probably has thermal vision."

Cosay stared at it, and asked, "That's been up there the whole time?"

Braaten said, "It could've been watching us since we got here."

Widow said, "It could've followed us from the resort."

Atland asked, "Is that possible? The resort is like five miles away."

"Of course it is. A ten thousand dollar drone's got quite a range on it. It could go five to ten miles," Widow said.

Sheriff Vedely glanced at it, and then back at the gate. He said, "Let's ram it. We gotta get in there."

Widow glanced at the camera over the gate, and said, "I don't think it'll be necessary."

Suddenly, the camera moved. The motors inside it whirred, letting out the slightest sound. But they heard it in the stillness. The camera rotated in its cradle until the lens pointed at them.

Something beyond the iron gate clicked, and a mechanical arm moved and pulled the gate wide open. They all stared at it, stunned. Sheriff Vedely was the most stunned. He said, "What the hell?"

Widow said, "Sheriff, I think we're going to need more firepower."

Sheriff Vedely turned to him, pointed at Cosay's vehicle, and said, "Get back inside. Keep your mouth shut, or I'll have Atland put you back in cuffs."

Widow stared at him, offended and frustrated. But he said nothing. They got back in their vehicles and followed Sheriff Vedely onto the property. The driveway was long. It looped through thick trees and a leafy canopy. The driveway was covered in leaves and light snow. Lights on spear-tipped stakes were on each side of the driveway, illuminating the path.

The trees ended abruptly. The trees used to go farther, but they'd been chopped down. It went from heavy tree cover to nothing but stumps to no trees at all. In the middle of the clearing was Vedely's house. It was all dark oak and gray stone.

Cosay said, "I never even knew this was here."

Widow said, "Of course not. You grew up on the reservation. This whole neighborhood was built away like this, so none of you would know it existed."

The house looked to be two stories, but could've been three. It could've had a basement. It was hard to gauge the square footage, but Widow guessed nine or ten thousand. To the left, there was a four-car garage. It was attached. There were two chimneys. One smoked, and one didn't.

Thirty feet in front of the house, an American flag flew high on a flagpole. The driveway ended in a paved circle. Part of it led to the garage and part led to the front door. A black Cadillac Escalade was parked near the porch. Two motorcycles and an old truck Widow hadn't seen before were parked near the garage. The motorcycles were the same ones from *The Ranchman* bar. Billy's guys were here. But no Billy, or at least, no Billy's truck.

They circled and parked. Braaten turned his SUV in such a way as to block any vehicles from going in or out of the driveway. They got out and met at the rear of Sheriff Vedely's SUV. He popped the cargo door open and handed out bulletproof vests and pump-action shotguns to everyone except Widow.

Widow said, "Give me a gun. You'll need my help."

Sheriff Vedely said, "No way! There's no proof that you're a cop."

Braaten said, "Cosay's armed."

Sheriff Vedely said, "She's a Fed. Widow is a nobody, a Nakai. He shouldn't even be here."

Braaten stared at him in confusion. He didn't know the word Nakai. Widow knew it.

Cosay said, "I vouch for Widow."

Sheriff Vedely turned to her, and said, "You probably shouldn't even be here. Your sister is potentially in there. If they took her."

Widow said, "Your brother is in there. And you're here."

"End of discussion. It's my show," Sheriff Vedely said, and pointed at Widow but looked at Cosay. "If he goes in, he's your responsibility. Now, let's go." Angrily, Sheriff Vedely turned and led the march to his brother's front door. The deputies followed.

Cosay looked at Widow, and shrugged. Widow said, "Stay frosty in there. If any of these guys blink, you shoot them first."

They fell in line behind the deputies. Widow took up the rear, unarmed and with no bulletproof vest. Sheriff Vedely and the deputies climbed the steps to the front porch. Widow stayed on the ground. Cosay stayed on the steps. The deputies flanked Sheriff Vedely. They kept the shotguns ready, but they didn't take up offensive positions like they were about to breach.

Sheriff Vedely reached a gloved hand up and knocked on the door. The door opened fast on the second knock. A bald man stood in the doorway. He didn't just stand in the doorway; he filled it. He looked more like a rock monster than a man. The guy's neck and shoulders were broad and thick. He wore all black—tactical pants, sweater, jacket, and boots. And his face was painted in black and green camo paint, like a commando about to embark on a night mission.

The deputies jumped back a foot as the bald man opened the door. Two of them raised their shotguns and aimed in the bald man's direction. But he was unarmed. He didn't raise his hands in surrender. He didn't flinch. Not a muscle moved. He stood there as if he were a tree planted in the floor.

Sheriff Vedely said, "Who the hell are you?"

The bald man didn't answer the question. Instead, he said, "Come in. Your brother is in the back." And he turned and disappeared into the house.

Sheriff Vedely turned back to his deputies, and motioned them to lower their shotguns. He said, "Wait for my signal. We don't know that the girl is here." Then he paused a beat, and said, "But stay on your toes."

Widow stayed quiet.

Cosay didn't. She said," Sheriff, this is insane. Let's rush them now! They have my sister!"

"We don't know that for sure. We don't even know that she was really taken. It's Widow saying that. This is my town, my jurisdiction. Now, if we see her and she's being held against her will, then we'll do something. Right now we're operating with suspicion. Once we know more, I promise you we will react," Sheriff Vedely said, and spun around and entered the house.

Atland, the other deputy, Braaten, and Cosay entered the house behind him. Widow stayed a step back. He glanced up at the sky. The drone hovered overhead, nearly silent. It buzzed on four rotors. It was painted black to match the night sky, and it virtually succeeded.

Widow stepped over the threshold. The drone vanished over the house the moment he did. He left the front door open behind him.

The interior of the house was something to behold. The foyer was large and grand. There was a mudroom to the right with boots and shoes in it. Widow noticed a pair of cowboy boots that looked like Billy's.

None of the others took off their shoes. And Widow wasn't about to do it either. After the foyer, huge floor-to-ceiling windows lined the exterior walls. Dark oak floors and ceilings made the place especially dark at night. Dim light showed the direction they were expected to walk. Sheriff Vedely led the way, like he'd been in the house a thousand times before.

Next they passed through a large, empty living room, and an enormous kitchen. After that, they entered a wide hallway. Dead animal heads and antlers were displayed as kill trophies throughout the house. There were a lot of open doors with nothing but darkness and shadows beyond the thresholds.

Finally, they ended up in a large study. A fire roared and crackled in a rock fireplace. There was a large mahogany desk in the room's corner. A dim light emitted from a desk lamp on it. The room had a bookcase and several leather armchairs.

The bald man stood at a thick glass slider at the far wall. He opened it and walked outside. Sheriff Vedely followed him, and the deputies followed him out. Cosay waited for Widow. She whispered, "I got a bad feeling."

"You and me both," Widow said.

"Should we turn back?"

Widow glanced behind him at the shadows and the darkness. He said, "I don't think we could if we wanted to. Let's see what happens. If Aponi's here, we'll get her back."

Cosay nodded and went out through the slider door. Widow followed. The bald man stood outside the slider and closed it behind them. He was now at their rear, which Widow didn't like. But he appeared to be unarmed.

They stepped out onto a massive rock terrace, which thrust out one floor over the backyard below. Tall outdoor heaters were placed around the terrace to heat it up during the winter months. Luxurious patio furniture was set around the terrace.

The back of the property was even better than the front. The view was breathtaking. There was a grand forest behind the property, to the north and east. Widow wasn't sure where Vedely's property line ended and the forest began. Beyond that were mountains. To the west was the lake. Widow glanced at it. Vedely's property had several hundred feet of lakefront. He saw a walking path, lit up by more of those spearhead lights on stakes. At the end of it, there was a pier. And at the end of that were a couple of expensive speedboats, docked in front of a boathouse.

The rock terrace was enormous. It faced west to north. A metal railing surrounded it. Below the terrace, the grounds were shrouded in darkness. Widow glanced over the edge, looking around the best he could from his position. He saw the tops of three tall wooden poles, like pillars that held nothing up. He couldn't understand their purpose. Below the lit-up peaks of the poles, Widow heard faint murmuring. It was low and nearly inaudible, but sounded almost like whimpering. Maybe it was a water feature, bubbling over?

There were only two men on the terrace other than Sheriff Vedely and his deputies, leaving Widow to wonder where Billy and his friends were. He'd seen the motorcycles out front.

The bald man walked around the sheriff and deputies, Cosay and Widow, and went to stand next to a man seated on a patio sofa. The seated man had a device in his hands. Part of the device lit up his face. It was his cellphone inserted into a gaming controller. He stared at the screen, and thumbed two sticks. And pressed a couple of buttons.

Sheriff Vedely said, "Alton?!"

The seated man put a finger up, gesturing for them to wait. He thumbed the controller and watched the screen. Suddenly, the drone came buzzing down to the terrace. It flew past him and landed on a tray on a table. The man put the controller aside and stood up.

The man said, "Hello, Brother."

Alton Vedely looked like his brother, only without the mustache. His hair was gray and thick. He was taller than Sheriff Vedely by two inches. He was thin, but muscular. And his stubbled face was painted the same as the bald man's. He also wore all black, a similar getup to the bald man's, like they were going on a night raid.

Alton Vedely walked over to his brother. He reached out like he wanted to hug him. Sheriff Vedely stood there frozen, like Alton was a ghost. Alton said, "Can I get a hug, dear brother?"

Sheriff Vedely asked, "How long have you been back?"

Alton lowered his hands, and said, "I've only been here for a little while. Sorry I didn't call. It's business." He stepped over to the railing, turned around to face all of them, and put his hands into his jacket pockets. He started to fish something out.

Atland and the unknown deputy raised their shotguns and pointed them at Alton. Braaten and Cosay stayed where they were, not moving, but constantly glancing around for anything to happen. Widow shuffled behind them and made his way to the edge of the terrace. He looked out over the railing. All he saw was darkness. But in the darkness, he saw movement. At the bottom of the wooden poles, he saw movement on the left one and nothing on the other two. *What was down there?* he wondered.

"Relax. I'm unarmed. We both are. I'm not getting a weapon, just this," Alton said, and pulled out a gold flip lighter and a cigar. Sheriff Vedely nodded to the deputies, and they lowered their shotguns. Alton lit his cigar, puffed it, and pocketed the lighter. "So, what can I help you with?"

Sheriff Vedely said, "I don't understand. You're here and don't tell me?"

"I apologized, Brother. Now, why're you here with your men, and," Alton said, glanced at Cosay, then at Widow, "these other folks?"

Widow wondered if Alton recognized Cosay. They'd grown up in the same town, but he didn't seem to recognize her, not like a guy who hasn't seen a classmate in two decades. Maybe he genuinely didn't remember her?

Sheriff Vedely teetered on the edge of emotion. His estranged brother was back in town, unannounced, and now he might have to arrest and interrogate him. Sheriff Vedely snapped out of it, and said, "Did you do this?"

Alton said, "Do what? I'm afraid you'll have to be specific?"

"What's Gray Ghosts?" Sheriff Vedely asked.

Alton glanced at him. There was a glimmer of happiness on his face, like he was proud of his brother for figuring it out. Alton said, "You're not supposed to know about that."

"What is it?" Sheriff Vedely asked.

"Gray Ghosts is my enterprise. We offer military solutions to the problems of foreign peoples, and sometimes to the Pentagon."

Sheriff Vedely asked, "Then it's true?"

"What's true?" Alton said.

"You murdered all those people?" Sheriff Vedely asked.

Alton said nothing. He just puffed on his cigar. Widow watched the bald man, who stared back at him. The bald man didn't flinch. He didn't look anywhere else. He stared into Widow, like when two grizzlies in the wild pass each other. The bald man's eyes said: *stay in your territory and I'll stay in mine.*

Alton said, "Brother, I implore you to stay out of it. My business is about national security. Yours is to police this community."

Sheriff Vedely stared at his brother, dumbfounded, shocked, and heartbroken. He said, "Father always loved you more. You know that. Don't you?"

Alton said nothing.

Cosay couldn't control herself anymore. She raised her shotgun, pointed it at Alton, and shouted, "Where's my sister?"

Atland and the unknown deputy stood there, unsure of what to do. They waited for orders from the sheriff. Braaten also stood by. Widow inched back. He was unarmed and didn't want to be in the crossfire, in case Alton had lied about being unarmed. Widow watched the bald man. He knew that if the bald man made a move, then he should make one too. But his move would be to crash back through the slider, find cover, and then procure a weapon. Looking at the slider, he wasn't sure he could even crack it. The glass was thick. He hoped not to find out.

Calmly, Alton puffed the cigar. He maintained eye contact with his brother. He said, "Take your guys, and just turn around. Go back to your job. Go back to your little life."

At first, Widow thought Sheriff Vedely would tell Cosay to put her gun down, but he didn't. He glanced back at her. At least, that's what Widow thought. But he wasn't glancing at her. He was looking away from his brother. There was a tear in one eye. Quickly, he took his hand off his shotgun and wiped the tear away, then put the hand back on the shotgun. He faced Alton, and said, "Did you do this?"

Alton said, "Walk away, Derrick."

Cosay shouted, "Did you take my sister?"

Sheriff Vedely said, "Answer her!"

Alton paused a slow, menacing beat, and asked, "You're really going to do this?"

"Where's Aponi?" Sheriff Vedely barked, and a second later, he teared up, and asked, "Did you kill all those people?"

Alton sighed, stepped away from the railing, and left the cigar to burn out on a table. He said, "Okay. Follow me. I wanna show you something." Alton glanced at the bald man, and then at Sheriff Vedely. "Come on, Harvey. Oh, this is Paul Harvey, one of my associates. This is my brother." They didn't shake hands. Harvey nodded at Sheriff Vedely, and that was all.

Alton walked to a set of heavy wooden stairs, and took them down to the grass in the backyard. Harvey followed, and the rest came down after. Widow stayed last.

At the bottom of the stairs, there was a walkway split by a fork. Two paths diverged. The left went down to the boathouse. Alton turned right. They walked for ten yards and found themselves in total darkness. Widow's eyes adjusted. They weren't far from the poles and the whimpering sounds, but that was drowned out by the murmuring and rustling that took place to their right.

Two more steps forward, and a new sound dominated their ears. It sounded like the crunching of plastic.

Alton said, "Light it up, please."

Suddenly, a firepit burst to life and flamed up. They stood at the back of the house on a lower patio area. The dirt from the back-yard edged up against a long square-shaped concrete slab. On the slab was a firepit, and several chairs and benches. Five men lounged around the fire, drinking beer. At least, two of them were. There were beers on tables next to everyone. Widow imme-diately recognized three of them. They were the two motorcycle guys and the skittish guy—Billy's men, without Billy.

The two motorcycle guys sat across from a fourth and fifth man. The skittish guy sat between the fourth and fifth guy.

The fourth and fifth men were new to Widow. He'd never seen them before in his life. But he recognized them, in the kind of way a cop in normal clothes stands out. They were like Alton Vedely and Harvey, in the same way that SEALs are like other SEALs. The fourth and fifth guys were average-sized men—average height, average weight. The only two notable things about them was that one was Asian, the other black, and both were dressed the same as Alton and Harvey—all black with the black and green camo face paint.

Widow stepped closer into his group. The ground under his feet crinkled again. He looked down and saw what it was in the fire-light. It was plastic, a lot of thick plastic. The entire back patio was covered in plastic, like it was being remodeled. Widow stared at it and traced it with his eyes all the way past the men to the back of Vedely's house. Against the back wall, he saw something else. There were stacks of paint cans. *Was Vedely having his house painted?* Widow speculated.

They were big cans, like the ones needed for house painting. Dry paintbrushes rested in an empty can. A few wet brushes hung to dry from a post. Some colors were marked on the can's labels. Widow squinted his eyes and saw two of the labels: one marked black and one marked red.

The deputies fanned out around the sheriff, like they were preparing for a firefight. Sheriff Vedely asked, "What's this?"

Widow looked back at the men on the sofas. Something was wrong with them. Something was wrong with Billy's men. The skittish guy acted different, unusual. He behaved out of character, like he was a totally different person. Widow gazed into his eyes, his expression. The skittish guy wasn't skittish. He was completely still and ghostly white. He stared at Widow. The black guy and the Asian guy couldn't see the skittish guy's face because they faced the motorcycle guys. The skittish guy mouthed something at Widow. But Widow couldn't understand what he was trying to say.

Alton Vedely answered, "These are some of my guys. They're the best of the best. Our services are sought all over the world. But being the best comes with a price. There's a key component to how we stay so good. It's our training. Do you know what sets us apart?"

Silence. His brother said nothing.

Alton Vedely continued, "We train in all areas of combat, making our services better than the competition."

Sheriff Vedely said, "What are you babbling about? I asked you a question! Did you kill people? Did you take Aponi?"

"Listen, Brother. I'm explaining it to you. My men are elite. I attribute that to their training. And their training includes shooting long-range and mid-range, close-quarters combat, knife work, tracking, rendition, abductions, hunting, killing, and intense interrogation tactics. Our clients hire us because we're the best. And to be the best, our simulations have to be real."

Sheriff Vedely asked, "Intense interrogation?"

Widow said, "He means torture."

Alton Vedely said, "Who is this guy? Who are you? You're not Jason Dessen. That's for sure."

Widow didn't respond.

Suddenly, more murmuring sounded from out in the darkness. Widow glanced in the murmuring's direction. There was something moving on the poles. At least, there was something on the left pole. He saw nothing on the other two. Then he saw a hump in the middle of the field. It was like a dark boulder. He wasn't sure what it was. A hedge? Maybe. He looked back at the skittish guy. He was still mouthing something.

Alton turned back to his brother. He said, "This is your last chance to walk away, Brother. Take it or leave it."

Sheriff Vedely replied, "I'm not leaving here until I get answers."

Widow looked at the skittish guy, who mouthed, "Help us." Widow turned back to the hedge and the poles. He focused on them, trying to see what they were.

Alton sighed, and said, "Lights."

Suddenly, bright lights clicked on below the middle and right poles in the dark part of the yard, washing over them. All the poles were aligned like the three crucifixes at Golgotha, where Jesus was crucified on the hill.

The far right post was empty. A rope dangled from it like someone had been tied up there. Dried blood stained the wood and the threads of the ropes.

A naked corpse hung from the middle post. Blood was caked all over various wounds on its chest. Huge black bruises patched over the body, like it'd been beaten. Its limbs were contorted and bones were broken. Several fingers and toes had been severed with gardening shears. The shears lay beneath its feet in the grass. The severed toes and fingers were piled in a heap next to the shears.

The broken bones. The severed digits. The blunt force trauma. None of these were the cause of death though. The cause of death was the four arrows in the chest. They were still there, poking out. There was blood on the shafts where they stuck out of the dead body.

Two of the arrows had landed directly inside of a fading yellow circle painted on the corpse's chest. The other two had landed off-center inside of red circles. The corpse was a naked woman. Her face was frozen in an expression of complete horror. She'd suffered immensely.

Cosay's eyes shot open wider, and she shouted, "It's Cassie!" She raised her shotgun, pointed it at Vedely. No one reacted. Vedely didn't flinch. He put up his finger again, tauntingly, mockingly, and said, "Wait for Aponi."

Cosay froze.

A third bright ground light clicked on, illuminating the far left post. A young girl dangled, secured to the post with ropes. She struggled against them, but couldn't move, couldn't speak. Her hands and feet were bound by the ropes. She was gagged. It was Aponi Cosay. She bucked and wiggled desperately, trying to free herself, but it was no good. She was there until someone took her down. Tears of fear welled up in her eyes. Her makeup ran. She looked terrified, but otherwise she appeared unharmed.

Cosay saw her sister, and racked the action on the shotgun in case there wasn't a shell in the chamber. There had been. It ejected out of a port on the side of the gun. She didn't care. She aimed it at Alton Vedely. The others drew their weapons and pointed them at Vedely and his men.

Vedely shouted at Cosay, "Shoot that gun and your sister dies!"

Cosay froze, unsure if he had a trick up his sleeve or if he was bluffing.

Sheriff Vedely raised his shotgun and pointed it at his brother. He shouted, "Release her, Alton! I swear to God, I'll shoot you!"

"I'm sorry to hear you say that, Brother," Alton Vedely said. A single tear welled in his eye. "You were my brother, my family. But Gray Ghosts are my family now." Alton Vedely sidestepped, glanced past his brother, and nodded, like he was signaling to someone.

A shotgun fired behind Sheriff Vedely. The sound boomed. The shot sprayed across Sheriff Vedely's back, neck, and the back of his head. His vest prevented some penetration at the top part of his back, but not at his neck and head. Blood sprayed from his neck, out so far it splattered across Cosay's face. It stunned her for a moment. Then she screamed, just one quick shriek. She spun around and raised her weapon at the shooter. Widow turned to look at the shooter. The deputies froze where they were, all but one—Braaten.

It was Braaten who had shot Sheriff Vedely in the back. In a quick arc, he jerked left, pumped the action, and pointed his shotgun at Cosay, who pointed hers at him. They stopped, deadlocked in a Mexican standoff. They yelled at each other in cop voices, using cop-trained words.

Time slowed down. Widow glanced at Alton Vedely. Vedely stood there, completely still, unfazed, a man at peace in the carnage. Widow glanced at Vedely's guys. Harvey pulled a handgun out of a planter. He raised it and aimed at Widow, but didn't fire. The fourth and fifth guys stood up, both armed with handguns, and both aimed them at the motorcycle guys. They weren't worried about the skittish guy, or Widow, or the deputies.

Widow wondered, *why?* But he found out a split-second later.

A loud gunshot boomed across the field, from the trees. Widow spun and stared at the location. It was high in the trees, as if from a deer stand. The shooter fired two more times. Both boomed over the field and over Cosay's and Braaten's yelling.

Widow recognized the report on the first shot. It came from a high-powered sniper rifle. The first bullet ripped through the deputy whose name Widow didn't know. The bulletproof vest was useless. The bullet cut through his left shoulder from the side and ripped through his right pectoral muscle, and slammed into the plastic and concrete. Plastic blew up into a small dusty cloud from the bullet impact. Red mist hung in the surrounding air. Blood sprayed across the plastic on the ground. And now Widow knew why it was there. Vedely wasn't remodeling. He expected blood—lots of it. The first deputy didn't scream or make a sound, because he was dead before he hit the plastic. The bullet must've been huge. It tore him nearly in half. The impact sent him off his feet. He was flung forward, like a rag doll. His head slammed into the plastic and the concrete beneath it. He hit so hard that if the bullet hadn't killed him, the head trauma from slamming into the ground would have.

The second bullet was a headshot. It tore through Atland's head, left to right like the first bullet. It entered his left ear, disintegrating it, and exited through his right ear, blowing the right side of his skull and face completely off. Brain and bone exploded out into the air and splattered across the plastic.

Atland's body cartwheeled, and splatted on the ground. Blood and brains oozed out of his head, like out of a piñata that's been cracked open. Both deputies were dead in seconds.

The third bullet was meant for Cosay. But Widow had dived for her at the sound of the first bullet. He slammed into her, knocking the shotgun clean from her hand. He pushed her to the ground and covered her body. He glanced back at Vedely, who looked displeased and shaken for the first time since Widow'd met him. Vedely spun and faced the shooter. He waved his hands up above his head, like he was signaling a ship offshore to come and rescue him from a deserted island.

Harvey pulled out a radio and spoke into it. He said, "Not the girl! No more!" And the shooting from the sniper stopped.

Cosay pushed Widow off her, scrambled to her feet, and drew her SIG Sauer P229R. She aimed it at Vedely. She nearly squeezed the trigger. But she knew once she did, the others would definitely kill her. No question. That was fine with her. She was willing to die to kill him. That question had been settled in her mind six-plus years ago, the day she made the kill promise to her dead mother. But she didn't squeeze the trigger. She froze because of a new question that entered her mind. If she shot Vedely, they would kill her, but they'd kill Widow too. Was she willing to sacrifice Widow for revenge? And what about Aponi?

Widow scrambled to his feet behind her. He didn't stop her. If she killed Vedely, he knew they were both dead. Still, he didn't stop her. He glanced around. Four guns pointed at him and Cosay—Harvey, the unnamed Gray Ghosts, and Braaten. And there was the sniper. Impasse. No way out. Widow raised his hands in surrender, something he usually didn't do. But he had no choice. It wasn't just his and Cosay's lives on the line. Aponi was there too.

Braaten kept his gun trained on Cosay, and stepped directly to her. He lined his shot up to blow her head clean off if he pulled the trigger.

Vedely turned to Cosay. He stared into her eyes. He walked toward her, toward the SIG. He stepped closer to the barrel. He said, "Go on! Shoot me! Avenge your brother!"

Cosay's face changed to the color of rage. She wanted to squeeze the trigger. She wanted to blow Vedely's head off, to watch him die. But she couldn't.

"I figure we're even. I killed your brother. And you killed mine. Oh, I know you didn't shoot him. I didn't shoot yours either. But I'm just as responsible as you are. If you had left it alone, that journalist over there," Vedely said, and pointed at Cassie Fray's corpse, "she'd be alive still. If you'd stayed out of it, my brother would still be an ignorant sheriff, unaware of my business. But you couldn't leave it alone. And I get it. Believe me. Every action we make has consequences. If I hadn't employed Billy Tabaaha, he'd never have convinced your little brother to take part in our hunt."

Billy Tabaaha? Cosay thought, realizing that Billy sold her brother out. He'd lured in Mika, and probably the others, to this maniac.

Vedely said, "I ordered the hunt. See, we hunted your brother at night. It was like this night. We set him loose, into those woods north of the lake. It's over fifty thousand acres of rugged forests. People don't go there much. It's untouched by man. It's a perfect killing ground. We told little Mika that if he made it to the Canadian border, then he could escape us. And we hunted him like an animal. He never made it."

Cosay's finger squeezed the trigger part of the way. Sweat ran down her brow. She wanted to pull it. She wanted to watch Vedely's head explode. But she couldn't.

Vedely said, "You shoot me. They'll kill your little sister."

Silence.

He said, "If you wonder whether we've raped her?"

The Gray Ghosts and Braaten chuckled around her. All of them pointed their guns at her and Widow.

Vedely said, "The answer is no. We haven't. However, my guys raped your reporter friend. Excuse me, podcaster friend. We raped her. We tortured her. And we shot her with arrows. The arrows were for target practice. My method of training them requires squeezing the life out of every opportunity. First, Billy and his idiots brought her to us, after they had some fun with her. Then, we tortured her for information. It's part of the training for the Gray Ghosts. Sometimes we get hired to get information from targets before we kill them. You'd be surprised how often our customers are government agencies. Especially America's."

Cosay stayed quiet. She continued aiming at him.

Vedely said, "Of course, we had to kill Billy. His incompetence put us into the light. Then we had to kill Ms. Fray's boss and recover her research. Now, I'm told you have some of it. But we'll get that from you."

Cosay said, "It's too late! You're exposed! I shared evidence with others—cops."

Vedely smiled, and said, "You mean those idiots in the Air Force? Don't worry about that. They got nothing. And you didn't share what you got with anyone. They'd have taken away your opportunity to find me. Nothing is more important to you than that. I can see that. It's written on your face. Your friend told us everything. I know about your little vendetta against us, against me. Well, here I am. Do it. Squeeze that trigger."

Cosay stared into Vedely's dark eyes. She wanted to shoot him.

Widow said, "Lou, you pull that trigger, we're all dead."

Braaten said, "Drop it, Lou."

Cosay glanced at Widow, and then Braaten. She shot Braaten a glance that sent chills down his spine. He had made her list.

Vedely said, "Enough of this. Curtis, light."

Suddenly, another ground light clicked on. It lit up the hedge-shaped object that Widow thought might be a boulder. It was ten yards in front of Aponi. But it wasn't a hedge or a boulder. It was a man, a sixth Gray Ghost. Like the others, he was average height and weight, with a muscular frame. He was also dressed in all black with the same camo face paint. He had a weapon. In an action that was so fast Widow nearly missed it, the sixth Gray Ghost wrenched one arm back like he was pulling something and aimed at Aponi. He held a compound hunting bow. He'd drawn the string and had an arrow in place. He aimed it at Aponi.

The sixth Gray Ghost called out, "Ready to fire!"

Vedely stared at Cosay, and said, "What do you think? Should I give the order? He might miss her."

Cosay broke eye contact with Vedely and glanced over her shoulder at her sister. Aponi wriggled and squirmed to get away, but she couldn't. Her skin turned a shade of sheer white.

Cosay immediately dropped her gun, and shot her hands up. "Okay! Okay!" she said. "I give up!"

Vedely smiled.

Braaten said, "She's got a backup gun too. It's in an ankle holster."

"Get it," Vedely said.

Braaten lowered his shotgun, approached Cosay, bent down, raised her pant leg and took the other SIG, and picked up the one she'd dropped. He glanced up at her. She spit on him, and said, "Traitor!"

Angrily, he wiped the spit off his face and stood up. He said, "Money goes a long way." He backed away, and threw both of her guns off into the darkness.

Harvey walked over to his boss and handed him the radio. Vedely clicked the talk button, spoke into it, and said, "Gordon, all's good. Get to the dock. We'll meet there."

Gordon was the fifth man, the sniper. He replied, "Got it."

Vedely handed the radio back to Harvey. Then he ordered Braaten to check Widow and Cosay for any more weapons. Braaten smiled, looked at Cosay, and said, "You get that freebie. You spit on me again and I'll do tenfold to your sister. I've been eyeballing her for a while now."

Cosay asked, "That was you harassing her the other night?"

"And you're the one who interrupted," he said, then he patted her down. And it was thorough. He checked everywhere. He inspected her curvy areas more thoroughly than the other areas. Cosay winced in disgust. Widow felt anger, but stayed calm.

Braaten moved on to Widow, checked him over, and pulled out his passport and toothbrush. He left everything else in Widow's pockets. He gave Vedely the toothbrush and passport. Vedely opened the passport, looked at it, and said, "Well, Mr. Jack Widow." He stared at the toothbrush. "Why do you carry a toothbrush?"

"He's a hobo," said Braaten.

Vedely nodded, tossed the toothbrush onto the plastic, looked over the passport, flipped the pages, and said, "You've been to a lot of places. More than me. I think. What's up with that? You travel a lot, hobo?"

Widow stayed quiet.

"Well, you're gonna like what I got planned for you, Widow. Both of you will."

CHAPTER 27

The Gray Ghosts left Braaten behind to babysit Aponi, with strict instructions not to touch her. Which he'd reluctantly follow because he knew that if he disobeyed Vedely, he'd end up on that empty post with a gut full of arrows. So Braaten stayed behind, drinking a beer on the terrace, overlooking Aponi. He sat with his feet up and the shotgun laid across his lap. He was above the carnage of his dead coworkers. Their corpses and body parts bled out across the plastic.

He wasn't sure what was in store for him. Since he'd helped murder his boss and the other deputies, his becoming sheriff was probably out the window. Maybe not. Vedely was skilled and connected and rich. Somehow, they'd brainstorm a plan to cover it up. And if not, then he'd leave the country. He'd vanish and go live on a beach in Mexico, or somewhere else. Vedely was paying him enough money to do anything he wanted. But what he wanted right then was Aponi. He'd been watching her from afar. And she looked so good. But he'd have to wait. For now.

* * *

Several miles out on the lake, the two speedboats stopped over the deepest part of the lake, as one of them had on Wednesday night. Vedely, Curtis, and the Asian guy rode in the first speedboat with Harvey at the wheel. Cosay was handcuffed behind her back and her ankles were duct-taped together. She hurt from being bounced around on the floor by them driving fast across the lake. Water had splashed across her body. Her clothes were wet and clingy. It soaked her hair. And she was terrified.

Gordon drove the other boat. The black guy sat in the passenger seat. Widow was handcuffed, along with Billy's men. A long chain linked them together, like a chain gang. A pile of cinderblocks lay next to them on the floor. Widow was linked to one end of the chain and the cinderblocks were at the other. He didn't want to think about what the cinderblocks were for.

Widow stayed quiet. But Billy's guys begged and pleaded so much that the black guy duct-taped their mouths shut. He left the tape off Widow. He commented how impressed he was at Widow's calm demeanor. Widow replied, "If I'm going to die tonight, then what's the point?"

The second speedboat had stopped five yards from the first. They drifted closer to each other, and the black guy tossed a line over to the first boat. Curtis caught it and reeled the boats close together.

Vedely climbed from the first over to the second. He stood in front of Widow and the others. Billy's guys were on their knees, still pleading for their lives. Which was pointless because of the duct tape and the kind of man they were dealing with.

Vedely barked an order at the black guy to stand the others up. He and Gordon hopped to it and got them on their feet. Only the skittish guy stayed curled up, like his mommy would come and save him. The black guy hauled him up and held him there.

Vedely stood in front of them, like he was giving a speech to his platoon. The bikers and the skittish guy feared for their lives. It was obvious to Vedely. But Widow stayed quiet. He didn't react. He didn't huff and puff about it, didn't plead. He simply stood there, awaiting his fate, like he accepted it.

Vedely stared at him. He asked, "Why aren't you afraid?"

Widow stared back at him, and said, "Afraid of what? Of you?"

"You don't think I'm to be feared?"

Widow said nothing.

Vedely said, "They're afraid."

"They should be. They're going to die."

"And you're not?"

Widow glanced over Vedely's shoulder at the first speedboat. Harvey, Curtis, and the Asian guy stared back at Widow. Their faces blended into the darkness. He saw only the whites of their eyes. He looked over at the black guy and Gordon. And then he looked back at Vedely, and said, "You're the ones who are going to die tonight."

Vedely belted out a laugh, and said, "Really? You're funny. I don't know who you are or anything about you. But you're different. You'd have made a good soldier, under my command. Too bad."

Widow stayed quiet, glanced at Cosay.

Vedely saw it, and said, "Don't worry about her. She'll get the same fate as her brother. Just so you know, she'll have a fighting chance, like her brother. We're going to hunt her. Don't worry. My men won't have guns. It'll be bows only. That will suit her. Don't you think? An Indian killed by bow and arrow is a fitting way to go. Of course, if we catch her, then she's fair game. Spoils of war, Widow. We'll have to practice some of our other methods on her, like we did with the podcaster. Does that make you angry?"

Vedely grabbed Widow's chin hard, and redirected Widow's gaze so he stared directly at Vedely.

Widow said, "Are you trying to talk me to death? You run your mouth too much."

The skittish guy chuckled. Vedely glanced at him, and he went quiet.

Vedely released Widow's chin, and asked, "Ever heard of drown-proofing?"

Widow knew exactly what it was, but he said nothing.

Vedely said, "It's a SEAL training technique. You've heard of the SEALs, I'm sure. What they do is, they throw you into a deep body of water with your hands and legs tied. And they train you to survive. But I'm not going to tell you how it works. That'd spoil the fun."

Widow glanced over his shoulder at Cosay. She'd wobbled over to the port side of the first speedboat, grabbed the gunwale, and hauled and shimmied herself up enough to see Widow. He shouted, "Stay alive! I'll come for you!"

Vedely looked back at Cosay, then at the black guy. He barked an order at him. He said, "Do it."

Widow inhaled and exhaled several times fast, like a man who'd just breathed oxygen for the first time in hours. It was a freediving technique that enabled freedivers to expand their lungs in order to hold significantly more oxygen.

The black guy and Gordon threaded past the row of prisoners, lifted the cinderblocks and threw them over the edge. They sank immediately. Widow inhaled one final time, taking in a huge amount of air. Then he held it. The chain clattered off the boat after the cinderblocks. It jerked the skittish guy first, followed by the two bikers, then Widow. The weight of the cinderblocks and the chain dragged them all down into the lake's dark depths.

CHAPTER 28

Vedely and the others watched over the sides of the boats with sadistic joy in their eyes. Cosay pushed herself up against the gunwale and looked down in terror. Widow's was the last face to peer up at them, before he sank into the darkness and vanished. The lake swallowed him up. Cosay felt her hopes dashed. Her heart sank. Her shoulders slumped, and she slid back down and fell onto the floor of the boat. Hopelessness consumed her. She was on her own.

After a long minute, thunder rumbled in the distance. Vedely stepped away from the edge of the boat. He glanced up at the sky. A bolt of lightning charged the horizon with a single flash. The night sky died back to blackness. Vedely looked at his watch, and said, "Okay boys. Let's get this show on the road. I'd like to avoid that weather."

Vedely walked across the second speedboat's deck and climbed back into the first boat. He turned back to the black guy and Gordon. He said, "You two stay here. Give it another five minutes. Make sure he doesn't come back up."

Gordon said, "You don't think he can do that?"

The black guy said, "No way will any of them survive."

A couple of tiny bubbles rose to the surface, breached it, and popped over the spot where Billy's men and Widow had sunk. Vedely glanced at them. He said, "Better make it ten. No! Fifteen minutes. Then join us. You know where."

Gordon glanced at the black guy. They both shrugged. Fifteen minutes was insane. They didn't want to miss any of the action. They wanted to go out on the hunt for Cosay. They all knew that the first one to catch her got first go at her. Unless they killed her with the arrows first. Either way, they didn't want to miss the fun.

But neither man protested. They stayed in the boat, and waited.

Vedely sat in the passenger chair next to Harvey, and ordered, "Let's go."

The first speedboat jumped and took off over the water like it was nothing.

* * *

They rode in the speedboat another couple of miles, until Vedely said, "Here. This is good."

Harvey nodded, and eased back on the throttle. The boat slowed. Harvey pulled it close to the shoreline and killed the engine. The Asian guy walked to the port edge and leapt off the boat into the shallow water. He grabbed the gunwale and pulled the boat through the water, closer to the shore. Then he walked up on shore. Curtis lifted a metal ramp the size and shape of a plank, and shoved it off the gunwale to the Asian guy. He grabbed it, and pulled and walked it up on dry land. He dropped it. It was a makeshift catwalk to the boat. Harvey stepped over Cosay to the stern, grabbed an anchor, and tossed it overboard. Vedely stepped on the ramp and crossed over to dry land. He carried the drone and the controller with him.

Harvey leaned over Cosay. He pulled out a large hunting knife. He held it up for her to see. The blade was stainless steel and razor-sharp. The blade glinted in the moonlight. Another lightning bolt fired across the sky to the north. The flash lit up Harvey's camo-painted face. He smiled sinisterly at Cosay. Then he reached down and slashed the duct tape around her ankles. She kicked at him, but he swatted her away and stuck the blade at her throat. He stared into her eyes, and said, "Quit, or I'll gut you now!"

She believed him. He was serious. He would do it. She stopped kicking. He sheathed the knife and grabbed her handcuffs, and hauled her to her feet. He spun her around and pushed her to the ramp. He forced her onto it, and said, "Walk!"

Cosay walked to the shore. Harvey followed close behind her. They stopped on shore. He kicked her legs from behind, forcing her to her knees. He said, "Stay!"

Vedely got the drone up and running. It launched into the air. He sent it off on a test run. It was programmed to zoom around for a square mile radius to map out the terrain and spot any forms of human life. The process was automated, but it took some time. He turned back to Cosay. She watched the other men as they came off the boat with four sets of compound hunting bows like the one Curtis had threatened to kill her sister with, and quivers of arrows. They were like the ones that killed Mika, more than six long years ago. And these were the men who murdered him. But what was she going to do?

Widow was dead. She had watched him go over the side, into the lake.

She had to stay alive. She had to fight, but she'd have to wait for her chance. If she ever got it.

Several minutes later, the drone reported back. Vedely said, "Looks all clear." He turned to Cosay. Harvey stood behind her, watching her. The Asian guy and Curtis flanked her. They all had compound bows. They stood around her, towering over her small frame. She glanced around at them. She was terrified. *Is this what Mika felt?* She asked herself.

Vedely said, "Get the glasses."

Harvey hopped to it and went to a crate on the boat. He opened it, and pulled out four sets of the same item. He returned and handed them out, saving one for himself. Each slipped one on over his head. Now they were all wearing high-tech night vision goggles.

It was then that Cosay realized she was going to die.

The Gray Ghosts huddled around her, breathing, but saying nothing. They were hyping themselves up in a sick and twisted way. It was ceremonial, ritualistic.

Finally, Vedely said, "Listen up, Lou. Here's the ground rules. We're going to uncuff you." He grabbed her cuffs and jerked them up, and stared at her watch. "Normally, we give an hour head start. That's what we gave your brother. However, I don't wanna get caught out here if it rains. Plus, I figure a resourceful sailor and NCIS agent like yourself doesn't need an hour. So, you got thirty minutes." Vedely glanced at Harvey and snapped his fingers. Harvey pulled the handcuff key out of his pocket and handed it to Vedely, who unlocked her cuffs. He tossed the cuffs and key back to Harvey, who pocketed them. Vedely said, "Once thirty minutes has passed, one of us is coming after you. After an hour, we all go. And here's a bonus, just for you."

Cosay lowered her hands to her sides. She wanted to punch Vedely. But that wouldn't do her any good. She just listened. But Vedely said something that changed her entire life.

He said, "Harvey's coming after you first. And you know why?"

Cosay stayed quiet.

Vedely said, "He's the one who killed your brother."

Harvey said nothing. He stood behind Cosay. She felt his breath on the back of her neck. She froze, and stared straight ahead.

Vedely sidestepped, pointed north, and said, "Tick tock. Get going."

Harvey shoved her hard. Cosay took two long steps forward and spun around. She stared at him. Harvey smiled, and waved at her, tauntingly. He had killed her brother. He was the one she'd promised to kill.

Cosay turned and ran north into the forest, not knowing that she ran the same trail her brother ran nearly seven years ago.

CHAPTER 29

The lake swallowed Widow's chain gang one by one. Each of them sank deeper and deeper. Widow sank with his hands out in front of him, like he was diving down. His handcuffs were the last on the chain, and he was cuffed in front, which caused him to be dragged down head first. He glanced behind him, up toward the surface. He saw the moonlight fade. And the stern lights on the second speedboat disappear above him. He sank deep, and he sank fast. He had no idea how deep the lake was. It could've been a hundred feet or a thousand. He hoped it was closer to a hundred.

He looked down and saw the bikers. He could hardly see the skittish guy beyond them. Their fast descent disturbed the water, causing it to get murky. The bikers' frantic struggles to free themselves bubbled the water. Widow burst through the cloud of bubbles as he descended. They sank and sank. It felt like forever.

Finally, the cinderblocks landed on something. He used his hands to fan his way out to the side. He looked down. The blocks had landed on the hull of an upside-down, sunken boat. That was his best guess, because it was hard to see exactly. But he saw that beyond the boat there was more darkness, making him afraid that the lake went deeper. And he didn't want to sink deeper.

Widow pulled on the chain and forced his feet downward. He adjusted himself so that his feet were beneath him. He felt the closest biker panicking and thrashing around wildly, desperately. He was running out of air. They all were.

Widow looked around. He tried to stay calm, keeping his movements slow and controlled. He needed to keep his energy consumption low. He was a trained SEAL. Widow wasn't a record holder in holding his breath, but he knew he could hold it a lot longer. The Navy trained SEALs to hold their breath for two to three minutes. But Widow knew guys who could go six and seven minutes. He had read about a freediver who held his for twenty-five minutes back in 2021. And that diver was a fifty-six-year-old man.

Widow wasn't going to get to twenty-five minutes, not even close. But he figured maybe he could get five or six, if he had to. Maybe. He was sure he could do three minutes. Hopefully he wouldn't need to find out what his limit was.

He looked at his handcuffs. They were standard police-issue. It would've been great if he had a key. But he didn't. He looked around. Maybe there was something in the wreckage of the boat below him. Or maybe there was something useful in one of the pockets of his three drowning companions. He had to check. It was probably best to wait for each of them to drown first. But the clock was ticking. So, he let his legs float back up and he grabbed the chain and began pulling himself down the line.

Widow stretched one hand in front of the other as far as he could. The handcuffs limited his reach. But he kept going. Slack from the chain increased as he went deeper. He pulled and towed himself downward, like climbing a rope, only in reverse.

He got to the first biker. The guy thrashed and flailed. He was drowning. He turned blue. Widow waited. But he didn't have to wait long. The guy drowned in seconds. His eyes were wide open. His mouth was wide open. The life inside him was gone just like that. His corpse floated to the end of the chain.

Widow grabbed on to the dead biker and pulled himself down until he was behind the corpse. Then he began searching the guy's pockets. He found nothing but pocket lint and cash. He had to move on to the next guy.

Widow pulled himself farther down the chain. It was harder, because now he was hauling himself and the dead biker. He kicked his feet behind him to keep them both from floating back up. He grabbed the chain tight, keeping the slack behind his grip. If he slipped, he'd float back up and have to start completely over.

Suddenly, something changed. The water turned darker. It was blood. The blood drifted into his eyes and across his face. He turned his head to the side to avoid it. He kept pulling and swimming downward. He got through the blood and saw what it was from.

The second biker had stashed a switchblade in his boot. The boot floated past Widow slowly, like driftwood. The second biker had sawed off his own thumb. It also floated away. *That's an idea*, Widow thought.

The biker saw Widow coming at him. He had one free, thumbless hand. He switched the knife to it and swiped at Widow.

Widow nearly released his grip on the chain, which would've sent him floating back to the top of the chain gang. Which he couldn't let happen. He couldn't afford to waste the time to get back down.

The biker swiped again. The darkness and the cloud of blood made it hard to see. Widow barely dodged the knife. *How was he holding it?* Widow wondered. The guy had no thumb. But then he saw how. The biker held the knife in a clenched fist, between his index and middle fingers.

The biker stabbed, but Widow kicked and darted to the side, avoiding the knife again. The biker came in with another slash. Widow blocked it, grabbed the biker's arm and heaved himself downward. He propelled down until he was even with the second biker, towing the dead biker behind him. The dead biker's head came close to the second biker. He stared at his friend in horror. He screamed under the water, nearly releasing his knife.

Widow scrambled behind the second biker, dropped the slack in the chain, and wrapped it around the second biker's neck and pulled. He pulled as hard as he could. The chain looped around the biker's neck like a hangman's noose.

Widow kicked his feet down, planted a knee in the biker's back, and strangled him with the chain. The guy thrashed. He slashed at the darkness in front of him with the knife. Widow didn't know why at first. Then he realized the biker's brain was out of oxygen. His vision was not good. He had seen his biker friend and thought it was Widow.

The first dead biker floated out in front of the second biker. The second one slashed at the dead one two more times, but the attacks were slow. His energy was fading. Finally, the second one died.

Widow released him and grabbed the switchblade. The blade wasn't small enough to pick the lock on the handcuff, but it might come in handy. He put it his mouth, gripping the blade with his teeth. He checked the second dead biker's pockets. Nothing. Then he swam farther down, pulling the two dead bikers behind him. He grabbed the chain to help pull him down. The dead bikers behind him were heavy. His arms ached from the effort. But he kept going.

Widow pulled himself and the two dead bikers all the way to the bottom of the chain gang. He stopped above the skittish guy, the last one on the chain.

The skittish guy had turned blue, but was still alive. Sheer terror shone through his eyes. He looked like he had seen a ghost. He was more scared than anyone Widow had ever seen before. It wasn't because of Widow. And it wasn't because he was about to drown.

The skittish guy looked at Widow, and then downward at a twenty-five degree angle below him. Widow followed his gaze.

Floating less than ten feet from them, Widow saw why the skittish guy was so terrified. He had seen a ghost, after all. Suspended and floating from a different chain and a different pile of cinderblocks was another dead body.

The corpse wore a familiar leather cowboy jacket with fringe and beads. It wore the same bolo tie Widow had seen on Wednesday afternoon. It was Billy. He was dead. His eyes were wide open. A look of utter terror stretched across his face. His mouth hung open. A fish swam out of it. His nose was all bandaged up and stapled. His tan skin was pale white.

Widow stared at Billy. He looked at Billy's broken nose, at the bandages and staples, and he knew how he was going to free himself.

Widow glanced back at the skittish guy. But the skittish guy didn't look back at Widow, not with life in his eyes. He was dead. He'd taken his last breath after seeing his boss dead in the water.

Widow closed the switchblade, pocketed it, and heaved the chain and the dead bodies behind him. He kicked as hard as he could. It was slow going, but he was moving. He swam and kicked until he was at Billy. He grabbed Billy's chain with one hand, holding the chain with the three dead guys with his other hand. When he got a good grip on Billy's chain, he released his own chain. The slack shot back and the corpses floated back up. They pulled at him, but he held tight to Billy's chain.

Once his grip was secure, Widow used one hand to hold himself in place, and the other to rip a staple out of Billy's nose. The skin was mushy and pruned. Parts of Billy's flesh came right off and floated into the water. Widow yanked out two staples. He only needed one, but he took two in case he broke one. He inspected one. He squeezed it, to make sure it would bend. Satisfied, Widow released Billy, and clenched a fist around the staples like his life depended on it. Which it did.

The dead bikers and skittish guy snapped him away from Billy. He floated back up faster than he'd climbed down. Widow whipped up to the limit of the chain and floated there. Four dead people stayed below him.

Widow kicked, and flapped his empty hand. Then he stabilized himself. He opened his other hand. He'd lost one of the staples on the way back up. *Shit*, he thought. But it was fine. It just meant that this one had to work.

Widow grabbed the staple with both hands, and squeezed it on both ends. It was hard, not because he wasn't strong, but because he was exhausted from the effort it took to get the staples. He closed his eyes and squeezed with all his might. Then he felt it. The staple bent. He opened his eyes. He bent the staple into a jagged but straight enough line.

Widow stuck one end into the handcuff keyhole. He felt his lungs starting to ache. He'd spent a lot of energy to get the staple. And now it had to work. He had no options left.

Widow jostled the improvised lock pick around for a long, long time. He was running out of air. Finally, pay dirt! The lock clicked. And one of his hands came free. He almost dropped the staple in his excitement. He took it and picked the other cuff's lock until it clicked, releasing him.

Desperate for air, Widow swam as hard and fast as he knew how up to the surface. He kicked and paddled. His lungs ached. His muscles felt like they were on fire. He swam for what felt like an eternity. Then he saw it. Moonlight. And stern lights from the second speedboat.

Rejuvenated, Widow kicked harder. Finally, he broke the surface and took a deep, deep breath of air.

* * *

THE BLACK GUY'S name was Roberts. He and Gordon sat on the second speedboat sharing a marijuana cigarette and chatting casually, like drowning four guys in the lake was just another day at the office. They talked loud, careless about who might hear them, because they were out on Sawyer Lake at night, without a care in the world. No one was around. Or were they?

Suddenly, Roberts and Gordon froze. They both heard the same noise. It wasn't loud, but it was obvious. It sounded like splashing, like someone crashing through the water's surface.

Roberts said, "Hey man. You hear that?"

Gordon stood up, and said, "It came from the stern, starboard side." Roberts stood up, took a puff off the joint, and handed it to Gordon. Adrenaline spiked through their veins, swiftly, like their brains kicked into high alert. The splashing sound startled them. It came from the spot on the water where Widow had gone over the edge with the others.

The two Gray Ghosts scrambled to the edge of the boat and stared at the water. It was dark. Gordon took a puff off the joint and kept it in his mouth, holding it with his lips. Then he grabbed a flashlight, clicked it on, and shone it on the spot where they heard the splash. Water rippled and waved, like someone, or something, had just breached the surface and then dove back down.

Water bubbles gurgled and popped in the flashlight's beam. The two men stared under the surface, trying to see if there was someone there. But the water was too dark. The flashlight beam penetrated, but only a few feet down.

Something moved in the same spot. They both saw it. More water bubbled. Roberts pulled his gun, aimed it at the spot. Then something surfaced. It was a cowboy boot, floating and bobbing on the water.

Gordon said, "It's just a boot, man." He retracted the flashlight and clicked off the beam. Just as he did, Roberts saw something large and long. It swam fast under the surface toward the boat. He saw it for only a split-second, and then Gordon turned the flashlight off. Roberts said, "Wait! There's something down there. I saw it."

After another puff from the joint, Gordon said, "Nah. Your mind is playing tricks on you."

Roberts said, "Turn the light back on! I'm telling you I saw something big!"

Gordon clicked the flashlight back on, walked to the edge, and stopped next to Roberts. Roberts aimed his gun into the water. He leaned closer, trying to see. Something moved under the surface. It was just a flash, but they both saw it.

With the joint hanging out of his mouth, Gordon said, "What was that?"

Roberts leaned closer to the water. He was halfway over the side of the boat. His arm held the gun outstretched to the water. His finger was on the trigger. He said, "Where did it go?"

Suddenly, two hands crashed through the surface of the water just beneath them. The first hand clamped down on Robert's wrist, just above the gun, and jolted it to the side. Roberts pulled the trigger. The gun fired wildly into the water. The second hand burst through the water holding something. It was a switchblade. It glinted in the moonlight, but only for a fraction of a second.

Gordon went for his gun, but fumbled the flashlight, missing what happened next. But what happened was Widow stabbed Roberts in the neck, and yanked Roberts' arm back down with him.

Widow pulled the Gray Ghost under the water. He twisted the knife as he did. And stared into Roberts' eyes. Panic and terror raced across Roberts' face.

Widow released the switchblade, wrestled the gun away, and ducked under Roberts' dying body. Gordon got his gun out, and redirected the flashlight's beam back to the water. He saw big ripples from the commotion. He saw a blurry figure under the surface. It looked like two men. One was thrashing about. The joint dropped from his mouth and landed on the deck.

Gordon aimed his gun at the two forms in the water. He paused, because he didn't want to hit his friend. Which was which?

Widow was under the surface of the water, and below Roberts. Roberts struggled to pull the knife out of his neck. He gripped it with both hands and jerked it out. Blood oozed out and floated around his head.

Gordon couldn't make out which guy was which and now the water was filled with blood. He took his chances. He fired blindly at both forms. The bullets cut through the water and shot into Roberts' back.

Gordon stopped firing, and leaned over the side to survey what he'd hit.

Widow stayed beneath Roberts, using his body for cover until the shooting stopped. Gordon leaned over the boat and stared down at him. Widow raised the dying Gray Ghost's gun and returned fire. He shot at Gordon twice. Bang! Bang!

The first shot missed completely. It was off target by inches. But the second one blew Gordon's brains out the back of his head. The guy's head bounced up from the impact. Blood and brains exploded up into the air. And that red mist burst around his head. Then the guy's dead body slumped forward, and hung over the boat's gunwale.

Widow swam to Roberts, grabbed the switchblade, and yanked it out of Roberts' hands. He glanced at the guy's face once. Roberts' eyes were wide open, and he wasn't moving. He was also dead.

Widow climbed into the boat, past the other dead one. He dropped onto his back and stared up at the sky and just laid there a long minute, catching his breath. He was exhausted. His body ached. He just breathed.

After several minutes, Widow got up. He was wet and cold, and shivering. His clothes were soaked, making it far worse. He stripped down to his birthday suit and searched the boat. He found several items of interest, including two compound bows with arrows.

He pulled Gordon's body up just to check his clothing tags for sizes. Nothing would fit him. He glanced at Roberts' floating corpse. Roberts was bigger than Gordon, but his clothes still wouldn't fit Widow. It wouldn't matter anyway, because Roberts' clothes were all wet.

Widow found a marijuana cigarette, and was tempted to light it up. He'd earned it after all he'd been through. However, he hadn't smoked that many joints in his life. And most of those had been while undercover. When maintaining his cover, an undercover operative can't just decline the offer to hit a joint. And there were a few times, in his youth, when he'd smoked. Once he did it to impress a girl.

However, he wasn't interested in it at this age. Plus, there was a significant danger. How would he know it wasn't laced with something much worse? So he tossed it overboard. He took Gordon's gun, which was the same as Roberts' but it was dry. He ejected the magazine from the wet one and tossed it onto the deck. He counted the remaining bullets, and set the extra magazine and dry gun down on the passenger seat. He found a lighter in Gordon's pocket, and a cellphone. And nothing else of interest.

Widow found a couple of water canteens. One was short. It was only sixteen ounces. He unscrewed the lid, checked it, and it was empty. He found a gas can filled with extra gas. He poured some into the canteen, along with some stuffing he cut out of the passenger seat with the switchblade. Then he used the lighter and lit a fire inside the canteen. He set it in a cup holder to keep it stable when the boat rocked on the water. It didn't rock that much, but he didn't want the canteen to spill over. He stayed there for a while, drying off and warming up next to the small fire.

Once his adrenaline slowed, the cold hit him like a punch in the gut. He warmed near the fire longer than he wanted to. But it was necessary.

After several more minutes, he felt okay. His body temperature had risen closer to normal. And he stopped shivering. He took out the cellphone. It was passcoded, but had facial recognition turned on to unlock it. He took it over to Gordon's corpse, raised the guy's head out of the water, faced the phone to it, and unlocked it. Since there was a bullet hole in the front of Gordon's head, he hadn't been sure it would work. But it did. Widow tossed Gordon overboard to float next to his dead friend.

He called Steslow's number. Steslow answered. He sounded sleepy. Widow had wakened him up. Steslow said, "Hello?"

Widow spoke, cold shivers in his voice. He said, "Reed, it's Widow. I don't have time to explain. So listen up. You ready?"

"Widow? Yeah. I'm listening."

"I found Lou."

"That's great!"

"Listen, Reed. I'm out of time. Call Cress when we get off the phone. Tell him to look up Gray Ghosts and their Pentagon contracts. Tell him they've been committing high crimes all over the world and we can prove it. But Reed, tell him they got a nineteen-year-old girl hostage. She's being watched by a corrupt sheriff's deputy named Braaten. Are you getting all this?" Widow said, and paused.

"Getting it."

"They've kidnapped Lou. I killed two of them already. I'm going after her now. We're at a place called Sawyer Lake. The girl's named Aponi. She's at Alton Vedely's house. It's northeast of the resort. Call the state police and get them out there. Don't forget to tell them about Braaten. He murdered the sheriff. We saw it. Got it?"

Steslow said, "I got it. But Widow, wait for us."

"Gotta go. Just get the cops to that house. Save her. I'm counting on you," Widow didn't wait for a response. He clicked the phone off and tossed it into the lake. It was useless to him now. He wasn't going to cut Gordon's head off just to unlock the phone again.

Widow set his clothes near the small fire, hopped in the driver's seat, and throttled at top speed. He headed northwest, and hoped he'd see some sign it was the right direction.

CHAPTER 30

Cosay ran through the thicket of shrubs and high grass and tree branches. She pushed through desperately. They'd given her a thirty minute head start. But it might as well have been thirty seconds. It wasn't much help for her. She was no kind of outdoorsman. She knew some basics, like how to make a fire, find shelter, etc. But that was about it. She could thank three years in the Girl Scouts for that. Which her mom made her join when she was a kid. Her mother's intention was to help Lou meet other girls off the reservation, to help her assimilate better with more people. It was also to help her learn more domestic duties, like baking cookies. However, Lou hated those activities. She gravitated more towards the adventure side, like getting her badges in camping events. That was a long time ago. But some of the lessons stayed with her.

Cosay ran as far as she could. She kept her pace fast, but steady. She figured the Gray Ghosts' objective was to get her to wear herself out. They would probably kill her, but she wasn't going down without a fight. If she could, she would escape and find a way back to the lake. Maybe she could steal their boat. She needed to get back to Aponi. If she couldn't steal their boat, then she'd walk all the way back. It'd take all night, but if the Ghosts didn't find her, they'd keep looking in the woods and not pay attention to the lake. That could give her the time she needed to walk all the way back.

She might be better off backtracking and turning south. If she could get back to the roads on the reservation, then she could signal someone and get the tribal police involved. She just had to come up with a plan and execute it. Right now, she needed to put distance between her and Harvey. So, she continued north, away from the lake, and away from the Gray Ghosts.

* * *

HARVEY DIDN'T WAIT thirty minutes, like they'd promised Cosay. He was geared up, had his hunting bow and his arrows and his night vision goggles. He left his gun back on the boat. The Gray Ghosts' training program was broken up into lessons and exercises. Part of the night hunt exercise was to hunt with the designated weapon, which was a bow. All he had were the arrows and a hunting knife. More than he needed to kill some Indian woman. That was after he had finished with her.

Harvey had tracked her for a half mile so far. He glanced down at her tracks in the dirt and snow. He could catch her within ten minutes, if he chose to. But he had fifty minutes before the others would follow him. Plenty of time. And once he got her, he could take her to a secluded area, before the other Ghosts could find them.

* * *

WIDOW DROVE the boat for what felt like an eternity. At one point, he'd seen lights to the northeast, but it turned out to be some drunken locals doing a little night fishing. He headed due west for a while, and then saw the heavy forest to the north, towards Canada. He figured that's where they would go. It looked to be the most secluded part of the lake. As he got closer to shore, he knew it was where they went because there were lots of *No Trespassing* signs. The signs warned that the land was designated as a wildlife preserve. Visitors were not allowed without a permit.

Widow slowed the boat, scanning the woods. He rode on for about ten minutes, and then he saw something. It was smoke, over the trees. He stopped the boat, killed the lights, and put out his small fire. He didn't want to give away his position or alert them he was coming.

Widow checked his clothes. They were dry enough, except his underwear. He left them off, but put everything else back on. Then he gathered everything he needed and made a pile on the passenger seat. He watched the smoke and scanned the woods again. He saw an inlet that led to the shore. That had to be the way they went. He throttled the engine to a low rumble and headed inland.

The inlet narrowed and snaked, like a river. He followed it and the smoke in the sky, until he saw firelight through the trees, just over the lakeside grass. There was a large fallen tree with holes in it. They'd made camp on the other side of the log.

Just around the bend, Widow saw their speedboat. He saw one guy sitting at the edge of the boat on some kind of makeshift metal catwalk. The guy was occupied.

Widow slowed the boat and cut off the engine. He let it drift in the water. The current was weak, but guided the boat toward the camp. Widow looked at what he had and made a plan.

He stepped up on the driver's seat and stretched out as tall as he could. He scanned the camp, staring at the guy on the boat. He tracked their footpath up to the fire. Two more guys came into view. They were conversing. They had quivers of arrows strapped to their backs, and compound bows in their hands. They wore night vision goggles on their heads, with the goggles up.

Vedely was serious about hunting Cosay. The face paint, the bows and arrows, and night vision goggles left no doubt. One of the guys talking by the fire was Vedely. The other was the Asian guy. Both men stood facing each other. The one on the boat had hair, which made him the one called Curtis.

Widow took extra time to see everything. He scanned the camp-site again, and the other boat. Two people were missing from the scene—Cosay and the bald one, Harvey.

Widow figured they must've given Cosay a head start and now she was running for her life in the forest. Probably to the north-west, away from the lake, which was where they wanted her to go. Widow also reckoned that Harvey was already on her trail.

Widow was out of time. It was now or never. He studied the scene one more time, measuring the distance between Curtis and the others. It was too close for a bullet, but far enough for a silent kill. And the two dead Gray Ghosts had been kind enough to leave Widow their bows and arrows.

Widow removed his jacket, the one that the widow in Seattle had given him. It was possibly ruined because it wasn't waterproof, and he was wearing it when he sank hundreds of feet into the lake. It was mostly dry, but its integrity looked more suspect than it had when she'd given it to him. He felt a little bad about that. But the reason he removed it was because the color stuck out in the dark. He also removed the flannel shirt, and went down to his black t-shirt and blue jeans. He was freezing, but didn't care because he was going back into the cold lake anyway.

Widow grabbed one set of the bows and arrows. He climbed up on the bow of the boat and knelt on one knee against the railing. He steadied himself. The boat drifted onward, closing in on the other one. It was a hundred feet away. Widow watched Vedely and the Asian guy, making sure they didn't turn around and spot him. His eyes darted back and forth between the three men and the two positions. He had to watch all three men. If Curtis turned around, he'd spot Widow. Same went for Vedely and the Asian guy.

The boat drifted on. Seventy-five feet. Widow waited. Fifty feet. Widow grabbed the bow and loaded an arrow, laid it on the shelf. He waited. Thirty-five feet. Widow drew the string, aimed, and held it. The tension strained his arm muscles more than they already were from his swim in the lake. But he held it. Twenty-five feet, then twenty.

Widow whistled, just loud enough to get Curtis's attention. Curtis sat on an empty cooler, tuning his bowstring. He heard the whistle, stopped, and stood up. The bow was in his hand. He turned around to the right, and looked for the source of the whistle. He froze. He saw Widow, facing him from the other speedboat. He opened his mouth to speak, but didn't. He wasn't sure who he was looking at.

Widow released the string, which instantly relieved his arm muscles. It also sent an arrow flying. The arrow flew straight through Curtis's open mouth and stuck out the back of his medulla, severing his basilar and vertebral arteries. The arrow didn't pass through him, not all the way, but the arrowhead came out the back of his head. It was covered in blood and brains and flesh.

Curtis never finished his thought. He stood for a long second, and then slumped forward. He plopped into the grass. Widow glanced at Vedely and the Asian guy. They'd heard nothing.

Widow put the bow back into the boat. He took his boots and socks off, tossed the painter from the bow into the lake, and eased himself into the water. He grabbed the painter and swam, towing the boat to shore. He reversed it so that it faced back out of the inlet to the lake, found a tree branch, and tied it off.

Widow climbed back onto the boat. He dug more stuffing out of the seat and duct-taped it to a couple of arrowheads. Then he poured gas into the canteen, and dipped the arrowheads into the gas. He left the arrows there to soak. He took the remaining gas in the can and left the boat. He walked quietly over to Curtis' corpse and the first boat. He dragged Curtis' dead body onto the first boat and sat him in the driver's seat. Then Widow searched the boat, and found another gas can, filled with gasoline. He braced one foot on the corpse and yanked the arrow out. He tossed the used arrow, brains and all, into the water.

Widow set Curtis' dead body up to look like he was alive and facing away. Widow had to duct-tape part of the corpse to keep it in position. Then Widow doused the entire boat with the gas from both cans. He covered the corpse, the seats, the floor, and the metal walkway.

Widow glanced at Vedely and the Asian. They were looking at their watches. Time was running out. Widow turned back to the driver's seat. The keys were in the ignition. Which he had counted on. Then he fired up the boat. The engine boomed to life. The motor rumbled as it idled.

Widow glanced at Vedely and the Asian guy. He had gotten their attention. They were coming back to the boat. The Asian guy shouted, "Curtis, what gives, man?"

Widow slipped off the boat and into the water, and swam fast and hard. He returned to the commandeered boat, hauled himself on board, and spun around and watched the other boat.

Thunder clapped in the distance. Vedely and the Asian guy glanced at the horizon. Widow scooped up the bow and the two gasoline-soaked arrows and hopped out of the boat onto dry land. He crouched down and crept slowly toward the other boat. He stayed low in the grass.

The Asian guy walked towards the boat to check on his friend. The Asian guy called out, "Hey, Curtis!" No answer.

Vedely followed close behind. The Asian guy crossed the metal catwalk and boarded the speedboat. Widow inched closer. Vedely stopped at the end of the catwalk and called out, "Curtis, come on. Let's get going."

Curtis didn't reply.

Widow inched closer, stopped, flipped the extra arrow, and stabbed the nock end into the dirt. He shelved the other arrow, and waited. *Come on, Vedely*, he said to himself.

The Asian guy stepped closer to Curtis, and stopped. He waved his hand in front of his nose, turned back to Vedely, and asked, "What's that smell?"

Vedely boarded and joined him in the middle of the boat. He sniffed the air and said, "It smells like gasoline."

Widow stood up, pulled Gordon's lighter out of his pocket and lit the business end of the arrow. It ignited and flamed up. The firelight was obvious in the darkness. Vedely and the Asian guy turned to look. They saw the flame, but didn't react. At least, not fast enough.

Widow took several giant steps forward, drew the string, aimed at the corpse, and released the string. The fiery arrow flew through the air and stabbed through their dead friend's chest. The corpse ignited. Blue flame engulfed the dead body in seconds. Then it engulfed the boat and Vedely and the Asian guy.

Widow watched the two of them panic, and dance, and burn. They screamed, and ran around like chickens with their heads cut off. There was water right there, surrounding them. But when you're on fire, you don't think.

Widow ran back and grabbed the second arrow, lit it. He walked back toward the boat and aimed and shot one of the fiery dancing men. He wasn't sure which, but he hoped it was Vedely.

Widow dropped the bow, took out Gordon's pistol, and fired at both men. He hit both of them. Two shots hit the one with the arrow sticking out of him. And the other guy he hit at least once. He aimed at the other guy again, and readied to shoot. But just then the fire reached the boat's gas tank, and it exploded. A fireball erupted and lit up the tree line. The backdraft kicked Widow off his feet. He fell into the mud. The men's bodies flew into the air. Some of the debris was body parts.

After the fireball exploded, the flames evened out, and the boat burned until it sank into the water. Widow jumped to his feet, aimed the gun at the fire, and waited for movement. Nothing moved. He walked the shoreline to the boat. He surveyed the fire. There was nothing. No movement. No sign of survivors. The only thing that was still there was part of the metal catwalk.

Bodies floated in the lake. They were charred and still smoking. None of them were intact, not in one whole piece. It was hard to count them. He tried to verify that he got Vedely, but none of their faces were recognizable.

Widow left the boats and the dead Gray Ghosts, and entered the campsite. He cleared it with the gun out. There was no sign of anyone. He walked the perimeter, and found nothing to tell him which direction Harvey or Cosay went. No boot prints. Nothing. The snowfall was too light and the thick canopy of autumn leaves above blocked a lot of it.

Widow pocketed the gun. The cold air turned his exhalations into white vapor. He needed to get warm. But there was no time for that. He tried to think of a plan. *How was he going to find Cosay?*

Widow searched the camp for clues. Maybe they had a map lying around? He didn't find a map, or another coat, which would've been helpful. But he found his passport, which made him happy. But not his toothbrush, which made him a little sad.

The sadness was fleeting because he found Vedely's drone. It was parked on a rock, next to its controller. And he smiled. Vedely's phone was attached to the controller, and the screen was on.

Widow wasn't an expert with drones. Normally in his SEAL platoon, one of the tech experts was assigned to the drones. But he got the gist of it.

Widow ran back to the second speedboat, past the sinking boat and the corpses, and boarded. He grabbed the last of the roll of duct tape and returned to the camp. He took out Gordon's gun, checked the magazine. There were five rounds left. He had a crazy idea. And he asked himself one question: *How much does a handgun with five bullets weigh?*

* * *

Cosay ran uphill in the dark. She was completely lost. She knew it. At first, she had a good grasp on where she was and the direction she was heading. But now the sky was dark. Clouds covered most of it. There was moonlight, but that didn't help her gauge the direction. If it did, she didn't know how to do it. Her watch told her she was out of time. Soon, they'd all be searching for her.

She had to rest. Her legs and feet ached. Her muscles screamed at her to stop. And she was panting.

At the top of the hill, she turned back and looked over the forest that she'd run through. She saw smoke in the distance. It might've been two or three miles away. It could've been the Gray Ghosts' campfire, but there was a lot of smoke. Something big was on fire.

Then she saw him. There was a dark figure coming up behind her. She caught just a hint of him. It was fast. One second he'd been there. And the next, he'd passed through the trees below her. But it was a Gray Ghost. She knew it. It was Harvey, or one of the others. She glimpsed him again. The dark figure moved in slow. Moonlight glinted off of something on his face. He was wearing night vision goggles.

He was gone again. He darted in and out of the trees like he was stalking her. And he loved it.

Cosay panted. Her chest heaved. Her heart raced, like it would burst and kill her. She forced herself to keep going. She ran up a hill, topped it and found herself in a field. The hilltop was more prairie land.

The hill had deceived her. The trees continued, but far from her. The mountains stood beyond that. She wasn't going to make it. There was nowhere to hide. She stared into the blackness to the north. Even if she had the strength to run that far, she didn't have the will. She was beaten.

Cosay dropped to her knees and just breathed. Maybe Harvey would kill her quick? No. Of course he wouldn't. He would attack her. She'd put up a fight, but Harvey would eventually overpower her. Then he'd have his way with her. Maybe the others would too. She was going to suffer in unimaginable ways. She knew it now. She accepted it.

At least when it was all over, she'd be free. She would see her baby brother again in the spirit world. The one her mother always taught her about. She'd see her mother again. They would all be reunited.

Cosay stared at the ground. Her breathing caught up. Her heartbeat slowed. Her vitals returned to normal. She waited for him, the man who killed her brother, her mother. He'd kill her next.

She waited. Then she heard him. Wait. It wasn't him. Something buzzed in the distance. She craned her head and looked back over the trees. She couldn't see it.

She stood up, walked back to the edge of the hill. She looked down at the trees, where she'd seen him. She couldn't see him, but she knew he was there. In the dark. Watching. Waiting. He was taunting her.

Then she saw it. The little black object flying in the air. It darted towards her quick, like a bug. It was Vedely's drone. She didn't hide from it. She just stayed where she was.

The drone flew overhead, almost missing her. Then it stopped. Its flight was clunky, like it was being operated by a gorilla with brain damage. The drone circled around the hill and came back to her.

She glanced down, back into the trees. She saw him this time. Harvey stared back at her with the night vision goggles down. He had a compound bow in his hand. He could've shot her with an arrow. But he didn't. He waved at her, instead.

Harvey shouted, "I'm coming for you now. I hope you're ready."

Cosay stayed quiet. She glanced up and couldn't see the drone anymore, but she heard the buzzing. She stepped back away from the hillside, and searched for it.

Harvey shouted, "I'm climbing the hill now. And when I catch you, it's going to be the most pain you can imagine. I won't be delicate. Not like I was with the others."

Suddenly, the drone slammed into her butt. She spun around, tried to swat it away. But it rose to her eye level. She heard footsteps behind her. Harvey was gaining ground. He was on the hillside, not far away.

Harvey called out, "You're going to get it worse than that podcaster. I'm so excited. I can feel the adrenaline pumping in my veins."

The drone hovered within Cosay's reach. It started to make sounds. She heard static like on a radio. And then she heard a voice. It buzzed over a small speaker on the drone's belly. It was Widow. He said, "Harvey is close."

"Widow?"

"He's very close. I spotted him in the trees."

Cosay said, "I know. How did you… are you alive?"

Harvey closed in. He shouted, "Who are you talking to, love? Are you saying your last prayers? I hope so. You better be."

Widow's voice was staticky. He said, "Take the gun. What, do I gotta spell it out for you?"

Cosay glanced at the drone. Something was hanging from it. Something was duct-taped to the bottom of it, below the speaker. She grabbed it, and ripped it off. It was a gun.

Harvey spoke. He was right behind her now. Maybe ten or fifteen feet away. He said, "You waited for me. For that, I'll try to be soft, at first."

Cosay said, "I waited for you, so I can kill you." She spun around, saw Harvey walking toward her with the bow at his side and the night vision goggles down. And she shot him in the chest, and neck, and face. She squeezed the gun's trigger until it clicked empty.

The drone clunked its way up and over her shoulder, and over to Harvey's fallen body.

Cosay joined it. She stared down at him, the man who killed her brother. He gurgled blood. More blood bubbled out of five bullet holes. Three shots to the chest. One to the neck. And one to the face. She watched him gurgle a long second, and then she watched him die.

Cosay fell to her knees. She dropped the empty gun. She cried in relief. She cried for her brother. She cried for her mother. And she cried for herself. She'd done it.

After a long moment, she got back up and looked at the drone. Then panic set in again. She said, "Widow, my sister?"

"I called Steslow. The police should already be there."

Cosay asked, "The others?"

"Dead."

"Alton?"

"He's dead."

Cosay said, "Are you sure?"

"He blew up with two others."

Cosay closed her eyes, breathed another sigh of relief.

Widow asked, "I'm at their campsite with the boats. Can you make it back to me?"

"Yes. I'll be slow. My feet are killing me."

"My whole body is killing me. Come back. I'll help guide you with the drone," Widow said, and signed off.

* * *

IT TOOK Cosay over ninety minutes to backtrack to Widow. Partially, it was because she moved slowly. She limped because of a swollen ankle. But mostly it was because Widow kept running the drone into trees.

They took the second speedboat back into Sawyer Lake. Finding their way to Vedely's house was easy because of the blue and red police and emergency vehicle lights flashing across the lake.

When they got there, Widow docked the boat at the pier. Cosay flashed her badge to the state cops and the tribal police. She walked through the crowds of firemen and cops, searching for her sister. There were people everywhere. Most wore uniforms. Some were neighbors or locals or reporters.

Eventually, she saw Aponi from a distance. Aponi sat in the rear of an ambulance. A blanket was wrapped around her. Makeup ran down her cheeks. She looked a little bruised, a little scared, but overall she was fine.

Widow followed Cosay, but stayed twenty feet back, giving her space. Cosay ran to her sister. Aponi saw her, and leapt to her feet and out of the blanket. They ran to each other and hugged and cried.

Widow stayed back. He thought it was the happiest moment he'd seen in recent memory. The reuniting of two sisters. But he was wrong.

An old man pushed through a crowd of spectators. He looked familiar. It was Mr. Cosay, Lou's father. He wore the same clothes Widow had seen him in several hours ago.

Mr. Cosay walked slowly over to his daughters. Aponi saw him first. She let go of her sister and ran to him. He hugged her tight.

Widow stayed back. Blue and red lights flashed across his face. He watched.

Lou Cosay stayed where she was. She stared at her father. He shifted Aponi to one arm, then beckoned Lou to come to them. Slowly, unsure, she joined them. Mr. Cosay grabbed her and pulled her to him and hugged both his daughters. Tears streamed down his face.

Widow couldn't hear what was said. But it looked like Mr. Cosay was saying he was sorry, over and over, to Lou. She hugged him. They cried. A family reunited. This was the happiest moment Widow had seen.

CHAPTER 31

Widow slept in the next morning. He stayed in his room at the resort. Cosay stayed in her old bedroom in her childhood home, with her family. They'd stayed awake, answering questions from investigators into the early morning hours. Widow avoided the questions. He walked away before any cop identified him. He didn't say goodbye to Cosay. He figured he would stick around another day, and see her when she was free.

Widow showered, and brushed his teeth with the brush from the traveler's kit he had purchased. He needed a replacement brush for the one he liked. That was on today's agenda.

Widow got coffee at the resort's lounge, and eggs and toast. He stopped by the front desk. The woman behind the counter told him that Aponi wasn't scheduled to return to work for a couple of days. He left something with her for Aponi. Then she pointed him to a local clothing store, because they didn't have a thrift store in town. Widow left the resort, kept his keycard in case he returned. Which he might. He hadn't decided yet. He'd had enough of Sawyer Lake, but he wanted to see Lou before he left. Just to check on her.

Widow walked into town. The weather was gloomy. Thunder rumbled over the lake. Gray clouds covered the sky, and lightning flashed occasionally. So far, it hadn't rained. No snow either. Which he was grateful for.

Widow walked in the cold with no jacket. He left the bomber jacket behind, in the hotel room closet. Maybe someone would come along, find it, and give it a new home. Even though it was ruined. He still felt bad about that. But it was what it was.

Widow found a clothing store. He went in and came back out. They didn't have clothes that would fit him. One of the cashiers pointed him to a big and tall shop down the street. He went there instead, and found some new clothes. The store was western-themed. Which meant that he ended up wearing clothes that any cowboy would be proud to wear. *Whatever*, he thought. *When in Rome*, and all that. But he skipped the cowboy hat and bolo tie.

Widow walked through the town, killing time. He passed the sheriff's station, which was swarmed with state police vehicles and police tape, like it was a crime scene now. To get out of the cold, he ended up back at the bookstore. He sat at a table, drank more coffee, and picked up Fray's book. He finished reading it by the early afternoon.

Widow stared at her author bio and picture one last time. Then he was interrupted by an old friend.

Capt. Reed Steslow walked into the bookstore, and over to Widow. Steslow wore street clothes—a warm coat, button-down shirt and tie, and jeans. Widow stood up from the table when Steslow was a yard away.

Steslow said, "I knew I'd find you here."

"What're you doing here?" Widow asked, and shook his hand.

Steslow looked Widow up and down and side to side, and said, "Look at you. You went through hell last night, and not even a scratch. Although, you may have brain damage. Look at your clothes."

The two men sat down at the table, and Widow said, "These clothes are in fashion around here."

"Maybe they were, back in the 1850s."

Widow smiled, and asked, "You know everything that happened?"

"I got the gist of it from Lou's debriefing with the state police. And what we found out about the Gray Ghosts."

"You have access to that?"

"Cress does. The NCIS opened an investigation this morning. I'm sure the FBI will want on board as well. And probably a half-dozen foreign police agencies. You really kicked a hornets' nest. But it'll all get sorted out in time, I'm sure."

"You know, I was thinking. There's gotta be more Gray Ghosts out there. Someone killed Bret Prawat and ransacked his studio, and that happened in New York last night. I doubt it was one of the guys I met. Do you know how many are out there, still?"

"No idea. You worried about looking over your shoulder? I wouldn't if I were you. Nobody could find you if they wanted to."

Widow said, "Not me, but the Cosays they could."

"I wouldn't worry. Vedely's dead. Any remainders are scattered. I'm sure they'll get rounded up, at some point."

"You didn't answer my question. What're you doing here?"

"I came to see Lou, and to check on you. I had to make sure you weren't too badly beat up."

"You really got it bad for her? Can't say that I blame you. She's an amazing woman. Good cop. A great sister. Any man would be lucky."

Steslow said, "You ever think about getting back in? You're suited for this line of work."

"No way! I like the life I got now."

"I'll be right back," Steslow said, and got up, went to the coffee counter, and ordered. A couple of minutes passed, then he returned to Widow's table but didn't sit down. He held a card-board four-cup drink carrier in one hand, filled with four cups of to-go coffee.

Widow looked up at him, and asked, "Going somewhere?"

"We're going somewhere."

"Where?"

"Come on. I'll tell you on the way."

"I don't know. The last time I went somewhere with you got me into this mess."

Steslow said, "One of these coffees is for you."

"Who's the extra ones for?"

"Come with me, and find out."

Widow got up from the table, took his book, but downed his coffee and tossed the cup into a trash bin. Then he followed Steslow out of the bookstore and onto the street, where a black Escalade was parked. Two guys in black coats and matching scarves, wearing sunglasses, stood at opposite ends of the SUV like they were Secret Service, which they might've been, because the rear door opened and Secretary Adam Cress stepped out.

"Widow. It's good to see you again," Cress said, and put a hand out for Widow to shake. Widow took it, and shook it.

"Nice to see you. What're you doing here?"

Cress said, "We couldn't get the girl to the medal, so we brought the medal to the girl."

Steslow joined them, and said, "We're surprising Lou at her farm. We'll do a little low-key medal ceremony and give it to her."

Widow said, "That's a nice surprise. She'll like that. But maybe you guys should wait a couple of days. She's been through a lot."

Cress said, "It's gotta be today. My schedule is booked up for weeks. This is all the free time I have."

Steslow said, "I already talked to her old man on the phone. He invited us. He invited you too."

"Me?" Widow asked.

"He said it was the only way we'd get his blessing. You have to go. He said something about feeling bad about almost shooting you with a shotgun?" Steslow said.

One of the Secretary's guards signaled to Cress by tapping on his watch. Cress saw it, and said, "We better get going. I gotta be on a plane in two hours."

One of the agents climbed into a third row of seats, in the back. Widow hopped in the middle row, after Cress. Steslow climbed in the front passenger seat. And the other agent drove.

Steslow handed coffees out. There were four of them. One for everyone but one of the guards, who hadn't requested one. Widow drank his pretty quickly, before they reached their destination. He thought, *Maybe the Cosays will have more.*

They drove through the town, to the lake, and turned left. They followed the road along the lake, passing traffic headed into town. There was no one fishing or boating on the lake today, but many people from the reservation drove into town. Widow figured everyone had heard the news by now that something crazy went on in Lake Hills. The rumor mill turned. Locals had heard about Braaten murdering his boss. He'd been arrested by the state police. He'd die in prison.

People drove by the sheriff's station just to check it out. It was only natural.

It thundered in the distance again. Cress stared out the window at the sky. He saw dark clouds rolling in. He said, "Looks like rain. I hope that doesn't affect my flight."

Widow stared out his window, said nothing the whole trip, except twice when the driver asked which way to turn.

They drove on and found the Cosay farm. They pulled into the driveway, passing the spot where Widow had seen Lou Cosay parked, watching him, just two afternoons ago. They drove the winding driveway, passing the dead tractor in the field, the horses running free, the family cemetery, and the run-down greenhouse. At the farmhouse, Cosay's old dog came running from around the side of the house. He barked at them as they drove up.

The Cosay farm was the same as when Widow saw it the first time, but also different. There was activity and life in it. Lou Cosay's Range Rover was parked next to the two old pickup trucks. Cress' driver parked off to the side, near an old tree.

The entire family stepped out onto the porch. The old man's hair was long and gray. There was something in it. He wore a combination of Native American and western cowboy clothes—a sweater, tattered blue jeans, cowboy boots, and a tribal print scarf. No hat. And no shotgun this time.

Aponi wore clothes that were more apt to whatever young American girls were into. It was a short dress, with a leather jacket, and a scarf like her father's. She also wore jewelry. And there was something in her hair. More important than what she wore was how she looked. She looked healthy, happy, and alive. It was a far cry from when she was tied up to that post.

Lou was the standout here. She wore an indigenous dress, similar to what Widow had seen other Mokani women wear around the reservation. Her hair was done up. Both of the girls and the old man wore Mokani headbands with feathers in their hair. Aponi had one feather. Lou had two. And their father had three.

They stood on the porch and watched the Escalade with tinted windows pull up. Lou knew whoever was in the SUV must've been friendlies, because her dad didn't greet them with his old shotgun. Except, he greeted friends that way too. So whoever was in the Escalade must've been close family or the President, and she wasn't sure the President wouldn't get the shotgun-welcome.

Lou had suspicions about who was inside. She watched the Escalade park. Two Secret Service-looking agents got out, and held the door open for their passengers. Steslow got out. She saw him, but didn't acknowledge him yet. Adam Cress got out the back, and she was surprised, nearly shocked to see such an important person. But it was the last passenger who made her smile.

Widow stepped out of the Escalade, coffee-less, which made him a little grumpy. He followed Steslow and stepped around the Escalade. Steslow waved at Lou. She waved back.

Their father descended the steps, and greeted Cress. They shook hands. The old man wouldn't let go. For him, it *was* like meeting the President. Adam Cress was the most important man he'd ever met, as far as political stature.

Both women stepped off the porch and ran toward Steslow, passed him, and hugged Widow. They threw their arms around him, one on each side, and squeezed him.

"Whoa. What's all this for?" he asked.

They let him go. Lou looked at Steslow, and greeted him, and hugged him too. Aponi hugged Widow again. He put one arm around her, and hugged her back. She let go, and said, "I just wanted to say thank you. For saving my life, and all."

"I didn't save it. Your sister did. Thank her," Widow said.

"I will. Thank you," Aponi said, smiled at Widow, and walked over to join her father in meeting the Secretary.

Lou thanked Steslow and directed him to the house, but stayed behind. She hugged Widow again. Then she kissed him on the lips. It wasn't a big, passionate deal, but it was far from innocent. He kissed her back with the same mixture of pleasure and friendship.

After, he asked, "What's that for?"

Lou let go of him, and said, "I wanted to, is all."

"Okay."

"Come on, meet my father. Properly, this time," Lou said, took Widow's hand, and brought him to meet her father. The Catahoula Leopard dog barked, and ran around them all in circles, like he was herding them.

* * *

THUNDER RUMBLED, and lightning cracked across the horizon. The sky was gray outside. It was like day into night in minutes. Cress' guards stayed in or around the Escalade.

In the farmhouse, they piled into the living room and kitchen. Widow leaned on a corner wall, drinking Aponi's homemade coffee. It was so good, he considered trying to rope one of them into marriage, just for the coffee. Cosay's father stood at the kitchen's edge. Aponi watched the action from behind a kitchen countertop. She had her phone out, camera facing the living room. She recorded their little ceremony. Steslow stood behind her, leaning on the opposite counter, and watched. Lou stood center of attention in the living room, in front of the old furniture and the fireplace. A fire crackled behind her, warming up the house. Pictures of the family in better days, and larger by two more members, adorned the mantle above the fireplace. Mokani blankets and art decorated the whole house.

Cress stood, his back to the onlookers, and faced Lou Cosay. He held up a navy-blue leather box. The lid flipped open like a large wallet. Gold trim etched down the front of it. There were words etched in the same gold. They read: *Navy Cross* in the center with big bold letters, and *United States of America* at the bottom corner, in a smaller font.

Cress presented Lou with the medal. He gave the speech Widow had heard before. A tearful Lou accepted it. She gave a short speech. Everyone cheered and congratulated her. Steslow had a cold beer in one hand, and a shot of whiskey in the other. He raised the whiskey to toast Lou.

Widow eyeballed him, because just a few days ago he told Widow he'd quit drinking. Steslow had mentioned he was sober now, implying that he was in recovery. Widow asked, "I thought you weren't drinking anymore?"

Steslow said, "Very rarely, Cress and I throw caution to the wind and we'll have a drink. It's only on special occasions. And not more than once, maybe twice a year. It keeps me sane, Widow."

Widow didn't say anything else about it. Steslow and Cress were grown men. Maybe breaking his streak for special occasions worked for him. Whatever kept him sober most of the time. Widow didn't judge.

Widow toasted with the coffee that Aponi had made him. She toasted with a beer. Her father let her have one on special occasions. Their father toasted with a bottled water because he proclaimed he would stop drinking, now that Lou was back in his life. Cress joined in with another whiskey in a shot glass. And Lou did the same.

They sat around talking and having a nice visit. The afternoon turned into late afternoon. Cress had planned to leave, but his flight had been delayed. Bad weather. So he stuck around. Although, Widow wasn't sure he believed the excuse. Cress followed his first shot of whiskey with a second one. He seemed to be having the time of his life. Running the entire Navy was probably hard. Why shouldn't he have a little fun?

An hour before sunset, the thunderstorm consumed the sky. Rain hammered the farm. The father got the girls to go out with him to round up the loose horses. They had to stable them back in the barn.

Aponi and Lou threw on their rain slickers and coats. The old man put on his coat and hat and took his shotgun out with him.

Cress asked, "What's the gun for?

The old man replied, "Coyotes."

Lou said, "We get coyotes. When it rains, they seek shelter. Sometimes they try to find it in local barns, where they can snack on our animals." She smiled at Widow, joined her family, and headed out into the rain. Their dog ran out behind them.

Cress and Steslow had no experience with horses, so they stayed at the kitchen table, drinking a third shot of whiskey, and swapping sailor stories. Widow had ridden horses before. He volunteered to help, but the Cosays waved him off. They didn't need his help, Lou told him. She said it might take fifteen or twenty minutes, max. So Widow stayed behind, and relaxed on the sofa. He listened to the rain, and Steslow and Cress talking, which turned into singing old sailor songs to see if the other could finish. Occasionally, they included Widow with a question, or asked him to finish a limerick.

The agents couldn't help. It was outside their operational parameters. They blasted the heater inside the Escalade, while rain hammered the exterior.

Time passed. Fifteen minutes, then twenty, and then thirty. Concerned, Widow finished his coffee, went to the sink, pretended to dump out the mug, and stared out a window above the sink. He angled his head to see the barn. The rain poured, making it hard to see three feet in front of the window.

He set the mug down, and stepped away. "I'm going to go out there and see if they need some help," he said.

Steslow said, "Let them be. What the hell do you know about horses?"

Cress started to get up, and said, "Let's go help him." He didn't make it up. He stumbled back into his chair, and started laughing. Steslow laughed with him.

Steslow said, "You probably should stay sitting, old friend." They laughed.

Widow stopped at the door and said, "I'll be right back." And walked out.

Outside, the rain battered down. He was soaked within seconds, reminding him of when he was in the lake. Which he'd like to forget. He pulled his beanie down over his ears, keeping them as dry as possible.

Widow put a hand up over his eyes to shelter them from the rain. He glanced at the Escalade. It was parked far from the house and the barn. He couldn't see the agents. But he heard the car stereo playing. He saw the interior lights on. And their silhouettes moving around like they were having as good a time as Steslow and Cress.

The dog barked, somewhere near the barn. Widow followed the barking. He tunneled through the thick wall of rain toward the barn. He stopped. He saw something in the distance. It was huge. He headed toward it. It looked like a vehicle, but it was running around the field.

Widow pushed forward and saw three more of the same big object. Whatever it was, it ran around like wild animal.

Then he heard it. It stampeded toward him, wildly. He launched himself to the ground, just in time to dodge it. It was a horse with an empty saddle. Maybe one of the Cosays fell off their horse?

Widow scrambled to his feet. He pushed toward a group of horses farther in the field. He figured that's where the Cosays were. The father was old. Maybe he fell off his horse. Maybe they needed help. Widow pushed on. The rain made it slow going. The cowboy boots weren't treaded for walking in the mud. He nearly slipped twice. He got within fifteen yards of the horses. He saw no one. No one was in the saddles. No one attended to them.

Widow turned back to the greenhouse and the barn. The family dog barked, but it was faint. Not because he was far away, but because the weather muffled the sound.

Widow pushed on. On the way to the barn, he nearly tripped again, but this time he'd stepped on something. He moved aside and stared down at the mud. It looked like a log or a stick. But there was metal. He knelt and picked it up. It was the father's old shotgun.

Widow looked at the ground below him. There were human tracks all around. It looked like a scuffle had taken place. He looked closer, counted the tracks. He counted and Lou's were obvious. They were tiny women, and tiny women usually have small feet. The father's was one pair of boot prints, but whose were the other two?

Widow followed the tracks. Then he saw someone being dragged by the women. Widow followed.

Widow walked until he heard the dog barking louder. He stopped following the tracks because he knew where they went. They went straight into the barn. The family dog had been thrown into the greenhouse. He barked, and clawed at the door.

Widow started to let him out, but then he heard something. A woman screamed. It was Aponi. He spun around. She screamed again. It came from inside the barn. The doors were pulled closed. Lights flickered under the doors and around the edges and through the cracks in the old barn.

Widow ran through the rain and stopped outside the door. He heard voices. He inched himself close to the door, found a crack, and peeked inside. He saw Lou. She was tied to a post. Blood trickled down her nose, like she'd been slapped in the face. Her father was toppled over. His face was in agony. He hadn't been slapped, but somebody had gut-punched him good.

Aponi had her wrists tied together. Her face was just as scared as it had been when she was on that post. She was bent over a pile of old saddles.

Two men were inside the barn with them. Both were dressed in black. One of them was a big white guy Widow had never seen before. He was armed with a tactical shotgun. Widow didn't recognize the brand. Not through the rain, and distance, and a crack in the barn. But it looked police-issued, and upgraded with a bunch of aftermarket modifications.

There was another man in there with them. He had no gun. He had a big hunting knife in one hand. The blade shimmered in the low light. He could barely hold the knife. One of his hands had no fingers. And the one holding the knife only had half an index finger and a thumb.

His face and neck and head were red and puffy. There were huge gaps in his skin. One large gap on his cheek showed the inside of his mouth, like a window. Most of his teeth were there. But his gums were black. One of his eyes was completely burned, leaving his pupil white as paper. Half his hair was burned off his scalp. Only a third of his face was still there.

It was Alton Vedely. He was alive. The other guy must've been the Gray Ghost who killed Prawat in New York. He must have been on his way to Shadow Lake when Widow killed his friends.

Alton had survived the fire. He spoke. His voice was unrecognizable. His vocal chords were charred. His voice sounded grizzly, and deep, and monstrous.

The father tried to get the shotgun from the big guy. The big guy clocked him in the stomach with the butt of the shotgun. He said, "Stay down, old-timer. The next time, I'll kneecap you." He pumped the action. Crunch-crunch. The sound sent shivers down Lou's spine. She knew what kind of men they were. She begged her father to stop, to stay where he was. She spoke to him in Mokani. Her father tried to get up. The Gray Ghost aimed at him. He said, "Don't do it, old man."

The father couldn't get up. He was in too much pain. He fell back onto his butt. The Gray Ghost lowered the shotgun.

Vedely stared at Lou. She winced at the sight of his face. He said, "You killed my family. Destroyed my face. And took away the spoils that are mine." He raised the knife and showed it to her. Then he pointed it at his groin. "In case you're wondering. It's still there. I think it works. Not sure though. But you'd better hope it does. Because if it don't." He showed her the blade again. "I'm going to use this on your sister instead."

Lou screamed, "Widow! Help us!"

Vedely raised his fingerless hands into the air, and joined them. "Widow! Widow!" he shouted, and stopped. He lowered his arms. "No one is coming for you. But don't worry. After we kill you. We'll get him too. And the others out there."

Vedely moved to Aponi. He said, "Don't fight me. The harder you struggle, the worse I'll make it."

Aponi cried, but didn't kick or struggle. Vedely used the blade to pull her dress up. He got behind her, and tried to undo his zipper. But he couldn't. He said, "Aponi, turn around."

Slowly, she turned around, looked at him, horrified. He said, "Take it out for me."

Aponi winced, but started to do as she was told.

The other guy stepped back, and turned to watch. Which was the chance Widow was waiting for. He stepped back, moved to the barn doors, and opened the shotgun. It was an old double-barreled Browning. He checked the shells. He had two rounds. *Better make them count*, he thought.

Widow eased one of the barn doors open a crack. He slipped in undetected, and snuck to the right, staying in the shadows of the horse stalls. He crept behind the big guy, raised the Browning, and tapped the guy between the shoulder blades with it. It was a hard double-tap with the barrel. Widow stepped back, aimed, and said, "Turn around slowly!"

Vedely froze the second he heard Widow's voice. He raised his nubbed hands. The knife fell out of his grip, not because he dropped it on purpose, but because he no longer had the grip strength to raise it any higher.

Aponi saw Widow, released Vedely's zipper, and scrambled away from him. Lou and her father both stared at Widow. He was drenched in water, standing in darkness, and holding a double-barreled shotgun. Lou was relieved, but also a little scared of him.

The Gray Ghost turned around slowly.

Widow said, "Toss the gun."

He tossed it.

Widow craned his head, looked at Lou's father, who stood behind the big guy. Widow said, "Move away from back there."

The father moved clear. The big guy watched him, and the wheels in his head started turning. He realized why Widow had asked the father to move away. But it was too late.

Widow shot him in the gut, one barrel. The last Gray Ghost flew back off his feet as a large hole blew through him. Guts and intestines and blood sprayed across a pile of hay. The Gray Ghost was dead.

Widow turned to Alton Vedely, who started to plead and beg. Widow said, "Save it." He turned to Aponi, and said, "Get the knife, cut your sister loose."

Widow lowered the shotgun. Because what was Vedely going to do? Go for a gun hidden somewhere? He couldn't hold it, let alone pull a trigger.

Widow glanced at Lou's father, and tossed him his own shotgun. The father aimed it at Vedely, keeping him standing there with his arms up. Widow grabbed the tactical shotgun that had been dropped by the Gray Ghost. It was better suited to his taste.

Aponi cut Lou free. She ran to her father and hugged him. So did Aponi.

Vedely stood there, terrified of what would happen next.

Lou released her father and turned to Widow. She said, "Now what?"

Widow tossed her the tactical shotgun. She caught it. Widow stepped back, and said, "Promises are meant to be kept."

Lou nodded. She glanced at her father. He nodded. Then she looked at Aponi. And she nodded. Aponi stepped to her father and helped him stand straight. She took hold of the old Browning as well. They stood, holding the gun together.

The Cosays aimed their shotguns at Vedely, the man responsible for their brother's murder, for their mother's suicide. They shotgunned him to death. Execution by firing squad.

Whatever pieces that didn't burn up in the fire were gone now.

* * *

THEY LEFT the dead men in the barn. Widow and Lou rounded up the horses in the rain. The dog helped. It took them less than fifteen minutes to do it. It turned out the horses wanted to return to their stables as badly as Widow wanted coffee.

Aponi helped her father around to the back entrance of the house, which led into his bedroom. She patched him up and cleaned herself off.

The agents in the Escalade never heard a thing. And Steslow and Cress chalked up the shooting to coyotes.

The agents drove Steslow and Cress to the resort, where they all got rooms at a deep discount after Aponi called it in.

Widow stayed behind. He spent the night on the Cosays' family sofa. Although Lou had informed him that her door was open, if he wanted to sleep in her bed. The temptation kept him up all night. But he never took her up on the offer. Which he would regret later. He knew it. He accepted it.

The next morning, the sky was clear. Widow ate breakfast with the Cosays. Aponi made him some of that frybread he'd missed out on. It was delicious. He offered to help them bury the bodies. But Lou told him not to worry about it. They had neighbors who knew how to bury things that needed burying.

At ten in the morning, Widow shook the old man's hand. He petted the old dog. Aponi hugged him, and also kissed him on the lips. She gave the same reason that Lou gave him. *She just wanted to at least once.*

Lou drove Widow out of the reservation. They drove towards Minot. An hour west and south, and they stopped at the cloverleaf of US 83 and US 52. Widow said goodbye. Lou kissed him again. She told him to call her sometime.

Widow got out on the shoulder of US 83's southbound lane. He waved at her, and watched her drive away. He watched her until she was gone from sight.

At the same moment, Steslow and Cress climbed into the back of the Escalade to head to the airport, and take their separate flights in separate directions. Steslow had a coffee. His head ached. He said, "Adam, I'm not drinking again."

Cress said, "You've said that before. We both have."

"This time I'm serious."

"Me too," Cress said. Suddenly, he felt something underneath him. He shifted in the seat, reached underneath him, grabbed it, and pulled it out. It was a water-damaged paperback copy of Cassie Fray's book.

Three nights later, Aponi Cosay's father drove her to work because he didn't want her to go out alone, not for a while. She didn't complain. She kissed him goodnight. He reminded her that Lou would pick her up when she got off. Aponi went into work, clocked in, and sat at the front counter. The night was slow, and boring. She played on her phone. But got bored with it. She looked in the back office for some busywork, and found a note, addressed to her. It read: *A guest left this for you.* Under the note was a paperback copy of *Dark Matter*, the book Widow had read.

She opened it. There was no inscription, no message from him. Nothing.

THE SHADOW CLUB

The beginning of his career. The end of her life.
Go back to when Widow was twenty-two.
Coming 2023

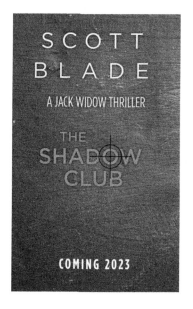

(Actual cover to be revealed in 2023)

THE SHADOW CLUB: A BLURB

AMAZON BESTSELLER Scott Blade returns with a new action-thriller featuring Jack Widow, in 2023.

Annapolis. The US Naval Academy. The beginning of his career. The end of her life.

Go back to when Jack Widow was twenty-two, in his last week at the Academy.

A dying woman asks Widow to help solve the cold-case murder of her sister using the help of a secretive club of the world's best investigators. Only this club holds a dark secret.

The secret club appears to be for justice on the surface. But at what price?

Preorder Jack Widow book 19.

Readers are saying about Scott Blade and the Jack Widow series...

★ ★ ★ ★ ★ Scott Blade's Jack Widow is so good, my biggest complaint is having to wait for the next one!

A WORD FROM SCOTT

Thank you for reading KILL PROMISE. You got this far—I'm guessing that you enjoyed Widow.

The story continues…

The next book in the series is *THE SHADOW CLUB*, coming in 2023!

To find out more, sign up for the Scott Blade Book Club and get notified of upcoming new releases. See next page.

THE SCOTT BLADE
BOOK CLUB

Building a relationship with my readers is the very best thing about writing. I occasionally send newsletters with details on new releases, special offers, and other bits of news relating to the Jack Widow Series.

If you are new to the series, you can join the Scott Blade Book Club and get the starter kit.

Sign up for exclusive free stories, special offers, access to bonus content, info on the latest releases, and coming-soon Jack Widow novels. Sign up at ScottBlade.com.

THE NOMADVELIST

NOMAD + NOVELIST = NOMADVELIST

Scott Blade is a Nomadvelist, a drifter and author of the breakout Jack Widow series. Scott travels the world, hitchhiking, drinking coffee, and writing.

Jack Widow has sold over a million copies.

Visit @: ScottBlade.com

Contact @: scott@scottblade.com

Follow @:

Facebook.com/ScottBladeAuthor

Bookbub.com/profile/scott-blade

Amazon.com/Scott-Blade/e/B00AU7ZRS8

BOOKS BY SCOTT BLADE

The Jack Widow Series

Gone Forever

Winter Territory

A Reason to Kill

Without Measure

Once Quiet

Name Not Given

The Midnight Caller

Fire Watch

The Last Rainmaker

The Devil's Stop

Black Daylight

The Standoff

Foreign and Domestic

Patriot Lies

The Double Man

Nothing Left

The Protector

Kill Promise

The Shadow Club

Printed in Great Britain
by Amazon